HEIR OF BLOOD & FIRE

MARINA LAURENDI

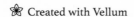 Created with Vellum

CASTLE ILLONA

PRAXIAN SEA

VOD

BAEGAR

TIR

SOLTERRE

PRONUNCIATION GUIDE

- Zadyn- Zay Den
- Jace- Jay S
- Sorscha- Sor Sha
- Marideth- Mae Ri Deth
- Dover- Doh Ver
- Cece (Ceec)- See See | Seec
- Igrid- Ee Grid
- Gnorr- Nor
- Prophyria (Furi)- Pro Fury A | Fury
- Ienar- Eye Nar
- Urhlon- Er Lon
- Aerill- Air Ull
- Wyneth- Win Eth
- Myr- Mer
- Naiad- N Eye Ad
- Stryga- Stri Ga
- Aegar- Aye Gar
- Hyrax- Hi Racks
- Aeix- A Ex

- Vod- Voh D
- Tir- Tee Er
- Solterre- Sohl Tair
- Iaspus- Ee As Pis
- Hysphestus- His Fest Us
- Iterre- Ee Tair
- Erastin- Ee Ras Tin
- Stygian- St Eye Gee En
- Markade- Mar Kaid

RECOMMENDED PLAYLIST

- Chapter 1: *Scott Street* by Phoebe Bridgers
- Chapter 3: *DVD Menu* by Phoebe Bridgers
- Chapter 15: *Cruel Summer* by Ana Done
- Chapter 18: *Sour Patch* by Ruby Waters
- Chapter 19: *ICU* by Phoebe Bridgers | *My Fun* by Suki Waterhouse
- Chapter 20: *Grow Up Tomorrow* by The Beaches
- Chapter 22: *Chaise Longue* by Wet Leg | *Gasoline* by HAIM feat. Taylor Swift
- Chapter 23: *Little Chaos* by Orla Gartland
- Chapter 24: *The Wire* by HAIM | *The Way It Was* by The Killers
- Chapter 25: *Guilty As Sin* by Taylor Swift
- Chapter 27: *Bite The Hand* by boygenius
- Chapter 28: *I Love You, I'm Sorry* by Gracie Abrams
- Chapter 31: *Risk* by Gracie Abrams
- Chapter 33: *Ode to a Conversation Stuck in Your Throat* by Del Water Gap
- Chapter 38: *Moon Song* by Phoebe Bridgers

- Chapter 41: *Devil Like Me* by Rainbow Kitten Surprise
- Chapter 42/43: *Nothing's Gonna Hurt You Baby* by Cigarettes After Sex

Official Spotify Playlist- HEIR OF BLOOD & FIRE #1

For my dad and for anyone who has ever been afraid to fly.

1

"**I**'m so tired it's not even fucking funny."

Adam breezes over to me and flings himself against the wall next to the bar, his voice flat with that *I'm so over this shit* tone.

It's a tone I know all too well.

It's two o'clock on a Monday afternoon and I've had a total of one and a half bar guests. The first left me a breath mint as a tip and the second just asked for a water and directions to the bathroom. It hasn't been a total waste of an afternoon, though. In the five hours I've been here, I've had so little to do that I downloaded a new book on my phone and am already halfway through it.

The story isn't unlike the others I've devoured lately. Shameless romantasy—usually involving an obscenely beautiful male, a badass heroine who makes you feel pathetic in comparison, and a battle against evil forces that inevitably results in the main characters saving the world and banging angstily in a run-down inn.

You know, all your favorite tropes.

I toss Adam a polite smile and laugh, grasping at straws for a response. I won't stoop so low as to mention the weather.*

Connecting with others has never been second nature to me. I'm sure people think I'm strange—the girl always more interested in reading than social interaction. It's not that I'm anti-social. I actually don't *mind* conversing with people—making small talk, the whole nine yards.

I just prefer imaginary worlds to the one I'm living in.

I'm still relatively new to town, and I'm not drowning in friends. Far from it. I had a few growing up, but there was only ever one person besides my dad that I could trust and truly rely on.

Annie.

We met in college, and it felt like we had known each other in another lifetime. She was infectious and passionate. Alive. But then a few years after we graduated, she disappeared. The last time we spoke, she sent me a text saying she was staying in Germany with her hot Belgian fiancé and that she'd be in touch.

That was years ago. I eventually stopped trying.

I come to work and see the servers off in the corner, giggling over inside jokes. I see them flirt with our managers—both parties seeming equally chummy and at ease with one another. That kind of camaraderie can only come from openness and trust and self-assurance—none of which I'd particularly pride myself on these days.

Propping my chin on my hand, I swipe my finger across my phone's screen, eager to get to the next chapter of my book.

Maybe it's because my love life is so devoid of...well, *existence* that living vicariously through these characters is all I can do to remain hopeful in the face of constant disappointment.

---

* Cue: *Scott Street* by Phoebe Bridgers

I've done my time on the failed relationship circuit. Being a lifelong hopeless romantic has only skewed my idea of what love looks like into something idealistic and unobtainable. There was the bar manager when I was nineteen. The lawyer when I was twenty-one. The pilot at twenty-three. And a handful of unmentionables in between.

And then there was Jack.

I didn't just think I loved him. I *knew* I did. Because when it ended, I fled the state. I would have made a fool of myself for that man.

And I couldn't do it.

I don't think I ever stopped loving him. Not really. It's been two years and even after all this time, the thought of kissing someone else makes my stomach churn.

And I know I shouldn't be looking for fulfillment in the form of a man and that I have to love myself first and foremost and wait for when I least expect it. Basically, I need to live my life like it's a fucking Pinterest board of inspirational quotes. But let's face it, happy people who have traveled and lived and found their soulmates aren't chanting "live, laugh, love" over and over to themselves and crying into their dinner.

I want someone to love. I want to *be* loved.

There was a time after my dad died when I was afraid of what that meant. But my loneliness has since curbed that fear. I was so close to having everything I ever wanted. If I hadn't been so stubborn and scared, I could have actually been happy.

But I was an idiot and let it all slip away.

I just want a good story to tell in the end. I want to get to the last chapter of my book so that I can have that "aha" moment. The moment when it all clicks into place. When I realize what I, as the narrator, have been too blind to see from the first page. Maybe I realize that what I wanted was always right in front of me. Maybe I find that place where I truly belong. Maybe I fall in love with the mailman or the guy who comes to fix my apartment appliances when they break.

I don't fucking know.

So here I am. New home. New job. New job that I *hate*, but new job all the same.

"Did my ticket come through?" Adam's voice snaps me out of my haze.

I hadn't even noticed it printing. I rip it free and get to work on an espresso martini.

When I left New York two years ago, I made my way down to Florida, stopping in sleepy towns and staying a few months at a time as my savings dwindled. I couldn't bring myself to care. About *anything*.

Grief had me twelve shades of fucked up. It was as if everything I once cared about suddenly faded into grayscale, the vitality drained, leaving only the bones of my old life behind. I was blindly stumbling around, searching for color in cheap motels and dirty dive bars—searching desperately for the girl I was before losing the person I loved most in this world.

I ended up in Jacksonville this past August, right around the time The Black Rose opened and they hired me on the spot. It's a far cry from the dream job I fumbled at one of the top women's magazines in the country, but beggars can't be choosers. I was told I'd make good money as a bartender here, although I've yet to see it reflected in my bank account. I have a couple of regulars. Most of them misogynistic middle-aged men who I secretly hate.

"Here you go," I say to Adam, sliding the drink across the bar.

"Thanks, girl." He drops a few coffee beans in it and saunters off to a two-top by the French doors.

The January day is nice enough to have the patio doors

open, the breeze cutting the scorching heat. He sets the martini down in front of two handsome men in expensive-looking suits.

I wonder what their story is. Are they brothers? Are they lovers? What do they do for work? Are they here on vacation? Are they perhaps Secret Service on their lunch break?

I have to stop.

Everything I see serves as grounds for creative material—millions of great ideas collected in a Word document saved on my computer. The problem is, I can't seem to do anything with them. I read and read, and then I try to write because what else can you do with an overactive imagination and a tanked career in journalism?

Of course, it's not easy to write anything substantial when you feel like your life is in the gutter.

"Whatcha reading?" Zoe sneaks up on me, whisper-shouting in my ear. I gasp, nearly jumping out of my skin as I shoot her a sharp look.

"Jesus," I breathe, my heart rate slowly recovering. She claps a hand over her chest and laughs.

"So jumpy today." Leaning over the bar, she quirks an eyebrow at my phone. "Are you reading smut? At work?! *Serena!*"

I roll my eyes but allow a small smile. Zoe's got one of those endearing, absurd, always saying-something-crazy types of personalities I've always envied. She says the first thing that comes to her mind and can make conversation with a brick wall. Sometimes I'm stunned by how much she reminds me of Annie.

"Not smut," I clarify, "but is it even a finished book if there's no steam?"

She offers another loud laugh that sounds like wind chimes. "I've never seen anyone read so much."

"What else is there to do while I'm bar-sitting?" I say, shrugging my shoulders.

"Do you see those guys over there?" She leans in, lowering her voice and discreetly pointing over my shoulder. "Freaking *gorgeous*. I think that one is an influencer."

I follow her gaze toward the dark-haired man at Adam's table and study his profile. From where I stand, I can tell he's stunning. Black hair that spills over his forehead with model-like cheekbones and eyes a remarkable shade of sea blue. He lazes in his seat as he says something to his handsome friend with the mushroom brown hair and blue-gray eyes.

"What would an influencer be doing in here?" I scoff, leaning my elbow against the service bar. My eyes lock with his and I avert my gaze, turning back to Zoe as she sifts through a stack of crinkled cash.

"Fourteen dollars today. And I spent forty on happy hour last night, so that's how my week is starting off!" Stuffing the wad of cash into her apron, she gives me a sardonic look and is off to charm one of our managers with a bounce in her step.

I cast a glance around the nearly empty restaurant, heave a sigh, and turn back to my book.

2

Tatler's Books is a small local hole-in-the-wall bookshop owned by a sweet elderly man with soft tufts of white hair. Age has slowed his steps but the twinkle in his big brown eyes and the soft wrinkle around his smile are warm and youthful.

The chime on the door sings as I push it open, announcing my arrival. The musky smell of old books pervades the air, filling my heart and head with a deep sense of calm. My shoulders relax as I take in the familiar spot I've frequented every week since I moved here. The bookshop has been here since the early 80s. The floor is checker-tiled near the entrance with a dark green carpet blanketing the shelves on either side of the main aisle. A chipped dark wood checkout counter sits at the epicenter of the small shop. Eclectic paraphernalia and B-movie posters from the 1950s decorate the yellow-tinged walls.

A spot of white pops into my vision, peeking out from one of the aisles. Mr. Tatler breaks into a wide grin.

"Serena," he says.

"How are you, Mr. T?" I smile back. I've always found interactions with elderly people to be easiest for me and oftentimes the most genuine.

"Fine, just fine, my dear. What brings you in today?" He cradles a stack of hardcovers in his frail-looking arms.

"Oh, just general displeasure with the modern world—what else?"

He huffs a short laugh. "I see we're gonna need something stronger than decaf." Sighing, he nods his head for me to follow.

This has become our little tradition. I come in, Mr. Tatler brings out two coffees and we sit in the two worn leather chairs near the classics section which have clearly seen better days. I never see anyone else in the store which is a relief, actually. Mr. Tatler and I became fast friends, bonding over our love of fiction and mythology. I know that the shop has been in his family for generations but business must not be thriving, since the last time it was updated was probably the late 90s. But I don't mind. I think it adds to this place's charm.

He places the steaming styrofoam cup in my hands. Then, sinking into the worn brown leather, he holds up a hand for me to begin.

"So?"

"So what?" I lift the steaming cup to my lips and blow.

"What's the story this week?"

"No story, just self-isolating as usual. Hence, coming here to hide among the new releases."

He chuckles. "Nice try. You're not getting off the hook that easy. What's so terrible that you have to hole up in this rotting building with a decrepit old man?"

"I've just been thinking about the past a lot," I admit. "Nothing has turned out the way I planned. It feels like the only time I can escape my regrets is when I lose myself in a book."

I raise my eyes to his, feeling self-conscious. Saying it out loud feels kind of embarrassing.

"There is nothing in this world worth feeling regret over. It keeps the past alive, but always out of reach. Don't torture yourself." He pauses. "Maybe what you need is some friends your own age."

I laugh. "People think I'm weird. Anti-social. And they're probably right." I hesitate before continuing. "I think there's something broken in me. I *try*, but I can't relate to most people. Everyone makes it look so easy. They laugh, and they joke, and they all seem so *light* compared to the way I feel inside. I mean, I feel more connected to my favorite book characters than I do to people I know and they're not even real. How ridiculous is that?"

I pause, studying my hands wrapped around the warmth of the cup. "Sorry, I don't mean to dump all of this self-pity on you."

He leans forward in his chair.

"There is absolutely nothing wrong with you, understand? You're not broken. Your heart is kind and generous. You're wise beyond your years. And you must never forget that you possess a very rare, child-like wonder inside of you. The kind of wonder that allows you to see beyond what is and glimpse what could be. You see a world of ideals, a world of possibility. You, my dear, have a wanderer's soul."

A wanderer's soul.

It sounds beautiful, but I know it's just a fancy way of saying I'm a hopeless dreamer. And look where it's gotten me in life.

He smiles. "You're meant for more than any of those people can imagine. Your life is going to be bigger than even you know."

"Are you kidding? There is nothing exciting or big about my life."

"So change it." He shrugs.

"Easier said than done. I have a job. Bills to pay. I can't just go off and have these wild adventures in order to find myself like they do in books and movies. This is real life—I'm not some heroine."

"But what if you are?" he asks, studying me for a long minute.

"This feels oddly like a therapy session. Would you like to collect payment now, or are you going to bill me at the end?"

"Listen. I've lived a long time." His brown eyes fix mine in a serious gaze. "Many lifetimes, or so it seems. Your only regret in life will be to remain in the shadow of the person you want to be. When you close your eyes and see the story of your life, who are you? Who is that young woman that you feel you are failing to be?"

The air is suddenly thick, the silence unending.

"I—I don't know," I whisper. He shakes his head.

"Yes, you do. And as long as you are afraid to admit it to yourself, you will not be happy. You will not be fulfilled."

"Wow, tell it like it really is, Mr. T." I blow out an aspirated breath.

"What is it you want out of your life, Serena?"

I take a second and think about it.

I want a lot of things. I want a do-over of the last ten years. I want to live in a world where my dad is still alive. One where my sister and I still speak. One where I don't sabotage myself and my dreams. One where I am in control. Where I know myself and my strength. One where I am a force of nature. The main character instead of the wallflower side character that you don't think twice about.

As if hearing all of my inner dialogue loud and clear, he stands and says, "I know just the thing."

~

MR. TATLER GESTURES for me to follow him. Placing my coffee down on the wobbly side table, I trail him to a peeling gray door at the back of the shop. He fishes a small keyring from his pocket and jostles the door open to reveal a secret staircase.

"What's up there?" I ask.

"My prized books. Some first editions, special editions. I suspect you are in need of something sturdier than your average paperback."

I follow him up the stairs and wait as he keys open another door.

"Why have I never seen this before?" I ask as he holds it open for me to pass.

"I don't keep this open to the general public."

I didn't think this place could be any cozier—any homier—but this second floor is even more charming than the first. Dark mahogany bookshelves line the walls. In the center of the room are two large glossy wooden reading tables and chairs. Large windows framed by thick cobalt curtains sit on the far wall, bathing the room in buttery sunlight. The smell of old books is mixed with something that reminds me of shoe polish, of fresh leather. The whole room gives off an air of rich academia.

"This is beautiful!" I trail my fingers along the multicolored spines as I pass by, not recognizing any titles. "I had no idea this was up here."

"That's the idea now, isn't it?" He smirks when I glance his way.

"So, Doc, what do you recommend? First edition of *Pride and Prejudice*, or will it be a signed copy of *Anna Karenina*?" I tease.

"Neither, I'm afraid." He pulls his hands from his pockets and strides over to the far wall where a tall glass bookcase stands nestled in the corner. It shimmers in the light of the sun —spotless, without a speck of dust. Inside the glass case is a heavy book of the deepest purple with silver leaf detailing a shape that resembles a winged creature.

Something seems to hum from that direction. A nearly imperceptible vibrational pull.

"It sings to you," he says, barely louder than a whisper.

Easing open the case, he removes the beautiful volume and smooths the cover in his crinkled hands. He places it down on one of the large reading tables and pulls out a chair for me. I knit my brows together as I slide into the wooden seat.

"This." He taps a finger on the book cover, peering down at me. "This is what I would recommend for your particular ordeal."

"Mr. T, I was just venting about my life. It's no big—"

"I know I am not mistaken," he cuts me off, "in thinking you desire more from your life. And that life desires more from you."

"Mr. T, I appreciate you trying to cheer me up, but what is this?" I tilt my head, staring up at him.

"Open it," he says. I flip open the heavy leather-bound cover. The lining is a velvety black material, and as I turn the first page of cream-colored parchment, I realize it is blank. As is the second page, the third, the fourth... I glance up at him, perplexed.

"It's blank."

"Look closely. It is not blank, even though it is unseen."

Okay, dude, I'll bite.

I squint, seeing nothing. "I'm looking closely," I sing, drumming my nails on the table. "Still not seeing anything."

"Your story lies between the folds of these pages, waiting to be revealed. To be discovered. To be lived." I shake my head, not understanding his cryptic riddles.

"But how do I read it if I can't see anything on the page?" I persist.

"You need only ask."

"Are there magic words or something?" I chuckle to hide my growing exasperation.

"Perhaps." He moves around the table to stand across from me. Then, nodding toward the book, he urges, "Look again."

My jaw falls open as I stare down at the ink beginning to form on the page. I marvel at the sight, transfixed.

"How did you—"

He holds up a cautionary hand, interrupting my train of thought. "Say the words only if you truly seek a life beyond the bounds of the mundane. What comes next is not for the faint of heart."

His words fill me with trepidation, sending a wave of goose-bumps down my arms. I blink, glancing from his face back to the spreading ink. My eyes widen further as a silent request etches itself onto the page.

Read me. Speak me. Sing me.

I would look upon the world as it were. To see what is unseen. To know what lies beyond the veil.

The words strike an inexplicable sense of foreboding within me. Yet I can't tear my eyes away from the page.

Serena.

I gasp, pushing back from the heavy chair. My name's

sudden permanence on the parchment fills me with a deep sense of unease, bordering on dread.

"Okay, very funny," I say, an edge of panic lacing my words as I stare him down. This is beginning to feel less and less like a practical joke or innocent magic trick.

"I didn't bring you here for a laugh."

I swallow hard. My intuition is tugging at me, flashing warning signs that it's time to leave. Something is not right about this.

Studying him closely, I realize that he isn't all that short. His shoulders are not as sunken as I thought, his body not as frail. And then it dawns on me that I don't know this man that well. While his stature is still far from imposing, I am now aware that he has led me upstairs behind locked doors and is spewing fanatical nonsense at me with a frightening degree of conviction. My palms grow clammy at the prospect of a homicide with my name on it.

Rushing for the door, I mutter, "I have to go."

I scurry past him and yank at the handle, but the door is locked. I try again before whirling to him.

"Unlock the door," I command.

A sudden sharp pain shoots through my fingertips and up my forearm, rooting me where I stand. I cry out and grip my right arm as the spasm works its way higher and higher. He remains watching me, unfazed by my outburst.

"What the fuck is happening?! Are you doing this?" I shout, holding up my searing arm.

He just watches, offering no answer. Trembling from the pain, I wrestle the door handle with my good hand.

"Open this door!" I cry, panic threatening to choke me.

"I'm afraid I can't do that."

I turn to face him, pressing my back against the wood.

"What do you want from me?"

"Say the words."

"*What?*"

"Say the words, and you will be free."

What the actual fuck.

"If I say the damn words, you'll stop whatever you're doing? You'll let me go?" I bark, fighting to keep my voice steady.

He inclines his head in a silent dare.

I approach the table with caution and slide the book toward me. The pain is now lancing through my other arm and up my shoulder. Bracing my throbbing hands on the cool table, I recite the words on the page.

"*I would look upon the world as it were. To see what is unseen. To know what lies beyond the veil.*"

My heart thunders as I glare back at the old man. At the face that, at one point in his life, might have been handsome. But those kind brown eyes now hold something strange and secret. Something dangerous.

I open my mouth to say something but am distracted by the steam rising from below me. A sizzle crackles in my ear and I jump back, feeling a flood of heat roll off the book. Only it isn't coming from the book.

My hands have left a detailed imprint where they branded the wood. Steam hisses as it touches the cool air, and the entire table seems to vibrate. The book begins to glow like a hot coal, eager to leap from the fire and wreak havoc on the world.

"Oh my god," I breathe in horror. "Oh my god, what's happening to me!" My throat tightens to the point of pain as hellfire scalds my uplifted palms.

But something catches my eye beyond my burning hands. A small, slow metamorphosis.

Mr. T's features begin to melt, to shift. Wrinkles begin to smooth, sagging cheeks right themselves against gravity, thin lips grow full, pink and plump. Patches of white hair warm into burnished waves that flow like an ocean tide bathed in sunset. Bony arms form smooth, lean muscle and the person before me stands tall, his figure no longer that of a non-threatening elderly bookstore owner.

A vital young man now stands before me, looking beautiful and fresh as springtime. The only thing recognizable about him are those brown eyes. Only they burn brighter now, the irises like melted chocolate. That sparkle has returned accompanied by an air of mischief.

In a matter of seconds, Mr. Tatler is gone, replaced by a beautiful stranger.

I let out a blood-curdling scream.

3

My appendix burst when I was nine years old.

One second, I'm in my friend's backyard playing popcorn on her trampoline, and the next, I'm doubled over, screaming in pain, being rushed to the ER. My dad squeezes my hand while nurses bustle around the room, readying me for surgery. Then I'm being wheeled into an OR, shrinking back from the harsh fluorescent lights overhead. Someone tells me to count backward from ten. I think I make it to seven before the world drops out from beneath me and there is nothing but sweet, empty silence. Darkness welcomes me into its velvet arms and pulls me into a dreamless sleep.

Coming out of that sleep, my body and mind are reluctant. I do not want to return to the light. Anxiety laces my blood as the anesthesia wears off, leaving a sticky panic in its wake. My heart is beating too fast. My thoughts race to make up for lost time, unleashing themselves one after another like a swarm of locusts as my stomach lurches. My eyes fly open, and I am gasping.

This feels a lot like that.

I blink, trying to somehow clear away the image of the figure standing before me. But no matter how many times my eyes open and close, the Mr. Tatler I know is gone.

Something about this is very, very wrong. But I don't plan on sticking around to find out what.

I lunge for the door again, ready to barrel right through it, but Mr. T—this stranger—springs to life in one graceful step. He's fast and agile as he grips my arm and roots me to the spot. I gasp at the sudden movement in such stark contrast to the old man who scuffles his feet when he pads across the bookshop floor. His hand feels so large wrapped around my bicep, his grip firm but not painful.

"Who are you?" I peer up at him, trying to wrestle free. "Let me go right now!"

"It's too late for that."

Even his voice is different. Softer, richer, like honey. Staring up at him, I notice the slight point at the tip of his ears.

What the actual.

"Please," I beg. "I don't know what this is, but I can't be here —I can't! Please!"

I don't even know what I'm saying, what I'm begging for, but I'm bordering on hysterical.

"I'm not going to hurt you." Something like pain flashes in his eyes. "But I can't let you leave, even if I wanted to."

He glances toward the heavy tome, still glowing eerily on the table.

I have to get out of here. *But how?*

He's gotta be over six feet tall. Even if I managed to swipe the keys from his pocket, he would have me pinned in an instant. I don't have any weapons on me, and even if I did, I probably wouldn't know how the hell to use them.

Except.

I did just scorch my handprints onto the wooden table. Maybe not of my own volition, but...

Before I think better of it, I clamp my fingers around his thick forearm and will myself to bring forth whatever fire seemed to flow from me a moment ago. I squeeze my eyes shut, my entire body clenching in effort.

"That's not going to work on me."

I peel my eyes open. A smile spreads over his lips as if he finds my effort cute.

"Sit down. We don't have much time," he says with gentle firmness.

"The fuck I will," I spit.

"I need to explain."

"Explain what you *did* to me?" I shove my hands in his face, but his grip doesn't loosen.

"What the hell is this? Where's Tatler?"

"I am Tatler. It was a glamour."

"Hah!" I bark. "Oh, it was a *glamour*? You think I'm an idiot?"

"I think you're in shock and denial. But either way, I need you to listen carefully." He holds me by the shoulders and locks me in an intense stare. I have no choice but to look up into his warm brown eyes.

"In a few moments, you will be summoned."

"What the—"

"Keep your eyes open and watch your back, wanderer. You won't be alone."

As he gazes down at me, black mist begins to materialize and curl around my ankles. The shadows kiss up my legs and cloud the room until we are almost completely ensconced in darkness.

There's no time to run, to hide, or to fight.

I watch from above as if my soul is detached from my body,

seeing myself unable to move. The book glows brighter now—white hot. That is the last thing I see before the darkness engulfs me and rips me from all I know.

~

I'M FALLING.

Wherever I am now, it is not of this world. *My* world. I unleashed Pandora's box when I spoke those words. And now I will pay.*

Malevolent winds bite at me as I plummet, nipping at my face with fierce aggression. There is the feeling of something tearing inside of me. I am being ripped open from my very chest, where my heart lies. The pain is like nothing I've felt before, and somewhere during my fall, I thankfully lose consciousness.

I'm woken by the distant sound of rustling leaves and men's shouting voices. Something warm and wet tickles my cheek. I crack my eyes open to find a furry-faced creature with a delicate black nose and familiar brown eyes licking my face.

The shouts grow closer as the animal nudges me, head-butting me with a sense of urgency. I struggle to my elbows, trying to recall how I ended up on the floor of this unsettling, whitewashed forest. Milky leaves crunch beneath me, blanketing the ground along with something else—something white, smooth, and hard. The jagged sticks leave impressions on my arms as I force myself upright.

Trees the color of freshly fallen snow surround me, their barren branches reaching so high they disappear into the thick clouds.

My head snaps toward the sound of heavy gallops.

---

* Cue: *DVD Menu* by Phoebe Bridgers

Something is coming. Someone. *Many* someones.

"This way!"

I whirl in time to see a massive black horse racing toward me, with a dark armored soldier astride.

He casts out his hand in my direction and before I can blink, a large net is around me, sweeping me off my feet. The horse begins to drag me across the forest floor, threatening to take the skin off my back. My scream is silenced by the guttural sounds coming from the strange lupine creature that woke me.

It has the narrow snout and fluffy tail of a white fox, only its size is that of a wolf. I've never seen anything like it.

But decoding this fox is very low right now on my list of figuring out what the *fucking fuck* is going on.

I watch as it leaps, razor-like fangs bared, and latches onto the rider's neck with alarming accuracy. He topples as his horse skids to a stop. Grappling for one of the sharp sticks on the ground, I quickly saw through the net, tearing it wide enough to slip through. I break free in time to see four more dark soldiers galloping toward us.

The soldier and the feral creature are still locked in a face-off, the lithe wolf-fox snapping his jaws at my opponent.

He's incapacitated. This could be my only shot to run. But I find myself unable to move, unable to abandon the odd animal defending me so fiercely.

A sharp yelp bursts from its mouth as the soldier knocks it back with his heavy boot. He starts toward me, but the animal is relentless—scrambling between us with bared fangs as the other riders dismount and approach with inhuman speed. Before I can react, my arms are pinned behind my back, and I'm forced onto my knees.

"Don't touch me!" I shout and am met with a hard slap to my face. I don't even see it coming.

The force knocks me sideways. Pain blossoms across my

cheek, and a metallic taste coats my tongue. But my forest friend is there, in front of me, growling like a rabid dog. Snarling in the face of the strangers, defying certain death.

One of the helmeted soldiers loads an arrow into a bow and aims at the creature.

"No!" I gasp, scrambling to knock it out of the way.

I'm too late.

The arrow whizzes past me and lodges itself in the creature's chest. It collapses, its cries of agony cracking my heart. I rush to its side, not knowing what to do but knowing I must do something as it stills beneath my hands.

Pull it out, something inside of me whispers.

With no time to second guess, I rip the arrow from its limp body. I whirl toward the soldier as he pulls his elbow back, a second arrow at the ready.

A large hand on his chest halts him.

"Stop."

The voice is deep and commanding.

"But Captain—"

"She goes unharmed. Take her to the king."

The man hauls himself onto the largest horse and rides off while I am bound at the wrists and ankles, thrown over the side of a glossy black steed, and held there by a faceless armored brute. I try to fight, try to resist, but it's useless.

As we ride away, I strain to look back at the wounded animal. Blood leaks from its chest, staining the white-floored forest crimson. I squeeze my eyes shut, unable to bear the sight any longer. There's nothing I can do now.

"Where are you taking me?" I demand.

"To pay a little visit to the king, witch."

"Witch?" I scoff. "You can't be serious."

He doesn't answer.

"Where are we?"

"Bone Forest. But I'm sure you already knew that."

"This isn't happening. How did I—what happened..."

I trail off, trying to make sense of the past ten minutes. I make zero.

"Please, please, stop. I need help. I think I'm a long way from home. I don't know how I got here. Whatever it was, it was an accident. Please, just tell me how to get home."

"Quit your babbling, witch."

"I said, I'm not a witch!"

"You'd best hold your tongue before the king. He doesn't take kindly to mouthy little females. No matter how pretty."

My stomach twists.

We travel on at a swift speed for what feels like hours. Each gallop sends me bouncing with a punch to my gut. I crane my neck to take in my surroundings.

We've passed through the strange whitewashed forest and into one of familiar greens and browns. Night blackens the sky, the moon casting an eerie glow over all it touches. I have no idea how my captors can navigate the narrow space between trees at a pace like this.

I'm filled with apprehension as we reach a portcullis built into the side of a massive mountain. It rises noisily as we proceed and are swallowed up by the crag. The gate lowers behind me, sealing me in. And likely sealing my tomb.

I can barely see through the dark, but these men seem to have no trouble at all as they dismount and pass the horses off to a worker dressed in ratty clothes. I'm pulled from the saddle and the bindings at my ankles are slashed. A wave of dizziness hits me as I'm jerked upright.

"Walk, witch." The rider grabs me by my bound arms and marches me into a dark cavernous tunnel.

Flaming lanterns line the walls of the narrow corridor, guiding us deeper into the mountain. A chill rolls through the air, wafting from the other side of the stretch, where a soft bluish-white light gleams with promise. We reach the source as I am guided into a glittering cavern of light and refraction.

Diamonds, uncut and raw lace every inch of the space. Massive stalagmites that hold every color of the rainbow jut from the floor. Crystalline icicles drip from the cave's towering arches, dagger-like and dangerous. Pools of water curtain the walkway on which we now stand, the light coming from beneath a mesmerizing sea-foam green. The entire space is sharp, lethal, and filled with searing beauty. I stand breathless, in awe of my surroundings.

But despite the marvelous sight, my gaze is drawn elsewhere. My heart flutters as I am guided toward a raised dais where two figures wait on crystalline thrones carved into the rock itself.

My eyes land on the man. His familiar brown eyes and thick brows, straight nose, and dark hair the same shade as mine.

It can't be.

It's just an optical illusion created by the lights and the rocks.

But then I'm a foot away from him being forced onto my knees, and there is no mistaking that face as he rises from his diamond throne and takes a step closer, peering down with a stern expression.

He nods his head once, and I'm wrenched to my feet to find myself face-to-face with my father.

4

My father.

He's *alive* and standing right in front of me.

What is he doing here? Why is he wearing a crown?

"*Dad!*"

Tears spring from my eyes as I fling myself toward him, ready to throw my arms around his neck and never let go. Instead, I'm met with two razor-sharp spears angled directly at my rib cage. I stumble back so as to not impale myself on the guards' weapons as they take up a menacing position between us.

"Dad, it's *me!*" I cry out in disbelief.

His gaze is cold and hard. Unflinching—as if I don't exist.

"It's *Serena.*"

The unnaturally beautiful woman seated on the throne behind him rolls her eyes, looking bored as she mutters, "Good gods, Derek, one of your bastards?"

I search my dad's face. It's set in hard lines—jaw tense, brows creased. His dark beard is longer and thicker than I've ever seen. His hair falls past his ears. And on his head sits a crown that looks heavy and cold. Shining silver, spiked with dew drops of diamond and onyx that devours the light. He has meat on his bones. He looks sturdy and strong. Healthy and whole.

My heart lurches.

It's Dad.

Power bubbles in the space around him. I can feel his presence like a pressure in the air. It's palpable. My eyes snag on his ears, where I notice a small arching point where there should be a rounded curve.

"No bastard of mine, wife." His voice is icy, showing no indication of emotion or even recognition.

"Ah," she denotes, dangling a lithe arm over the side of her diamond throne. "Just a common whore peddling for attention then." Her words lash out like a whip to slap me across the face. Dad says nothing.

Does he really not recognize me?

He turns and starts back toward the throne, his dark fur-lined cloak trailing behind him.

Off to the left, a female silhouette draws my attention. I notice the shimmer of her diamond and opal tiara before I lock eyes with my sister. Sam.

This can't be real. *Where the fuck are we?*

"Why do you insist on wasting my time with these inconsequential audiences, Captain?" Dad drones.

One of the armored guards steps forward, removing his black metal helmet. When he speaks, I recognize his as the voice in the forest—the one that stopped the other guard from rendering the killing blow on my furry defender.

But I can't look at him. I can't move. I can't pry my eyes away from my undead father standing before me in furs and a crown.

"I would not dare waste your valuable time, my King, had I not thought it a matter of great importance."

"Then, by all means, keep me in suspense no further." Dad drops into his seat and waves an impatient hand, urging the guard to continue. He clears his throat, and Dad follows his gaze to the remaining guards standing off to the side, silent and stone-faced. He dismisses them with a wave, leaving me behind in a room of familiar strangers.

"She appeared in a cloud of shadow smoke at the edge of the Bone Forest. My men and I brought her straight away. Sire, it's possible the girl may be a witch."

The woman lazing about in her seat straightens, planting her heels on the floor, gripping the throne's glittering arms with her razor-sharp nails. She leans forward, suddenly very interested in the conversation.

"A witch, you say?" Her icy eyes gleam as they peer into my own.

Her beauty is arresting. Eyes so blue they nearly burn silver, framed by hair black as night. Her silken locks are woven into an elegant golden crown inset with diamonds and rubies, leaving her strange ears to peek through. She studies me carefully from head to toe, her knuckles turning white from her vice-like grip on the throne. "Derek."

He inclines his head, eyeing me warily as he rises to his feet again.

"She's human," he says suspiciously. "Shadow smoke. You're sure of this?"

The captain nods.

"Was she alone?"

"She was found with an *OrCat*."

"A familiar?"

"Kill it," the queen snaps. Dad shoots her a piercing look.

"These are *my* lands. You know the law. No harm shall come to a familiar on Aegean soil."

"Even that which belongs to a common whore witch?" She scowls with distaste.

"Your Majesty, the creature attacked one of my men. It was shot in defense before I could intervene," the captain says from beside me. My father's eyes snap to him as he inches closer.

"Tell me you did not *kill* the *OrCat*, Captain." His words are clipped and quiet, making his rage seem all the more terrifying. "Where is it now?"

"Left in the forest. The shot was only meant to incapacitate while we delivered the girl."

"Pray to the gods it still lives. Send out a search party and have it brought to me. *Alive*. Do you understand?"

"Yes, sire." The captain bows low.

Dad tosses a careless nod in my direction. "Have her put in a holding cell until Gnorr can examine her. Bind her with blood ore."

"She needs to be questioned," the severe woman behind him protests.

"And she will be." The sharpness of his tone leaves no further room for debate.

Tossing the guard a curt nod, he turns his back and starts toward the empty throne where my sister waits, silent and unaffected. I don't dare call out to her—plead with her to see me, hear me, help me. Her imperious gaze remains fixed on the man beside me.

Before I can protest, my arms are yanked forward. The bindings are replaced by two heavy shackles the color of rust, the color of...oh my god.

I'm going to throw up. It's dried blood.

Nausea roils inside of me as I'm gripped around the arm by a rough, callused hand and dragged into a corridor to the right, away from my dad and sister. Away from the only familiar faces in this place. I'm towed down what feels like a million stairs before we reach another passageway.

"Please," I entreat the guard hauling me forward.

When he doesn't answer, I dig my heels into the ground and rear back with all my might. Resisting against his grasp is futile. With his impressive height and strength, he lifts my arm higher, forcing me onto my tiptoes where I have to fight to keep my feet beneath me.

"Look, I'm not a witch, I swear. I don't even know where I am or how I got here. I just want to go home. I opened that stupid book and—"

My foot catches a snag in the floor causing me to lurch forward. The guard jerks me upright.

"Jesus H. Christ!" I squeal.

"Hold your tongue, witch. I'll not have you hauling hexes on me, blood ore or not."

"I told you I'm not a witch! My name is Serena Avery. That was my father in there. You have to take me back. I need to speak with him."

"The king is your father, is he?" His eyes remain fixed straight ahead as he gibes, "And Queen Ilspeth is my mother."

The two guards trailing us let out a chuckle. I preen my head to scowl at them. They have matching faces and the same flowing auburn hair. Twins.

We reach a dark, dimly lit cell with iron bars. Inside sits a plain wooden chair with leather straps secured to the armrests. One of the twin guards steps forward and unlocks the door, holding it open.

"Just tell me where I am. Please. I don't belong here," I entreat my captor. He looks at me for the first time, and I gasp.

"You're right, you belong in here."

With a swift shove, he retracts his grip, and I career face-first into the ground. The uneven stone bites into my cheek-bone. Shaking fingers lift to my face. They're tinged red when I pull them away.

"See to it that she settles in. I'll be back," he says to the twin guards before disappearing down the hall.

Tears pool in my unblinking eyes. The salt stings the cut on my cheek as they fall.

"*Jack*," I croak after him.

5

I knew I had too much to drink. But who cared? Everyone there was over-served, and that was fine because it was New Year's Eve, and we were all just going to crash on whoever's living room floor this was anyway.

I didn't know many people there. Annie's friend, Dee, practically forced us to come. But the flood of champagne had my body singing. They were all so beautiful in their shiny metallic dresses and little sequin numbers. The boys looking sharp in button-down shirts and black pants, streamers and confetti dusting their shoulders. I loved all of these strangers, this throng of people revolving around me, beaming like a sexy disco ball while I danced directly beneath shrouded in good times and good vibes. I was so gone that I was actually giggling to myself as I peered over the balcony railing, waving down at the people in the streets shouting, "Happy New Year!"

I didn't hear him creep up next to me. I felt the brush of a shoulder against mine and turned.

Though the image could have been less blurry had I not

been so intoxicated, I'll never forget seeing him for the first time.

Dark hair falling just past his ears, eyes an intense honey color, and a tiny silver hoop piercing his full bottom lip. He wasn't dressed in finery like the rest of us. Dressed down in a worn leather jacket, dark jeans, and boots, he put everyone to shame with casual ease. I could just make out the hint of tattoos licking up the strong column of his neck, peeking out above the collar of his black T-shirt. He was a walking warning sign screaming, *"CAUTION."* But those honeyed eyes locked with mine and we started to laugh. Over nothing.

I don't remember what we talked about but he never left my side that night. We stayed up talking long after everyone else had scattered and passed out, covering every surface, nook, and cranny with their drunken bodies. I woke the next morning with one of the worst hangovers of my life, fully clothed, with a pair of heavy, tattooed arms wrapped around my waist.

I tried to disengage from him without jostling him awake, but he tightened his grip, pulling me flush against his chest as he whispered in my ear, "I don't know your name, but I'm pretty sure I told you I loved you last night."

I giggled through the raging headache. "I think you did."

He sighed happily. "Well, I'm psychic, so it wasn't complete bullshit."

"Well, then maybe you can tell me if my car is gonna make it another year or if I should trade it in while I have the chance?"

"Oh, you don't believe me?"

"Not even a little."

"You'll see, baby. I'm gonna marry you." He planted a sweet kiss on my neck and sat up. "After I take you to breakfast."

∼

FIRST MY DAD, then my sister, and now…

Jack is here. *My* Jack.

This can't be real. It just can't. This *has* to be a dream.

But that was *him*. Only not.

He seemed even more beautiful than the last time I saw him. As if that were humanly possible. Those eyes that used to remind me of honey were now liquid gold. His hair was shorter than when I last saw him—cropped closer on the sides with enough left on top to spill over his forehead in a roguish, lazy way, leaving his high cheekbones and strong jawline to shine.

Had he always been so tall, so strapping? *Captain*, they had called him. He clearly didn't recognize me either.

How is it possible that no one recognizes me?

The twin guards haul me up and heave me into the chair, securing the leather restraints around my forearms. The moment they're gone, I fight against the thick straps, jerking my arms to no avail.

Roughly half an hour later, a long shadow appears down the hall. Jack breezes into my cell, face hard as stone as he slides on a pair of black leather gloves.

"Alright, witch. I'm going to ask you some questions," he says absentmindedly, as if this were a doctor's visit.

He stops in front of a small wooden table near the wall where he uncovers a series of silver knives. My stomach tightens.

"Answer them truthfully, and this will be relatively painless for you. Lie to me or neglect to answer them, and I don't think you'll find the alternative enjoyable."

"What do you want from me?"

"*Oh.*" He turns to me, eyebrows raised, his voice dripping in sarcasm. "I think you're mistaken. *I* ask the questions here."

He circles me, slowly sizing me up before stopping in front of me, hands folded behind his back.

"Who are you."

"My name is Serena Avery. I don't know how I got here—"

"Ah, ah, ah." He holds up a hand. "Let's not get ahead of ourselves. One step at a time. Serena, is it?"

"It is," I bite.

"What were you doing in the Bone Forest?"

"I told you, I don't know how I got there. I don't know anything."

He tuts.

"See, I think you do." Shaking his head in disapproval, he picks up a serrated knife and holds it up to the light, examining it like a serial killer.

"I'm telling the truth. I have no idea how I got here."

"You know, for a human, you're not ugly," he muses, lowering the knife to my cheek. I hold my breath.

"Not exactly a compliment," I mutter, chancing a look up into a set of dazzling golden eyes.

"I didn't say you were beautiful," he specifies. "It's a plain face. But an interesting one. However, I think I can make it even more interesting."

His voice sends traitorous chills down my arms as it leaves his mouth. He crouches before me, leaning over my lap with the knife still pressed to my cheek. He tickles it along my skin, teasing the pain that will come if he applies just a touch more pressure.

"I have no reason to lie to you," I say evenly, my eyes holding his.

"Don't you?"

"No."

"Are you a witch?"

A laugh bursts out of me as I stare at him. He stares back, unblinking and unamused.

"Oh, you're serious?"

"I'd like to show you just how serious I am," he murmurs, gently dragging his knife up the inside of my leg to stop above my knee. The sound of my scream echoes down the cavernous hall as he sinks the tip into the meaty part of my thigh.

He makes no move to pull the it out. Instead, he holds it in place with the tip of his long pointer finger.

"Don't waste your energy all at once. We're just getting started. Now tell me how a human came to appear in the Bone Forest by way of shadow smoke?"

"I don't know what the fuck you're talking about!" I growl, tugging at my restraints. A red splotch blooms around his knife, drenching my jeans in blood.

"Red blood." He clicks his tongue. "Not a promising start. Is it a glamour?"

His knife digs in the slightest bit more, and a high-pitched yelp tears from me. I force myself to smile and laugh through the searing pain.

"If this is your idea of flirting, you're gonna have to do better than that."

His upper lip curls back in a snarl.

"I'll be straight with you. You're only here because you're suspected of being the last Blackblood witch."

"On what grounds?"

"Well, let's see—is materializing in a cloud of smoke with a rabid familiar grounds enough for you?"

I shake my head, exasperated. "Again, I don't know what you're talking about."

"If you just cut the act and tell me the truth, this can be over."

"And then what? Will you let me go?"

He gives a noncommittal shrug. "I haven't decided yet."

"Look, just tell me what it is you want to hear because I truly don't know."

He pauses, and for a moment, I think he might believe the sincerity of my words. But instead, he shoves the knife all the way through my leg to the hilt.

I wail before my body goes into shock. Blood splatters his dark leathers as he wrenches the knife free and stands, wiping the blade on his pant leg. He stares down at me with icy indifference, ignoring the pool of blood gathering at my feet.

He must have hit a major artery because I'm getting dizzy fast.

"I'm going to bleed out if you don't help me," I breathe, my head lolling back as I struggle to remain awake. His image starts to blur beyond my blinking eyes. The last thing I see before they close is his knife slicing through the leather restraints before bending to scoop me up in his arms.

6

I wake on a cot in the same cell, a thin blanket draped over me. Heart racing, I rip it back to examine my leg.

It is healed completely.

It's impossible. I shake my head, dumbfounded. The massive burgundy stain on my jeans is proof enough that I didn't imagine it. But there is no deep gash, no scratch.

Nothing.

I scramble to the iron bars, pulling and pounding them until my hands are bloody and bruised. I shout until my voice is hoarse from crying out for my father like a child waking fresh out of a nightmare. Exhausted and heartbroken, I sink to my knees.

I don't make it back to the cot.

I curl up in the fetal position, shivering on the cold, hard floor as hot tears stream down my face. A dull ache forms in my chest as I replay the earlier interaction between me and my dead father. The overwhelming shock of seeing him alive and healthy catches up to me in a raging flood of emotion. The sobs shake me relentlessly as I flip back and forth between terror, confusion, and strange joy.

Because I thought I had said goodbye to my dad forever.

That is the only silver lining to this sordid mess. Seeing his face again.

Even if he doesn't recognize me. Even if I die in this cell waiting for him to come.

A small white dot darts into my vision, slipping beneath the barred door of my cell. A flash of light erupts, sending me sprawling back toward the stone wall. The tiny white mouse is replaced by a male form. I find myself staring into the warm brown eyes of a young Mr. Tatler.

And his totally naked body.

I open my mouth to scream, but he rushes forward, clamping a hand over it and crouching in front of me.

"The guards will hear. If they find out I can shift in here, they will have me removed. I'm not going to hurt you," he says, his voice hushed. He slowly eases his hand from my lips, watching my reaction.

"Where are your clothes?" I hiss. I don't intend for that to be the first question out of my mouth, but the amount of skin he's showing makes it kind of difficult to form a coherent thought.

"You humans with your shame." He shakes his head and does a quick sweep of the room, snatching the thin wool blanket off the cot and draping it around his waist. With his lean, muscled chest and arms still bare, it isn't much of an improvement to my poor concentration. His eyes catch on my bloodied pants and widen in horror.

"What happened?" he demands, dropping down to brace my thigh in his hands.

I shove his hands away.

"I was strapped to a chair, tortured, and accused of being a witch."

"They tortured you?" The color leeches from his face before something like rage takes over.

"Yeah, and I'm guessing it had something to do with your little stunt with the book," I growl. "How did you just do that? You were a *mouse*."

My head swims as I search for answers in those eyes, those familiar brown eyes.

I gasp.

"In the forest, that *fox-wolf* thing that tried to save me, that was you?"

He presses his lips together—his answering silence confirmation enough. My gaze shoots to his chest, where the arrow pierced him. I reach forward instinctively to check for the damage. He gently encloses my hands in his before I can touch him.

"I'm alright. You pulled the arrow out before the paralytic spread. I was able to heal myself."

"Heal yourself?"

I stare at the tiny pink mark above his breast where there should be a gaping hole. The skin is perfectly smooth. My eyes snag on the small tattoo across from it. Over his heart are two overlapping circles joined with a small star in the shared space.

I wrench my hands out of his grasp.

"What are you? Where the *fuck* are we?" The questions tumble out of me like an avalanche.

"We're in my home, Solterre, world of the fae."

World of the fae.

I blink and give that a moment to sink in.

"That *fox-wolf* thing from the forest is called an *OrCat*. And yes, that was me. I'm fae." He turns his head to the side and tucks his silky, caramel-colored hair behind his ear. His slightly *pointed* ear. "And a shifter."

"A shapeshifter? You're fae...and a shapeshifter?" I repeat mechanically.

"I'm sorry you had to find out like this. About all of it." His expression is sincere.

I don't trust it.

But with the wall at my back and his half-naked body so close, I have nowhere to retreat. A beat passes while I stare at him, grasping at straws for any logical explanation for what's happening, but it's getting harder to deny how very real it all feels.

"What did you do to Tatler?"

His brown eyes hold mine as he takes a steadying breath. "I am Tatler. Just as I have been many people to you."

I wait with narrowed eyes.

"I have been Tatler. I have been Annie Arnold, I've been your third-grade math teacher, the health inspector for The Black Rose, and many, many others. My name is Zadyn. I am your familiar, blood sworn to you at birth to protect and guide you. I have been with you your whole life, though unbeknownst to you."

"You've been posing as different people in my life ever since I was born?"

He nods.

"That's impossible. Annie? One of my best friends?" I gape.

There is no way. *No way* she could have been this person all along.

Although, she did drop off the face of the earth pretty abruptly. I remember thinking it was strange at the time, but I just chalked it up to her being happily married in a foreign country. My heart sinks at the possible truth of his claim. Shaking the thought from my head, I force myself to stay present.

"Why am I here? Why is my dad here, my sister, Ja—" I

swallow abruptly. Saying that name will just trigger the water-works all over again. "Why is my family here, and why don't they know me?"

He sighs, leaning back, palms splayed on the stone floor. His abs threaten to distract me from the rising panic.

"The world of the fae is like a mirror to the human world. A parallel universe. People here may seem familiar, but do not mistake them for the people you know—the people you love—despite any appearances. You must treat them like strangers, or else it can cause a ripple effect that alters nature's course," he warns.

I shake my head in opposition.

"I need to speak with my dad. He'll recognize me if..."

The stranger—Zadyn—shakes his head, his eyes filled with regret.

"I'm afraid that won't be the case. The king has an entirely different set of memories, a past absent of you. That isn't the man that raised you."

I blink back idiotic tears.

"In this world, your father is King Derek Accostia, one of the five fae kings of Solterre. This is his kingdom, Aegar." He pauses, no doubt reading my crestfallen expression.

"And my sister?

"Her name is Sorscha. She's the king's only living heir, born from his late wife, Queen Margot. Queen Ilspeth is her stepmother."

The image of the cold, beautiful female on the diamond throne beside my father flashes through my mind.

"This is insane...why am I here?"

"In this cell or in this world?" he asks earnestly.

"Both!" I shout, my voice clamoring against the walls. "Why am I being tortured for information?! Why am I being called a witch?!"

"The Kingsguard must have seen the shadow smoke in the Bone Forest when we arrived. They brought you here because they think—they hope—that you're the last Blackblood witch."

"Are you kidding? That's literally insane. Why would they think that?"

"I was getting to that part," he says almost guiltily. Fixing him with a death glare, I lean in.

"What. Part."

"You were born in the mortal realm," Zadyn begins slowly, readying me for the shoe I know he's about to drop. "But you possess the last drop of black blood left in this world, in all worlds."

"Meaning *what* exactly."

"Meaning that you are the one and only living descendant of the Blackblood clan."

I don't know what that means, but a wild laugh bursts from me because I'm sure, I am *positive*, that I hit my head in the bookshop and none of this is really happening. I shove to my feet to pace around the small cell while Zadyn watches me carefully from the ground.

"Are you alright?" he asks after a moment.

"I think you're sorely mistaken. I was born in the *human* world, on this little planet called *Earth*—I believe you've heard of it? My father was not *fae* or '*Blueblood*,'" I use air quotes.

"Blackblood," he corrects.

"And my mother may be a witch, but she sure as shit isn't the kind you're referring to. Both parents perfectly human, okay? Just like me." I gesture to my disheveled, bloodstained body.

"Your lineage has no bearing. Black blood isn't hereditary; the magic chooses. You were chosen across worlds, across time."

"How did you—never mind. This is all a pipe dream. I've

completely lost my shit." I toss my shackled arms up and slide down the length of the rough, uneven wall. "Oh, well. Guess I don't have to file taxes this year on account of insanity."

"This is very real." Zadyn scoots closer and places a large hand over my drawn-up knee, peering into my eyes. The warmth in his beautiful face is almost enough to combat my speeding heart and growing anxiety.

Almost. But not quite.

"Don't you think I'd know if I was a witch?" I hiss. "I have no supernatural abilities. I never *have*, and believe me, I've attended my fair share of middle school sleepover seances."

"You *are* the last Blackblood," he affirms. "You may not know it yet, but you have great power within you."

Shaking my head, I counter, "And why should I believe a word you say? You've lied to me my whole life, and you expect me to just believe I was chosen by some voodoo bullshit to be a witch? Maybe you're just as crazy as I am."

My gaze falls to the heavy shackles encircling my wrists.

"Look at me."

Reluctantly, I do as he says.

"I'm telling you the truth. You were chosen. Just as I was chosen to be your familiar, to guard you, and deliver you here safely. This mark—it brought me to you." He points to the tattoo on his chest.

"Your tattoo?"

"It's the mark of a familiar," he explains. "It appeared when you were born."

Absurd. So fucking absurd.

"The mark acts like a compass, guiding me to you. You were glamoured at birth to blend in with the humans of your world. Your magic was repressed, your appearance muted."

"*Blend* in with the humans? I *am* human. Why would I need a glamour to blend?"

"You may have been born in the human world, but you aren't human. Witches are native to Solterre."

"There's no way." I slide my fingers into my hair, gripping it by the roots. "There's just no way. You're trying to tell me that I'm not human? That this isn't my real face? That I have *magic* inside me?" My voice rises with growing hysteria.

"Yes. Exactly."

"Oh my god," I groan, knocking my head against the wall. "Can this nightmare just be over already?"

"I know this is a lot. I never intended to deceive you." He sounds truly regretful. I crack an eye to peer at him.

"We'll circle back to the lying and deceiving part." Blowing out a long breath, I stare up at the dark ceiling. "What do they want with me? Are they going to kill me?"

"No." Surprise flashes in Zadyn's eyes. "King Derek needs you. For the dragon. He's been searching for centuries—"

"Centuries?" I repeat, making sure I heard him correctly.

"The fae are immortal," he says, shrugging his shoulder. "Most of us have lived far longer than you can even comprehend."

I jerk forward, coming nearly nose-to-nose with him.

"Oh, I think I *comprehend* that just fine. What I *can't* seem to comprehend is how and why I am now stuck in a mirror world where my own father locks me in a dungeon because he wants to use me and my *black blood* to what? Slay a dragon?" I spit.

"Not to slay, never to slay."

He shakes his head, his eyes reverent.

"To ride."

I stare at him in utter disbelief.

He presses on, rushing his words as if I'll stop him at any moment.

"This world hasn't seen a Dragon Rider for thousands of years. The Blackbloods were the *only* ones powerful enough to wield dragon magic without being torn apart. There is only one left in our world, and you alone are capable of bonding her. All five kingdoms have been hunting for you for ages."

"A literal witch hunt." I swallow hard in utter disbelief. "For me? Why?"

"Many reasons, the main one being that a dragon is an invaluable war weapon."

I close my eyes and pinch the bridge of my nose.

"This is a mistake. I'm not a Dragon Rider, and I can't be a witch. It isn't me. You've got the wrong girl."

"I don't, and whether you want to admit it or not, neither do they. I know who you are. I've been there all your life, and I'll be there every moment from now until your last breath. My life is tied to yours."

I shake my head and fall silent, trying to process all this information. I hear what he's saying, but it's not making any sense. A magical world with fae? With witches? Dragons? It's impossible.

After a few moments of fighting back tears of confusion and frustration, I force myself to look back at Zadyn.

"How can I trust you? How can I believe you when all of this"—I gesture around me—"is straight out of a fantasy book?"

His gaze falls to my bloody fists. Gently pulling me forward, he places his hands over mine. Warmth spreads through my palms and up my arms as I glance from our joined hands to his long, lowered lashes. When he pulls back, my shackled hands are as good as new. I stare up at him, awestruck.

"All stories are rooted in truth. No matter how outlandish. You were always meant to be here."

"I just had a knife jammed in my leg! I'm trapped in a dungeon with you, waiting to see if I'll live or die! Not feeling very welcome here at the moment!"

"I won't let anything happen to you," he says matter-offactly. "Besides, they would never truly harm you. You're too valuable to them. They're likely only keeping you here until they can confirm your identity. All you have to do is prove you are who you are."

"Well, that's not gonna be very easy since I don't have magic, and I just learned I was a witch two seconds ago!"

"Slow down." He reaches out, placing a gentle hand on my knee. "Take a breath. You're trying to process everything. I know it's a lot. You're taking it better than I expected, actually."

I glare at him, and he slowly retracts his hand.

"How did you even get in here?" I ask after some time.

"Shapeshifting has its perks," he shrugs. "Tiny spaces, tiny body."

He opens his mouth to say more, but the sound of footfalls outside the door distracts him. A bright light flares, and once again, I'm seated across from a little white mouse.

One of the twin guards with hair like burnished copper unlocks my cell and drags me down the corridor. Zadyn scurries behind us as I'm ushered up endless sets of stairs and hallways that open up to a castle so stunning my mouth drops.

Like the diamond cave, every surface of the high arching hall sparkles brilliantly. I gape at the polished blue-white marble floors and pillars, the ceilings lined with diamond chandeliers that dangle overhead with no visible suspensions, the windowed walls that peer out over shadowed hills and black waterways glittering with night. In the distance, I can vaguely make out the twinkling lights of a city in the valleys below. I'm so distracted by my surroundings, I barely even notice as I'm yanked to a stop.

The guard knocks twice on the door before us. "Madame Gnorr, I've brought the girl."

"Send her in," a voice calls from the other side.

The door opens to a small infirmary. A slight, elderly

woman in flowing gray robes turns to face me. Her face is so wrinkled I can barely make out her eyes. She must be a thousand years old. Her hair is concealed beneath a matching headpiece, displaying her gently pointed ears.

"Have a seat here, child." Her voice is warm and inviting as she gestures to one of the clean cots lining the wall.

I move toward her, my eyes darting around the room, taking in the shelves of colorful vials, the stacks of folded linens, and the small wooden work table scattered with scrolls and parchment.

"Privacy, if you please, Sir Maxim," she says to the guard.

He clears his throat, dipping his head. "I'll be outside."

The door closes, and a small silence ensues as the ancient-looking fae assesses me, hands folded in front of her.

"A familiar," she regards the white mouse at my ankles.

"How did you—"

She smiles knowingly. "How rare they have become. Treasure that bond."

I swallow as she turns her back and moves to open a wooden cupboard.

"Are you going to torture me, too?"

She whirls to me in surprise, taking in my bloodstained pants.

"No, child. But mark me, I will be having words with the captain about that," she promises. "My name is Gnorr. I've been the king's healer for fourteen hundred years. Long before King Derek was born. I served his father and his grandfather before him. I am not here to harm you, child. I am only meant to examine."

"You want to know if I'm a Blackblood."

She nods. Moving closer to me, she lays a gentle hand on my shoulder, prompting me to sit back on the cot. In her other hand, she holds a vial of fizzy blue liquid. She places it in my palm and gives me an encouraging nod.

"Drink."

"Not unless you tell me what this is," I protest.

"You will sleep and I will search." She taps my forehead twice. "Here."

"I'm not letting you into my mind." I shake my head.

"I promise to leave everything as I find it." She smiles, amused, lines crinkling her ancient face.

I dare a glance down at Zadyn.

Can I trust her?

In answer, he zigzags between her skirted legs, weaving between her frail ankles.

Take that as a yes.

I watch her warily as I gulp down the shimmering blue liquid, praying she didn't just feed me a melted Tide pod. It tastes sickly sweet. Like pears and cough syrup. Before I can form another thought, I'm out cold.

I don't know how long I'm down for. But when I wake, staring up at the ceiling, my head throbs. I blink and let out a loud gasp when I see Zadyn in his fae form perched beside me, watching over me intently.

"There you are," he says.

"You're not miniature," I croak, pushing up to my elbows. My throat is dry as sandpaper.

He chuckles. "Madame Gnorr is ancient. She knows what I am. She can be trusted."

"I gathered. What do you think she saw in my head? What was she looking for?"

"Her gifts are unique. That's why she's been in Aegar's employ for over three generations. She is a special kind of healer, a sensor. She reaches out into people's minds and, well, senses them. She can even transmute pain when necessary."

"So, like an empath," I say.

"Yes, but with the ability to alter emotions. She was getting a sense of you, sifting through memories and feelings."

"How intrusive."

"Better her than one of the Kingsguard torturing it out of you some more."

I roll my eyes.

Voices sound from outside the door and I freeze, straining to listen. Hearing my dad's deep voice, I race to the door, ready to fling it open but Zadyn is there in an instant, his hand closed over my wrist. He shakes his head and lifts his pointer finger to his lips. I hold his gaze as we eavesdrop on the conversation.

"Well? Is she a witch?" Dad asks in his familiar husky voice.

"I could sense witch blood in her, Majesty. Though it was very quiet."

"Black blood?" he presses.

"That I cannot glean, sire, not upon a first attempt, even with the elixir. There is a heavy glamour over her, one that I may only hope to undo in time. I do know that she is not of this world. She comes from the human realm, as she claimed."

A pause ensues. I hold my breath.

"Could she ride? With the proper training, of course."

"I cannot say with certainty, sire. The glamour is too thick. It would be a danger to the girl's life if she attempted to bond the dragon without black blood."

"She bleeds red," says another voice I recognize as Jack's. My heart clenches.

"I have seen glamours affect eye color, skin color, blood color, even scent. Magic is a very powerful thing. I would rule out nothing at this point."

"And this doe-eyed, lost little girl act? Is she mad or just a convincing actress?" Jack asks. "How many Blues have come forward over the years claiming to be the Dragon Rider to satisfy their own inflated sense of pride? How many idiots have lost their lives trying to wake her?" he says in disgust.

"I sense disorientation in her, Majesty. She is frightened and fatigued. If she is a Blackblood, she certainly isn't aware of it. It would take a skilled witch to be able to fool a sensor such as myself into a false reading."

"Not to mention it would be an act of treason," Jack adds with a bite to his voice.

"I have been at this longer than you have been alive, young Captain," she says lightly. "I sense no malice from her. Instead, I sense a tenderness for you, my King. She has told all that she knows."

"What do you propose we do with the girl?" the king says.

"She needs to be questioned further."

"I disagree, Captain. Torturing the girl isn't going to do any good in waking her magic or prying out answers she doesn't have. Put her to work around the castle. Keep eyes on her. Her magic will show itself in time. In the right environment, a *safe* environment," she says pointedly, "she may blossom and prove to be the one you seek."

"And if she's a danger?" Jack presses.

A long silence ensues.

"She poses no threat to the crown. Not to you, my King, nor to the princess."

"Very well, Gnorr. I thank you for your services and counsel," Dad says. His voice grows more distant, echoing off the walls. "See to it she's moved into the servant's quarters, Captain. And that she is kept comfortable. Have Sir Warryn guard her."

"Sire, what of—"

"See it done."

The hall goes silent.

I try to decipher Zadyn's expression before the door flings open. I jump back and nearly trample the short-haired white cat that crops up behind me. As I steady myself, I look up to see Madame Gnorr and Jack standing in the doorway. Watching me.

"Oh, good, she's awake," Jack says dryly, earning a soft smack in the stomach from the healer. He tosses her a look and then fixes those molten eyes on mine.

I should hate him. But even after he stuck a knife in my leg, it takes everything in my power not to run to him, to throw my arms around his neck and drink in that woodsy campfire scent I would know anywhere. But he regards me with not even an ounce of familiarity. It hurts to breathe under the scrutiny of his gaze.

"Come," he commands me in a cold voice. He doesn't wait to see if I obey.

I follow him, struggling to keep up with his long strides as I'm led to the servant's quarters. They smell better than the holding cell, but not by much. Jack pushes open the door to a small living space with a single bed shoved against the wall and a rickety-looking three-drawer dresser across from it.

"Home, sweet home," he croons as I step inside.

He doesn't seem to notice the small cat that slips into the room behind us as he waves a hand, and the restraints on my wrists clank to the floor.

"Change out of whatever it is you're wearing and put these on." He pulls open a drawer and tosses me a bundle of drab-looking garments. I catch them reflexively, staring at him without restraint until he notices.

"Problem, witch?"

"N—no," I stammer. "You just look like someone I know."

"Lucky him." He hurls the words like an insult as he takes in my disheveled hair, torn clothes, and bruising face.

"Dress quickly and meet me outside."

Without another word, he leaves me alone with Zadyn. I

begin to undress and then pause, my shirt halfway over my head.

"Turn around, you."

He purrs and leaps onto the bed, burying his face in his paws. As I pull my pants off, my phone goes tumbling out of my back pocket. I scramble to pick it up and try to get a signal. Nothing.

Jack knocks on the door to hurry me along. I stuff the phone under my pillow and start to dress.

The clothes he gave me are straight out of the Medieval Times costume department: a long sleeve, shapeless gray shift dress, and a lace-up brown leather bodice.

I frown at my Nikes. I'm guessing servants here aren't allowed to wear name brands. I slip them off in exchange for a pair of slippers lying in the corner. My hair feels like a rat's nest as I thread it through the elastic around my wrist and tug the ponytail tighter.

"Let's do this," I say, more to myself than to Zadyn.

With a steadying breath, I step into the hallway to begin my first day as one of my dad's employees.

7

I'm shown to the kitchens where bustling bodies rush around shouting friendly orders back and forth. Next, we visit the washrooms where the laundresses are dipping garments into large vats of water and hanging them to dry on lines of string stretched across the room. As we make our way down the hall, Jack barely answers any of my questions with more than one word.

"When can I see the king?" I ask. The question has burned me since I saw his face in the crystalline throne room. Jack doesn't deign to answer me.

"Where does my—" I cut off abruptly, clearing my throat. *Smooth.*

"Where does the princess reside?"

He peers down at me, his face a mask of disgust as I sidle up to him.

"That's none of your concern, witch."

"Oh, come on," I whine.

"What business would a *servant* have with the princess?" he asks condescendingly.

"I never thought I'd see the day where you talk down to me."

The words slip past my defenses as I shake my head. Then Zadyn's warning flashes in my mind—not to mistake these strangers for the people I knew.

He stops short, slowly turning to me.

"I'm sorry, what makes you think you've earned my respect?" he spits.

"Everyone deserves respect and you know it." I lift my chin, holding my ground. "I'm still waiting for an apology for the knife you stuck in my leg, by the way."

"Listen, witch." He stalks up to me menacingly, and for the first time, nothing of the man I loved remains in that hardened face.

"I brought you before the king solely out of protocol. But I do not take kindly to outsiders under the same roof as *my* king and *my* princess until they have proved themselves to be of no threat. Everything about you is screaming suspicion. And my gut is never wrong. You're lucky a knife in your leg was all I gave you for your silence. You make one wrong move—" He holds up his pointer finger in my face as he glowers down at me. "Just one, and I'll have your head in a basket. Blackblood bitch or no."

Without another word, he turns and stalks away. I can't get my legs to move. I can't follow him. And he doesn't turn back as I watch him disappear around a corner.

I FIND my way back to my room, guided by Zadyn's uncanny sense of direction. It must be late now, well past midnight. Or maybe it's morning. Who knows? My mind is too scrambled to care.

I collapse face-first into the bed, not expecting it to be cushy, but also not expecting it to be hard as a rock. I groan as the impact reverberates through my aching body.

Zadyn curls up in a little ball on the floor beside by bed. I debate asking him to shift. I know I should be demanding answers right now, but I don't have the strength to talk. To think. My mind is overloaded, my body exhausted. The second my eyes close, sleep drags me under.

Three brisk knocks jar me from my heavy slumber, sending my heart into a thundering sprint. My entire body tenses as I jolt upright.

"Rise and shine, missy!" a cheery voice calls from the hall.

I remain frozen. Three more knocks jostle my door.

"Open up, missy, or I'll have to come in there."

The melodic lilt is unthreatening, but I make my way to the door and crack it open to find a tall, freckled redhead with a sweet, round face and teal eyes staring back at me.

"How do you do this morning, miss?" She tilts her head, her gaze skipping from my ratty hair to the unlaced bodice twisted around my torso. "Oh, dear, now this won't do. We've got to make haste, or we'll be late for morning chores!"

She pushes into the room and swiftly moves behind me, righting my bodice and lacing it so tightly I think I've lost two inches around the waist. She makes quick work of braiding my hair before tossing me the gray slippers from yesterday. My hands shoot out, snatching them from the air.

"Oh good, you *are* awake." She smirks, holding the door open. "Now, come along."

I blink and follow her, still unable to find words.

"Cute kitty." Her voice brightens further as she glances down at Zadyn's feline form. I fall into step beside her, noticing the tiny arched ears beneath her own thick braid.

"I'm Igrid." She smiles warmly as we walk toward the

kitchens. "I've been assigned to show you the ropes around here. I hope we'll be good friends. It's been so long since we've had anyone new at the castle. I've grown bored of all these dull faces."

I stifle a laugh. Because every face I've seen so far in this strange world is uniquely beautiful. Some may be non-conventional, but each one is captivating in its own ethereal way. Even Madame Gnorr, in her old age, had an odd beauty to her.

"Well, are you going to tell me your name, miss?" She looks down at me, her button nose scrunching as she gasps. "Oh, dear gods, are you mute? Don't mind me—I'm a proper idiot!"

"No," I finally find my voice. "No, I'm not mute. I just think I'm still in shock."

"From what, may I ask?"

"It's a long story. One I'm even having trouble believing."

We reach the kitchens and Igrid directs me to pick up one of the polished silver serving trays, heavy with a variety of fruits, nuts, and cheeses. My stomach begins to rumble, and I realize that I haven't eaten since breakfast yesterday before I fell into another world. Before I learned that I'm of witch heritage and that I've been glamoured since birth.

I still don't quite believe it or understand it.

I follow Igrid up through the castle, into an ornate yet cozy dining room. A rich cherry wood table for eight takes center stage among the intricately woven carpets scattered around the floor. The far wall is made completely of glass, overlooking a terrifying drop into an unseen abyss.

We set our trays down on the table as more servants filter in with teas and cookies and all kinds of delicious smelling breads. As we line up along the wall, I take in the splendor of the uncut diamond light fixtures overhead, suspended in the air with no strings, no wires. They must be held in place by magic.

A hush settles over the space as the striking female from the throne room, Queen Ilspeth, breezes through the door, her glittering gold skirts flapping behind her. I'm oddly fascinated by the way she moves. I always thought queens moved with slow, elegant grace. But her movements are feline, prowling, and sharp. A coiled snake ready to strike at any moment. She acknowledges no one as she sits at the head of the table at the far side of the room.

A moment later, my sister is ushered in by three pretty young women, who I can only assume are her ladies-in-waiting. They curtsy to the queen before taking their places near the princess.

Sam is dressed in a simple but lovely dove gray gown with fitted gossamer sleeves and a belt of opal around her waist. Her hair, an enviable shade of light brown, falls in gentle waves past her chest. I want to shout her name—make her acknowledge me. But I know that even one outburst—one wrong move here—could get me killed. The captain as much as said so.

Dad appears next, and I can feel his presence, his power, enter the room a moment before he does. I wonder exactly how that power manifests in this alternative version of him.

He, too, does not look at me. And I'm still pinching myself because no matter how bad this situation is, my dad is here. He's alive in this world, and I don't care if he knows who I am because I thought I would never see him again in my lifetime.

And if this all goes to hell in a handbasket, at least I will have gotten to see him one last time.

The captain enters behind him, his expression serious. He's without the armor today, dressed in a black long-sleeve tunic with billowy sleeves. Its ties are unlaced, falling softly over his tan chest. Tight leather pants hug his legs before disappearing into riding boots. The belt at his hip conceals a dark longsword with an onyx hilt and a matching dagger. He ignores my presence completely.

I'm surprised to see that Jack takes a seat at my father's right-hand side, directly across from Sam.

"Come along, missy." Igrid nudges me to curtsy, and I follow her from the room.

She finds things to talk about while showing me the ropes around the castle. I listen, grateful for the distraction. After another hour or two of work, we head to the kitchen to find it empty and slide onto a wooden bench beneath the table. I sigh, stretching my arms over my head.

"Are you ever going to tell me your name, miss?"

"Oh, I'm sorry, yes. It's Serena. Serena Avery."

"What an interesting name. It's lovely."

"Thanks."

"So, Serena Avery, how did a human come to be working as a servant at the castle? I haven't seen one of your kind in ages," she lilts, her voice melodic with a slight accent.

"How did you—" I start, but she gives me a knowing look.

"Wild guess." She smiles warmly, tapping my rounded ear. "But your scent is different somehow. Not exactly human, but not fae either, something else. It's quite singular." She eyes me, her interest piqued.

"Oh." I nod, not sure if that's a compliment or an insult. "I've been asking myself the same thing. I uh—I'm not from here, originally."

Technically, it's the truth. I just hope my vague answer fends her off from further questioning.

"Not from Aegar?"

"No, I mean not from *here* here. Solterre?" I whisper, leaning into her.

She gapes at me, stunned. "How did you get through the portal?"

A portal? A flash of hope sparks to life in my chest. Maybe I could get home through a *portal*.

"A little thing like you—how did you manage to get past the Guardians?"

"The Guardians?"

Her eyes widen into saucers. "Boy, you really aren't from here, are you? The Guardians are the wardens at the portal, tasked with keeping out travelers from other worlds. I wouldn't sick them on my worst enemy."

Before I can answer, she glances down at Zadyn, who's weaving circles around my ankles.

"Goodness, is that a loyal creature." She smiles, setting down a tray of bread and cheese in front of us.

"He's my familiar."

Crap.

That's probably not something I should be blabbing about.

"Your familiar?" Her teal eyes glitter. "Then that means...oh, you are no ordinary human, are you, missy?"

"Not according to the people that locked me in a dungeon less than forty-eight hours ago."

I loose a sigh as I pull apart a piece of bread, holding it out to Zadyn. I don't know the last time he ate, but I'm sure he must be hungry as I am. He nibbles it, licking my fingertips with his little pink tongue. He really is adorable like this.

Igrid scoots closer to me on the bench. "We're alone now. No nosy ears. Let's have your story, then."

She lays a gentle hand on mine and eyes me expectantly.

I assess her, wondering how much would be okay to reveal. I could really use someone to hash this out with, and something is telling me that she can be trusted.

I lay it out for her, sparing no detail. Zadyn doesn't try to stop me. Maybe he understands that I need to process this with someone else, someone not directly attached to the situation.

Igrid's jaw is slack by the time I get to the end.

"Good gods, you're the last Blackblood witch." She leans back, her whisper reverent. "That explains the scent."

"You say that like it's a good thing, but they're treating me like a prisoner until I can prove it."

"It would be a very good thing! Blackblood witches were once considered the highest of royalty. They were fierce warriors and the High Queens of this world before they became extinct. Well, *almost* extinct," she corrects herself. "Haven't you ever heard the prophecy?"

Her eyes widen in realization as she tilts her pretty head.

"Of course you haven't—you only just got here! Many hundreds of years ago, the High Seer foretold that one last Blackblood witch would come to claim the last remaining dragon on Solterre. I guess that's you." She regards me fondly, her cerulean eyes twinkling.

"Igrid—" I angle myself to face her head-on, tucking one leg beneath me. "Even if it is true and I am a Blackblood, I'm not a warrior, I'm not a High Queen, and I don't have any magic. I'm perfectly ordinary. I'd be the last person you'd want to be your Dragon Rider."

"It's not entirely up to you, you know." She sits straddling the bench to face me fully. "The magic chooses. And so will the dragon, of course. If you are worthy, she will bond you."

"And if I'm not?" I counter.

"You'll save us all a lot of trouble and die."

A cold voice murmurs from the doorway.

Jack is casually leaning against the archway, arms crossed over his broad chest. I stare at him, barely even registering his words. Zadyn's tail brushes my ankle, and I break the intense eye contact.

"Captain." Igrid rises and curtsies. I do not.

I can feel his eyes burning into me from across the room as I study the grooves of the table and count the seconds.

"May I be of assistance?" she asks.

"Thank you, Igrid, but no. I'm simply here to make sure the witch behaves." He gives me a smug little smirk, crossing one ankle over the other.

"Have I given you reason to believe I won't?" I mutter under my breath. He somehow hears it.

"I'm not one to leave things to chance," he retorts.

"How boring."

I feel Igrid's shock as she snaps her head down to me. I dare to lift my eyes to Jack's, holding my breath for the nasty comeback. Instead, he gives a dark chuckle and saunters over to the table, sliding onto the bench across from me.

I fight the urge to fidget.

"Please, don't let me interrupt." He gestures for Igrid to sit and continue. "Where were we? Oh, that's right. The history of witches. As if you don't already know."

"I don't," I object. "Do you think I really *chose* to be here?"

"It's possible." He folds his hands neatly on the table. "Wouldn't be the first time a commoner posed as a witch to get inside the castle."

"Well, I didn't," I hiss. "I don't know what makes you think you know or understand me, but you're pretty judgmental for someone who doesn't have the full story."

"Oh, and what's the full story?" he challenges, leaning forward.

"The full story is that before yesterday, I didn't even know that fae or witches existed. I had never heard of *Blackbloods*, and I certainly didn't know that I would be tortured and kept here against my will until you figure out if I can be your precious Dragon Rider. So if you're going to sit here accusing me of having an ulterior motive, then you can turn around and march *straight* out that door. It's you people that want to use me for your own personal gain. Not the other way around, *Captain.*"

The liquid gold in his eyes seems to simmer. Beneath the rage, they are hypnotic. Igrid does not dare breathe beside me.

"I'll let you in on a little secret." He leans in further and drops his voice, making him seem all the more threatening than if he were to bellow at the top of his lungs.

"I believe you do carry witch blood in you, like Gnorr said. But I also don't believe you're the last Blackblood. I think you're just another little liar looking for glory. An imposter hoping to scheme your way into a position at the king's side. I don't believe that the gods would bless a human-born brat with a single drop of black blood. I don't think they would waste a moment's thought on you, let alone choose you as the last Dragon Rider. You are nothing. You are no one."

His whisper hangs in the air between us as I absorb his words. He rises wordlessly and heads for the door.

"If I'm no one, then why did you bring me here?"

My voice rings out of its own volition, strong and sturdy, causing him to stop mid-stride. He angles his head over his broad shoulder. Without turning fully, his next words directed at Igrid.

"I entrust her to your watch. Should she cause any trouble, I will hold you personally responsible, Igrid. You won't enjoy the consequences."

Just before he passes the threshold, he addresses me.

"Oh, and witch, if I hear you've been running your mouth about this to anyone else, I'll sew it shut myself."

He stalks away, and I slowly turn to look at Igrid, my eyes wide.

"Gods, he's mean. But so damn beautiful." A slow smile spreads across her face as she collapses onto the bench dramatically.

I force out a long breath. "He really does not like me."

"He's the captain for a reason. He's overprotective to a fault."

"And alarmingly self-righteous," I add, rolling my eyes.

"Yes, well, he's a favorite of the king, but that comes with its own set of burdens."

"I just don't get it." I push out of my seat to pace around the kitchen. "I didn't ask to be here. They must think I sent myself here using magic, but that's not what happened. If I could just talk to the king and explain all of this—"

"You won't get an audience with the king unless he requests one." Igrid shakes her head.

"Or unless I do something to get his attention." I slide my gaze her way, leaning against the butcher block counter. As I chew my bottom lip, my mind sifts through a wide spectrum of possibilities ranging from mild to bat-shit crazy.

Igrid studies me warily. "Serena—"

"I'm not going to do anything stupid," I vow, glancing toward the door. "But he needs me. Which means I have the upper hand here."

"What are you thinking? You've got a wicked look in your eye, missy." Her brows slant in suspicion.

"I don't know," I admit, drumming my fingers on the counter. "But I'll think of something."

8

A guard approaches Igrid and me midday and trails us the rest of the afternoon. His name is Sir Warryn. He's young-looking—younger than Jack at least—and his features are delicate, boyish, and beautiful. He keeps quiet mostly, to my relief. I don't think I could handle another hateful guard.

By the time I return to my room, my feet are aching from being pinched in those flats all day. All I want to do is curl up in bed and watch *Vanderpump Rules*.

Then I remember.

They don't have that here. They don't have TV. Or Instagram. Or anything.

Before the door fully shuts behind me, Zadyn is there in his male form. He pushes it shut the rest of the way as I sink into the mattress face-first.

"Any notes?" I ask dryly, my voice muffled by the blanket. His brow ticks up as he comes to sit on the edge of my bed.

"I can save them for when you don't look ready to rip off someone's head," he offers.

"I'm just tired." I roll onto my back, staring up at the ceiling.

"I know you are. Aside from that, how are you feeling?"

I appreciate his concern. I mean, no one else has stopped to ask how I'm settling into this new world. But I haven't fully forgiven him for lying to me for years.

"I feel...numb. Confused. Alone. I never thought I would see my dad's face again. I got so excited because I thought—" I swallow the tightness in my throat. "I thought it was really him. Now I just feel...devastated."

Zadyn's eyes turn down in concern. He slides closer and takes my hand in his. I gaze up at him, tears stinging my eyes.

"You are not alone. I know you won't be able to trust me right away. But I'm here. No matter how overwhelmed you feel, I hope you can believe that I won't let anything happen to you. You never have to pretend around me. Your safety and your happiness are mine to ensure."

His words and warm touch ease some of that tension in my chest.

"Will they hurt you if they find you here?"

"They're welcome to try. But I'd rather leave the element of surprise in case we end up needing it." He offers a wide, dimpled grin that I can't look away from.

If Tatler had an adult grandson, it would be the beautiful person sitting before me with the kind eyes and heartfelt smile. I reach out without thinking and brush my fingers against his smooth face. He tenses, watching me carefully.

"It was so real." I let my hand fall to my side, and he relaxes.

"Most glamours are woven with that intent."

"So, this is your true form?"

"The one I was born with." He nods. "Shifting was nearly impossible in the human world, so I relied on glamours instead."

"It's strange to think you've been so many people in my life. And I never knew, never even suspected."

He offers an apologetic smile. "I wanted to tell you. So many times, but you weren't ready. For any of this."

"I'm not ready now. I don't think I'll ever be."

"You are. Trust me. You may not know me the way you thought you did, but I know you. I know the blood of a warrior witch clan runs in your veins. Your strength runs deeper than you could ever imagine."

"It's all just too much." My voice is barely even a whisper.

"What can I do?" he offers, eyes searching mine.

"I—I don't know." I sit up. "There's still so much I don't understand. Igrid mentioned this prophecy earlier...what I don't get is how I can be this Blackblood witch when I'm not even from your world."

"You may have been born in the human world, but it was Blackblood magic that placed you there for safekeeping until it was time to return here to your true home."

My true home? This is *not* my true home.

"So what you're telling me is that while I look human...I'm not." I shake my head in confusion. "But my parents—"

"You were essentially planted in your mother's womb."

"That explains why we're nothing alike," I mumble.

"They're still your birth parents," he amends. "But your blood, your *true* blood, is black."

Witch. Blackblood. Not human.

He continues on.

"The prophecy Igrid was telling you about foretold the coming of the last Dragon Rider. But there was another part of the prophecy that the High Seer only sold to the highest bidder. Only a few were privy to that knowledge."

"What was the other part?"

"That the Dragon Rider wouldn't be born here, on Solterre.

That she was hidden in another world for protection. The king was one of the few who knew. He and my parents."

"Your parents know the king?"

A muscle in his jaw ticks. "They were all friends."

"Then maybe he'll see you, maybe he'll listen to you," I point out, but he shakes his head.

"I don't know the male. I want to do some spying first. Make sure the king's intentions are pure."

"And if they're not?"

"Then I'll get you out of here," he says without hesitation.

"I thought you said they wouldn't truly hurt me."

"You are an asset to them. But I'm not willing to gamble when it comes to you." A chill shoots through me for some reason. I pivot, breaking his intense gaze.

"Why did the captain say he thinks I'm a witch but not a Blackblood?"

"He probably thinks you're a Red or Blue."

I stare at him blankly.

"Say more."

"At one point in time, there were three clans: the Redbloods, the Bluebloods, and the Blackbloods," Zadyn outlines. "Reds are the most common. Their power is slight, drawing mostly from nature. The Blues have a higher concentration of magic in their blood, so they can essentially siphon off themselves and others. But the Blackbloods"—his eyes sparkle as he leans forward—"were, by far, the most powerful and most feared."

I find myself leaning in too, my interest piqued.

"Banshees, necromancers, shadow walkers—all black-blooded. They were warriors with a unique ability to serve as conduits for obscene amounts of power. That's why only a Blackblood would be fit to be a Dragon Rider. For a Red or Blue to channel a dragon's power, they would be incinerated instantaneously."

Yet they want *me* to attempt it? *Lovely.*

"Before Solterre was split off into five kingdoms, it was one unified land ruled by three Blackblood High Queens. They were the most fearsome creatures in the world, up until the time they were killed off."

"What happened to them?"

"They were destroyed by the god that created them."

I raise my eyebrows in surprise.

Zadyn continues along his previous train of thought. "To maintain the balance of power within nature, the witches feed on their own kind."

"I'm sorry, what? No, no, no, I draw the line at cannibalism." I scoot back toward the wall, shaking my head vehemently.

"It sounds worse than it is," he rushes to explain, holding up a hand. "The Bluebloods drink red blood, and the Blackbloods drink blue."

"What do the Reds drink?"

"They don't need to drink. They draw power from the land and celestial events."

"So the Blues and Blacks are like vampires?"

"Vampires aren't real." He laughs, and I stare at him blankly.

"That's what they said about fae. About witches," I snap.

"Well, whoever *they* were, they were wrong. Blood sharing has become quite civilized over the last thousand years. Blackbloods only need to drink a few times a year unless they're gravely wounded or depleted of magic."

He must read the horror on my face. "But none of this is anything for you to worry about right now."

"But what if it is?"

He shoots me a quizzical look.

"Blackbloods need to drink blue blood to stay strong and to keep their magic working, right?" I wait for him to confirm with a nod. "If I really am a Blackblood...what if I can't access my power because I've never drank before?"

Zadyn stares at me in awe.

"As disgusting as it sounds," I say, "maybe I need to drink."

I can see the lightbulb go off in his head.

"I can't believe I didn't think of it before! Brilliant," he says, bounding off the bed.

"You think it will work?" I ask, hope rising in my voice.

"Actually, I do. Your power has been suppressed from the glamour, from years of living in the human world. Your magic wanted to avoid drawing attention, so it buried itself inside of you. We just need something to trigger it. If Gnorr can't undo the glamour, this is our next best shot."

"Do you know any Bluebloods willing to donate to the cause?"

He thinks for a moment. "The Blues and the Reds have all migrated away from these lands."

"Maybe the king can pull a few royal strings." I shrug. "He wants me to prove that I'm a Blackblood, but I can't do that without the necessary tools. The captain is his right-hand man. Maybe I can get him to hear me out."

Zadyn stands across from me, arms folded over his broad chest, nodding in agreement. I stifle a yawn.

"Your body needs rest," he says, his voice lullaby-soft.

"I know, I know," I grouse. I'm so tired, I could fall asleep fully clothed.

As if reading my mind, Zadyn opens a drawer and pulls out a simple white sleep dress. He faces the door while I quickly undress and slip the thin fabric over my head.

"Decent," I inform him, slipping my feet under the sheets. They're closer to sandpaper than Egyptian cotton, but hey, beggars can't be choosers.

Zadyn takes a seat up against the wall, his long legs drawn

up to his chest. My gaze skims over his profile as his thick lashes drift closed, and he tips his head back. I take in the tan skin, the faintest touch of freckles dusting his cheeks and nose. The slight stubble over his well-defined jawline.

"That looks uncomfortable," I point out, nuzzling deeper into the pillow.

He cracks an eye at me and shrugs. "I've slept on worse."

"We can share," I offer.

I don't know at what point over the last two days I began to trust him again, but against all reasoning, I do. I know in my bones he would not hurt me. His brown eyes flicker toward the tiny single bed.

"If you shift, you can fit. Seriously, it doesn't bother me," I add, sitting up and patting the space near the foot of the bed. He watches me for a moment, then stands.

With a gentle tilt of his head, he says, "Goodnight, Serena."

He shifts between blinks and leaps up onto the bed with feline grace. His tiny paws pad over my blanketed feet before he curls up, a bundle of white fur at the foot of the bed.

My mind sifts through a thousand thoughts as I close my eyes. Part of me feels like I should be planning my escape instead of going to sleep. Zadyn has promised me safety, but how can he be sure they won't hurt me? That they won't risk my life for their own gain?

To stay around these people would be painful. Like compulsively picking at a scab over and over. But my mind keeps going back to the king who wears my father's face. To leave without knowing this man, without understanding why he looks the way he does, why the princess and the captain look the way they do...it would drive me crazy.

I can't unsee what I've seen or unlearn what I now know. I have to know them.

If curiosity killed the cat, I'm a dead woman walking.

9

I go through the motions for the next three days as Igrid's shadow. Each morning I wake, I become farther removed from the idea of making it back home. The harsh reality that, whether I like it or not, I'm here begins to take root. Fighting to make sense of it and even fighting against it feels futile. But maybe, just maybe, if I can be who they want me to be, or if I can at least fake it well enough to survive, maybe after this is all over, they'll let me go home.

Home to a world where my dad, my favorite person, my sweet, loving, never-hurt-a-fly in his life, dad is gone. One where my sister and my mother are estranged from me.

It's been nearly two years since I've spoken to them. My parents divorced when Sam and I were kids. I stayed with Dad while my mom and Sam moved to the West Coast and promptly forgot that we existed. When Sam chose a college in Manhattan with a campus eight blocks from my apartment, I did my best to salvage our relationship. I saw Mom once when she came to visit her in the city. We went to dinner. It turned into a screaming match between the three of us and I walked out, cheeks red from embarrassment and wet with tears.

I knew my dad had regrets about Sam toward the end of his life. But unlike my mom, he always tried. He called. He sent birthday cards and Christmas cards and gifts for every occasion he could think of. How many times had I seen him pick up the phone only to be sent straight to voicemail? She barely ever returned his calls. Barely ever returned his love. And still, he found a way to blame himself for it.

So I came to resent her. My mom, too.

She was worse. Never calling to check in, to ask how his treatments were going. Neither of them even visited in the five years he was sick. Never even offered to help when I put my life on hold—my *career* on hold—to take care of him.

They had the nerve to show up at his wake, though. And the hell I gave them outside the funeral home made the New York dinner look like *ring around the rosie*.

I had just lost my best friend. I was unhinged. Feral.

And that was the last time we spoke.

I've gone to therapy. I've worked on that resentment, that anger and bitterness, and for the most part, I let it go. But something about seeing her at my father's side here...

I feel a strange sense of envy. How cruel can the universe be? Why does she get to be his daughter after all this, after everything...and I don't? I'm the one who took care of him. I'm the one who knew him, who loved him so fiercely that when he died a light went out in me that never rekindled.

The way she barely acknowledged him in the throne room and at the dining room table...it sparked that anger in me again. Because not only does she get to be his daughter. But I can bet she takes it for granted every day of her royal life.

"Are you alright, my lady?"

Sir Warryn's voice jars me from my thoughts. His eyes fall to my hands, and it's only then that I become aware of the white knuckle death grip I've been inflicting on this poor, innocent broomstick.

"Sorry," I apologize, easing up on my clutch. "I'm fine."

I sweep the broom across the hall's impeccable marble floor. In the light of day, the majestic snow-capped mountains are even closer than I realized, standing just beyond the floor-to-ceiling windows.

"Why don't they just use magic to clean this place?" I mutter.

"Oh, they do." Sir Warryn faces me, hands folded behind him.

"Then why am I holding this broom?" I lean on the tip of the broomstick and level a look at the young guard. He clears his throat uncomfortably, a timid expression on his handsome face.

"The captain said you were to do things—manually."

"I'm guessing you made some polite revisions to his order. Come on, what else did he say?"

"Until you reveal your own magic, he said, you shouldn't have the *'privilege of benefiting from ours.'*" His face is pained as he rushes to explain. "Not all of us share in his sentiment, my lady."

I offer him a smile. "I know, Sir Warryn. Thank you for your honesty. And your kindness."

I continue sweeping the broom back and forth along the empty corridor.

"I don't have any," I finally say, earning an inquisitive look from the young fae. I meet his gaze. He's mostly lanky, not a lot of muscle. His shiny, black armor fits him loosely, like he hasn't yet grown into it.

"I don't have any magic. Not that I know of."

"But Madame Gnorr all but confirmed you are a witch."

"Yes, a witch with no magic. Even if I do have it, and it's just dormant inside me, I don't think I can access it on my own."

"Why not? Have you ever tried?"

"Not really. I'm from the human world. We don't have the kind of magic that exists here."

"There are no witches in the mortal world?" he asks, raising a brow.

"Some call themselves witches, but I don't think the magic is anywhere near comparable."

The magic here is a little more potent than manifesting your dream life from a vision board.

"Maybe with the proper training, your power would manifest," he concludes. I nod in agreement.

"Tell that to the captain. He's insistent I do it all on my own. He's got it in his head I came here with some hidden agenda."

"The captain is wary of outsiders. He takes his role very seriously, but that is what makes him a great leader. He was Princess Sorscha's sworn protector for years before he was moved up to Captain of the Kingsguard. The king values him like a son. He has a good heart once you get to know him."

I snort.

"Well, as I don't plan on getting to know him, I doubt I'll be seeing that good heart anytime soon. He's convinced that I'm impersonating the last Blackblood, for god knows what reason. I don't see why anyone in their right mind would lie about that all so they could ride a dragon."

"You'd be surprised. There have been countless Bluebloods and even some Reds that have come forward over the centuries claiming to be the last Blackblood witch so they could have a shot at bonding the dragon."

"Why?"

"Personal gain, the favor of kings. Bonding a dragon is the

greatest test of strength and power. There is no greater honor for a witch."

"But I thought only Blackbloods were strong enough."

"Exactly, which is why every attempt by a Blue or Red has ended...unsuccessfully."

"I see. Are there any other witches at court?"

If there are others in the castle, maybe I don't even need to plead with Jack to get me that blue blood.

"Well, most of the Redblood covens have migrated south to the Mydlands of Aeix. No one knows where the Blues disappeared to. So, I believe you are the only one here. It was a gods-gift that the Kingsguard found you alive in the Bone Forest. How was it you came to our lands, by the way, if not through your own magic?" he asks.

"Happy accident, I guess. You said it was a gift that they found me alive? Why is that?"

"The Bone Forest is full of lethal shadow creatures. The Mara. They come out at dusk. They can't stand the light."

"Those were...those were actual bones?"

"The Mara have an insatiable hunger. They feast on fear and pain, leaving behind only the bones of their prey. They find those quite indigestible."

I suppress a gag. I had been rolling around in a heap of human bone that day I arrived in Aegar.

"You've gone pale, my lady." Warryn approaches me looking concerned.

"I just can't remember the last time I had some water."

His eyes widen. "Stay here, I'll return shortly," he tells me and is off before I can protest that it's not necessary.

Zadyn's feline form is curled up on a window perch, basking in the sun.

"Did you hear that? Your little escapade with that book almost got me eaten by a shadow creature. Some pet you are."

He gives me a mild hiss, flicking his tail against the wall. For the past three days, he's been snooping around the castle as an array of small, inconspicuous creatures and insects, trying to listen in on the king's conversations and learn his plans for me. So far, he's found nothing incriminating.

The faint echo of footsteps sounds from around the corner. I follow them, unable to stop myself. Zadyn hops off his perch and trails me to the end of the hall. Pressed flat against the wall, I strain to listen.

"...forced entry...dead at the portal in Hyrax," says a voice I don't recognize. I miss the beginning of his sentence, but the last part is clear.

There is a portal in Hyrax.

But who knows how far away it is? I can't exactly google it.

"How many?" Jack's deep voice sets off a flutter in my stomach. I roll my eyes at myself.

"Two Guardians dead. The healer says the other may never regain consciousness. Its mind was shredded."

"And the travelers?" he asks.

"Only traces were left behind. Whatever crossed over certainly made it into Hyrax."

"And you have no idea what they are? Or where they came from?"

"No, Captain, I have my spies searching along the Hyraxian border, but for them to have taken on the Guardians...they must be creatures with an unnatural amount of power. Hyrax is sending a watch to stand in for them."

Jack is silent for a moment.

"Ready a troupe for tonight. Bring the hounds. I'll not risk those creatures making their way into Aegar."

His footsteps grow closer as I scoot away from the wall, feigning busy with my task. He stops a few feet away upon seeing me. I dare a glance in his direction. Disgust addles his features as he approaches.

"I could hear you, you know." He circles me leisurely, hands behind his back. "As if that weren't enough, I could smell you."

He wrinkles his nose.

"We can't all have the privilege of daily baths, especially those of us with '*no magic of their own.*'"

My smile is a sneer. He chuckles.

"Is it my fault you're a defective witch with no power of her own? Besides, I figured it wouldn't hurt for you to learn a little discipline." He jerks his chin toward the broom in my hand.

"Yet you seem to have no regard for it yourself."

He stops to look at me.

"You expect me to produce magic without knowing the first thing about it. I need to be taught. Otherwise, I'm just wasting my time here."

"You're mistaken in thinking you have a choice in the matter."

"I'm not part of your court or your kingdom. I'm not your prisoner."

He prowls closer, his face a mask of calm cruelty.

"As long as your feet are on Aegean soil, you are a subject of this kingdom. And you will abide the orders of the king, or you will face death."

"Could you stop being an ass for one second and listen?" I ask. "There are things we need to talk about. You, me, the king. I know you need me. But you have to be willing to help me help you. Help your kingdom. And I can't do that if you just shove me down in the servant's quarters, out of sight with no direction, and expect me to prove myself. Don't you see how unfair that is?"

He chews the inside of his bottom lip, eyeing me with quiet rancor. I dare a step closer.

"I'll put it this way. If you don't help me to be the one you so desperately want, then you'll never get your Dragon Rider."

I hope he doesn't call my bluff. Because for all my big talk, I myself am not fully convinced that I'm the one they want. The one they need. That I could ever sit on top of a living, fire-breathing dragon and fly it like a chopper.

I wait for the captain's answer, expecting him to either give me a yes or no. Instead, he imparts me with one more dirty look, turns on his heel, and disappears down the hall.

My temper flares as I stare after him in disbelief.

"Fuck this."

I throw the broom on the ground. It clatters loudly as I stomp all the way back to my room. I've already slammed the door behind me and begun stripping off my bodice when Zadyn transforms before me.

"What are you doing?" he asks.

"I'm going home," I say sharply.

"Serena."

"No, Zadyn. Don't try to calm me down—don't try to convince me otherwise. I am leaving this place. I tried. I really did. I tried to stay for them, but I don't belong here."

"Oh, and where do you suppose you'll go?" he challenges.

"To Hyrax. To the portal."

"You'll never make it. It's too far, and you heard what they said in the hall. Something came over, left two Guardians dead, and shredded the other's mind. You have no idea how hard that is to do. They are death machines built to stop anyone who tries to cross into this world. There is something out there, something bad."

"But that's why I have you, isn't it? My blood-bound protector?" I quip and pull the shift over my head. I don't pause to see if he's looking. I really don't care.

"No. It's too dangerous. Let's just take a second and talk about this."

"You said you want what's best for me—you want my happiness," I point out as I brush past him in nothing but undergarments and yank open the top drawer to fish out the clothes I came here with.

"I do, but—"

"This is what I want. I want to go home. That is literally the only thing that will make me happy."

"No, it's not, and you know it," he pleads, sitting on the bed and staring up at me beseechingly. "Don't tell me you aren't the least bit curious about all this. You can lie to me all you want, but at least be honest with yourself before you do something rash."

"The only rash thing would be staying here and seeing what's in store for me," I snap, angrily shoving my leg through my jeans.

"What of the king?" he presses.

"Of course, I want to know him." I whirl on Zadyn, half-dressed. "How could I not? I want to understand why he looks like my dad. I want to be close to him no matter who he is, but I don't belong here. This place is cruel. This world is cruel. I'd rather be alone in my world than here with the people I love looking at me like nothing more than a piece of gum on their shoes." My voice cracks as tears threaten to overtake me. I shake them away and tug my jeans over my hips.

I can feel Zadyn's gaze burning into me.

"This is about the captain. You're letting him drive you away."

"It's about all of it, all of them!" I say more defensively than I intend.

"Just give me one more day. One more day to make sure

they won't risk your life, and then I'll go before the king. I will make him listen. We can't make it to Hyrax. It's too far on foot." He runs his hands through his smooth hair.

"So we steal a horse." I shrug as if it's the simplest solution in the world when, in reality, I've never even ridden solo.

"It's a five-day journey from here without stopping. The second they notice you're gone, they'll have patrols out to drag you right back. And you heard the captain. They're riding out to Hyrax tonight."

"If we leave now, we can beat them there. This is my best shot to go home," I point out.

"You don't know how to use a portal, Serena. It's not that straightforward. Shadow smoke is one thing, but the portal... traveling between worlds is dangerous. There are too many spaces in between. It's too easy to fall through the cracks and be lost forever. The force alone can tear you apart from the inside out."

I recall the feeling of being ripped open when I was transported here. That searing pain is unforgettable.

"If you're really that desperate to leave, then we need to find another way."

"I can't stay here another minute. I have to try." I shove my head through the neck of my T-shirt and sit on the bed beside him to slip my sneakers on. Zadyn says nothing for a long time.

"Are you going to try to stop me?" I ask.

His eyes meet mine, and there is anguish in them. He's torn.

"If I did, I doubt you'd listen. As much as I'd love to talk some sense into you, your mind is made up. I won't force you to stay if that isn't what you want. Even if this plan is the most idiotic and ill-advised I've ever heard."

I sigh and run my hands over my face, thinking of Jack's expression as he stalked away.

"He won't even acknowledge that I need to see the king, that I need to talk to him," I say, shaking my head. "I can't. I can't do it. Are you coming, or am I doing this alone?"

"No," he says, taking my hand. "Never alone."

10

I leave the horse stealing to Zadyn. He has me wait behind the stables while his little white body disappears inside. There is the brief sound of a scuffle, and a moment later, he emerges triumphant on one of those giant black steeds, wearing the stolen clothes of a stable boy. He waves me over and slides down, taking the heavy packs of supplies he managed to procure off my shoulder and lifting me into the saddle. He re-mounts in one smooth motion and shifts closer to me, his chest pressed against my back.

"Are you comfortable?"

I nod. "Comfortable as I can be."

"It's not too late to change your mind," he points out.

It's a Hail Mary, but I'm standing firm.

"I'm not changing my mind."

He sighs, tossing his head back to the heavens. "Gods, be with us."

Zadyn steers the horse in the direction of the massive gates up ahead. I glance around at the unfamiliar courtyard.

"This isn't the way I came in."

"They took you round the back," he explains. I take in the line of armored guards stationed on either side of the gates.

"Will they give us a hard time?" I whisper.

"Just don't say anything, okay? And don't move."

My heart locks in my throat as we slow to a stop before them.

"I have business in Iaspus," Zadyn says smoothly.

"What business?" the guard asks in a gruff voice.

"The king requires a new Stygian horse, a gift for the princess. I'm to meet with a foreign breeder there."

"Very well." He nods, and the gate slowly opens. I remain deathly still, but the guard doesn't seem to notice me at all.

"Good day." Zadyn kicks the steed, and we take off in a gallop that sends my hair flying back from my face.

"Can I talk now?" I ask once we've cleared the front gates and are halfway down the mile-long stretch of tree-lined road.

"Yes," he says in my ear. "I had to throw a glamour over you so he would let us go. As far as he could tell, I was alone."

We head toward a thick forest of brilliant green.

"We'll ride until dark. I won't risk going anywhere near the Bone Forest after dusk."

"How do we reach Hyrax?"

"The safest route will take an extra two days."

"And the other way is?"

"We cut through the Bone Forest and head north, past Skull Valley."

"And how do we find the portal? Do you have any idea where it might be?"

"I have a good guess."

He doesn't offer to elaborate.

"We'll take the shortcut. Through the Bone Forest," I tell him, expecting him to protest. I can almost hear him weighing the pros and cons in his head. But he says nothing.

We ride on in comfortable silence, his arms wrapped around me to keep hold of the reins. My lower back begins to stiffen a few hours into the ride, and I wonder how the hell we're going to keep this up for another two full days. I lean into him for support, his body a blanket of warmth behind the harsh winds.

We reach the top of a large hill, and I dare a glance back.

"The castle, oh my god," I breathe. "It's beautiful from here."

"You've never had the full view."

"They brought me in through the side of a mountain," I recount.

"The castle is built into the mountain and the diamond caves." He points at the jagged peaks of the gargantuan mountain between the many spires and reaching towers. I shake my head at the magnificent infrastructure.

From the hilltop, I can see all that the mountain obstructed from view when I entered. It glitters like a diamond in the distance. Made of windowed walls and pale stone with sparkling grains. A shining beacon of serenity.

"The mountain is a fortress—nearly impenetrable from the outside. And since the city is south, it, too, is protected behind it."

We ride on until we reach trees a familiar shade of white. I recognize those tall, scraggly trees—their ethereal, leafless branches like long, thin spikes that disappear into the sky.

The Bone Forest.

"Why are we stopping?" I ask as we slow a few yards away.

"We'll make camp here," he says.

"It's not dark yet. We have at least another hour before the sun sets," I protest, but he's already dismounting.

"I'm not willing to risk it. You don't know the things that lurk in that forest."

"You brought weapons, didn't you?" I nod toward the dagger at his hip.

"A dagger will do nothing against the Mara."

"We don't have any time to waste. The Kingsguard could be looking for me already."

"I suggested we wait until morning, but you insisted we leave tonight. This is the trade-off."

"Zadyn," I start. But he lifts his hands to help me down.

"I'm not debating this," he says, his brown eyes gazing up into mine. "I won't risk your safety by doing something as reckless as entering the Bone Forest at dusk. It's a no."

There's a sternness in his voice I've never heard. I bristle at his sudden bossiness.

"If you won't go with me, I'll go myself."

He grips my waist without another word and yanks me off the horse. I fall into him hard, and he pins me to his chest to keep me from crashing to the ground.

"If I have to tie you to a tree to prevent that from happening," he says softly, an inch away from my face, "I will."

I blink, and he releases me. My knees buckle, feeling like jelly after hours of riding. He doesn't try to steady me.

"I'm going to gather wood for a fire," he says, knotting the horse's reins around a nearby tree. I watch the muscles of his arms flex in the process. He reaches into his belt for the dagger and presses it into my palm, closing my fist around the silver hilt.

"I'll be back soon. Don't make me regret leaving you alone." He squeezes my hand, and with a warning look, disappears into the green forest behind us.

I gaze up at the sky, shielding my eyes from the sun. The moon isn't even visible yet. No oranges or pinks to indicate an oncoming sunset.

One thing Zadyn clearly hasn't learned in all his years of

knowing me is that I don't like being told what I can and can't do. I look around and listen for any sign of him nearby. When I hear nothing but my own heartbeat and the soft song of birds overhead, I throw one of the packs over my shoulder and turn to face the Bone Forest.

Squaring my shoulders, I take the first few steps into the whitewashed forest and continue on to the music of age-old bones crunching beneath my feet.

~

I REALLY HOPE *I'm going the right way.*

I push down the growing sense of unease building in my stomach as I trudge forward through bleached leaves and ancient bones. The sparse forest is surprisingly disorienting. With every step I take, I'm swallowed up by pale trees and milky bones. It's like moving through a blizzard—eerie and bewildering.

I glance backward.

I should be able to see the green beyond the edge of the forest where I entered, but the second I stepped foot in these woods, the outside world disappeared. The path behind me is blurred and hazy—a light layer of fog masking everything else from sight.

No sign of green. No sign of Zadyn. No sign of life.

I haven't heard so much as a bird chirp since I've entered the forest.

It's suddenly overcast, and I'm starting to worry that I might not make it out of here before dark. I pick up my pace, refusing to let doubt enter my mind, but my fingers clutch the dagger tighter.

Serena.

I hear Zadyn's voice in my head as if he spoke my name

directly into my ear. I twist around, my heart leaping out of my chest. But I'm alone.

Did I just imagine that?

My stomach tightens as I scan the unnaturally quiet expanse. I force myself to keep walking, my senses now on high alert. After a few steps, I hear it again, louder this time.

Serena.

I turn once again.

Nothing. Nothing but unending silence.

"Zadyn?" I call cautiously.

I'm here!

I spin in a circle. "I don't see you. Are you wearing a glamour?"

I'm here. Follow my voice.

I try to do that.

Keep going, I'm right here.

I apprehensively drift closer to the source, the pounding of my own heart ringing in my ears.

"Zadyn, can you just come out? This is freaking me out."

Don't be afraid. I won't let anything hurt you. Just a little further.

The sun is setting. There's no denying it now. It's all but disappeared, the faint wash of a water-colored sky quickly fading to black. Worry settles into my chest.

"I'm not afraid, I'm annoyed. We don't have time for games." My voice is edged with panic.

But I do.

I freeze, feeling an ice-cold breath on the back of my neck. It sends a chilled shiver down my spine. I whirl around, only to be faced with the horror-inducing realization I already suspected in my bones.

"You're not Zadyn," I choke.

Towering above me is a dark, shadowy figure in tattered

robes that float on an invisible wind. Its large hood swallows its face, revealing nothing but a depthless abyss. Black feathered wings extend from its back, arching high overhead. An angel of death. It reeks of rotting flesh.

The Mara.

It lifts a long, bony finger. Black nails, three inches long and sharpened to lethal points reach toward me.

I don't hesitate before plunging the dagger into its chest.

11

I'm not sure why I thought stabbing it would really work.

Instead of feeling flesh give way beneath the sleek blade, I strike something hard, like stone. But when I try to pull the dagger free, it refuses, lodged between...a ribcage?

I don't wait to find out.

Abandoning the dagger, I break into a sprint.

A dark, chilling laugh echoes through my head. My heart threatens to burst from my chest as I pump my arms, running faster than I ever have in my life.

Without warning, a cold hand grips the neck of my shirt and yanks me back, tearing the fabric clean off my body.

Sharp, jagged bones dig into my bare back as I hit the forest floor. Scrambling backward, I look up to see the Mara clutching my tattered shirt in its bony hands. It inhales loudly, lifting the rag to its obscured face.

"Mmmm, your fear smells divine," it purrs, its putrid breath stinging my nostrils.

I grapple for anything to use against it. My hand closes around a long, thin bone, and I snap it over my knee, screaming at the backlash of pain that follows. I hold up one of the spiked ends with trembling hands.

This motherfucker's about to eat me alive.

"Oh, no, no, no. Now this won't do. I want to taste your fear. I want to taste your *pain*," it hisses, death personified.

"You're gonna have to try a little harder than that, Casper."

"Sweet thing." It drifts closer with eerie grace. "You've yet to see me try."

Scrambling to my feet, I try to run again. A piercing pain forces me to cry out as I look down at the thin bone embedded in my thigh. On instinct, I pull it out. Blood spurts from the wound.

The Mara groans in pleasure at the smell, moving closer. It lifts its cement-white fingers to draw back its heavy hood. Long, stringy raven hair falls free as I peer into a gaunt gray face, so sunken it's nearly skeletal. It has no lips, only a gaping black hole of a mouth. Its eyes bulge from within the deep sockets—the black pupils so dilated they swallow up all the white.

My heart lodges in my throat as I blindly scramble away.

I make it a few feet before the creature is upon me, tossing me onto my back and squatting above my chest, pinning my arms beneath its spindly fingers. I'm unable to contain the scream that bursts from me.

I holler relentlessly. I can't stop. I can't *make* myself stop.

Then the forest floor disappears beneath me, and I'm suddenly standing over my dad's hospice bed, staring down at his frail, weak body—tubes in his nose, needles in his arms. I cry out, trying to clear the image from my head.

"This isn't real."

I back away, but I'm met with a wall of muscle. I spin around, and Jack—no, not Jack—the *captain* towers over me. He grips my face with one hand, and for a split second, it is the gentle caress of a lover.

Then his lips pull back, bearing sharply pointed canines. His smile turns violent, bloodthirsty, as he drives a knife into my gut.

I wail, nails digging into his shoulders as I struggle to stay upright. He twists the knife, and pain like I've never known decimates me. I crumble to the ground.

My hands are wet with my own blood.

Jack withdraws his blade with jarring force, and I fall back, unable to scream or breathe or think.

His molten eyes glitter triumphantly as he lifts the blade to his cruel mouth and slides his tongue up the edge, lapping up my blood.

My *black* blood.

"Please," I sob, horrified by the sight. "Please stop."

That's better, the death voice speaks into my mind.

I struggle to keep my eyes open. My fingers and toes begin to fall asleep. Spots decorate my vision. I know I'm losing too much blood. This is how I die. I should have listened to Zadyn.

Icy hands wrap around my throat, but everything is black now. My jaw clenches as I brace myself for the death blow, but a moment later, the frozen grip disappears.

I force my eyes open.

I'm on the forest floor. I clutch my stomach, expecting to find warm, thick liquid pooling there. But there is no blood, no fatal wound.

A high-pitched screech makes me clap my hands over my ears. I struggle to my elbows, still weak and disoriented as three armored males on imposing black steeds dash into view, swords drawn and blazing with white light.

I recognize that shining black armor. Those horses.

The Kingsguard.

Another grating sound bursts from the Mara, its eyes growing red and swollen. It tears at its own face with razored claws as the Kingsguard surrounds it. Two of them lift their swords, angling them toward the third soldier in the center. He raises his own sword high into the sky, and as he does so, bright bolts of lightning spit from the swords of the other two guards. The white lightning strikes the raised metal blade, and it vibrates with energy. A blast of blinding light erupts like a tidal wave through the dark forest as he brings the electrified sword down through the Mara's head. The very ground shakes as I throw my arms over my eyes, unable to bear the brightness of a thousand suns.

The screeching sounds cut off abruptly. I slowly peel my eyes open, the intense light having eased to a soft glow.

The tallest of the guards dismounts and races over to me, crouching by my side. He rips off his helmet, and a mess of dark hair tumbles out. Golden eyes lock on mine.

I scramble back, gasping.

"You're hurt," he says, reaching for me.

"Get away from me!"

"Where are you bleeding from?" He inches closer, scanning my body.

"Don't touch me!" I shout. "You tried to kill me!"

Surprise crosses his face before his expression softens.

"No, no, it was an illusion. The Mara—" He shakes his head. "Let me help. On my life, I won't hurt you."

I'm pretty sure that the fae are allowed to lie despite the many stories stating the opposite. I have no time to debate before Zadyn sprints into view. He slides onto the ground beside me and grips my face in his hands.

"Are you hurt?" His frantic gaze travels over my face, my body, my bloody leg. "What did you do to her?" he snarls at Jack.

"I'm fine," I answer for him.

In a flash of movement, Jack has Zadyn on his feet, a dagger pressed to his throat. The handsome red-headed twins move to restrain Zadyn and he turns on them with a ferocity like I've never seen, baring two razor-sharp canines in threat. Jack's blade nicks his neck, and a thin line of blood beads on his tan skin.

"Stop!" I scream. "He's my familiar. Let him go."

Jack waits a beat before releasing him. The twin guards ease back and I can breathe again. They look down at me, and it dawns on me that I'm sitting here bloody and topless in front of four men, in just a bra. Either noticing my embarrassment or my shivering, the captain removes his cloak, extending it to me. I take it cautiously, monitoring his every move.

"She said you tried to kill her," Zadyn growls as he lowers himself back to me, tearing a piece of fabric from his sleeve and bracing my thigh in his hand. I wince, my fingernails digging into his shoulder as he begins to bind it.

"The Mara illusioned her. We arrived just in time. Found her pinned beneath it, screaming her head off. What were you thinking, letting her run off into the Bone Forest alone after dark?" Jack grills him.

Zadyn snarls. I can feel the anger rolling off him. I put a hand to his chest in warning.

"It was my fault. He told me to stay where I was, and I wandered off."

"Evaded by your little witchling," Jack tuts, shaking his head. "Some familiar."

Zadyn is all but quaking with rage.

"I'm sorry." I clutch his shirt, trying to pull his attention from Jack. "I should have listened. I'm sorry."

He finally tears his burning gaze away, his eyes softening when they land on me.

"I got back, and you were gone. You had me terrified." He

shakes his head. "This place is a vacuum. I couldn't hear you, couldn't even pick up your scent."

"As much as I'd love for you to have this little heart-to-heart here and now, I would advise we save it for when we aren't sitting ducks," Jack pipes, earning another glare from Zadyn. I glance over at the tattered robes strewn across the forest floor. The Mara, however, is nowhere in sight. "I'm sure it has a few friends who would be thrilled to meet us."

"Is it dead?" I ask as Zadyn helps me stand.

"It's dead," Jack confirms.

The light, Sir Warryn had said. It couldn't handle the light.

I try to take a step, but Zadyn scoops me into his arms, carrying me toward the waiting horses. Normally I would protest, but I can barely put any weight on my leg right now.

The twins mount their steeds. Only one is left remaining.

"She can ride with me," Jack offers, brushing past us.

"Absolutely not." Zadyn makes no effort to set me down.

"I'm not going back to the castle."

"We'll discuss that when we get somewhere safe," Jack says, patting the saddle.

Neither Zadyn nor I move. He pauses, looking back at us.

"Would you rather the two of you walk? It's just a ride. You can go with Max," he tells Zadyn, jerking his chin toward one of the twins. "Or Mal, if you prefer. Come on, friend, I won't bite her."

Jack flashes him a condescending smirk, and he tenses, tightening his grip on me.

"Zadyn," I say, snapping him out of their little pissing contest. "Put me down. It's only a ride. I'm fine."

He stares Jack down another second before giving in.

"I'll be right behind you," he assures me, helping me into the saddle. The warm smell of a campfire hits me as Jack scoots closer, reaching around me to grip the reins.

"You need to hold on, witch. This won't be a leisure ride." He takes my hands and places them on the reins just above his. His voice tickles my ear, and I want so badly to lean back into him. To rest my head on his shoulder. To have his arms pull me back against him.

But I can't. And he won't.

He kicks the horse and leads us through the forest at a punishing pace. I bounce so hard that my hips leave the saddle with each gallop. Just when I think I'm going to fly clean off, Jack's arm presses against my stomach and locks me in. I settle on his lap as he roots me to the horse and pulls me flush against his hard body. It's tough not to let his nearness get to me. Him holding me like this doesn't mean what I want it to. It doesn't mean anything at all.

We make it to the edge of the Bone Forest without another hiccup. I loose a breath of relief as the horses touch down on rich green grass.

A camp is already set up in the center of a large clearing by the time we stop. A handful of horses graze beneath thick-trunked trees while a pack of gray bloodhounds snooze beside the crackling fire. Five or six guards occupy a fallen log, holding skewers of dark meat to the flame. My stomach rumbles at the scent.

Jack helps me dismount, and I pull the cloak tighter around myself. It's better than being topless, but it's open down the front and doesn't offer much protection against the elements.

"I'll find you a shirt," Jack says quietly. He ties up his horse as Zadyn approaches.

"Come on, let's get you warmed up."

I lean on him for support as we make our way to sit by the fire. I'm given a piece of meat to nibble on, and someone passes a canteen of water around.

"You and that Bone Forest," says a deep, husky voice.

I glance up and am met with the auburn-haired, green-eyed twins. Identical, chiseled faces of elemental beauty peer at me from across the fire. One wears his hair twisted up into a man bun and the other lets it flow over his shoulders.

"Thought you would have learned the first time," the man bun on the left says with a wink. I quirk an eyebrow.

"Hello, nice to see you again." He dips his head. "I'm Max. And *this* is Mal." He claps his brother hard on the shoulder, knocking the skewered meat in his hands to the ground. His twin slowly turns to glare at him.

My eyes dart between the two of them.

"We're twins," Max explains.

I nod.

"I hadn't noticed."

Max bursts into a loud, infectious laugh. Mal does not join him. He just watches me silently, intently, with preternatural stillness. It's a little unnerving.

"She's funny. The witch is funny, Cap," Max crows.

Jack walks around him, ignoring his epiphany as he extends a blousy white tunic to me and stalks away, silent and aloof.

I twist my torso, facing the trees so as to not flash tit at the circle of guards while I slide the top over my head. The shirt fits me like a dress and smells deliciously like Jack. I turn back to the hoots and hollers of the fae males around me and flip them off, earning their respect in the process.

I lock eyes with Jack. He doesn't smile or join in his men's jovial quips. He sits across the fire, quiet and brooding, his molten eyes looking like a part of the flame itself. A glowing ember in the night.

"And you," Max says, wagging a finger at Zadyn as he chews loudly. "You must be the rabid *OrCat* Mal shot in the forest that day. Glad to see you made it. Had we known—"

Zadyn lifts a hand, sparing him. "You didn't know. It's fine. It didn't even scar." He directs that last part at the stone-faced Mal, who eyes us up before returning his gaze to the fire.

"I'm furious with you, you know." Zadyn lightly nudges my shoulder as he takes a sip of water.

"I don't blame you," I admit.

"You could have been killed—"

"Zadyn, please. I can't do the lecture. Not tonight. I know everything you're about to say, and you're right. I'm sorry if I scared you."

He laughs. "That's putting it mildly."

After we finish eating, Zadyn insists on checking my thigh wound. He cuts through my pant leg with a small knife before dabbing it with a dampened cloth.

"I can't heal it before it's properly cleaned. If it's infected, it will just seal it in," he explains.

The bleeding has stopped, thankfully, and I pray it doesn't get infected out here in the wilderness. For all the magic in this world, I don't think they've mastered the art of modern medicine.

Zadyn and I have to share the only extra bedroll in the camp, and I'm grateful for the warmth of his body near mine. By the time we lay down, my body feels heavy and exhausted. But my mind is not so willing to rest. I toss and turn while Zadyn sleeps peacefully at my side.

Wired and frustrated, I sit up and glance toward the still-blazing fire. Jack is the only one left there, taking the first watch while the rest of the camp sleeps. He stokes the fire with a stick, eliciting soft crackles in the quiet night. His gaze locks with mine, wordlessly beckoning me.

I find myself walking toward him. He watches every step. I slip the cloak from my shoulders and hold it out to him.

"Thank you," I say. He shakes his head, eyes sliding back to the fire.

"Keep it. You'll freeze without it."

Not in the mood to argue, I slide the heavy wool back over my shoulders and take a seat beside him. He quickly schools the surprise on his face into indifference.

"How did you get to me so quickly?"

The angles of his face are made even sharper by the shadows and the dancing firelight as he stares into the flames.

"We were heading north toward Hyrax when we heard you screaming," he explains. "You're lucky we had just stopped to set up camp when you were attacked, or we wouldn't have gotten to you in time."

I lower my eyes while I pick at my nails.

"I should thank you for saving my life."

"I'd do it for anyone," he says without looking at me. "The better question is, what were you doing in the Bone Forest when you should have been at the castle?"

"Needed some fresh air."

He chuckles.

"Or you heard my conversation in the hall earlier and went searching for the portal." Jack peers at me, face half illuminated by the crackling fire. "You're either incredibly stupid or incredibly brave."

"Actually, I'm just tired of everyone refusing to hear me out and treat me like a human being."

His dark brows arch in surprise.

"Oh, you know what I mean. I did what I had to do. Or tried to, at least."

"You would have been quite disappointed if you had made it to the portal, only to find that it's out of commission for the foreseeable future. Whatever passed through that gate did a solid job of making sure no one else could."

"So, why are you and your men heading there?"

"To scout the area, try to figure out what was strong enough to destroy two Guardians and stop it from invading these lands any further. I had planned to travel north with my men, but now that's changed."

I tilt my head in confusion.

"I'm escorting you back in the morning," he clarifies.

"I meant what I said. I'm not going back." I hold firm. "Besides, don't your men need you?"

"I'm not their mother. They can handle themselves."

"Then let us go north with you. Zadyn and I will make ourselves useful. I promise."

He looks at me with those golden eyes, and every part of me feels electric. "What's in it for you?"

"Honestly?" I say. "I'm hoping you'll help me find another way to get home."

"And defy direct orders of the king by abetting your escape? No, thank you."

"Am I a prisoner then?" He doesn't answer. I shake my head. "You don't understand—I don't belong here. This isn't my world."

"If that were true, I don't think you could have found your way here even if you tried. Despite where you were born, this is where you ended up. I'm not letting you out of my sight until I know more."

I groan in exasperation.

"I tried to run. I tried to get away from you, from the king," I point out. "Doesn't that prove to you that this isn't some elaborate act? That I'm not just posing as a Blackblood to win the king's favor?"

He's silent for a moment.

"Or you just hate the food at the castle."

I roll my eyes.

"Why can't you just say you believe me?" I press, ignoring his joke. He gives me a long look and once again deflects my question.

"I, for one, think the food is pretty decent."

"I'm being treated like an object. Like I belong to the king, yet he won't even see me. I have no say in anything. And you don't help—with your constant doubt and derision."

"The king thinks you might be of use to him." He takes a swig from a canteen. "It's my job to make sure you're not a threat."

"Then let me prove to you that I'm not. But you can't expect me to help the king if I'm not getting something in return."

He turns his eyes to mine.

"The way I see it is you need me, and I need you," I say, not backing down from his stare. "You've been searching for the last Blackblood for centuries, and I want to go home. I'll do what he needs me to do in exchange for help getting back. *Safely.*"

He contemplates this for a while. "You need to understand something," he starts slowly. "This isn't a one-time favor he's asking of you. Aegar needs a Dragon Rider. It's a permanent position."

"It's a life sentence, you mean," I counter, leaping to my feet. "If you think I will give my life for a cause that has nothing to do with me, that I never asked—"

He clamps a large hand around my wrist, and I stop short. His eyes are softer as he stares up at me.

"He needs you. We all do."

His words take me off guard, but they hit their desired mark. The king needs me.

He needs me. Which means that some small part of him believes me. How can I turn my back?

The campfire crackles as he holds my gaze. Something

charged passes between us, and his reaction tells me he feels it too.

"Why is me trying to kill you one of your greatest fears?" he murmurs, his hand sliding from my arm. "The Mara show you visions of your deepest fears in order to feed on your pain and torment. You said you had a vision... of me trying to kill you."

I nod, swallowing thickly. "You plunged a knife into my stomach. And twisted it," I admit, staring at the ground.

"Why?" His gravelly voice is little more than a whisper. "Why would you fear that?"

"Maybe since you've been known to stab me in the past," I mutter under my breath, crossing my arms.

"If I wanted to hurt you, I would have. Certainly wouldn't have healed you afterward."

It was Jack that healed my leg after he stabbed it?

I stare into the fire, away from the scrutiny of his gaze.

"You're not convincing, you know." He stretches his long legs in front of him and leans back on his palms.

"I'm not trying to convince you of anything."

"But there's something you won't say." He narrows his eyes in challenge. "You're keeping secrets."

"Because I don't know you." I toss my hands up. "What do you want from me? You want to read my high school diary?"

"I want you to be truthful."

"I have been nothing but truthful. You just refuse to believe a word that comes out of my mouth."

"Can you blame me?"

"I've never lied to you," I whisper fervently. "But I don't trust you, just like you don't trust me. Even if I did tell you everything, you'd probably just choose not to believe me."

"Let me be the judge of that," he says simply.

I sit back down with a sigh.

"This is all new to me. A week ago, I thought Zadyn was a little old bookshop owner. My friend. Then he—he showed me this book. Basically forced me to recite these words, and next thing I know, Zadyn shifts into this hot guy, and I'm swallowed up by a puff of black smoke. I woke up in the Bone Forest, and you and your men picked me up. Zadyn snuck into the castle and explained everything. A week ago, my life was mundane—boring. I was blissfully unaware that magic was real, that the fae were real, and that, apparently, I'm a witch."

I try to decipher his expression.

"Do you believe me?"

He nods after a moment of pregnant silence. "You've never accessed your magic?"

"When I read those words from the book, my hands, they—" I look at my palms. "I all but burned a hole through the table. When I tried to do it again, nothing happened. I haven't been able to do anything out of the ordinary since then."

He's quiet for a long time.

"What made you think I might be a witch in the first place?" I ask, earning his steady gaze. "When you found me that day in the Bone Forest, you took me straight to the king."

"I was just following protocol. The king ordered every witch found in our lands to be brought before him." He scratches the stubble shadowing his sharp jawline as he studies the fire. I fight the urge to lean in and lick it.

Oh my god, I need to stop.

"I first suspected it when I saw the shadow smoke. That's how Blackbloods used to travel. They were called shadow walkers. They could leap from one side of the world to the other in a matter of seconds, riding the shadows. Not many Bluebloods can swing that." He pauses. "Also, from the way your *OrCat* friend was defending you, I assumed he was a familiar."

"Is that a witch thing?"

"Yes, only witches have familiars. Thousands of years ago, it was considered uncommon for a witch not to have a familiar. Now, it's the opposite. It's rare among the Reds and Blues."

"Do you think I made that smoke happen?" I ask. "I had just assumed it was the book."

"I think the book acted like a catalyst in getting you here," he says. "When you said those words out loud, I think you opened a door to our world and unlocked a part of yourself you didn't know existed."

I sit with this for a moment, studying the familiar planes of his face.

"I'll go back to the castle," I concede. "On one condition."

He sighs in vexation but motions for me to continue.

"You bring me to the king, and we all discuss this like sensible adults. Then I will decide to stay or go."

"Done."

"And you agree that this is not me working for you. We are all working together. And I need answers to my questions if I am to help you. We need to be open with each other, to trust each other. Do you think you can get the king to agree to that?" I ask.

"He values my counsel, so yes. I will speak to him."

"And can *you* agree to that?" I narrow my eyes at him. He gives a curt nod.

"Good. And I want to be moved out of that little four-by-four you call a room."

He sighs again. "Fine. That's three conditions, by the way. Would you also like to add a tutor to your list of contingencies? Your ability to count is seemingly impaired."

I smack his arm. He doesn't smile, but there's a dark glint of amusement in his golden eyes.

I resolve to give this an actual shot. I will stay to find answers. I will stay to be close to this alternate version of my father, even if he doesn't know me, even if he's the king and I'm a means to an end for him. I will stay until he can look at me with pride and love in his eyes.

Jack and I fall silent, staring into the fire until my eyelids begin to droop, and I drag myself away to sleep.

12

The next day, we start back toward the castle. I explain the change in plan to Zadyn, and I can see the immediate relief wash over him. I ride with him this time, but it doesn't make for a less awkward dynamic as the three of us make our way back.

One thing Jack and Zadyn at least agree on is that we take the long way back—*around* the Bone Forest.

A two-day trip.

No bathrooms, no beds, just the fabulous outdoors.

I hate to admit it, but as the shimmering castle appears in view, catching the sunlight with crystalline magnificence, I feel relieved. Soon, so soon, I will be off this damn horse. I just pray that my ovaries haven't been damaged beyond repair.

We reach the front gates and are relieved of our horses. I can barely feel anything from the waist down, but my thigh seems to be holding up.

"I'll speak to the king this evening, and we'll find you alternate sleeping arrangements. Rest today, witch. I'll come find you," Jack says as we make our way up the alabaster stairs leading to the massive arched doorway. I stare after him as he goes. Zadyn's hand on my shoulder snaps me back to reality, and I follow him to Gnorr's infirmary to have my leg inspected. It takes under five minutes for her to clean the wound with a strong astringent and heal it up completely.

When I hear a knock on my door the next morning, I expect to see a bright-eyed, bushy-tailed Igrid on the other side. I swing it open, a bed-headed hot mess, to find Jack waiting there instead. He greets me with a quick once over and a gruff order to follow him.

Back to his grouchy self, I see.

I quickly slip my shoes on and slide my phone into my back pocket while Jack's back is turned. I doubt it will be of any use to me here, and it's on ten percent battery, but it's the only thing I have from home.

Zadyn walks beside me, no longer bothering with the whole cat act.

"I take it the king agreed to my requests?" I ask as we make our way out of the servant's quarters and into a pristine hallway with marble floors so reflective I can see myself in them. We stop in front of an ornately carved wooden door. Jack steps through and holds his arm out.

"I trust the accommodations will be to your liking."

"Holy shit," I breathe, stepping inside. The room is bigger than my whole apartment in Jacksonville.

A canopied four-post bed with a luscious, lilac-colored comforter rests against the wall to my left. My fingers glide over the intricate vines carved into the whitewashed bedpost as I take in the rest of the room.

Sunlight spills through the arching windows above the plush, plum-colored nook. My breath hitches as I look up at the whimsical hand-painted sky on the ceiling, spattered with diamonds. They look like twinkling stars swirling around the giant amethyst chandelier in the center. The space is complete with cozy puffs, pillows, and floor cushions scattered across the ornate carpet.

"The washroom is through there." Jack nods to one of the doors to the right, behind the dining table for four.

"What's in here?" I ask, making my way to the door beside it.

"It's an adjoining suite," he says, glancing at Zadyn. "For you. I didn't think it wise to keep a familiar too far out of reach."

"Thank you, that was very considerate," Zadyn says, begrudging every word. I fight a smile, secretly thriving on their little drama.

"It's lovely, Jack," I say before I can stop myself. My hand flies to my mouth. "I'm sorry. I meant Captain."

"Jace," he says, and I think he might be blushing. He quickly lowers his eyes and then brings them back up to mine. "My name is Jace."

"Right, of course," I say quickly.

Jace.

He bobs his head once. "I'll leave you to bathe and dress. The king has agreed to speak with you this afternoon. I'll have Sir Maxim escort you."

"Thank you," I say, locking eyes with him. "Truly."

He gives me another one of his curt soldier nods and moves to the door.

"You'll be there, right? For the meeting?" I sound a tad too hopeful. Like a schoolgirl with a crush.

"I'll be there."

He bows this time and closes the door behind him. As I turn to face Zadyn, I'm surprised to find him already looking at me.

"Not bad, right?" I twirl around, gesturing to the obscenely beautiful room. "I severely underestimated my negotiating skills."

"I don't think they'd work half as well without your charm," he teases.

"I want to see yours." I start to move toward Zadyn's room when a petite fae female in a servant's dress enters with a small curtsy.

"Hello, my lady. My name is Pertha. I'll be attending you."

"Oh, hi. I'm Serena. It's nice to meet you."

Pertha smiles without fully meeting my eyes.

"I'll run your bath, my lady," she says before hurrying off to the bathroom.

"Oh, it's just Serena, not my lady!" I call out, but she's already disappeared.

"I'll leave you to it," Zadyn says, pressing his palms together and retreating toward his room. Taking another glance around my new living space, I let out a tiny squeal. I cannot *wait* to sprawl out on that bed.

The bathroom looks as if a spa and temple had a baby. It's massive. Floor-to-ceiling cream-colored marble. And the bath, *oh my god*. It's the size of a jacuzzi and could easily fit six people. College party girl Serena would have been all about this.

Pertha stands beside the steaming water, holding a towel folded in her arms.

"I'll take this," I say to her, placing it down on the stunning cut of marble vanity. "Thank you, Pertha."

She doesn't move.

"I can take it from here." I smile gently. "Thank you."

"Yes, my lady." She bows her head. "I'll be outside to help you dress."

"It's just Serena," I repeat as the closes the door behind me. "That's gonna take some getting used to."

I strip and step into the inviting waters. My eyes close as I lean my head back, gulping down greedy lungfuls of lavender and eucalyptus bath salts. The massive window before me offers a gorgeous view of a shimmering city in the distance. I make a mental note to explore it.

If I stay here.

Even though everything is so fucked right now, I can almost pretend that I'm on vacation at a five-star hotel in the Swiss Alps. All of it feels too good to be true. And that's probably because it is.

I stay in the bath until my fingers are pruned, marveling at how relaxed I now feel. My heart isn't anxiously racing. I'm not in fight-or-flight mode. I'm oddly calm.

I dry off, slipping into the champagne-colored silk robe hanging on the door, and dare a look in the mirror.

It's still me, but I seem lighter. Like there's a sunny aura around me. Same wavy chocolate brown hair that falls over my chest. Same brown eyes and button nose. My skin is still slightly tan from the Florida sun, making the freckles on my cheeks and nose even more accentuated. Tucking my wet hair behind my ears, I step out into the bedroom.

"So, what does one wear for a meeting with a king?" I ask Pertha. She moves to the armoire with modest grace and sifts through the choices.

"Here are some of the less formal options, my lady."

I don't bother to correct her this time. My eyes skip over the long, flowing skirts and shimmery materials.

"These are less formal?" I laugh. Pertha lays them out on the bed as Zadyn enters the room, his caramel-colored hair still glistening from his own bath. He pushes the wet strands from his face and locks eyes with me.

He looks good. Clean and fresh and inhumanly handsome in a close-cut brown jacket over a cream-colored tunic, dark pants, and boots that reach past his calves. He approaches the bed with the laid-out dress options.

"Help. I'm not used to these clothes," I tell him, toying with the frills on a baby pink number. "Fae wear this stuff every day?"

"High Fae in the king's court, yes," he says with an apologetic look at Pertha, who seems uninterested.

"Well, I'm a witch, so do you guys have any denim?"

Zadyn rolls his eyes and moves past me to select one of the dresses from the bed. He holds it up to my chest, tilting his head as he studies me.

"This one. It's the least feminine."

"Uh, alright." I frown.

Zadyn lowers his mouth to my ear as Pertha moves back to the wardrobe. "You're a Blackblood. You don't want to go there in pastels and ruffles. No one will take you seriously. Something more subdued, more mature, is better."

The dress is a deep, rich eggplant shade. It's simple, compared to the others. Clean lines, fitted long sleeves—mature. Not girlish at all.

I begin to undo my robe, and Zadyn's hand flies to shield his eyes.

"A little warning."

He stalks away to sit on the window seat with his back to me.

"Oh, relax. You've seen it all before, *Annie*. Spring break, Panama City."

"I didn't see anything. We were in the water," he grumbles, staring out the window at the frosted mountains beyond.

"Did you like having a woman's body? I'm sure the boobs were a fun little bonus."

He groans, turning beat red. "Can we not, please?"

"Let me have my fun! I'm just beginning to come to terms

with the fact that my best girl friend was actually a guy all along. The same girl friend who I skinny-dipped with on more than one occasion. Oh, and then there was that time we played truth or dare at the soccer team's party when we had to—"

"Serena."

The warning in his voice cuts me off, but I see the blush creeping up his tan neck. I can't help but chuckle at how easily embarrassed he is.

Pertha slides the gown over my head and begins to fiddle with the laces of the bodice. The dress fits me like a glove, hugging my arms, chest, and waist. The square-cut neck is modest, but sensual somehow, showcasing the length of my throat and the line of my clavicle. She slips my middle fingers through the little loops at the end of each sleeve, then ushers me to the vanity to comb through my damp hair.

"I can do it, Pertha. Thank you." Taking the comb from her, I begin to run it through my ends. She gives me a quick curtsy and exits the room.

"I don't suppose you have anything like texture spray in your strange little fae world?"

Zadyn barks a laugh, his arm dangling over his drawn-up knee.

"It'll never dry in time for this meeting. I'm going to go in there dripping like a wet dog."

He snaps his fingers once and I gape at my perfectly dried waves in the mirror.

"Neat trick," I say in wonder. "Can you touch up my highlights, too?"

"Don't push it."

On the vanity is an assortment of cosmetics in little glass tubs and bottles. I dust some pink over my cheeks and dab my lips with a red-tinted lip stain, blotting them together in the mirror. Once I lace up my heeled boots, I stand with my arms outstretched and give a quick twirl.

"How do I look?" I ask. "Fit for a meeting with dear old dad?"

Placing his feet on the ground, Zadyn turns to examine me.

"Perfect," he says.

A knock sounds from the door.

"Come in," I call.

The door opens to the wicked grin of a red-haired soldier. Sir Max stands tall and proud, bright green eyes twinkling with roguish mischief. He etches a low bow and says in that warm husky voice, "The king will see you now, *my lady*."

His words are a light tease as he takes a waiting step back into the hall.

I glance at Zadyn and take a big breath, readying myself to go head-to-head with my father.

13

My palms are so sweaty.

That's my predominant thought as Zadyn and I sit at a circular table in the council room, across from my dad—I've got to stop doing that—the *king* and the members of his small council.

At the round table sits the Master of Coin—a pale, High Fae male with long, lustrous, blue-black hair and narrowed eyes, called Lord Gronwen. Beside him is the High Priest, a bald fae in billowing blue robes whose soft, wrinkled skin makes him appear close to Gnorr in age. Across from him sits the king's Head of Records, Lord Conwell, a stunning male with golden-brown skin and electric blue eyes.

Standing behind my father's right shoulder is Jack. *Jace.*

Silence falls after the introductions, and the king watches me, his expression hard and unreadable. I'm wondering if they're expecting me to say something. I chance a look at Zadyn, and he nods his head in silent confirmation.

"For those of you who don't know me—which is all of you—"

Strong start.

"My name is Serena Avery. This is my familiar, Zadyn—" I glance at him, realizing I never learned his last name.

"Rhodes," he supplies.

The king's eyebrows raise as he leans forward.

"Not the Rhodeses of Cardynia?" he asks, narrowing his eyes.

"The very ones. I believe you know my father, Zorren Rhodes."

A laugh breaks through the king's stone-faced stare. It sounds so much like my dad that my heart twists to hear it again.

"Zadyn." He shakes his head in disbelief. "You're grown. You were just an infant when you left court. Your father," he recounts fondly, "fought beside me in every battle since we were seventeen. He was my oldest friend." A look of sadness crosses his features. "Gods, you look just like him."

Zadyn's jaw clenches, and I feel him tense beside me.

"When did it happen?" he asks quietly.

"Nearly a year after your departure." The king's regret is sincere. He rises to his feet, glancing between us.

"They said she was found with a familiar, but I never suspected...it worked then. You found her. I had my doubts when she first arrived, but this..." He trails off. "Why didn't you come to me sooner?"

"Frankly, I wanted to make sure you could be trusted not to harm her," Zadyn says.

"What worked?" I ask.

The king finally looks at me. *Really* looks at me for the first time since being here.

"Good gods. I had all but given up hope." He marvels at me, like a sideshow curiosity.

Rising to my feet, I demand, "Tell me what worked."

He motions for me to sit back down.

"There is much to explain."

I reluctantly sink back into my seat.

"Nearly two hundred years ago, we were at war with Vod. Their king, at the time, was a tyrant who sought to expand his reach overseas. They had been encroaching on our lands for years, spreading like a plague around this kingdom—stirring civil unrest, raiding and pillaging the poor villages. With their military numbers and fleets, we needed a sure-fire defense, something to secure our lands. After I inherited the crown from my father, I continued his quest to find the Dragon Rider with the help of your parents. We needed to end the war and ensure against all future ones." His gaze shifts back to Zadyn.

"We knew that with a dragon on our side, any attack on Aegean soil would be futile. Our enemies wouldn't stand a chance. We searched for centuries, to no avail. We had all but given up hope of ever finding her when we sailed the Erastin Ocean to consult the High Seer. Her price was steep, but we paid it. Our centuries of searching, she said, had been in vain. You were never here." He turns to me.

"She foretold the birth of a babe with black blood, hidden from sight by old magic, belonging to our world but not born to it."

I feel a chill run down my spine.

"Your mother"—he looks at Zadyn and swallows thickly—"clever as she was, devised a plan. We were unsure it would work, but it was a necessary risk. She crafted a spell, binding the life of her unborn son to that of the unborn Blackblood witch. She did everything to ensure the binding would hold across worlds, across galaxies. She gave her life to make it so," he says, his cold king's stare softening a fraction.

I peer at Zadyn, my mind racing. Zadyn's mother had magic? Was she a witch?

"One hundred and seventy years went by with no sign of the Blackblood. We found an alternative solution to end the war and smooth tensions with Vod. When your father took you from court for safekeeping, even I did not know the location." A dark look crosses his features. "Years passed, and then one day, he sent word that the mark had finally appeared on you. The mark of a familiar. And we knew she had been born." He gestures to where I sit, holding my breath.

A moment of silence passes before I slide my gaze to Zadyn.

"So your mother created this bond as a direct link to me in the mortal world?"

He confirms with a nod.

"Without your mother and her magic, there was no way to know if you had reached her once you'd been summoned. If you were safe. All we could do was wait and hope that one day you would return to us," the king says, almost to himself.

"With the very thing my parents gave their lives for, of course," Zadyn says with a touch of bitterness. A flicker of hurt skids across the king's face.

"They knew the cost, and they paid it willingly for the good of the realm," he says evenly. "It was our secret to bear. Your father took you from court to protect it and to protect you. We did everything we could think of to keep you safe."

"But not to keep them safe. They took the secret to their graves." Zadyn stares at the king with defiance in his eyes. "Don't pity me—I knew what I was coming back to."

A cool and unaffected mask slips over the king's face. "The fact that the two of you sit here before me confirms that your parents' sacrifice was not in vain. This is her. The last Black-blood witch."

It's my turn to speak up. "Except I can't touch my magic."

His eyes snap to me, nearly jarring me from my seat. The weight of his stare and the power rolling off of him is truly frightening. "What I mean is, I can't access it."

"The glamour is likely what's repressing it. Gnorr said as much," the king replies.

"Look," I sigh. "There's a lot we need to cover here. Before I agree to be your...witch."

"There is no agreeing or disagreeing with what you are. It simply is. This is your birthright. There is no denying it—you are a Blackblood. Whether or not you desire my protection and safekeeping in fulfilling your birthright, however, is up to you."

"Your protection and safekeeping got off to a promising start when you threw me in a dungeon to be tortured for answers I didn't have," I spit, gesturing to Jace. If I'm not mistaken, it's regret I see on his face.

I sigh, softening. "Listen, I can't cast spells or ride broomsticks or brew love potions—" Zadyn shoots me a look that says *not helping*, and I trail off.

"You will be able to do all that and more," the king says, dismissing my opposition. "When the witches died, their spirits released a large amount of energy. Their magic was given back to the land, the soil from whence it came. But with their final breaths, they threw part of that energy into preserving their line. They hid their magic in you and then hid you in your mother's womb. Your blood appears red to blend in with the humans you were raised by."

"I *am* human. Witch or not, I will *always* be human," I say with contempt, glancing around the room at the wary onlookers. Easing back on the bite in my tone, I continue, "Besides, that doesn't make sense. I was born thousands of years after the witches died."

"Time works differently in your world. You may not have had physical form yet, but you, your soul, existed in the ether well before you were even an idea in your human parents' heads. You exist because the Blackbloods willed it so. Their magic was strong enough to span across time and space itself. Serena." His voice softens, and there is a shift in his cold expression, making him look so...Dad. And the way he says my name...

"You are safer here than in any other court. If you leave, you will be found by others and forced into action. They will not treat you with the grace that we have."

"Oh, you mean the grace of holding me captive or the grace of allowing me to clean your filthy toilets?"

He chuckles in surprise. "You'll forgive us for taking precautions against a stranger in our home. We did not yet have the full story. You are both free to leave if that is your will, but make no mistake—you will be kept safe here."

"And will I be kept safe from the dragon you intend for me to ride, or is that too much to ask?"

He says nothing.

"I'll be honest," I begin. "I don't fully understand what I'm doing here. But I will help you with the dragon if you show me how. On the condition that you let me go home when my work is done."

He is silent for a long moment, weighing my bargain.

"I wish I could promise you that." His words are sincere. "But bonding a dragon is for life. You may be surprised how your mind changes after experiencing it for yourself. Aside from that, there have been...disturbances at the portal as of late. It would be unsafe to be anywhere nearby until we know more."

My heart sinks.

"The captain has informed me of your...demands." The king braces his hands on the table, leaning forward slightly.

Jace's eyes link with mine for a brief moment, his beautiful face set hard as stone.

"Requests," I correct, holding up my pointer finger. "None of which seem unreasonable given the fact that I'm about to devote my life for the foreseeable future to being at your service."

I smile sweetly. He expels a single laugh.

"We can agree that the future Dragon Rider will need training. Physical and magical." He sits back in his ornately carved chair and steeples his hands. My eyes snag on the slight arch of his ears —the only distinguishable difference between Dad and king.

Except for the frilly clothes, of course.

"You will remain under my care and protection so long as you train in those areas. You will report to the captain each morning for physical training."

"*He's* going to train me?" I ask, my eyebrows quirked. His upper lip pulls back in a challenging snarl.

"Train you and serve as your personal guard."

"Problem with that, witch?" he asks.

"No. It's perfectly fine." It takes effort to make my voice sound nonchalant as I redirect my attention to the king.

"Zadyn, you will tutor her in the ways of our world. History, court politics, magic. Teach her anything and everything that will prepare her for the journey she is about to embark upon."

His gaze shifts to me. "In your off time, you will both be active members of this court."

The king's Master of Coin—the man with the long black hair and sinister eyes—stirs in his seat. "While I think that a wise idea, Majesty, we should make sure we are all on the same page about what we tell the public. It is not often we welcome new court members. There will be talk about who she is and where she came from."

"He has a point, my King," the ancient, robed fae drawls in a soft, reverent voice. "Perhaps we could claim a distant relative of Your Majesty. Any ties to the crown would justify her being here and put stop to any rumors."

"Very well." The king nods. "From henceforth, you shall be known as Lady Serena Accostia. You will take the name of my kin. Your father was High Fae and a cousin of the king. He fell in battle, and your mother fled to raise you at a temple in the north. Both parents are deceased."

I flinch inwardly.

Serena Accostia. *Lady Serena Accostia.*

"You are to attend my daughter, the princess, as one of her ladies."

"Of course, there is also the matter of her appearance," Gronwen says with disdain, his black pupils scanning me. I want to shrivel under his accusing stare. "She hardly blends."

"Is there nothing to be done for the human glamour?" Lord Conwell asks.

"Even Gnorr could not reverse it. In time, perhaps." The king glances at him.

"Even in the human glamour, there is an odd resemblance..." The hairless High Priest trails off, eyes bouncing between me and the king.

"Mere coincidence," he dismisses.

"There is another solution. If we cannot undo the glamour, perhaps we can add to it," the High Priest murmurs, assessing me.

Jace eyes him. "You want to layer glamours?"

"Temporarily. If her identity is to remain hidden at court, then she should look fae."

"Why would we need to hide my identity?" I interject.

"Because if other kingdoms catch wind of your presence

here, they will come for you," Jace answers, eyes leveled with mine.

"Isn't the truth going to come out, eventually?" I ask the room.

"The most lethal weapons are the ones that remain concealed up until the very. Last. Second." Gronwen purrs.

I shudder.

"Do it." The king gives the High Priest a terse nod. He lifts a hand in my direction, and a soft breeze wraps around me. Before I can protest, he lowers his hands to his lap.

"What did you just do to me?" I hiss.

"Nothing drastic. Now you look the part." Gronwen smiles like the cat that ate the canary. I lift my fingers to my ears and gasp when I feel the slightly pointed tip. I glance at Zadyn, horrified.

"It's okay," he assures me. I relax a little and find my voice.

Turning to the king, I ask, "What do we tell people about Zadyn?"

"The truth. He is Zadyn Rhodes, Lord of Cardynia. Your birthright." He looks at Zadyn, who, in turn, bows his head in silent gratitude. "Speak of this to no one outside of this room. The only others privy to your true identity will be the guards I place on your personal detail."

"Zadyn and I had an idea," I say, earning the curious eyes of every male in the room. "You said that the glamour concealed my magic. But what if it was suppressed because I've never drank before?"

The room is silent.

"He said that the Blackbloods fed on Bluebloods to sustain themselves."

The king looks back to Jace. Something unsaid passes between them.

"Confer with Madame Gnorr on the subject. She may have sources."

"Sire." Jace gives him a dutiful nod.

"Is there anything else you'd like to discuss before this meeting adjourns?" the king asks me.

"Just one thing," I start. "My friend, Igrid, is a servant here. Can I request for her to be on my service?"

"Done," he answers quickly. "Welcome to the Court of Aegar, Lady Accostia. Your training begins at dawn."

14

When we are halfway to our rooms and beyond earshot of the small council, I turn to Zadyn.

"So, I think that went well."

"It could have gone a lot worse." His tone is flat.

"You didn't tell me the extent of your ties to the king." I glance up at him as we skirt down the lavish hallway.

His expression is indifferent as he says, "The ties were my parents' really. I was an infant when I left court. I barely know the king."

"He seemed to know you," I nudge.

Zadyn stares straight ahead as he speaks. "My father used to sit on his council. My mother was a witch. She helped from time to time." Finally turning his face to me, his jaw relaxes a bit.

"When I was young, my father told me what he and my mother did in order to bind me to you," he says, redirecting his eyes down the hall.

"My mother came from a line of powerful Bluebloods, and her father was High Fae. She knew—well, they both did—that in order for the binding to work across worlds, across time, a sacrifice would need to be made. Two lives, the seer warned them. She told my mother that if she tried to bind me against the will of the gods and nature, it would kill her and my father would die to protect the secret."

He pauses for a moment, swallowing. I watch him struggle to continue.

"I didn't expect him to be here when I returned. He prepared me the best he could. Told me to find you and deliver you safely to Aegar. But my duty has always been to you, before my king and my home. I couldn't hand you over without knowing beyond a shadow of a doubt that he wouldn't harm you for his own gain. I was just being cautious."

He shrugs as if it's no big deal that he cared enough about my safety to take extra precautions.

As if *everyone* is that loyal and considerate.

We're both quiet for a while. "I'm so sorry. About your parents."

"I never knew my mother," he says simply. "And it's been a long time since I've seen my father."

His parents *died* for the cause. So that I could find my way here—so that Zadyn could find his way to me. The weight of that fact sinks into my chest like a thousand-pound boulder.

Part of me knows exactly who Zadyn is. I've felt his presence my entire life. Even through a thousand different forms and names, there has always been an invisible thread, a connection, drawing me to him for as long as I can remember. So I know in my heart that he is good. That I can trust him. That he is a true friend. Maybe my only friend. He would defend me before the king if I said I really didn't want to do this. He would go against his dead parents' wishes, the king's wishes, if I asked him to. He risked everything to follow me to the portal to help me get home. And it's not that I want to do this, but it feels like I owe it to him, to the memory of his parents, to try.

And would it be so terrible to figure out who I am? If I have the power they're all saying I do lying dormant inside of me...I want to know. I need to know. Because I can't go back to living in ignorance. I can't unlearn what I've been forced to face. All I can do is make the best of an absurd situation.

"Lord Rhodes," an icy voice calls from behind us. We both turn to see Lords Gronwen and Conwell approaching us.

"Lord Conwell and I were just about to embark on a hunt with a few members of court. We wondered if you might honor us with your presence."

Everything about this guy is a warning. He's beautiful in the way all fae are beautiful. But his angular face, smooth ivory skin, and dark features remind me of a living, breathing vampire. Not the best of vibes.

"Thank you, gentlemen. Perhaps another time," he says politely and turns. I stop him with a hand on his chest.

"Why?" I ask, lowering my voice. "You should go. Get to know them."

"You shouldn't be left alone."

"I'll go find Igrid. I'm fine." He doesn't budge.

"Gentlemen, please excuse us for a moment." I pull Zadyn a few feet away. "Zadyn. I appreciate you looking out for me, but I can't live with someone attached to my hip. I need space to breathe. I'm safe. Plus, the king assigned Jace as my personal guard."

"I don't see him anywhere." He glances around to prove his point.

"If anyone touches me, the king will take a fit. You know that. You need to be a member of this court to keep up appearances. We both do. If you're always by my side, people are going to think something is up. You should go with them."

"But this place is unfamiliar to you."

"I promise you. I'm fine." I give his shoulders a light shake. He stands there, looking down at me with reluctance.

"Fine. I understand. I'll go with them. Be safe." His hand finds mine and gives it a gentle squeeze. I smile in encouragement.

Turning smoothly to the men, he says, "Shall we?"

Zadyn follows the waiting nobles and I start to make my way in the opposite direction toward my room.

"Congratulations on your promotion. *Lady*," a sensuous voice purrs in my ear.

I jump back, bumping into the wall beside me. Jace shakes his head. "What is *wrong* with you?"

"Many things," I retort, smoothing my dress. "You scared me."

"We need to work on your awareness. The fact that you couldn't tell I was behind you is not a promising start."

"I don't have your fancy fae hearing or your weird sense of smell." I bound off the wall and continue down the stretch of magnificent hallway. Jace falls into step beside me.

"Doesn't mean you should allow yourself to be caught off-guard, witch. We'll work on it."

Pursing my lips, I slide him a sidelong glance.

"Maybe it's just me, but that sounds kind of derogatory."

"You are a witch."

"But when you say it, it sounds like '*hey, scum.*'" I make a face, mimicking him.

"I did not call you *scum*," he protests as we pass beneath a sparkling marble archway.

"That's the underlying tone."

"How about 'lady' then?"

"How about Serena, you know, my *name*?"

"Serena." He gives me a look of disdain, testing out my name on his tongue. "I don't think it suits you."

I scoff, rounding the corner. "Your charm is truly astounding."

"So I've been told." He keeps pace beside me, shoulders back, hands folded behind him. "There is a ball tonight to welcome Prince Kai to court. All courtiers are expected to be in attendance."

"Who's Prince Kai?" I glance up at him.

"Queen Ilspeth's son from her first marriage to the King of Vod."

"Vod, as in the kingdom Aegar was at *war* with, Vod?" My eyebrows shoot up in surprise.

He nods. "King Derek wed the widowed queen as a peace treaty. Her eldest son, Kylian, is the current King of Vod. Prince Kai is second in line to the throne, and their younger brother, Kade, is third. You'll meet the other courtiers tonight, including the princess and her ladies. Remember to stick to the story."

"The princess won't ask any questions?"

A muscle in his jaw twitches. "I will speak with the princess."

"Are you going to tell her the truth?"

"As much of it as I can without endangering her."

"She's to be queen one day. Shouldn't she know these things?" I press.

"This isn't up for discussion." His sharp eyes land on me, and I struggle to read beneath that hardened expression. "Stick to the story. Even in the presence of the princess."

"Fine," I relent, making a face as we reach my room and he takes up post outside my door.

I turn to him, holding it open. "You're just going to stand there?"

"That is why I'm here," he says in an obvious tone.

"Okay, knock yourself out." I begin to close the door, but his large hand shoots out and stops its trajectory.

"I don't have to worry about you climbing out of a window and scaling the wall to escape, do I?"

"I'm past trying to escape. You have nothing to worry about."

He stares at me for a long time, and I stand in stillness as his gaze travels over my eyes, my nose, my lips. Then his hand eases from the door, and it slides shut behind him.

Alone for the first time in days, I explore the wonder of my room, trailing my fingers over the silk bedding, the colorful gowns peeking from the wardrobe, and the ornate spines lining the bookshelf against the wall. Picking out a foreign title, I curl up beneath the window. I make it two pages before I fall asleep.

15

The brisk sound of knocking causes me to nearly fall out of the window seat and land flat on my ass. I recover in time to see Igrid standing before me with a wicked grin on her face.

"Igrid! You're here. Thank god."

"Look at you, missy!" She does a spin, taking in the room. "Quite a step up from the servant's quarters, isn't it?"

She pauses, looking over me. "There's something different about you." Her eyes touch on my newly pointed ears, and she gasps, clapping two freckled hands over her bow lips.

"It's a glamour. Over another glamour." I roll my eyes and finger the arched tip. "I have a lot to tell you."

Taking up my seat at the window, I pat the empty space beside me. Igrid listens as I recap the events of the last few days, including our meeting with the king and his council this morning. I know this information is supposed to remain confidential, but Igrid is my friend and she already knows so much.

"I'm supposed to go to this ball tonight, I guess." I lean my head back and gaze at the snowy mountain peak ten feet from my window.

"For Prince Kai," she assents, her eyes bright. "I'm told he is quite handsome."

"I've never been to a ball in my life. The closest I've gotten is prom. And I hated it so much I left after five minutes."

"Your first time appearing before the entire court." She sighs dreamily. "We'll need to make you look your best."

"Good luck with that. I haven't plucked my eyebrows in three weeks, and I probably have a mustache."

"Oh, you haven't met my friends, missy. They're nothing short of miracle workers." Her copper brows waggle at me. "Come on. Let's get you into the bath and then we'll work our magic."

Igrid leaves me to bathe, my sore hips and inner thighs releasing their tension as I soak. When I emerge in the silky bathrobe, Igrid and two other maids are waiting in my bedroom.

I'm sat in a chair, and every square inch of my body is waxed. My skin stings from where it has been ripped raw, but then a pink-tinged lotion is applied to my naked body, and the redness and irritation disappear.

"They definitely don't have this stuff at European Wax Center," I mutter.

My hair is styled into a gorgeous half-updo, falling over my chest in tight waves that remind me of a medieval maiden's. Tiny diamonds are woven throughout like little stars among a dark sky of silken tresses.

I'm sprayed with the most intoxicating perfume I've ever smelled—something smokey and sweet. I notice that even my skin looks brighter—more luminescent—as I'm eased into the gown with utmost care.

The neutral-colored corset is strapless, fitted through the

waist and hips before pooling out around my ankles. Every inch of the dress is encrusted with tiny, iridescent beads that shimmer beneath the light. Whimsical vines peek out from beneath the strip of gossamer fabric stretched diagonally from shoulder to hip. With the dress just a few shades lighter than my tan skin, one might mistake me for being naked at first glance. But upon further inspection, I look like I belong to the elements, to the ether.

I gasp as I take in my reflection, surveying the dramatic winged liner, the shimmering iridescent powder dusted along my cheeks, and the full, mauve-tinged lips.

I've never looked more beautiful and probably never will again.

Usually when I look in the mirror, I see about a hundred things I wish I could change about myself—my slightly crooked button nose, the deep color of my brown eyes, the little bit of softness around my hips that always leaves me feeling self-conscious.

But studying myself now, I feel beautiful. I feel fae.

I turn to the females, beaming. "You three deserve a raise."

Igrid claps her hands and bounces in place while the other two break into slow grins. She slides a pair of sheer fingerless gloves over my manicured hands and adjusts my dangling, vine-shaped earrings.

"You're ready," she says proudly. There's a soft knock on the door to the adjoining suite.

"Zadyn?"

He props the door open and leans into it, studying me. My cheeks flush under his assessment, but I relax when he smirks in approval, one dimple making itself known at the corner of his lips.

"Nice work," he says to the three fae beside me, his eyes holding mine.

"Did you just get back?" I ask, smoothing the material at my thighs.

"A few minutes ago. I'll be fast."

Two knocks sound from the outside door.

"Come in," I call.

I immediately regret the decision when I see who stands there.

Jace is resplendent in what looks to be a royal guard's uniform—a black jacket with a high collar and thick silver embroidery, and matching pants with a silver stripe down the seam. On his sleeve is a silver royal crest, and at his side hangs a sheathed sword. He looks handsome and regal.

His golden gaze devours me.

"Well, don't you look fae?" he purrs.

I can't look away, can't even find words. I can sense the others' tension, but I can't break the spell.

"Are you ready?" he asks.

"Yes, but Zadyn—" I glance over and see the way he's eyeing Jace.

"Doesn't seem to be ready," Jace supplies. "I'll escort you. He can meet us there."

Zadyn looks back to me. "Go. I'll be there shortly."

I square my shoulders and take Jace's extended hand. His warmth spreads through me, heating my naked arms and face. He wraps my gloved hand around the crook of his arm, and I fight the urge to squeeze down on his muscles.

"If you play this right, you might fool everyone," he says quietly as we make our way downstairs to the party. I glance up at him and he looks away. But not before I catch his eyes skimming over my neckline and lower. "You certainly look the part."

"Can any of your compliments not be backhanded?"

"I wasn't complimenting you." His voice is flat.

"Oh well, fuck me, I guess."

His head whips around so fast I think it's going to fly off. The shock on his face is priceless.

"It's an expression," I explain. "It's just something people say in my world when someone is being a dick."

"I think you're the only one being a dick here."

"Oh, good, at least you know what that word means."

"Insufferable," he mutters.

"The feeling is mutual."

We continue in silence until we reach the Grand Hall, a room over half the size of a football field. We stand at the arching, open doorway, and I drink in the warm decadence waiting on the other side.

Tall candelabras are scattered throughout the space, dousing the room in a soft glow. Crystalline chandeliers hover over the lavish settees, chairs, and nooks scattered around the perimeter of the large dance floor. Tables and towers of endless refreshments, colorful drinks, and desserts line the walls. But most arresting is the sea of beautiful fae dressed in outrageously extravagant finery. The guests sport strange and lovely fashions one would see at the Met Gala—their outfits closer to works of art than to clothing.

It's a vision. A vision from a beautiful, *beautiful* dream.

We make our way over to one of the drink tables, and Jace picks up a glass of water.

"Being boring tonight?" I ask, wiggling my fingers over a flute of fizzy pink liquid. "I'm guessing this has alcohol in it?"

"You'd be correct in that assumption."

I pick it up and take a tentative sip. It's possibly the best thing I've ever tasted. I wonder if it has a lot of sugar in it. Maybe calories don't count when you find yourself in an alternate universe.

We stand together in silence, listening to the triumphant music rolling off the orchestra beside the dance floor. Unable to resist, I take a few more sips from my glass, then dare a look up at him.

"You know, you're much better looking when you don't talk," I say lightly, tipping the glass to my lips.

He eyes me, then the drink in my hands.

"Careful with that stuff." His disinterested gaze flickers back to the storm of ballgowns sweeping across the dance floor. "It's known to loosen tongues."

"My tongue's already loose," I boast, swirling the liquid in my glass. "Loose as a goose."

Glancing down at me with knitted eyebrows, he says, "I meant it lowers one's inhibitions. Makes you more susceptible to being truthful."

"Not unlike our liquor back home."

"I'm guessing this stuff is slightly stronger." He peeks down and that's when I notice my chest brushing up against his arm. I spring back quickly, facing forward as my cheeks burn.

"I lost my balance," I lie. He snickers. "Don't let it go to your already massive head."

"Don't be embarrassed. You're not the first female to press up against me. Certainly won't be the last."

"I was not pressing up against you—" My protest is cut short when I see the crowd turning to the majestic white carpeted staircase toward the back of the room.

The music halts, and a steward announces the king, queen, and princess as they appear under the gilded archway. The princess looks stunning in a rosy silk gown with flowers spilling over the bodice and down the length of the full skirt. The long sleeves are set off the shoulder, revealing her delicate neck and luminous skin. Her honey-brown hair is braided and curled around her sparkling tiara. She looks like spring personified.

I glance at Jace, who seems to be watching her descent with bated breath.

The music resumes once they reach the dais at the bottom of the steps, where four silver thrones wait. The princess sits, and the three pretty fae females I recognize from the dining room materialize at her side.

"Time to meet the princess. Officially," Jace says, turning to me.

My heart starts galloping. "Shouldn't we wait for Z—"

A gentle touch at my elbow cuts me off.

"Here," he says breathlessly, like he just ran here. His smile is dazzling, revealing a full set of perfectly white teeth.

My mind goes blank.

"Hi," I blurt.

He notices the pink drink in my hand, and his face falls. "You got into the Poison, huh?"

"Poison?" I spit.

"That's what we call it. Pink Poison. It's not actually danger-ous. I mean, it is if you ingest an ungodly amount, but even then, you'll just pass out and wake up with your head in a toilet," he clarifies.

"I'm gonna be honest, guys," I begin, a grimace taking over my face as I glance between the two of them. "I really don't want to do this."

"Do what?" Jace asks.

"See my sis—" I catch myself. "Princess. See the princess."

Nice save, idiot.

"Well, you're going to have to get over that, since you are now one of her ladies," Jace insists.

I let out a whiny whimper.

"Let's just get it over with," Zadyn suggests. Jace wraps a fist around my bicep, tugging me forward. I dig my heels into the floor and pull back.

"Do I have to stand there with her the whole night?" I complain.

"Dear gods, you are a *child*."

And to prove his point, I stick my tongue out at him. He yanks me forward and snarls in my face.

"Put your tongue back in your mouth," he growls, baring his teeth. Zadyn places a firm hand on his chest and glowers at him.

"I suggest you take a step back." He doesn't move. "Did you forget that your job is to protect her, not rip her throat out?"

"I think he'd rather throttle me," I tease, staring up into those intense eyes. He rips his hand away and swings it toward the dais.

"After you, *my lady*," he sneers.

I give him a phony smile and brush past him, making my way toward the dais, flanked by the two males. Jace steps around me and bows his head.

"Your Majesties," he addresses the three royals before us. "I'd like to present the Lady Serena Accostia and Lord Rhodes of Cardynia."

Curtsy, Jace mouths to me, and I cross my legs and dip into a pathetic half bow, half squat. I can almost feel his eyes rolling.

"Lady Serena and Lord Rhodes, meet Her Majesty, Queen Ilspeth Triori Accostia, and Her Grace, the Crown Princess Sorscha Accostia."

The queen inclines her head before directing her alluring gaze back to the bustling dance floor. Sam—Sorscha—stands in one fluid motion and takes a step toward me. I am rooted to the spot.

"Cousin!"

She flings her slender arms around my neck and squeezes. I freeze, shoulders tensing before repaying her with an awkward pat on the back. She pulls back, beaming, her features made even more lovely by her radiant smile.

"I'm so glad to make your acquaintance. My apologies for

not visiting you sooner. I only just learnt of your arrival. But here you are! And to stay, I hear. I am thrilled. We shall be great friends." Her eyes skim over my dress as she shakes her head.

"You are an Accostia indeed." Slipping me a wink of approval, she ushers me toward the females behind her. "You must meet my ladies."

The three fae curtsy with devastating grace. I try to mimic the motion but fail miserably.

"This is Ilsa, Marideth, and Clemence—Cece for short."

Ilsa, the slightest of the three ladies, is spritely and fine-boned. Her features are small and elvish, with large, round hazel eyes and pin-straight hair that falls to her waist. The auburn-haired Marideth is tall and lean, with cool gray eyes. Her face is unusual, but striking in its singularity. Clemence is devastating, giving even the princess a run for her money. Her body is that of a goddess, slender with perfect curves. Brilliant curls fall in golden tumbles over her shoulders and the rich green of her gown complements the wide-set eyes of a similar jade. High cheekbones and a plump upper lip complete the masterpiece. I instantly hate her.

"How—how do you do?" I fumble over my words.

The ladies all give polite smiles that tell me there will be a full pow-wow after hours to talk shit about me.

"Are you enjoying the celebration, dear cousin?" asks the king. Ilspeth shoots him a look.

"Very much. It's—" I'm at a loss for words. "Far grander than anything I've attended at home."

He and I share a knowing smirk.

"Where is home again?" The queen leans her chin on her delicate palm and fixes her sharp gaze on me. I wonder if she recognizes me from that day in the throne room. If she does, then she doesn't let on. The king tenses ever so slightly.

"She's northern, my love," he supplies. "She was raised at a temple with her late mother."

"Yes," I agree, struggling to lie convincingly. I shoot Zadyn a look.

Save me, please.

"And Lord Rhodes, I'm sure the ladies of court will be both overjoyed and devastated by your presence here," Sorscha says with a sickening amount of charm.

"You flatter me, Princess." He bows his head gallantly. "The honor is mine."

Sorscha turns to me again.

"There is much we must discuss. Come to tea tomorrow. But for now, let us dance and celebrate. Prince Kai is as skilled a dancer as they come." She holds my hands and squeezes. I manage a laugh of relief.

My sister and I don't speak, but in this world, I have a chance to be friends with her replica. Even if this isn't Sam, it feels like a free shot at a redo. I know that's what my dad would want. I smile at her.

"Second, only to the captain, of course," she modifies, tossing him a look over my shoulder.

"Really?" I can't help but blurt out.

"Don't look so surprised." The *"witch"* is spoken only in his eyes.

"Princess," Jace says, earning her gaze as he extends a hand. "Would you do me the honor?"

His kind tone is vastly different from the one he uses with me. She places her delicate hand in his.

"The pleasure is mine, Captain. Cousin." She nods to me in departure as they stride to the dance floor.

I look to Zadyn, unsure if we're supposed to stand here and make small talk with the unsocial queen and the princess's pretty acolytes.

"Go," says the king, gesturing to the sea of graceful bodies. "Enjoy the evening."

I nod to him gratefully before Zadyn leads me to the dance floor. He pulls me into his arms, one hand resting against my lower back and the other clasping mine.

"I'm not sure I can dance in this dress," I warn him.

"Indulge me." He smirks, shrugging. *

I roll my eyes but move my hand to his shoulder. I try to keep up with his waltzing, but between my coordination skills and the Pink Poison, I'm about as graceful as a baby deer.

"I learned some interesting facts on the hunt earlier."

"Really?" I ask, gazing up at him. Even in the heels, he's got at least a foot on me. "That's great! I knew you'd make a good *man on the inside*. What did you learn?"

He bends his head to whisper in my ear. I try to ignore the tingle that spreads down my spine when his breath meets my skin.

"Gossip, mostly. The queen wants to marry Sorscha off to one of her sons. Preferably the second. The first is already King of Vod and refuses to take a wife. Kai is a highly sought-after bachelor, but he's also a notorious ladies' man."

"The queen wants to marry Sorscha to her step-brother? That's weird. I'm guessing the king doesn't approve?"

"I think the prince's stay is going to be the deciding factor. Kai and Sorscha have been friends since childhood, but he only comes to court every few years to visit. With Sorscha next in line for the throne, this would be a power move for Vod. A king in their stronghold and king consort in Aegar."

He spins me around and pulls me close again. I try to catch my breath.

"I hate to say this—" I glance over to see Jace effortlessly

---

* Cue: *Cruel Summer* by Ana Done

twirling Sorscha as she stares up into his eyes. They both look like they were made for the dance floor, and I nearly lose my train of thought watching their grace. "But she doesn't seem like the ruler type. She seems like a princess in every definition of the word."

"I agree. And I think the king does, too. From what I gleaned, he's reluctant toward the match but is trying to remain realistic about his daughter's capabilities. She's a High Fae royal, which means if she marries and performs the Bloodfast ceremony with her spouse, she will come into massive generational power. But the king questions her ability to lead. Not that Kai would make a much better ruler. There have been numerous conversations with the council over this. They don't have faith in her leadership. But unless the king can find a suitable option soon, Sorscha will be engaged to the prince before he starts his journey back to Vod."

I imagine the situation of having to wed someone for political gain. Not for love. Not even for a green card. How sad it must be.

"And Gronwen and Conwell just handed over this information willingly?"

Zadyn shrugs. "I think they like to gossip."

"Do you think they're trustworthy? The council? They know a lot about my...situation. And Lord Gronwen—something feels off with him."

"I don't know if I trust any of them yet. But I think you're right about spending time with them. I'd rather have my enemies close, if that's what they are."

He spins me out, and at the last second, when I think I might lose my balance and go flying, he jerks me back in and catches me in a low dip. My breath whooshes out of me as I stare up at him, wide-eyed and wonder-struck.

"But the king trusts them. So there's also that to consider," he says in conclusion.

"You're good at this," I say as he pulls me to stand. The music finishes, and the crowd begins to applaud.

"I had nearly two hundred years of practice before I found myself in a world whose definition of dancing is gyrating and grinding."

I laugh. "I know, us earthlings are so uncivilized. But did you totally hate it?"

It's his turn to laugh now. "Oh, there were many drunken nights where I loved it."

"I bet the fae of your world would shudder to hear such a thing."

"I wouldn't be so sure. You should see the kind of dancing they do at the pleasure halls." He smiles boyishly, then leans in, his voice hushed. "And I can guarantee everyone at this party has been at least once in their lifetime."

I try to suppress my smile. "What makes you think that?"

"Because fae live for centuries. And after a while, life gets dull. It's an effort to keep finding meaning and pleasure in the mundane. The only way to stay sane is by trying new things," he trails off suggestively.

"How old are you?" I ask.

"Nearly two hundred."

"Wow." I chuckle.

"That's considered young for a fae!"

I shake my head, trying to wrap my mind around that.

"Two hundred years is still a long time. You must have tried it all by now."

He smiles warmly. "Not all."

"You look so young like this." I reach up and brush away a stray lock of caramel hair. It's the most beautiful color—strands of gold, copper, and brown blended together to create a warm, rich hue. He's got that effortless kind of hair that parts down the middle in a swoopy wave that you just want to run your fingers through.

"We age differently. If I were human, I would probably pass for someone in my late twenties, like you."

"How do witches age?"

"Depends, really. Redbloods age slower than humans, but not as slow as fae. Bluebloods and Blackbloods are similar to fae in the aging process. Once they reach maturity, the changes become infinitesimal."

"So I could—" I trail off, and he finishes for me.

"It's possible for you to live a very, very long life."

"I don't even know if I would want that. Time means nothing without people you care about. Who care for you," I say, letting my hand drop from his shoulder. He eyes me for a long time, weighing what to say next.

"There are people here who care." His words are firm, his eyes soft.

"I know *you* care. It's in your job description." I smile ruefully, my gaze catching Jace's from where he stands beside Sorscha. We both quickly look away before my eyes hitch on the dais.

A fae male looking a year or two younger than Zadyn is standing in front of the queen. She looks up at him as he speaks and then falls into the empty throne beside her. His posture is the male version of hers. Disinterested, lax, and bored to tears. But the way he sprawls his legs and leans back into the armrest is roguish and sensual.

"Is that the prince?" I ask, pulling Zadyn's eyes from my face. He nods.

"Have you met him before?"

"Not officially."

Something about the prince feels dangerous. A dark aura

rolls off of him and curls around me like an exotic snake ready to devour its prey. I can't break my stare. As if my thoughts summoned his attention, he looks directly into my eyes, holding my gaze too long to feel casual. I finally break away, turning to Zadyn.

"I think I need some air," I tell him.

He nods his head and we start weaving through the thicket of gorgeous fae. Their collective beauty, combined with the intoxicating music and romantic candlelight suddenly feels overwhelming.

We approach a pair of French doors leading out onto a stone patio. Just before we pass through, Zadyn is stopped by Lord Gronwen and a petite fae female with golden curls and a devastating heart-shaped face. He pries Zadyn from my grip to introduce him to some *"people he should know."* Swallowed by the small group, Zadyn strains his neck to keep eyes on me. I smile and wave him off, pointing to the door. He nods and resumes his conversation while I step out into the glorious night.

The air is perfect. Mild but not cold. I wonder about the seasons here and if they have them. I picture the grounds with a light dusting of snow over the massive trees and sprawling lawns. It would be beautiful.

The star constellations look completely different here. They dangle a bit closer to the ground. Shine a tad brighter. But the moon steals the show, a glowing orb that dazzles all who look upon it. I brace my hands over the smooth stone railing and breathe deeply as the dull roar of the crowd and the music thrums behind me.

"Who might you be?" purrs a voice like silk.

I turn to face Prince Kai.

Up close, he's truly devastating. Black hair that falls perfectly around his ears without any detectable styling, ocean blue eyes, and high cheekbones. He has a small scar under his left eye, but it just makes him look ridiculously sexy.

"Sorry, I don't talk to strangers."

Tossing my long hair over my shoulder, I turn back to face the flawlessly groomed hedge maze below. A dark chuckle and the sound of footsteps coast toward me as he takes up a spot at my side, assuming my exact posture. I do my best not to look at him, but the pull is strong.

"Tell me your name, and we won't be strangers anymore." His voice is pure, unadulterated flirtation. "Alright, I'll start."

He angles his body to face mine, leaning on the railing with one elbow. Amusement twinkles in his hypnotic eyes.

"Hello. My name is Kai. I don't believe I've had the pleasure. Your turn." He gestures with a hand for me to speak.

"You're the queen's son," I say.

"Is that a statement or a question?" He smirks, a singular dimple appearing on his cheek.

"Neither. It was an observation."

"Really? And have you made any other observations tonight?" He takes a step closer, and I fight the urge to inhale his scent.

"Perhaps how all eyes are on you this evening when they should be on me. It's *my* party, after all," he says with a teasing whimper in his voice.

"I had not noticed that."

"I did. My eyes were among the admirers."

"Your eyes tell me a lot, actually."

A fire ignites in those sea-colored orbs as his voice lowers. "And what do they say?"

"That you are highly presumptuous." He bites his lower lip as he stares at mine without restraint. "And pompous," I add.

He leans back, chuckling. "Maybe I, too, am merely observant."

"Is that so."

"Yes. In fact, I observed you staring at me inside. I observed you walking out onto this terrace. I'm observing the very look on your face right now."

"We've just met, and you claim to be able to interpret my facial expressions? My, my, you must be a mind reader."

"No, I'm just an expert on body language." His gaze travels down my entire length and back up. I can feel my body heat under his stare. He reaches out tentatively, with enough slowness that I can move out of reach if I want to.

I don't want to.

His fingers tilt my chin up, angling my face to his. Time moves a touch slower.

"Do you really believe I'm going to kiss you right now?" I whisper against his lips.

"I'm just testing your restraint," he whispers back, a secret smile in his voice. "You're doing exceptionally well. Most females in your position would have dropped their panties to the floor by now."

My hand shoots up to grip him by the face, chasing the lusty, glazed look from his eyes and replacing it with pure shock.

"I'm not like *any* of the females you know. I'm a *woman*."

I release his face only to bring my palm across his cheek. The slap makes a satisfying sound, though I know I didn't hit him hard enough to actually hurt. The shock on his face as he rubs the spot I struck melts into admiration, then respect, and then circles back to lust.

"You'll ask before you touch me next time."

He bites his lip to stifle his growing smirk.

A deep sense of satisfaction washes over me as I start toward the door.

"I didn't get a name," he calls after me, his voice lighter.

"You didn't earn it," I shout back, facing the party. I gather my skirts in my hands when I see Zadyn on the other side of the glass door, his face pale. He pulls the door open for me.

"What did he want?" he asks tightly.

I shrug. "A kiss, most likely."

"Of course," Zadyn says. "You shouldn't be alone with him."

"I'm not even going to attempt to explain to you how fundamentally problematic that statement is."

"No, I mean"—Zadyn shakes his head—"he's a siren."

My look of confusion prompts him to elaborate.

"He is High Fae," he explains. "But each bloodline has its own set of unique gifts. His line, Queen Ilspeth's line, is descendant of ancient fae water nymphs, also known as sirens."

"And what do they do? Lure people to their watery graves?"

"In some cases, yes. Their power lies in their ability to influence. They can seduce you with a single thought. Bend you to their will without lifting a finger. They're dangerous."

It makes sense. Everything about him made me want to run screaming and also tear his clothes off and lick him head to toe at the same time.

"Relax." I pat Zadyn's chest. "I didn't fall for it. We have sirens back home, too. We call them narcissists." I chance a look toward the patio, but Kai is already gone.

The rest of the night passes quickly. I people-watch from Zadyn's side, occasionally locking eyes with Jace and cursing myself every time I do. But then again, he isn't helping, looking all brooding and beautiful in his sleek uniform with his hair brushed back off his face to show off those elegant, proud lines and liquid gold eyes.

Ugh, I have to stop.

"I need a drink," I mutter to Zadyn and head toward the refreshments table. Turning too quickly, I nearly collide with a bouncing sister-princess.

"Cousin!" she says. "I want you to meet someone. This is our special guest, Prince Kai of Vod."

Arms linked together, she beams up at him. He bows low, his eyes glinting as he lifts my hand to his lips. My body shivers in pleasure and that deviant smile he wears tells me it was no mere coincidence.

"Is there something wrong with your eyes?" I ask, batting my lashes. It knocks his concentration, halting whatever siren magic he was trying to work on me.

The princess giggles, a delicate hand over her pouty pink lips. "Forgive me, my Prince. This is my dear cousin, Lady Serena Accostia. She's just arrived at court from the north."

"The pleasure is mine, *Lady Serena*. I hope I will be blessed with the opportunity to get to know you over the course of my stay."

"Kai, I absolutely forbid you from monopolizing her." She pulls her arm from his to slide it through mine. I look down at her, an inch or two shorter than me.

It's nearly impossible not to like this version of my sister.

"She is, after all, my kin—it's only right that I be the first to have her all to myself."

"Have no fear, Princess, I'm a patient male." He gives me another shark smile.

"I will, however, spare her for a dance. You are our guest of honor, after all," Sorscha quips.

"A charming welcome gift indeed."

The princess gives me a gentle shove and an encouraging smile. *Good dancer,* she mouths to me, then turns to Zadyn to pour her honey in his ear. Kai wordlessly tows me to the dance floor and wraps his arms around me.

"I'm not your welcome gift," I clarify as he pulls me into his warmth.

"I wouldn't dream of objectifying you in such a way." He knits his eyebrows together, his lips curled in amusement.

"I know what you are," I warn him as the music picks up. It reminds me of a polka—lively, fast-paced, and exuberant.

"I'm many things, my love. You'll have to be more specific."

"A siren. I know that you're a siren, so I would appreciate it if you would stop with that seductive eye thing you're doing."

"I'm not trying to seduce you." Leaning in so that his lips skim my ear, he whispers, "But when I am, you'll know."

Before I can protest, he's whipping me across the floor, the air leaving my lungs so fast I struggle to keep up. He lifts me and tosses me around like I'm a feather, and I suppress a laugh because, honestly, it's kind of fun. The princess was right. Kai's dancing skills make the grace of the other fae look second-rate.

By the time the dance is finished, people have stopped to watch him and his impressive maneuvers. That's when I notice we are the only two left on the dance floor. I can feel my cheeks heat under the gaze of a thousand foreign eyes. And when the last note of the song plays, triumphant and final, he pulls me to a stop and lifts our joined hands high in the air, presenting me. The crowd erupts into wild cheers and whispers of awe. Kai beams at his adoring public.

Without sparing me a second glance, he jerks me forward into another spin and releases me, walking in the opposite direction and leaving Jace to catch me around the waist before I hit the ground face-first.

"Impressive," he says, heavy on the sarcasm as I struggle to right myself. "Did you keep hitting the Poison after I told you to be careful, or are you always this uncoordinated?"

"Let's hope for your sake I'm not. You're the one who'll be training me come tomorrow morning."

"I'm positive I have my work cut out for me."

He sets me upright, and I'm aware of every place our bodies

connect. His hand around my waist, his shoulder beneath my palm, my elbow brushing his forearm. I swear I feel him glide his thumb up my hip where his hand rests.

"There you are," the princess lilts from behind us.

For a second, I think she's talking to me, but then I notice her eyes are fixed on Jace. Her three ladies stand behind her with Zadyn in tow, dwarfing them all with his height. "We're about to retire to my chambers for the after-party."

She winks at me.

"Invite only." The gorgeous blonde, Cece, smiles beatifically.

"Did someone say after-party? Thank gods, I'm getting harassed by every female here. Your court has grown insufferably handsy since the last time I came to visit, Princess." Kai sidles up to her, eyeing me up like a crocodile.

"Oh, please, Kai." She rolls her eyes affectionately and turns to me. "Are you coming?"

I'm sure I look as shocked as I feel. I open my mouth to answer, but Jace does it for me.

"Lady Serena has a tutor coming early tomorrow morning." He glances from me to her. Sorscha looks suspicious but doesn't ask any follow-ups.

"Very well," the princess says, her hands folded in front of her. "Perhaps you'll join us next time."

She smiles and turns to lead her entourage from our sight. Kai peeks back only to wiggle his fingers at me in farewell.

I turn to Jace, fuming.

"You don't speak for me."

"You're not going to the after-party. You have to get up at dawn tomorrow and every day after that. I doubt that's something you're used to, witch. It's already past your bedtime."

I dare a step closer.

"Do not make the mistake of infantilizing me again."

"Is someone sad she'll miss the fun?" he mocks me. "Don't worry, I'll give you a full recap in the morning."

"Why do you get to go?" I huff, crossing my arms.

"Who am I to refuse the princess? Besides, I enjoy her little gatherings." That stupid smug smile on his face has me glaring up at him.

"He's right, you do have an early day," Zadyn says. I groan in frustration.

"Not you, too."

"I know what I'm talking about. It's already late. Don't think I'll go easy on you because you're tired," Jace says sternly and steers me toward the door. "Come on, I'll drop you off on my way to the party."

"I don't need a chaperone. Besides, I have Zadyn—he's worse than a guard dog."

"I don't trust you not to get around him. And I definitely don't trust him to say no to you."

"You're a dick," Zadyn says from my other side. I throw my head back and laugh loudly. He shrugs, glancing down at my surprised face. "You live around a bunch of uncivilized humans for thirty years, you pick up a few things."

He flashes me a proud smirk.

We reach our rooms, and as Zadyn and I pass through my door, Jace leans in.

"Dawn. I mean it," he warns, disappearing around the corner. A moment later, he pops his head back in. "Oh, and leave the guard dog. No distractions in the ring."

He leaves without so much as a glance at Zadyn. I look at him and shrug apologetically.

"You'll have to find some other way to occupy your morning," I tell him, unclasping my earrings and tossing them onto the vanity.

"Sleep sounds like a pretty good use of my time after the

week we've had." He stands with his hands in his pockets, looking around the room. I kick off my shoes and groan with relief as I flex through my arches. Zadyn watches me for a moment, then moves to one of the shaggy ottomans in front of the window seat and perches there. "Come here."

I take a seat in the alcove across from him, and he reaches down.

"What are you doing?"

In answer, he picks up my foot and begins kneading the sore muscles.

"Oh my god, that feels so good," I groan. He laughs and shakes his head.

"You know you don't have to do that," I tell him after a moment of watching his skilled hands work. "I don't think foot massages are in the job description of familiars."

"I know I don't have to." He looks up into my eyes. "But I want to."

I quietly consider his statement.

"You have to be on your game tomorrow. Can't do that with crippled feet. Jace is tough. He's going to be hard on you, you know."

I sigh. "He's already hard on me. I just don't understand why he's so hostile toward me all the time."

Zadyn gives me a look, and I can almost hear him saying, *don't play dumb.*

I shoot him a look back that says, *I'm not. I genuinely don't understand.*

He lets out a mirthless laugh.

"It must be hard," he says after a while. "To be around him."

I don't answer right away. "It's hard to be around all of them."

"You still love Jack," he says, studying me. It's not quite a question.

"I don't know," I answer honestly. "I don't know anything right now. He's—he's not Jack. I try to remind myself of that every time I see him. They couldn't be more opposite." I marvel. "Same with Sam—or Sorscha. Here, she's this flouncy little party princess, impossible not to love. My sister is cold and removed, just like my mom."

"And the king?" Zadyn asks, hitting a pressure point. I wince. "Sorry."

"It's fine. Umm...the king, I'm still figuring out. I just never thought I would see my dad's face again."

"For what it's worth, I think you're doing great. You're handling everything considerably well."

"Thanks," I say flatly, thinking of all the ways I could be handling things better than considerably well. Zadyn's hands still.

"You should probably get some rest," he says finally.

"Put my foot down, and I will," I tease.

He releases it quickly, and we both get to our feet. Giving my shoulder a gentle squeeze, he heads toward his suite, pausing in the threshold.

"In case no one told you tonight—" His brown eyes roam over me, warming my body. "You looked beautiful."

Before I can say a word, he's closed the door, leaving me alone to contemplate the faerie tale I've fallen into.

16

Dawn comes faster than I could have possibly imagined.

Jace drags me from my room, still half-asleep. I mutter profanities under my breath as he ushers me through the castle and into a small arena-like space. A private training ring, he tells me. It's empty except for a rack of weapons and some training equipment.

I follow Jace to the center of the ring and stand watching him with my arms crossed, half listening as he says things my brain can't even begin to comprehend at this ungodly hour.

"Are you listening to me at all?"

His words finally crack through my morning stupor.

"I am, but all I'm hearing is blah blah blah swords, blah blah blah daggers, fee fi fo fum."

"You're not getting within ten paces of a sword until I deem you ready."

I scoff. "I've dealt with plenty of swords in my lifetime. Plenty of tools, too."

"You have experience with swordplay?" He crosses his cut arms over his chest.

"I do," I boast, stifling a yawn. "Just probably not the kind you're referring to."

He moves over to the rack of weapons and picks up two wooden longswords, handing one to me by the hilt.

Without warning or direction, he says, "Block me."

He twirls the sword in one hand, creating an arc over my head before drawing a path downwards. I drop to the ground to avoid the wood splitting me in two. Jace halts its trajectory an inch from my head.

"Are you nuts?!" I screech.

"Been a while since you handled a sword?" he taunts, flipping the practice blade over in an impressive maneuver and driving it into the ground. It sticks straight up.

I scowl at him, suddenly very awake. "A little warning would have been nice."

"I was moving at a quarter of my natural speed. That was pathetic." He extends a hand down to me, and I grip it, allowing him to haul me to my feet.

"There's no need to be rude," I tell him, dusting myself off.

"I'm just trying to gauge where we should start," he says with false naiveté.

"Well, I may not be an expert at swinging these things around, but I've taken a couple of self-defense classes. I work out, I'm in good shape, and I live a healthy lifestyle, for the most part."

"I'm not interested in your lifestyle. You're here because you need to learn how to fight. Do you believe your enemy will warn you before they strike on the battlefield?"

"Who says I'm going to be on a battlefield?"

He looks at me, dumbfounded and gestures around the empty arena. "What do you think you're doing here?"

"Training to be a Dragon Rider," I say simply, crossing my arms.

"It's a little more intricate than that." He eyes me. "You do need to learn how to ride. But first, you need to learn how to fight. You have to master hand-to-hand combat. And weaponry."

"Why do I need all of that?"

"Because you can't be a Dragon Rider without being a warrior. The two are synonymous." He pushes a breath through his nose.

"I'll phrase it this way. The only reason we would have need of a Blackblood on dragon-back would be to obliterate enemy forces. Which would mean we're already at war. It isn't enough to know how to defend yourself. You need to make yourself into a weapon—to think like one. So I need you to wake up and pay attention," he says a touch more gently.

"I'm listening," I assure him as he begins to circle me. My eyes follow his trail.

"Fae are ten times as fast and as strong as humans. Plus, many have the advantage of magic. Until we can figure out how to free yours, you are as good as mortal. And just as easily killed. You need to get strong. Learn to balance. Build muscle. Here," he says, crouching to grip my inner thigh.

"Here," he continues, rising to fist my bicep.

"And here." His hand flattens against my stomach as he disappears behind me. I suppress a shudder as his breath teases my ear. He drops his hand, and I immediately crave his touch again.

"You won't be able to stay seated if you're weak in those areas. Especially your core. We'll start by stretching you out and then going for a run. It will help with endurance and breath control."

"My endurance is good," I inform him. "I run pretty regularly."

"We'll see," he says, earning an eye roll from me.

He has me mirror a series of stretches, and when my limbs feel loose, we set off into a run around the castle grounds. Keeping up with Jace's fae speed proves to be an immediate and impossible challenge. He zips back and forth like a bolt of lightning, running literal circles around me. He's so quick I can barely detect his movements.

"Is speed your superpower?" I brace my hands on my knees and breathe hard—in through the nose and out through the mouth. He laughs, not even having broken a sweat. I pant and wipe at my slick brow, feeling pathetic.

"All fae are this fast. Faster, actually. I slowed my pace so you could keep up."

"Are you serious? I'm screwed! You expect me to take on a species that is by nature ten times as fast and strong as me? I don't stand a chance."

"You need to change your mentality," he tells me. "This is day one. This is a jumping-off point. You cannot get worse. You cannot get more unprepared. The only way this can go is up. And I will make sure you know what to expect in battle and how to defend yourself."

I nod my head.

"Let's go. No more breaks," he says, breaking into a jog. I suck in a breath and chase after him.

Tea with the princess is nothing like I expected.

I figured I would sit across from Sorscha and her ladies, sipping tea out of pretty porcelain, gossiping about court members in a lavishly decorated setting.

The lavishly decorated setting part I got right. Sorscha's chambers are double the size of mine, with sparkling marble floors and pillars. A polished silver partition with swirling patterns sections off the space from the giant bed. The arching, curtained windows reveal only the faintest sliver of daylight through the gaps in material.

Upon entering, I find a group of lifeless fae in various states of undress. My eyes land on a disheveled, silk-robed princess sprawled out on a salmon-colored settee, waving a tasseled fan with one hand and clutching her head in the other. Her feet dangle over Cece's lap, whose pretty jade eyes are bloodshot and drooping. The top of her bodice is unlaced, showing ample amounts of cleavage.

Ilsa is seated on the floor beneath the princess, sleeping lightly, head lolling against the settee. The white blonde poker straight hair that skimmed her waist last night is shorn in jagged lines just below her delicate ears. I notice a long lock strewn across the small coffee table among a mess of playing cards, spilled ale, gold coins, and uncut gems.

Sprawled across from the ladies in a high-backed chair is a worse-for-wear Kai. He dangles from his seat, a hand clutched over his mouth and chin as if fighting back nausea. His hair is mussed like someone ran their fingers through it, and his white shirt hangs fully unbuttoned, revealing a taut stomach stretched over a rippling six-pack.

It's hard to pry my eyes from that sight.

Seated beside him is another male I don't recognize. He tries to lift a teacup to his lips, but his hand trembles so badly that some of it spills over the side.

Oh my god. *They're hungover.*

I press my lips together to keep from laughing. No one has noticed me enter.

"Good morning!" I crow.

The room gives a collective groan of agony. Ilsa's doe eyes fly open. The male in the chair beside me jolts forward, the entire contents of the tea spilling onto the likely priceless carpet.

"Fuck, Dover," Kai moans, his eyes still closed. The princess makes an effort to sit up, then gives up, collapsing back into the cushions.

"Please don't yell," Cece whines, rubbing her temples.

"Oh, cousin." The princess turns her head to offer me a small smile, her honey-colored curls spilling over the armrest. "Hello."

Her voice lacks the musicality it had last night, but that's no surprise, given the state I found them in.

"Come and sit." She points to the plush ottoman nestled in between the settee and the male whose name I don't know.

"Dover, move over," she urges the stranger to my left.

"That rhymed," says Ilsa, her voice dainty and deadpan.

Dover scoots his chair closer to Kai so that I have a bit more room in the circle.

I notice we're short a female—Lady Marideth. As if reading my thoughts, Sorscha says, "She's still asleep."

"How was the rest of your evening?" I ask the princess knowingly.

As if in answer, a small white creature waddles through the cracked door to the adjoining suite and skitters across the floor, between the settee and chairs. Its top half is a chicken with wings, and its bottom half looks like a Pomeranian's. As if that weren't odd enough, its neck is bedecked in freshwater pearls and ribbons. It squawks loudly, earning a bout of disgruntled moans from the group.

"Don't drink and spell," Kai says, abs flexing as he stretches his long legs. "Nothing good comes of it."

"Veruca," the princess breathes, lifting a hand over the back of the armrest to signal the fae maid standing in the corner.

"Ask Gnorr for one of her special brews and have it brought up," she directs, eyes closed.

The maid nods and disappears.

"I'm sorry you have to see us in such an unbecoming state." She glances at me. "What a terrible first impression we must make. I promise we're not always this dull. Our gatherings can sometimes get rather...spirited."

"Especially when I'm in town," Kai pipes, fixing his cool gaze on me. "Morning, gorgeous."

I ignore him, turning back to the princess. "It sounds like I missed a rather eventful evening."

"Oh, it was legendary. I'm sad you had to miss it." She pulls the tie of her blush-colored robe tighter over her corset. I wonder if it's considered appropriate here for the males and females to be dressed down like this in front of one another. If it is, none of them seem to care. They look utterly unfazed, as if this is an everyday occurrence. The princess manages to sit up, planting her bare feet on the carpet.

"We snuck out," she whispers conspiratorially.

"Where did you go?"

"The princess wanted to see what a pleasure hall was like after hours," Kai answers.

"I had never been. Kai and Dover are always telling such wild stories. I just had to experience one for myself."

"We're never wrong, are we, Princess?" Kai drawls, his temple balancing on the tip of his pointer finger.

"We were wrong about that last line of Stardust," Dover mutters from beside me. "I've never crashed this hard."

"I'm fully depleted." Cece sighs, tucking her long legs beneath her. "I can't even feel my magic."

"I can't feel my face," says little Ilsa.

"Tell me, cousin, did you enjoy the ball last night? The

dancing?" the princess asks. "It must have been so different from your life at the temple."

"Vastly different." I nod and force a pleasant smile onto my lips. Lying has never been a strength of mine.

"It must have been tragically dull. Raised by a handful of priestesses," Cece drawls, her wide green eyes surveying me. "How did you end up there?"

You got this.

"I was born there." I should have spent more time working on a believable backstory. For this to work, it needs to be tight. I chew my bottom lip as Cece continues to dig.

"Was your mother a refugee, or were you just a bastard?" she asks nonchalantly.

"Cece!" Sorscha berates, her mouth agape as she tosses an appalled look at the gorgeous fae. Cece gazes at me unflinchingly, resting her delicate chin on two fingers.

She's got some nerve.

Sorscha pats my knee. "You don't have to answer that."

Before I can say another word, a loud thud sounds from the adjoining suite, followed by a curse. I turn to see Marideth practically fall through the door, wearing nothing but a flimsy white nightgown and a diamond choker. Her auburn hair lies in disarray as she clutches the door handle to regain her balance. She stares at Ilsa in horror.

"What in hell happened to *you*?" She gapes, gray eyes wide.

"I don't remember," Ilsa says, reaching up to finger the uneven ends. She doesn't seem to have any feelings about it, just remains perfectly blasé.

"She lost a round of do or die," Cece says, lifting a jagged-edged lock and dropping it in disdain.

"What is do or die?" I ask.

"Oh, it's loads of fun. We'll teach you at the next soiree," the princess says.

Marideth trudges over and bellies down on the carpet, throwing her face in Ilsa's lap.

"I'm never drinking Poison again." Her voice is muffled in her friend's underskirt.

"You tapped out early, Mar," Kai tuts. "I'm surprised at you."

She lifts herself onto her elbows to glare at him.

"Forgive me for not being able to hold my own next to two males who drink themselves stupid on any given night."

"He's right, Mar, you usually make it to sunrise," Dover pipes up.

"I made it long enough to win this from you." She wiggles her eyebrows and strokes her collar seductively.

"That was supposed to be a gift for Wyneth." Kai breaks into laughter. "Wait until she sees it on Mar. You're done for, Dove."

"His betrothed," the princess provides. I nod.

"Who here is really going to tattle?" Mar counters, unruffled.

"Your betrothed doesn't mind you partying in your underwear with a bunch of beautiful females?" I ask the handsome male beside me.

Kai breaks into a brilliant smile. Dover looks at me like a toddler caught with his hand in the cookie jar.

"Wyneth knows she's always invited to our debauched little gatherings. She just declines, declines, declines." Marideth stands, answering for him. She plops down in Dover's lap and lays a big kiss on his lips. I gawk at them. When she pulls back and wipes a thumb over her lips, his eyes are glazed.

"It suits you." He reaches up to run his fingers over the dazzling necklace. They stare at each other like they're the only two in the room.

The maid returns with a tray of tea and a slew of servants in tow, wheeling in carts of delicious-smelling food.

"Oh, thank the gods." Marideth leaps up, dashing over to the trays of miniature quiches, finger sandwiches, and colorful parfaits. Dover chuckles, shaking his head, some color returning to his previously pale face.

The maid places a steaming cup of tea in the princess's hands and sets the pot down on the small coffee table between us.

"I need to guzzle a whole pot of that before I can even stand," Cece murmurs in her silky voice. As she leans forward to pour herself a cup, her breasts nearly spill out of her dress, coming dangerously close to showing nip. Even in her hungover state, she's beautiful.

"So what happened after I passed out?" Marideth says, around a mouthful of food. She plops down onto the cushioned window nook.

Kai and Dover take turns recounting the night for both Marideth and me. I listen, one detail more shocking than the next. I hadn't expected fae lords and ladies to party like rebel teenagers sneaking booze and drugs into the basement for a co-ed all-nighter. They sip their hangover cure, launching into fits of laughter every so often, as they recall the hazy details of the evening. I smile in silence, listening to their comfortable banter.

"Shall we picnic later?" the princess asks the group after some time.

"How about tomorrow?" Kai suggests. "Dove and I are going riding with your father."

"Of course." She sighs. "You already know what this is about."

Setting her teacup down, she props her head on her hand and looks at him. His smile fades, replaced by something more somber.

"What do you plan to say?" she asks.

"Nothing unless he brings it up first."

Kai stands, moving toward the tray of food to pop a raspberry in his mouth. He stuffs his hands in his pocket, stomach muscles illuminated by the sunlight peeking through the half-drawn curtains. Sorscha twists in her seat to look at him.

"*Kai*," she cautions, a hint of annoyance lacing her tone.

"*Sorscha*," he mimics. "There's no point in worrying about what hasn't happened. He may say nothing. Besides, he thinks I'm a bad influence on you."

"You are," Marideth chimes from her nook, chewing loudly. They both shoot her a look.

When Kai speaks, his voice is reassuring. "We don't have to discuss this right now. I give you my word that I won't commit to anything before we talk it over, alright?"

She nods, the concern fading from her expression as she faces us again.

"So tomorrow? You'll come, won't you, cousin?" Her hopeful, wide eyes land on me. I can't help but answer with a smile.

"I'll be there."

I get to my feet and excuse myself, telling them that Zadyn is giving me lessons on how to be a proper courtier. I'm almost to the door when Cece's voice makes me turn.

"Bring your little lord friend tomorrow," she says evenly, her green eyes unreadable.

I nod and then immediately try to shut out the intrusive thoughts that pop up following her request.

17

If I thought physical training was hard, then trying to bring forth magic is like pushing a boulder up a hill in ninety-degree heat. My forehead is covered in sweat, and my fists are balled so tightly that my nails nearly puncture my palms.

We sit in the most astonishing three-story library I've ever seen. It's Beauty and the Beast on steroids. A winding spiral staircase sits in the center of the expansive room, leading up to second and third-floor wrap-around balconies. Each level is filled with books from top to bottom. Bright light filters in through the arched windows, revealing a breathtaking view of the surrounding mountains and blue sky. And then there's the rolling ladders. I only got to squeeze in a brief fangirl moment before Zadyn put on his serious face and sat me down to get to work.

I heave a frustrated groan, collapsing my upper body onto the reading table. Zadyn places a cool glass of water before me and I nod to him gratefully.

The source of my vexation is me trying to push a coin across a table with my mind. I try and try, and nothing happens.

Earlier, when I closed my eyes, slowed my breath, and sank into my body, as Zadyn directed, I could feel the tiniest thrum of magic stirring beneath my skin. It tingled like tiny pinpricks, but it wasn't painful.

That had felt like a breakthrough. We sit here an hour later, and it feels hopeless that I'll ever be able to do more than just be aware of my magic.

"The fact that you're exerting yourself like this is a good thing," Zadyn points out, sliding into the chair opposite me. "It means your body is trying to dip into that untapped well of magic."

"It's hard to explain, but it feels like there's a cap over the magic when I push really hard." I sigh and lean back in my seat.

"I mean, that makes sense. I know you don't think that it's major, but being able to feel your magic is a huge step. Could you feel it yesterday? Last week?" he prods.

"No," I admit. "But I want to actually do something with it."

"You will," he assures me. "Just be patient. We just started."

I think for a moment.

"You—the fae," I specify, "have magic, don't you? You can shift, and I've seen you heal me...how are witches any different?"

"Aside from the fact that witches are only female? All witches are part fae, but not all fae are witches. High Fae are typically blessed with one or two affinities, depending on their bloodlines and what region they come from. But they can't summon magic at will beyond their gods-given gifts the way witches can."

"So technically, I'm part fae?"

"All witch lineage can be traced back to the goddess Silva

and the original fae of Solterre, but since black blood isn't hereditary, the amount of fae in you is probably infinitesimal."

I grip my hair and groan, suddenly feeling overwhelmed. "There's so much to learn about this place. I feel like my head is going to explode."

"Not before your history lesson." Jace's voice carries from the door, filling the massive library.

I shake my head, frustrated.

"Twice in one day." I twist to look at him. "To what do I owe this displeasure?"

He slides smoothly into the seat next to me. "Don't lie. You know you're happy to see me."

Zadyn tenses from the other side of the table.

"As if." I toss my glamoured mermaid hair over my shoulder, the ends smacking him in the face. He swats it away and leans forward.

"How's the magic coming along?" he asks Zadyn.

"The awareness is there. Now we just have to access and channel it."

I turn to Jace. "Some of that blue blood would really come in handy right about now."

"I'm working on it," he assures me. We are all quiet for a moment. "There's a ceremony tomorrow night for solstice. Perhaps, if she participates, the tea will loosen some of the magic and make it more viable." He glances between us.

"What tea?"

Zadyn shakes his head at Jace. "No. I don't want her drinking *Urh* Tea. There are too many side effects, and there's a chance it might do nothing but make her sick."

"Hello, sitting right here. What is *Urh* Tea?"

"It's a very potent plant medicine that can make you hallucinate. Among a few other unpleasant effects," Zadyn explains to me.

"So, it's Ayahuasca," I conclude. Zadyn gives me a yes and no kind of look.

"What's Ayahuasca?" Jace asks.

"It's a plant medicine from my world that people use to guide them on spiritual journeys. It usually ends with people crying, puking, and shitting themselves."

"So it's not much different at all," he deduces. "What's the problem?"

"The difference is that she's in a vastly different environment, and drinking that tea when you're off-center can have consequences."

"Yeah, that, and I'd prefer not to puke or shit myself. What's this ceremony?" I look between them.

"It's a long-standing solstice tradition in Aegar meant to honor the Queen of the Gods, Aerill. It's one of two nights of the entire year when she is able to take physical form to be with her mate. When consumed on this night, the *Urh* Tea creates an excess of magic within an individual. I'm hopeful its properties will trip your magic, maybe even crack the glamour."

"And that's it? You just drink the tea?"

"Well, the High Priest leads you in ceremony, but essentially. The goal is to open your mind enough so that Aerill can bless you with her spirit."

"The purpose is to hallucinate seeing a god queen?"

"The purpose is to offer your body as a sacred vessel for Aerill to inhabit on the longest night of the year."

"So, there's a chance I drink this stuff and become possessed by a *goddess*?"

"It's considered an honor among the fae to serve their mother in such a way," Jace articulates, vexation edging his tone.

"Why does she need a vessel? Doesn't she have a body of her own?"

"She has no physical form. She exists in the ether as a spirit that resides inside the moon," Zadyn explains. I shake my head in confusion.

"All the noble families take part by selecting one member to participate in the rite. Of all the participants, Aerill only appears to one," Jace continues. "The king wants Sorscha to represent this year, but she has no real interest. I'm sure she'd be glad to yield her duty to her *cousin*."

He gives me a disdainful once over.

"*We made that shit up*," I whisper to him. "Do you really think I'm going to fool this goddess into thinking I'm royal or something? Won't it piss her off when she finds out I wasted her time?"

"*If* she even appears to you—which I highly doubt she will." Jace sighs. "It's not illegal for a commoner to participate, it's just rare. Besides, you're a Blackblood. That makes you... important. I don't think Aerill will be disappointed with the option."

Zadyn shakes his head, clearly disagreeing with this idea. But ultimately, he concedes to me. "It's your choice."

I look to Jace. "Is it safe?"

His expression is open. "Nothing is safe."

"But you think it will help unlock my magic?"

He nods. "It's worth a shot."

"Okay. I'll do it," I relent, tossing up my hands. "But if I do puke or shit, you're cleaning it."

He chuckles, rising to his feet.

"I'll run it by the king," he says and is gone.

"There's a lot we need to cover before tomorrow night."

Zadyn stands to face the back wall of books. He pulls a few thick volumes from their shelves and plops them on the table in a neat stack before me. A cloud of dust surges from the pile. I cough dramatically, earning a laugh from him. He settles back into his seat as I lift the first book and flip it open.

"'*The History of Solterre, Volume One*,'" I read. "I'll never finish this by tomorrow. Can't you just give me the spark notes version?"

"Oh, don't worry, you're getting the crash course." He flashes me a secretive smirk.

From what Zadyn outlines, Solterre was born from the magic of two mega-powerful gods named Urhlon and Aerill—celestial forms residing within the sun and the moon, respectively. The seed of their love fell onto a nearby star, and from that star, Solterre was created. The gods' magic transformed it into a world capable of sustaining creatures with long lives and magic—the first fae.

Urhlon and Aerill sent three of their seven children to preside over this new world. Myr—goddess of the hunt. Ienar —god of war and wisdom. And Silva—goddess of nature and the elements.

High Fae were the product of the gods' love affairs with the original fae created by Urhlon and Aerill. The children of the gods were gifted with ancient, highly concentrated magic. Special affinities. Urhlon and Aerill's other children visited the world often and sired countless lines of High Fae. But it was *Silva's* line that sired the witches when she mated one of the first fae males.

"So basically, I'm a descendant of Silva?" I ask.

"Yes, and no. Silva, with her elemental magic, and her mate Sturgis, created the Redbloods and Bluebloods."

"What about the Blackbloods?" I lean forward, engrossed.

"One of Silva's sisters, the goddess Adelphi, was rumored to have taken countless lovers over her long life. Supposedly, she had an affair with a fae male, and they pledged themselves to each other with the Bloodfast ceremony. She then discovered that her lover had betrayed her. He gave her blood to a fatally wounded Blueblood, whom he was in love with, to save her life. She became the first-ever Blackblood."

I nod as Zadyn continues.

"It was discovered from there that when you mix blue blood and the blood of a god, you get a creature of wild power—immortal like the High Fae, but stronger and faster, with godly magic and capabilities. That's why they made such skilled warriors. They were unparalleled."

"Why did Adelphi and her lover exchange blood in the first place?"

"The fae share blood as a form of...intimacy," he explains, color blooming on his tan cheeks.

"Drinking blood is fae foreplay?! That's disgusting!" I slap my hand down on the table.

"It's a little more nuanced than that. Back to what I was saying." The blush fades from his face as he gets back on track. "When Ienar learnt what his sister had accidentally created, he sought to breed a warrior witch-race to govern the lands for him. He fed his blood to a group of Blues, and they became the first-ever Blackblood coven."

"You said Blackbloods are chosen, that it's not hereditary. But I was never given god blood."

"Once the original Blackbloods were made, their magic simply chose others. Their power was not passed down through generations. It was born at random. Even so, they were a sisterhood—stronger than even the High Fae. Which was why they were the first rulers of Solterre."

"I see. So how do the dragons tie into this?"

"Ah, yes. The dragons." Zadyn lowers his voice and leans forward over the table.

"They weren't originally from this world. They came from a neighboring realm as the pets of Zed, Urhlon and Aerill's eldest son. On one of his visits to Solterre, he brought three dragons with him. While here, he attempted to seduce a Blackblood witch, and when she refused, he tried to force her. She escaped by stealing his dragon and burning him alive. There is no magic in all of Solterre more powerful than dragon magic. It is raw, undiluted power capable of wiping away entire worlds. The only thing capable of destroying a god."

Zadyn pauses, letting the weight of his words sink in.

"Zed had enslaved the dragons in his realm for centuries, tormenting and beating them into submission. Grateful for their liberation, the dragons pledged themselves to the Blackbloods and vowed to only bond Blackblood riders. That witch became the first Blackblood High Queen, Arden, paired with her dragon, Hyraxia. Arden appointed two of her sisters to rule with her. They bonded Zed's remaining dragons."

Zadyn flips through the book before me, stopping on a detailed illustration depicting three Amazonian-looking females soaring through the sky on the backs of massive dragons.

"It was the loyalty of the dragons that made Ienar truly afraid. The Blackbloods had already become a threat to him, between their power and their autonomy. So he wiped them from existence."

I glance up from the book. "Oh my god. That's terrible."

"Do not mistake our gods for benevolent creators. They are fickle and envious, with terrifying power."

"I'm sure their egos are through the roof." I shake my head, dropping my gaze back to the book.

"Ienar obliterated the Blackbloods and the hundreds of dragons they bred on our soil, but one survived. After her rider had fallen to Ienar in battle, she slaughtered him in a blind rage. Then alone, without her sisters or her bonded, she retreated to the Mountain of Hysphestus and vowed to sleep until the next Blackblood rider came to claim her."

"A dragon moonlighting as sleeping beauty. Wow."

"All fairy tales are rooted in truth." He shrugs.

"So, the last dragon and the last Blackblood?" I absorb.

"There have been poems, songs, paintings dedicated to you, *the Faceless Rider*."

"Are you serious?"

"Deadly. The people of Aegar have waited for you and prayed for your coming since the day the Blackbloods fell, and Arden, with her last breath, promised a reckoning. That reckoning is you."

Chills skitter down my spine.

"That's flattering and all, but I'm no Jesus Christ." I lean back in my seat. He chuckles and closes the book.

"Is—is the kingdom in trouble? Is that why people have been waiting for me?"

"The kingdom is stable for now, ever since Derek married Ilspeth and forged an alliance. With their kingdoms united, the others would be foolish to make a move. But there has been growing unrest in Aegar and whispers of rebellion for many years. A Dragon Rider standing with Aegar would solidify its stronghold and squash any chance of a coup, whether from rebels or a neighboring kingdom. You're the most wanted person in Solterre. Every kingdom is after you."

The weight of his words presses down on my chest.

"And what if I find a kingdom I like better and decide to fight for them instead?" I ask hypothetically.

"There's a reason we landed on Aegean Soil."

"Yes, because you're my familiar, and you're from here."

He shakes his head. "That may be so, but it was your magic that led the way, whether you knew it or not. I do believe you were meant to fight for my kingdom and that the ties between your father, your sister, and Jack are no mere coincidence." His brown eyes are intense as they hold my gaze.

"If you decided you'd rather freeze to death fighting for Hyrax, then I would be by your side, Aegean or not. But no matter who you decide to fight for, you serve a dual purpose. You represent a system of checks and balances for the gods. The Blackbloods were the only ones who stood a chance against them and protected Solterre from their unpredictable whims and tantrums. You alone have the ability to be the protector of not just one kingdom, but all of Solterre."

I blanch at his heavy words, struggling to comprehend how it's me he's talking about. It's *me* the fae have anticipated, written songs about, painted portraits of. *The Faceless Rider.* All when I don't even have the first clue of how to exist in this world. Right now, I'm a baby deer trying to learn to walk, but an entire *world* needs me to run...to fly.

Our conversation is interrupted by my stomach's insistent growling.

"Let's get some food in you." He stands, holding his hand out to me. "We'll pick this up tomorrow."

DAY two of training sucks just as much as day one. First, I got my ass handed to me by Jace. And then what little ass I had left got handed to me by Zadyn.

As promised, I attend the princess's picnic after my lessons. I bring Zadyn with me, as per Cece's request, relieved to have someone to lean on if the conversation falters. This is the most social I've been in years, albeit not entirely by choice, though the group seems amiable enough.

My jaw drops at the full view of the manicured grounds. We're guided outside—down a wide stone staircase, past the veranda, and onto the lushest, greenest grass I've ever seen. The maze I spotted last night lies up ahead of the cobblestone pathway. In the daylight, its beauty is breathtaking, the towering, sculpted shrubs adorned with delicate, bright-colored flowers. Beyond the maze, a vibrant garden frames a row of majestic fountains. The serene sound of trickling water tickles my ears as I take in the watchful stares of the marble statues looming above us. I turn to Zadyn, unable to contain my amazement.

"Are those your gods?"

"All seven, plus Urhlon and Aerill."

He points up at the fountain a few feet ahead, depicting an embrace between two figures. The female is wrapped in a toga-like garment; her crowned head leant back against the shoulder of a tall, robust male. His muscled arm is draped around her waist possessively, and in his outstretched hand, he holds an orb. The female bears its twin in her open palm.

"Sun and moon," he explains to me in a hushed voice. "They were the first mated pair."

"Really? I'm guessing that's a big deal here?" I ask, my eyes drinking in the detailed statues.

"It is. It's the equivalent of a twin flame." He stares ahead, the sunlight turning his caramel hair golden.

"Their love story is a bittersweet one. Without physical forms of their own, they can only be together two nights of the year when they use willing vessels."

"If they're the sun and the moon and if they have no physical form, then their children...?" I trail off. He understands what I'm getting at.

"No one really knows how or why, but the children of the gods have both physical and celestial forms."

"I see." I pluck a bright yellow flower from a nearby shrub as we pass by and lift it to my face, drinking in the sweet scent. "How are mates chosen?"

"Adelphi—Urhlon and Aerill's first-born daughter. Goddess of love."

"But I thought Myr, Silva, and Ienar, before he was killed, presided over Solterre."

"They did," he clarifies, "but when Solterre was created, each of Urhlon and Aerill's children christened it with a gift. Adelphi gifted the fae of the land with mates, created in the image of her parents' love. That was her contribution."

"Everyone has a mate here?" I ask, twirling my flower. Zadyn shakes his head, glancing down at me.

"It's become less and less common, as if Adelphi's gift faded with time. But they do still exist." Zadyn points to the fountain up ahead, bearing the likeness of an imposing, if not sinister, male.

"That one is Ienar."

The god of war is built like a gladiator with thick, corded muscles. He is armed for battle—a helmet resting at his hip and a longsword dangling from his free hand.

"How did Ienar defeat the dragons when their fire is the only thing that can kill a god? Wouldn't the witches have obliterated him?"

"He had the element of surprise on his side. They never even saw it coming until it was too late. Even though the Blackbloods were, for all intents and purposes, god-offspring, they were no match for an actual god."

A bout of laughter ripples off the group of royals ahead, catching our eye. Dover careens into the side of the fountain before Kai pounces on him and dunks his head under the water. He howls maniacally before letting him up. Dover crosses back to the ladies and shakes his head like a shaggy dog, spraying them and earning a thousand unamused complaints. I chuckle at them.

"They seem so carefree, don't they? Not what I expected at all." I look up at Zadyn.

"I don't think they're as carefree as they let on. Each of them has a name and a title, each their own set of unpleasant responsibilities. I think they savor their time together while trying to outrun who they are and what they were born to do. At least until they no longer can."

"That's sad. Not to have any choice in who you are and what you do."

"It gives us purpose," he counters. "Fae are a powerful species. Like witches. Without some kind of pre-destination, we would be nightmares. Some are, despite that. But you know what they say about idle hands."

We reach our desired picnic spot and pass the afternoon in the glow of the brilliant sun. I try to avoid thinking about the ceremony until we pack our things and head back toward the castle. With each step, my anxiety grows.

I have no idea what I've gotten myself into.

18

The Cave of Manthis sits at the base of a large mountain some ten miles north of the castle. We ride out before sunset until stars dust the sky, and we reach a large clearing. Countless members of court have made the trek to the cave. Cloaked High Fae gather near the small burning pyres scattered throughout the clearing. Their flames dance high and wild, casting the surrounding forest in an orange haze. My eyes are drawn to the mouth of the cave, where a soft greenish light glows from within.

"The king doesn't come to this?" I ask Zadyn as he lifts a hand to ease me from the horse.

"No. He usually stays in the castle and pays homage in his own way. Besides, only participants enter the cave, so once the initial rite is performed, the night can get rather boring for spectators. Especially when it's the longest one of the year."

Jace stands outside the cave, speaking with a few noble females. Zadyn starts toward him, and I lag behind, looking around for any familiar faces.

"Big turnout this year," a soft voice purrs in my ear. I whirl to find Kai standing behind me, his face bathed in flickering firelight.

"What are you doing here?" I ask, my tone coming out harsher than I intend.

"Enjoying the solstice, of course. Readying for the rite. But the better question is, what are *you* doing here?" His eyes roam over me as he stuffs his hands into his pockets.

"I'm representing the king's blood." I lift my chin.

"So fresh from the temple, you're still wet behind the ears." He flicks the pointed tip of my ear and I swat at his hand. "I'm curious. Why on earth would the king choose a long-lost cousin for the ceremony over his own daughter?" he muses. Though his voice is light and teasing, there is an air of suspicion behind it.

I steel myself, doubling down on the act.

"To relieve her of the burden, of course."

His brows lift in surprise.

"An honor, more like. Raised in a temple all your life, I'd think you'd know the distinction." He prowls closer, sizing me up. I force a fake smile onto my face.

"Is there something you want, Kai?"

"Yes. I want to know what you're really doing here." He takes a step closer, and I am forced to tilt my head to look up at him.

"The king wants me here. You're the foreigner," I say casually.

"My mother is the queen of these lands." A secretive smile works its way over his lips, like we've just shared an inside joke.

"And yet you're just the second son," I lilt, sounding a lot more confident than I feel. Desperate to avoid the scrutiny of his stare, I pull the hood of my cloak over my head. "No kingdom of his own to toy with, so here you are to toy with ours."

He chuckles, waggling his finger an inch from my face. "There's something different about you."

"You barely know me." I shift on my feet. "I bet you say that to all the ladies."

His eyes gleam as he says, "I don't need to know you to know that you aren't like us."

My stomach sinks. Kai is smart. It would be too easy for him to catch me in a lie and unravel the fragile story we've fabricated around *Lady Serena Accostia*.

I lean in close to his face, just a hair's breadth away, and whisper, "You're insane."

Without another word, I brush past him, beelining toward Zadyn and Jace. They turn to look at me as I approach.

"Kai knows something is up," I breathe, my eyes darting back and forth between the two males.

"What do you mean?" Jace's brows cinch together.

"He knows I'm...different. He's suspicious."

They both crane their heads toward Kai in the most obvious way.

"Well, don't look now!" I hiss.

"I'll find out what he knows," Jace says, eyes still fixed over my shoulder. "You need to focus on the ceremony. Go in there with a clear mind and level head when you enter that cave. If you drink the tea in a state of paranoia—"

"I'll have a bad trip?"

"Something like that."

"Is Kai participating, too?" I ask, stopping him as he moves to step around me.

Jace nods, glancing down at me. "Yes. Truly, there is nothing to worry about. Kai may be a hothead, but I've known him a long time. He's not a bad guy."

"Can we trust him?" Zadyn asks Jace.

"Yes." A peal of bells chimes from inside the cave. "It's starting soon. You should head inside."

He strides away as I cast a rueful glance toward the cave's entrance.

"You can do this," Zadyn encourages, taking hold of me.

"What's the worst that can happen?" An unsteady laugh works its way up my throat as the cloaked fae begin to filter inside.

"You puke and shit yourself." His smirk succeeds in easing some tightness in my chest. "I'll be waiting for you out here."

He smooths his hands over my arms, and I force myself to swallow.

Then I turn and file into the torchlit cave beside the fae nobles, taking in the rough-hewn cavern adorned with soft carpets and throws. A large cauldron occupies the center of the space, heating over a pit of green flames and filling the air with a pungent scent that reminds me of frankincense.

The High Priest waits beside the fire, his flowing white robes stained green by its soft glow. Once we've all settled onto the floor cushions, he lifts his arms to the heavens and begins to chant in an unfamiliar language.

Ancient Fae.

I turn, expecting to see Zadyn standing behind me, but all I see is the dark of the night beyond the mouth of the cave. I face forward again as everyone draws back their hoods. Glancing around the circle of about thirty fae, I notice a few familiar faces—Kai, of course, as well as Cece and Ilsa. Neither seems to notice me.

The fae bow their heads and recite a collective prayer. My mouth moves with them, forming ambiguous shapes in attempt to blend. When I catch Kai watching me from across the circle, I quickly tear my eyes away to stare at my crossed legs.

The High Priest spoons the potent liquid from the cauldron into a large ceramic mug and makes his way around the circle. I watch as they drink and close their eyes, muttering what must be another prayer. When the priest stops before me and lowers the cup to my waiting hands, the smell is overwhelming. I grimace as I gulp down the hot liquid and mutter the fudged words. Then everyone begins to shed their cloaks. The females are dressed similar to me, in low-cut sleeveless shifts belted with a thin golden chain. The males are naked from the waist up.

I don't know when the room starts to blur and skip like a TV with a faulty connection. My lids grow heavy, and I find it hard to keep resisting. I decide to rest my eyes for just a second. I sink deeper and deeper until there is no chance of opening them again.

I ONCE WATCHED a documentary on Jim Jones and how, in the 1970s, he convinced 918 cult members to drink a lethal cyanide cocktail. It was called the Jonestown Massacre. Men, women, and children—all sheep led to the slaughter.

How many times had I been warned not to drink the Kool-Aid? How many times had I heard the expression?

And yet here I was, just throwing it right down the hatch.

What a fucking idiot.

Everything around me is black. Not just the kind of dark where my eyes need a minute to adjust. No, this is true blackness, void of color and light. I hear nothing, I feel nothing, like true sensory deprivation. I can't wiggle my toes or fingers. I can't smell or taste or touch as I search for my own body and come up empty.

Panic begins to rise in my consciousness, fear that I've been tricked, and now I'm going to end up with Jim Jones and his pack of idiots. I'm dying, if I'm not already dead.

But the sound of a voice pauses my meltdown.

"Hello, little witch."

The voice is buttery. If I could see its owner, I would guess them to be a sparkling, glowing, otherworldly creature. An angel.

"Have you come to make of yourself an offering for me?"

Unable to locate my own voice, I answer with silence.

"Speak," she commands gently. Suddenly, the word falls out of my formless being.

"Yes," I say, but then I think better of it. "What—what do you want with me?"

"This form pleases me. And I can sense the magic in your veins, the way it sings and begs for release. I can give that to you."

"You can release my magic?" I ask.

"I can do more than that. I can make a gift of our magic, to be inside of you always."

"Our magic?"

"Mine and my mate's," she supplies. "When we are joined once again on this the longest eve."

"Joined...how?"

"When we can touch and embrace. Make love."

Woah, hold on.

"You're going to have sex using my body?" I balk. "No way, I didn't agree to that!"

"You came here willingly; you drank the tea of your own volition." Her voice begins to crackle with power.

"I didn't know that was the purpose," I counter pathetically.

"I know why you have come. Just like I know all. I know your magic remains trapped inside of you and that you have come here in hopes that I will help you in exchange for your vessel."

"No," I whisper. "No, I'll find another way."

But something is wearing me down. First, a sense of calm, a sense of peace. Then a stirring in my core. Heat where my face would be.

"What are you doing?"

"Your flesh is weak. See how it craves to be satisfied? We can give that to you as well as your magic on a silver platter. My mate is very skilled. It will be a pleasure like you have never known."

"What is happening to me?" I breathe, feeling my formless body react to some unseen stimuli. The ache inside me grows lusty—needy—as I try to fight against it.

"It is the tea taking full effect," she says, her voice growing closer and more urgent. "The moon is at its high point. Stop resisting. Let me in."

"I said no!"

"Defiant child," she tuts. "My mate would be pleased to make love to this body. If you disappoint him, you disappoint me. And that means no magic for you."

"I don't care. Choose someone else," I say, my voice sounding breathy and unlike my own.

"Very well, young witch. But do not call upon our names for favor. We will not listen."

A gentle wind blows against me, and suddenly, I find myself back in my body.

My eyes are reluctant to open. I stretch out where I lay, a familiar thrum of pleasure coursing through me. Looking around, I see that there are a little less than half the bodies as before, spread out in peaceful sleep. The High Priest has gone, and all that remains of the cauldron's fire are a few simmering coals.

My body begins to steer before my mind can catch up. I rise from the ground and step out into the chilled night air in nothing but the thin sheath. My bare feet pad onto the grass, and the sensation feels decadent. Moonlight washes over me as I tip my head back, my long hair tickling the backs of my arms.

My eyes close as I smell something familiar. A campfire.

Jace.

I don't see him, but that scent is driving me *crazy*.

"Serena?" *

I turn slowly, expecting Jace, but instead find Zadyn leaning against the mouth of the cave, his body half-bathed in dying firelight. My stomach tightens as I take in his beautiful face. The warmth of his brown eyes, his tall, lean-muscled form, his large hands. I start to wonder what those hands would feel like on my waist, my neck, my ass. I want to know what they feel like on me, all over me. His eyebrows knit together as he takes a tentative step forward like he's approaching a wild animal.

And that's exactly what I feel like when I surge forward and push him roughly against the rock.

His breath leaves him as he hits the solid surface, and I marvel at my sudden show of strength. His eyes widen in surprise as I press myself against him. There's no mistaking what I want as my hand works its way up his smooth chest, pinning him back as he tries to lift off the rock.

"Serena, is that you?" he asks, breathless.

"Who else would it be?" I whisper, my hands roaming over his shoulders, his arms, up his neck. His throat bobs as he swallows.

"What happened? Are you alright?"

"I'm alright," I purr, shaking my head. "But I could be better."

---

* Cue: *Sour Patch* by Ruby Waters

He stares down at me, worry in his eyes. His big hands come to rest on my shoulders.

"Serena, stop," he says. "It's the tea. It's making you react this way. You don't know what you're doing."

"I know exactly what I'm doing. What I want." I push forward again, my breasts pressing against him. He lets out a tight sigh as his hands slide to my waist. When I think he's about to pull me flush against him, he pushes me back, holding me by the hips.

"I promise you, you don't." His voice is firm.

I stand there, locked in a stare-down with him, nothing but the sound of our breath and the low crackle of fire for miles. The strap of my shift slides down my shoulder, and his gaze tracks the motion, helpless as a moth to a flame. I smirk in satisfaction, knowing that a little skin is all it takes to drive a male—human or fae—to their animal instincts.

I watch him intently as I lift my hand to the other strap and slowly slide it down. He bites his lip, unable to look away. His head gives the slightest shake when he notices that my peaked breasts are the only thing keeping the thin material from pooling around my waist.

I take the opportunity to rest my hands over his and guide them upward from my hips.

"Touch me."

He shakes his head and closes his eyes, trying to hold onto some semblance of restraint. I can feel it thinning, like a tether about to snap. I just have to push a little farther...

"Don't you want to?" I tease.

My palms press against the rock as I lean in and plant the smallest kiss in the place where his neck meets his shoulder. A shudder racks through his body as I close the distance between us, pressing my legs, my hips, into his. I start to move, giggling at the frustrated sigh he heaves.

"*Serena.*"

"Jace is right. I don't think you know how to say no to me." I lick the column of his neck from the base up, stopping just below his ear lobe. He tastes and smells amazing. "Because I don't think you want to."

"Fuck," he mutters under his breath. "We're not doing this."

I grind my hips against him, playing dumb. "Not doing what?"

"This isn't what you really want. You wouldn't do this if you were sober."

I grind into him again, and he stifles a groan. I can feel him hardening against me.

"Like I said, we're not doing anything." I lean my head against his shoulder and slide my hands down his chest, over his hard stomach, reaching toward his belt. "Yet."

His hand lashes out and wraps around my wrist, stopping me. I tug against it, but even with this newfound sense of strength, I'm no match for him.

"You're right," he says, twisting his other hand into my hair and forcing me to look up at him. The dominant move sends another wave of desire through me. "I don't want to say no to you. But I am."

He holds me there for a moment before I break out of his grasp. Anger and frustration momentarily override my lust as I snap, "Fine. Have it your way. I'll find someone else."

"Serena, wait—" he starts, but the moment I think of running, my feet have already carried me deep into the forest. I'm faster than before, dodging the trees with little effort, unaffected by the darkness. Adrenaline courses through me as I follow that familiar scent.

I find Jace bent by a small stream, bathed in moonlight. He crouches beside his dark horse, stroking its head as it drinks.

My heart clenches. And so does something else.

His head snaps up when he hears me approach. He slowly rises to his feet, watching each determined step I take. I can tell I've caught him off guard because he forgets to put on that mask. The one that keeps people at arms-length. The one of the stern and stoic captain. The one that hides who he really is beneath it all. The one that guards his heart.

"Serena," he says. Before he can form another word, my arms are around his neck, hauling him to me.

The kiss bursts through me like a match meeting gasoline. Every part of me is on fire. My fists close around his hair, and I'm surprised when he doesn't immediately push me off the way Zadyn did. But I can't even think of that right now because I am *consuming* Jace. And he's consuming me right back.

His lips part mine, and I open for him, rising onto my toes. His fingers braid through my thick hair, rooting me to him. I whimper against his mouth, and his arm wraps around my waist, pulling me closer. I am squished against his chest, unable to get down a breath, and I think there's no better way to die than suffocated, starved for air and for space, by this dark angel under the moonlight.

I bite his lower lip and taste blood. He actually growls. I go into a frenzy, clawing at his shoulders, trying to climb him, to get closer and closer until there is no space between us, and I am buried beneath his skin.

"Slow down, little witch." He chuckles, cupping my face. I swat his hands away. "You feel strong."

"I'm faster, too." And to prove my point, my hand shoots up to grab him by the throat. Not hard enough to choke him, but hard enough for him to feel my newfound strength. The surprise in his stare quickly darkens into desire. I slowly bring him closer to me, at a teasing pace, testing. When his lips are a breath away from mine, I hear a twig snap.

"Are you fucking kidding me," Zadyn's voice calls from behind me.

"What do you want," I toss back, uninterested.

"Were you just going to take advantage of her? Let her do whatever she wants?"

"No, that's your job," Jace quips. Zadyn shoves him from my grasp, too fast to register. All I see is Jace stumble back into his horse.

"Easy. It was a joke." He holds up his hands. "I had it under control."

"She was about to eat you alive. And you were going to let her."

"Hey! I knew what I was doing," I snap.

"Oh, please, Serena, no, you didn't. You would never throw yourself at me like that—and certainly not at *him*," he growls at Jace, who straightens, dusting himself off. He glances between the two of us.

"If it bothers you so much, then maybe you should have given me what I wanted instead of acting like a jealous prick!" I spit at Zadyn. He gives a humorless laugh.

"*I'm* the prick, yeah, for wanting to protect you when you're clearly not yourself. For stopping you from making a mistake like this one."

"Oh, please, we kissed, whoop dee doo." I swirl my pointer finger around in the air lazily.

"She went to you first?" Jace asks Zadyn.

"Yes. Although if she had seen the horse first, I'm sure she would have propositioned him, too."

"Oh, fuck you, Zadyn!" I hiss. "I told you I knew what I was doing—that I was in control. I wish you'd stop treating me like a fucking baby. A baby that can't do anything in this world— that can't even do magic, or walk, or breathe, or want to have sex! I can do whatever I want, despite what you think I should or shouldn't do, all because you're sworn to me with some stupid possessive bond. You think you have the right, but you don't!" I shout. "You don't."

A long, tense silence ensues as Zadyn and I glare at each other, and Jace watches from the side.

"Come on," Jace says after a few moments. "We should head back. You're going to crash soon."

"I feel fine. I want to stay," I bite.

"Then find your own way back."

He turns to mount his horse and gallops off without another word. I catch a flicker of hurt on his face before he's swallowed up by the dark woods.

Is he upset with me?

"You can hate me all you want," Zadyn starts, his voice hard. "But I'm not going back without you."

We stare at each other confrontationally for a long moment.

Then I shake my head and stalk off in the direction Jace rode a moment ago. We make it back to the clearing, where Zadyn silently lifts me onto a horse and then settles in behind me. I hear soft moans coming from inside the cave.

Sounds like they're having a good time. Good for them.

It's tense and uncomfortable the whole ride back, neither of us breathing a word. As we approach our rooms, I see Jace standing outside my door—his posture upright, his icy mask of indifference resurrected. He doesn't bother to look at me.

I pause when I hear Zadyn warn him in a hushed voice, "She might try and get out in the middle of the night."

"So take care of her like she wanted, and she won't. Better her familiar than a stranger."

Zadyn scoffs. "Like you were about to if I hadn't interrupted?"

"You shouldn't insinuate such things."

"Hey," I snap at them. "Don't talk about me like I'm not

here. If I want to go out in the middle of the night, I will. If I want to fuck someone in this hallway, I will." They both eye me silently. "Don't worry, I'll let you watch."

"Go to bed," Jace says, his voice sounding somewhat tired.

"We'll talk about this in the morning. All of us." Zadyn throws Jace a pointed look, which he doesn't bother to return. We slip into our rooms without another word.

I'm still riding high on the tea, but the initial buzz I had when I came out of that cave is quickly fading. I flop onto my bed, sad and horny.

I DREAM ABOUT ZADYN.

Of his scent—a cool mixture of black tea, cedar, and bergamot. I dream about his hands, his arms, and his restraint hanging by a thread. I dream about my body pressed against his and how it feels when I drive my hips into his.

My eyes flash open, and I sit up with a loud gasp.

Oh my god. That wasn't a dream. That actually happened.

I tried to fuck Zadyn last night.

Oh my god, Jace, too. I tried to fuck both of them within a span of five minutes. And *both* had rejected me.

What was I thinking? What came over me?

My door flies open, and Jace storms in.

"Are you alright? I heard you gasping," he asks, his voice strained. I nod through the pounding headache and force a dry swallow before a wave of nausea works its way up my stomach. I launch myself out of bed and sprint toward the bathroom, shoving Jace out of the way in the process.

"Serena?"

I throw myself down over the toilet just in time to empty the contents of my stomach. My body shakes as I heave violently. A pair of cool hands graze the nape of my neck, gathering my hair behind me as my stomach lurches again.

"What the fuck," I groan into the toilet.

"Puking and shitting," Jace supplies, his hand tracing small circles on my back. I press my face into the cool porcelain and breathe hard. "You're alright."

"Last night, I—" I try to apologize but am interrupted by another surge of vomit. I'm still spitting the foul taste from my mouth when Zadyn's tight voice sounds from behind me.

"Is she alright?"

"It's a normal response. Her body is just trying to dispel the tea."

I slump back against the massive tub, my eyes closed, trying to focus on my breathing. Someone dabs my face with a cold washcloth, smoothing it over my sweat-slicked brow and dry lips.

A glass is placed in my hand, and Jace says, "Swish it around and spit."

I obey, swirling the minty liquid around my mouth, trying desperately to wash away the horrid aftertaste of last night. Then I'm being lifted and carried toward the bed. I don't protest. My whole body feels empty and limp, like jelly.

I curl up under the covers, my teeth chattering.

"I feel like a junkie," I whine.

"I'll have Gnorr brew you a tea," Jace says.

"No!" My eyes fly open. "No more tea. Just let me lay down a few minutes."

Jace perches beside me on the bed as Zadyn comes to stand above us, arms folded over his chest. They watch me, wearing twin expressions of concern.

"You guys—" I try to sit up and wince at the effort it takes. "What happened last night..." I shake my head. "My behavior was completely out of line."

"It's okay," Zadyn says. "You weren't yourself."

"I knew what I was doing, but I had this, this uncontrollable, insatiable lust. It was like nothing I've ever felt before. I couldn't even think straight or see beyond it. I was an animal. I'm so embarrassed."

"There's nothing to be embarrassed about." Zadyn pulls a chair up to the bed and sits. "The tea does that. It makes you starved for sex."

That's right.

"Oh my god," I whisper. "I saw her—I saw Aerill. She spoke to me."

"What did she say?" Jace asks.

"She...she wanted to use me as a vessel. She promised me my magic and some of her own if I let her..." I trail off and glance between them.

"Oh, you two are dead." I shake my head at them, furious.

Jace's lips press into a thin line.

"You didn't think I should be told that the point of this little ritual was to be possessed by Aerill so she could turn me into her husband's personal *sex doll*?" I can almost feel the steam coming out of my ears.

"He's technically not her husband," Jace mutters under his breath. I whack him in the arm.

"What the hell were you thinking keeping that from me?"

"We thought it was pretty self-evident," Jace retorts.

"To who?!" I shout. *Idiots.*

"We told you that the point of the ritual was for them to take physical form so they could be together for one night out of the year," he explains. "If I had realized how naïve you were, I would have spelled it out for you." His brow arches.

"I'm not naïve; it was just never explained to me explicitly! Forgive me for not putting two and two together after being thrown into a world where everything is upside down, and my brain is already fried from the insane plot twists that just keep popping up around every corner. You expect me to be thinking straight? I'm surprised I haven't completely *snapped* yet! You should have spelled it out for me. I was completely blindsided," I fume. "Would you really have whored me out just to access my magic?" My gaze shifts between the two of them.

"No, of course not. I'm so sorry." Zadyn looks sick to his stomach. "That wasn't—"

"You're right," Jace cuts in. "We should have been more direct. But we knew you'd be given a choice in the matter. It wasn't up to us to decide for you. Aerill presented you with that choice, and you chose. Clearly, you didn't accept."

"No. I didn't. She promised me magic for what she wanted me to do, and I said no. Sorry for botching your plan," I say a touch bitterly.

"That wasn't our plan." Jace leans forward. "We had no intention of you accepting her offer. To be frank, I thought there was little chance she would even appear to you. We just hoped that the tea would trigger your magic. When you came out of that cave, you were stronger."

"Faster, too," Zadyn says.

"That was from the tea?" I ask.

"Well, yes, the tea readies your body to receive Aerill and to—"

"It turns you on," I supply for Zadyn.

He nods gratefully. "It enhances things."

"Oh, it certainly did."

"Those effects are temporary, but we hoped it would act as a catalyst for you."

"They could have been permanent if I wasn't caught so off guard," I say.

"Would you have said yes to her otherwise?" Jace angles himself toward me. "Correct me if I'm wrong in saying this,

Zadyn, but neither of us had any intention of you whoring yourself out for magic. Trust me, if you had said yes to Aerill, the two of us would have put a very abrupt end to the experiment."

My eyebrows knit together as I try to unpack that statement.

"We would have never allowed you to go through with it," Jace says, golden eyes searing into me. "We only wanted to see if the tea could trip your magic."

"And what if she had forced me?" I counter.

"She cannot force you. It only works if you consent."

I glance between the two of them.

"I'm still pissed at you two."

"We're still pissed at you," Jace says with a shrug.

"If I had known I was going to be a sex demon when I walked out of that cave, I would have chained myself up. *That* you could have at least warned me about." I cross my arms, cringing at the memory of how I behaved.

"We tried to tell you, but you were rather determined." Jace chuckles. My cheeks heat, and I bury my face in my hands, thinking of Zadyn trying to pry my hands from his body.

But Jace?

When I crashed into him, he kissed me back with a ferocity to rival my own. The small cut on his lip is enough to send a new flash of emotion through me—a cocktail of desire and shame and secret satisfaction.

"I know it's no excuse," I begin again, "but I really wasn't myself."

"We know," Zadyn says.

"No, you don't. Aside from throwing myself at both of you, I said things I didn't mean. Terrible things that were completely unwarranted. I was just frustrated and riding high on the tea."

Zadyn studies his hands. "I know. It's okay. And I'm sorry

for not being more direct with you. We both are. It won't happen again." I return his sheepish look with a smile.

"Good. And I won't try to maul you again. Either of you." I meet Jace's eyes and suck in a breath. "Can we just agree to never speak of this again and move on?"

"Already forgotten." Jace stands. "I'll give you the morning to recover. We can train in the afternoon."

"What?" I protest. "I just puked my guts up! Doesn't that warrant a sick day?"

"Not on day three of training, it doesn't." He smiles, amused by my reaction. "I told you I'm not going to coddle you."

"Whatever."

Zadyn stands. "I'll bring that brew up for you." He smooths my shoulder and follows Jace from the room.

I close my eyes, snuggling into my pillow. I'm asleep before Zadyn returns with the hangover cure.

19

Two months pass by in the blink of an eye, and I rarely think of the world I left behind. I don't have the time or the space in my mind to occupy anything but the present moment.

I train with Jace every day until I have muscles in places I never have before. Until I can run for miles without stopping. And until I can take down a fae using nothing but my own body. He's tough on me, but he's a damn good trainer, I'll give him that.

I learn about Solterre and its inhabitants—the fae and other species. Monsters and dragons I thought only existed in the books I read. I learn the history and geography from Zadyn, as well as their customs and ways. But my magic remains dormant. Aside from mastering the art of lighting a small candle with my mind, I'm as good as human. And I still pass out sometimes when I do it.

Gnorr tries to track down a Blueblood contact, but the entire clan has relocated and centralized in secret. No one knows where they all disappeared to. She searches for alternatives to unbind my magic in the meantime.

I barely see the king, but Jace relays his restlessness. Time is against us. The longer I spend here under this false identity of Lady Accostia, the bigger the risk of being found out. Of being hunted by the other kingdoms.

That fear looms over me like a hanging sword. Not to say that my treatment here upon arrival was exactly hospitable, but I don't think the other kingdoms would hesitate to use whatever means necessary to bend the last Blackblood to their will. I've come to feel safe here. Comfortable even.

I try to avoid letting my mind skip too far into the future and what awaits me—the impossible and life-threatening task of bonding a living, fire-breathing dragon.

My afternoons and nights are spent as part of the princess's regular entourage, partying and kicking up harmless mischief. I come to look forward to their intimate revelries of pure, unadulterated fun. We play like children, singing and dancing with abandon, celebrating for no reason other than being alive. It helps me escape the harsh reality of what I'm really doing here. Besides, being in the company of royalty has its perks. The gowns, the jewels, the decadent luxuries. But despite the material benefits of being Lady Accostia, it's the actual company I enjoy most.[*]

For the first time, I feel like I have friends. Despite the worries hanging over my head, I find myself laughing and joking. Lighter of heart than when I arrived. In a way, it's the most normal I've felt in a long time. They offer me a temporary reprieve from the weight that's been thrust upon my shoulders. And for that, I'm grateful.

Jace, however, is not so quick to offer me the same reprieve.

---

[*] Cue: *ICU* by Phoebe Bridgers

I roll over my shoulder and land on one knee, my arm releasing the dagger into a smooth, straight line that slices the air. It was intended for Jace's head, but instead, it skims past him, shoring a few stray hairs off the side. He gives a wicked smirk and advances fast as lighting, appearing behind me. I turn, throwing my weight behind a sloppy punch, which he easily evades. Palming my outstretched fist in his calloused hand, he twists my wrist behind my back, sending a shooting pain up my arm. I rear my head back with all my might, slamming it into his chin as he loses his balance and releases me. I take the opportunity to land a rare punch to his jaw before dipping low and sweeping his legs out from under him. Rivulets of sweat skate down the back of my neck as I straddle him. I pull my fist back for another blow, but he spins us in the blink of an eye.

My back meets with the hard dirt of the training ring, and I groan in pain, arching in response. Jace slams into me, pinning me beneath his strong hips. I wriggle beneath his weight as he cages me between his arms and angles a dagger above my breast. Heat rolls off his body as we stare into each other's wide eyes, fighting for breath, and for that split second, his rough touch feels intimate. I bite my bottom lip to keep the traitorous smirk off my face. Jace's eyes narrow on the slight movement before he snarls and pushes off me.

"That was total shit. You're not focused."

How can I be when you look like that?

Sisyphus's karmic retribution was pushing a massive rock up a hill every day for all eternity.

Jace is my rock.

I watch his sweat-slicked body move across the ring, each step confident and assured. Even more torturous than the obstacles and drills he puts me through daily is being forced to bear witness to his perfectly lethal body in action. To spar with it. To be pinned helplessly beneath it. How can I not be distracted when his hands are constantly on me, correcting my posture, stretching my body out, putting me flat on my ass? It's taking sexual frustration to a whole new level.

"You're extra cranky this morning." I lie star-fished on the ground, staring up at his stone face. "What's eating you?"

He doesn't answer.

"You know, it's rude to ignore people when they're talking to you. Were you raised by wolves or something?" I grumble.

He turns to me, his face vicious.

"You know, it's rude to make assumptions about people's upbringings," he snaps.

"Woah. Okay, sorry. I didn't know it was a touchy subject for you. Probably because I don't know much about you at all." I sit up and give my barking legs a stretch.

He turns his back to me, striding to put away the scattered weapons, sweat beading on the tips of his dark hair. "You know nothing about me," he mutters under his breath.

"Because you don't let me. We've spent every morning together for months. We might as well get to know each other. Maybe it will ease some of this hostility."

"You haven't seen hostile yet, witch," he says. *With* hostility.

"So you'd prefer to shut everyone out? It's getting old. This act where you belittle me, degrade me, pretend not to care about anything. I don't think you're as tough as you pretend to be."

He heaves an annoyed sigh, tossing the weapon in his hand to the ground and turning to face me in a dramatic manner.

"What is it you want to know?" He holds his arms out.

"Anything." I pull my knees in, wrapping my fatigued arms around them. "How did you become Captain of the Guard?"

"The normal way. I worked for it."

"Were you a fighter before?"

"I fought in the king's armies, yes," he answers tightly, annoyance edging his voice.

"Have you..." I trail off, suddenly wondering if that's too personal a question to ask.

"Have I what?" He lifts his brows.

"Killed people?"

I hold my breath. He looks at me like I have a third eye.

"Yes, witch. I have killed before. It's sort of a requirement for winning a war."

"Right." I nod. "Of course it is."

"When the time comes, you'll do the same," he says, pushing his hair back. I jolt forward.

"Woah, woah, woah. I don't plan to kill anyone."

"Your destiny is to ride the last dragon left in Solterre. Killing comes with the territory. It comes with defending a nation."

"I can't." I shake my head. "I can't kill anyone."

"Why not?"

"Is that a serious question?" I sputter.

"Yes. What are you afraid of? What are you afraid will happen if you do?"

"I won't be able to live with myself knowing that I killed someone, that I took their life."

"Believe me when I say from experience you can. Not everyone is good." His eyes harden.

"That doesn't mean we should be the ones to decide who lives or dies."

"When the time comes, you'll be able to do it. When you're faced with the choice to kill or be killed, you will choose to kill. To survive. You will kill just like the rest of us vile creatures."

With that, he stalks off, leaving me to contemplate my destiny. What they're hoping I will become for the good of the kingdom.

A killer.

~

AFTER THE GRUELING training session this morning, it's the sweetest relief when I sink into the sea of blankets strewn across the expanse of plushy, fresh-cut grass.* I followed the princess and her entourage across the immaculate grounds— past the pristine flower gardens and marble water fountains, past the small temple near the edge of a thicket of giant cherry blossom trees, down a sloping green hill met with a shimmering pool of water. We set up our fortress of blankets and umbrellas near the water's edge.

I sprawl out, flexing my sore muscles against the butter-soft blanket. I breathe deep, noting how different the air feels compared to the air at home. Ours is thick—polluted with toxins. But here, the air is sweet, light, and thin. You can smell nature around you. The trees, the grass, even the water has a scent. I don't know if it's the whisper of my buried magic responding to this world, but everything has a slight charge to it. Every sunbeam on my skin or breeze that kisses my neck, every ripple in the water feels alive. Feels awake. And so do I.

I glance at my new friends, and marvel at how perfect they all look—individually, but also together. Dressed in complementary shades of white and cream and pink, they look like they stepped out of a Vogue photoshoot at Versailles. They belong to each other. And with the cap sleeved off-white corset and skirt, blush pink lace gloves, and wide-brimmed cream hat that Igrid insisted I wear, I fit right in.

"So, how are you finding life at court, Lady Accostia?" Marideth asks from beside me. Eyes closed, she lies on her

---

* Cue: *My Fun* by Suki Waterhouse

back, the sun dancing over her splayed auburn hair. Her silk-gloved fingers fiddle with the buttons down her beige bodice.

"Please." My head lolls to the side, squinting at her beside me. "Call me Serena. Court is *different*."

A soft chuckle slips through her uptilted lips.

"I'll say. I can't think of a more modest upbringing than a temple. I imagine this must be a big change for you."

"It's a welcome change," I lie smoothly.

I'm getting better at pretending. I don't know if that's a good thing or something to be concerned about. I know it's for everyone's safety, but I hate that I can't be honest with them about who I am. I feel a twinge of guilt anytime Sorscha calls me "*cousin*" or I have to play along with some falsity about my past.

Mar cracks one eye, sliding it in my direction as a peal of delighted squeals erupts from down the hill. Kai and Dover are calf-deep in glittering water, their cream-colored pants rolled up as they splash at Sorscha, Ilsa, and Cece. The ladies protest, skirts gathered in their arms above the water's opalescent surface. Dover's eyes catch on Marideth up the hill, and he dashes toward us. She squeals as he throws his body over hers, nuzzling sweet kisses along her neck until she swats him away.

"You're soaked, you fool!" she chides. He answers with a boyish laugh and a smacking kiss on her cheek before racing back to terrorize the three females downhill. I turn to Marideth, who watches him keenly, a small smile on her lips.

"You and Dover," I start. She looks at me, her expression open. "He's engaged."

"He's engaged." Her chest rises and falls with a heavy sigh. "Not to me."

"Why?" I flip onto my side to study her, propping my head up on one hand. "You two seem so—"

"We're mates."

My eyebrows lift at the admission.

"But he lives in Vod. I only get to see him when Kai comes to visit the queen. His parents arranged the marriage when he was three. They won't break it despite our many pleas."

"Who is she?"

"Wyneth?" Her eyes slide toward me. "A mealy mouse High Fae from Iaspis with more money than Aerill herself. The thing is, I could probably learn to tolerate her if she had a backbone and some dignity. But she knows about Dover and me—she has for years—and has never said a word. I could probably fuck him right in front of her, and she wouldn't bat an eye."

I choke on a laugh.

"It's true!" She mirrors my position, turning to face me.

"And she knows you and Dover are mates?"

"Everyone knows. We haven't exactly been discreet about it." She casts a glance in his direction. "His parents don't care; they want a cut of that diamond money. And hers just want her married off to a male with a good family name."

"That's awful. I'm so sorry."

"Don't be," she says, looking back to me. "We have no intention of stopping what we're doing. We're a mated pair by the will of the gods. Their parents are idiots to think they can stand in the way of something so strong. They'd sooner make a mockery of the marriage than break the engagement for us."

"You'll be his mistress?"

"I'll be his everything. They'll be married in name only." She falls silent for a moment, picking at the blanket. "If I have to give up the chance to marry so that I can follow him wherever he goes, then I will. If he has children with her, I will love them and treat them as if they were my own. It's a sacrifice I'm willing to make. There is no life for me without him."

I find my heart hurting for her.

"He's an idiot." She breaks the somber tone, shaking her head at him. "But he's *my* idiot. And he loves me."

The sound of footsteps rustling the grass draws my attention uphill. I twist around to see Zadyn making his way toward us. The sun washes over his caramel hair and tan skin, coloring him even more brilliant. I smile warmly as he approaches and sinks down beside me on the blanket.

"You made it," I say, sitting up.

"Apologies for being late. My meeting ran longer than I expected."

Zadyn was meeting with Gnorr this afternoon to research some theories on how to extract my magic.

"Lady Marideth." Zadyn nods to her in greeting. Marideth's eyes roam over him indiscreetly, top to toe, not even bothering to hide her blatant curiosity. Those steely gray eyes toss a knowing look in my direction. I tilt my head in confusion.

"Lord Rhodes." She tips her head before her eyes are pulled toward the tall figure stepping around the big umbrella above us. "And as I live and breathe, the Captain *himself*," Marideth crows, her voice dripping with sarcasm.

Jace stands above us, eclipsing the sun. I can't pry my eyes away.

"Marideth," he says in greeting. A curt nod is all the acknowledgment he gives me. For reasons I can't even begin to understand, he's still a dick to me when people are around.

I take that back. He's also a dick to me when people *aren't* around.

"Not feeling social today, or are you still recovering from last night?" Jace peers down at Marideth, his form an imposing shadow against a picturesque backdrop. She rolls her eyes dramatically, reaching for a grape.

"Be grateful I bowed out when I did. Or you would have lost your trousers to me in cards. Again." She pops the grape in her mouth and chomps it.

I was beat from yesterday's training, so I skipped out on the party last night. But it seems Jace attended. I've barely seen him at any of Sorscha's gatherings this month. Lately, he's full of excuses as to why he can't attend. Personally, I think he just tries to avoid being around me at all costs.

"Quite the party animal?" I squint up at him. His eyes are cold and his posture standoffish as he literally looks down his nose at me. I don't get a response.

Rising to my feet, I say to Zadyn, "I'm going to dip my feet in. Wanna come?" He nods and follows behind me. As I pass Jace, our shoulders brush.

"Wait." Marideth hauls herself up off the ground and stretches like a lazy cat. She grabs Jace by the arm and starts towing him downhill alongside her.

Kai greets Jace with a welcoming clap on the back as Sorscha, Ilsa, and Cece flock to Zadyn, who responds bashfully to their shameless flirtations. Making him blush has recently become one of their greatest sources of amusement. Beside us, Marideth shoves Dover into the water until he is fully submerged and flailing.

Looking around at these faces I've known for such a short time, I realize that I care for them. I never expected them to be this way. To be kids, moonlighting as adults, just trying to figure it out. Just like me.

I notice Sorscha tear her smiling eyes away from Zadyn to look at Jace. His head inclines toward the hill in silent invitation, and she quietly extricates herself from the pack to follow him. I try not to eavesdrop or stare, but I can't help glancing toward them as they make their way a few feet up the hill.

They stand surprisingly close to one another. Jace is talking, but I can't make out what he's saying. Sorscha nods, a curl falling loose from the chic, messy pile on her head. I hold my breath as he places a hand on her arm. It's a friendly gesture, but I find myself clenching my fists.

"Someone likes to watch," Marideth whispers in my ear. I start, but she just chuckles.

"I was just curious," I admit. "What's going on there?" My tone is casual. Nonchalant.

At least, that's what I'm going for.

"Exactly what it looks like." She plops a floppy hat over her brilliant hair. "They keep it kind of quiet, but Jace has been courting Sorscha for the past few months."

"What?" I sputter, facing her.

"They've been seeing each other," Mar explains. "The king has been pushing for a marriage between them, but the queen wants Kai to marry Sorscha."

"Oh?" My stomach tightens in disappointment. "And how do they feel about that?"

Their hands dangle close together, fingers practically kissing.

"Oh, they've been trying to talk their way out of it. Sorscha and Kai love each other, of course, just not in that way. But the king has politics to consider. Wed Sorscha to Kai and the alliance between the two kingdoms strengthens. On the other hand, making a Vod prince into king consort puts an awful lot of power in foreign hands."

My eyebrows knit together as I force myself to look back at Mar. "Why not wed Sorscha to a noble instead?"

"The king practically raised Jace. He fought in his armies for a long time and rose through the ranks exceptionally fast. Now he's on his way to being appointed Hand of the King. He would be a good match for Sorscha. The king wants her to marry soon, to produce heirs, and come into her full power."

The knife twists as I watch the two of them make their way further up the hill, her hand nestled in the crook of his arm. A peal of angelic laughter sounds as she beams up at him with the warmth of a thousand suns. The thought of the two of them producing heirs sends a shot of envy through me. Envy I have no business feeling because he and I can barely stand to be in the same room without ripping each other's heads off.

"Are you alright?" Mar lays a gentle hand on my shoulder. I nod.

"You don't hide it very well," she says with a knowing smirk.

"Hide what?" I tilt my head, looking at her.

She heaves an exasperated sigh, resting her hands on her hips. "I have eyes. I'll just say this."

She leans in. "Be careful."

20

I am seated across from the ladies at a wrought-iron table canopied by a massive umbrella. The shade is a welcome defense against the unusually hot day. The sun beams down in strong rays, making everything extremely bright.

Shielding my eyes, I look out at the lawn below the terrace, where Kai, Dover, and Zadyn are engaged in a game called *Signette*. From what I glean, it's similar to croquet, with the small wooden clubs.

The excess breeze from Sorscha and Cece's hand fans wafts toward me, and I welcome it with relief.

"Cousin," Sorscha says. I bring my gaze toward her. She jerks her chin in direction of the boys below. "What do you think of Kai?"

Marideth groans, ripping off her wide-brimmed hat and flopping her head onto the table. Cece gives a snarky chuckle under her breath. I glance between them, confused.

"Sorscha," Mar murmurs in warning. She holds up a pink-gloved hand that complement her sun-kissed cheeks.

"I was just asking!" Her doe eyes are wide with innocence as she turns to me. "He's rather handsome, isn't he?"

I glance back toward the lawn. Kai stands there, leaning on his club, his shirt and jacket unbuttoned, showing off his washboard abs. As if hearing the mention of his name, his attention snaps toward us. He offers a flirtatious smile that reeks of mischief before turning back to his game.

"He is. Unfortunately, man whore isn't my type."

The ladies burst into a laughing fit.

"Oh, cousin." Sorscha sighs, wiping the tears leaking from the corners of her eyes.

"For someone raised in a temple, you're rather sharp, you know." Cece eyes me.

"Not sure that's a compliment, but I'll take it." I sip my iced tea.

"Sorscha is desperate to marry Kai off during his stay, so she doesn't have to do it." Marideth gives her a knowing look. The princess sets her fan down on the table and sighs.

"Is that a crime?" Glancing between the ladies, she continues, "To want to see one of my oldest friends settled and happy?"

"Let's face it, he'll never be settled *and* happy. It's one or the other for Kai. Remind you of anyone you know?" Marideth raises her brows at Sorscha, who blinks before turning her attention back to the game.

"I don't know what you're talking about," she says, chin in the air. Mar rolls her eyes.

"Kai and I are old friends," she explains, "and while I can appreciate our similarities—"

"What she means is she can appreciate that they're the same *person*—" Mar corrects, bumping my arm.

"We are only friends," Sorscha emphasizes. "A match between us would never work. But that doesn't mean I don't want the best for him. And cousin, you are the best." She smiles proudly.

"I'm not really the marrying type." I press my lips together.

"Promiscuous?" Cece gibes, earning an elbow from Ilsa.

"Particular," I reply in a honeyed voice to rival her own.

"Well, if Kai doesn't pique your interest, there are dozens of nobles at court," Sorscha offers, brimming with excitement. She leans in. "What's your type?"

Cece cuts in before I can answer. "You and your little lord friend seem close." She swirls her iced tea, green eyes appraising me.

"Zadyn?" My eyebrows lift.

"Talk about dreamy," Ilsa lilts, smirking. Mar and Sorscha nod and giggle in agreement. I study Zadyn's impressive form as he lines up his club. He looks so laid-back with his sleeves rolled up to his elbows, the clean white of his shirt offsetting his tan skin. He pushes his caramel hair out of his eyes and strikes the ball. Kai and Dover cheer and clap him on the back. His answering smile is dazzling.

"Oh, we're just old friends," I say with a shrug. "My mother was his godmother. He spent a lot of time visiting us at the temple over the years."

We came up with that fib to cover for the fact that Zadyn and I are basically attached at the hip.

"Is that all?" Cece leans forward, resting her drink on the table.

"You've never..." Sorscha trails off, eyeing me conspiratorially.

"Oh my god, no." My laugh starts strong but fizzles out when I recall how I threw myself at him at solstice. That night, I found him completely irresistible.

There's no denying that Zadyn is gorgeous. He's the quintessential dream guy—attractive, kind, loyal. Exactly the kind of guy I *should* be with. But he's my familiar, which equals: off-limits.

Right?

"That's surprising," Mar says, leaning back in her seat. "I mean, look at the two of you." She gestures up and down my body.

"He does seem rather protective of you," Ilsa notes in her sweet little voice.

"It's because we've known each other a long time," I say in conclusion. Zadyn's eyes snag on mine, and he gives me a quick, dimpled smile, which I return with a wave. When I look back at the females eyeing me, they giggle.

All but Cece.

"WAKE UP."

A voice beckons into my dreamless sleep, barely a whisper down a long tunnel of heavy darkness.

"*Wake up,*" it sings again. Something soft tickles the tip of my nose. Light, muted giggles sound from far away.

"*Serena.*"

Warm breath ghosts over my ear, drawing out my name like a lyric in a song.

I jolt awake with a loud scream, eyes darting between the six bodies looming over me in the dark. My outburst causes them to shout in reaction, and we stare at each other, yelling in an endless feedback loop until Zadyn tears through the adjoining door, scanning for danger.

"What happened?" he shouts, cutting us off.

I gape at my cloaked friends huddled together beside my bed. All except for Kai, who is instead sprawled out on my bed twirling a feather in his hand. Moonlight glitters off his wide ocean eyes as he appraises my disheveled state.

"What the hell are you guys doing?! You scared the living shit out of me," I breathe, regaining a somewhat normal heart rate.

"We're going on a little field trip and wanted to see if you'd be inclined to join." Kai lounges beside me, crossing one leg over the other. He dusts the feather over my nose, and I snatch it out of his hand, tossing him a glare. His hands lift in mock surrender before folding comfortably behind his head.

"Come on, cousin, get dressed!" Sorscha all but dances over to my wardrobe and selects an outfit and cloak, tossing them onto the bed.

"You cannot wake a person like that." My statement is directed at the room. "I had just fallen asleep," I whine, thinking of the hell tomorrow's training is going to be.

"Oh, darling, did we give you a fright?" Kai whimpers, snatching his feather back from my unsuspecting grasp.

"Up you go." Marideth grabs me by the hands and hauls me out of bed, passing me over to Sorscha, who waits with a pair of flowing pants for me to step into.

"You might want to throw something on, as well." Marideth's steely eyes assess an attractively disheveled Zadyn, who stands there in nothing but low-slung sleep pants. He gives a curt nod and retreats to his room to dress.

"Where are we going?" I grumble, cranky as all hell, tugging the high-waisted pants over my hips.

"It's a surprise." Ilsa claps her teeny hands together beside an impatient-looking Cece.

Without warning, Sorscha and Marideth strip my nightgown over my head. I grab my bare breasts, shooting a glance at Kai, who's not even pretending to look away.

"Just when I thought you couldn't get any more beautiful,"

he croons, grinning like the Cheshire Cat as he teases the feather over his full lips.

"Do you mind?" I snap at him, still clutching my naked chest. In one languid movement, he sits up, bats those heavy lashes, and leans his pretty head on his hand.

"Ignore him." Marideth rolls her eyes, tugging a matching cap-sleeved cropped top over my head.

Sorscha passes me the cloak as Zadyn reappears far less naked, to the great disappointment of every female in the room. The door cracks open, and Jace pops his head in, his familiar face sending a shock wave of electric current through me.

Every damn time, I curse myself.

"If we're going, it has to be now," he says, golden eyes snagging on me before quickly looking away.

"We're ready." Sorscha tugs me toward the door, and we follow Jace down the hallway. He listens at a spot on the wall, knocks twice, and shoves it open to reveal a dark secret chamber. My friends file into the hidden corridor, brimming with excitement. Darkness envelops the passageway, and I cling to Zadyn, relying on his superior fae eyesight. Using the wall as a guide, we descend four flights of stairs deep beneath the castle. Excited whispers echo off the stone walls as we move further from the grounds.

A ladder waits at the tunnel's end, along with a small door overhead. Kai and Dover reach up to push it open, moonlight flooding in as they climb out. They help us onto soft, slightly overgrown grass.

We stand at the top of a large hill, peering down at a sparkling city of winding roads, glittering waterways, and rows and rows of pearlescent stone buildings. Bathed in brilliant moonlight, it waits below like a gem nestled inside the valley.

"Iaspus. City of Diamond," Kai announces from my side,

hands stuffed into his pockets, marveling down at the magnificent city awaiting us.

"Wow," I breathe in awe. Sorscha, Cece, and Ilsa breeze past, holding hands as they bound downhill, feet scrambling to catch up to the steep decline. Their voices disrupt the quiet stillness of the night.

"Come on!"

With a wink and a nudge to the ribs, Kai takes off after them, and I follow suit. A wild sense of freedom fills my chest as we career down the hill, arms outstretched to the clear expanse, laughter filling the air.

Breathless and windblown, we arrive beneath the towering diamond encrusted archway that marks the entrance into Iaspus. A childlike wonder overtakes me as we walk through the city, my arm linked through Mar's. We reach a busy intersection that leads us to a place they call the Markade.

Even at midnight, the Markade is bustling and alive, the streets crowded with fae. The cobblestone pathways are lined with white tents as far as the eye can see. Dozens of street vendors and tradesmen are posted up, selling goods of every kind, silks and fabrics, and confections that I've never heard of or seen before. Music drifts through the night air on a soft breeze, along with the intoxicating scent of exotic food.

At the edge of the street, we round an alleyway and step inside a building with an unmarked door. We are instantly met with lively music and the thick smell of beer. The old-fashioned pub is a revelry of spritely, expressive guests, clinking glasses, and merrymaking. They dance on top of the bar and the wooden tables, kicking up their skirts and stomping their feet in time to the trio of fiddles playing in the corner.

Kai leads us through the tightly packed crowd to the worn wooden bar and signals for a round. A stunning brunette in a barmaid's outfit saunters over to us, shaking her head at Kai.

"Marayah, my angel," he croons, leaning across the bar with a naughty smile plastered on his face.

"You've got some nerve showing your face here, *Prince*." The statuesque female wipes her hands aggressively on a bar rag and tosses it over her shoulder, eyeing him with suspicion. She stands there, fists pressed into the groove of her waist, clearly immune to Kai's charm.

"Don't be cross with me, my sweet." His pointer finger flicks out to tilt her delicate chin upward. "I do apologize for not telling you."

"Don't apologize to *me*." She rips her chin from his grasp, hissing at the unserious prince. "Apologize to the males you cheated in cards and swindled out of their pants."

"I'd like to swindle you out of your pants," he purrs.

"Gag me." Marideth makes a retching sound, sliding Dover's hands around her waist.

Seething at Kai, Marayah's eyes narrow, and her upper lip pulls back from her teeth, revealing two tiny fangs. For a moment, I think she might leap across the bar and throttle him.

Instead, the savvy barmaid rips the rag from her shoulder and snaps it at him before sashaying away. A moment later, she slides a round of beers down the bar toward us, casting a knowing look at Kai. The crowd of fae erupts into applause as the trio finishes a song on a triumphant note.

"Let's dance!" Sorscha tugs us toward the floor as the next tune starts up. We snake through the thicket of bodies and join the carefree fray.*

Kai hoists Sorscha up onto a nearby table, and she spins in time to the music, arms outstretched, skirt fanning out around her. She beckons for us to join, and before I know it, we are packed on top of the table, stomping and clapping and singing

---

* Cue: *Grow Up Tomorrow* by The Beaches

along to sailor's songs. All except Jace, who watches from below, grasping the hilt of his sword. His stiff posture and composed demeanor make him stick out like a sore thumb among the jovial horde. Every once in a while, I feel the heat of his golden eyes on me before casually glancing away.

We throw back round after round, losing track of time and basking in the anonymity of the crowd. When my hair begins clinging to my neck, I hop down from the table, eager for some fresh air.

I eventually make it outside to the cool relief of the night air. The breeze kisses my fevered cheeks as I close my eyes and tip my head back against the uneven stone. Through the wall, I can hear the muffled, rhythmic stomping of feet mingling with the sound of crickets coming from the empty field across the way.

A sudden laugh spills from my lips as the absurdity of my current situation flashes through my mind. I thought I was crazy to stay here in this strange world. But now the only thing that seems crazy is going back to a life of ignorant bliss.

A world without magic.

I may never get back to the girl I was before I lost everything that mattered. And maybe that's okay. Because I can slowly feel myself becoming someone new.

I can feel myself healing.

It's a strange and beautiful thing.

A slight movement pulls my attention toward a skinny stray cat lingering by the corner of the building. I approach it, extending a gentle hand. The harmless-looking creature works up a nasty hiss and scurries away.

"Alright, then." I straighten and turn to find that I'm no longer alone.

Standing at the opposite end of the building is a tall, hooded figure. Even though their face is concealed, I'm certain from the height and imposing form that it's a male. A dark energy rolls off of him, and I immediately get the sense that this isn't just another city dweller looking for a bit of fun inside an ale house. He stands eerily still, with definitive purpose.

I stare at him, paralyzed, like a deer in headlights. When he takes his first step toward me, I break into a sprint, tearing around the corner and into a crowded alleyway. I bump into people as I brush past, earning a slew of angry glances and curses. My stalker weaves through the crowd, determined but unhurried. I can tell that if he wanted to, he could catch up to me in three easy strides.

But he's hunting me like prey.

Knowing I can't outrun him, I mentally prepare myself for a fight. Jace has taught me well. All I need to do is buy myself enough time for the others to notice I'm missing. Enough time for them to hopefully find me.

I brace myself to turn and meet my hunter and instead collide with a hard body.

Blinking, I gape up at Jace.

"What in the seven hells are you doing?" he says sternly, gripping my shoulders.

"Someone's following me." I glance back toward where the hooded figure is now darting away. Jace instantly brushes past me, barreling after him. My legs fight to keep up with their fae speed as they round the corner and duck inside the bar. I spill through the door after them and spot the dark hood bobbing through the crowd. We trail him up a set of stairs and scan the congested hall. But the figure is nowhere in sight.

"He can't have gotten far," I pant, winded from the chase.

"Go downstairs. Get Zadyn and the others and go," Jace commands, something dangerous darkening his golden eyes.

"But—"

"Go, witch. I'm serious," he snarls, exposing two glittering white fangs. He darts around a corner and disappears, not bothering to make sure I obey. I turn toward the stairs, but something clamps down around my mouth and hauls me backward.

A split second is all it takes for my attacker to drag me through the nearest door. My screams are muffled beneath the tight grip on my mouth. I wriggle my face upward enough to bite down on the leather-gloved hand with all my might. Blood coats my tongue as my assailant curses and jerks his hand away. I throw a quick elbow to his rock-hard torso, but he absorbs it unflinchingly, dragging me backward around the waist toward the open window.

"Jace!" I scream.

A millisecond later, the door flies open, and Jace bursts in. The figure releases me, causing me to trip backward over his cloak. A small scrap of fabric tears free, trapped beneath my heel, before he leaps out the window. Jace wrenches me back before I career down after him.

"Are you hurt?" His concerned eyes roam over me. I shake my head, still stunned. We simultaneously dash to the window, but there is no sign of him below. He's gone. Vanished.

I bend to scoop up the scrap of cloak, turning it over and fingering the silky maroon underside stitched with gold.

"We're leaving. Now."

The patch slips from my hands as Jace tugs me toward the hall and down the stairs. "I leave you alone for one second, and you manage to pull trouble from thin air."

"It wasn't my fault. He was following me," I shoot back defensively.

"You shouldn't have wandered off in the first place," he growls, still gripping my arm.

"I was going downstairs like you told me to when he grabbed me from behind."

"That was my intent. I left you alone to lure him out."

"So I was the bait in your trap." I rip my arm away but continue to follow him. "Nice."

"I've been doing this a long time, witch. I know how to catch a mouse."

"Clearly not, because he got away."

"If I wasn't so worried you were going to trip and crack your skull open on the way back to the castle, I would have gone after him. But it seems you need round-the-clock supervision, so here I am."

I shoot him a scowl as we reach the bottom of the stairs.

"Where are the others?" I turn, scanning the crowd. No trace of our friends on the tables or by the bar.

"I can take a guess."

Jace leads us back up the stairs, around a corner, to the last door on the left.

As he cracks it open, the smell of flavored smoke wafts toward me. I nearly choke on the thick scent. Through the haze of vapor, I spy Dover, Zadyn, and Sorscha seated around a cards table beside four brawny, exotic-looking males.

I spot Cece, Mar, and Ilsa off to the side, engrossed in the game unfolding.

More males of intimidating stature are scattered throughout the room, passing what looks to be a large hookah around. Their leather vests are cut low to reveal their golden-brown chests and the tattoos snaking up their thick, muscled arms. Gold hoops are pierced through their ears, lips, and brows.

Each set of hypnotic kohl-lined eyes snaps toward us as we enter.

"Party's over," Jace says firmly. Dover's concentration breaks as he peeks up from his hand.

"We'll explain on the way, but right now, we need to go," I add. Zadyn is at my side without hesitation.

Sensing the underlying urgency in our tones, Dover pushes back from his chair and extends his hand for Mar to join him. "Gentlemen. You heard the lady."

Sorscha gets to her feet, but the hand of the large, stone-faced fae beside her shoots out to grip her arm. She struggles against him feebly.

"You can't just leave in the middle of a hand!" He tugs on her small wrist, wrenching her down.

Jace shoves forward, prowling as he frees his sword.

"Better than *losing* a hand, wouldn't you agree?"

In an instant, the group of hulking leather-clad strangers has jagged blades drawn. Everyone freezes.

"For your troubles." Dover slowly raises one hand while tossing a sack of coins into the middle of the table.

The male holding Sorscha barks a laugh. "That's not nearly enough to cover what you and your friend cheated us out of last time. Where *is* your little prince friend, by the way? I've been dying for a reunion." He gives a curt nod, and within a second, the males have Cece, Mar, and Ilsa around their waists, knives pressed to their throats.

"Surely your females are worth more than a few measly gold coins?"

"I'll give you one last chance before I really lose my temper, friend." Jace takes another step toward them, a crazy glint in his eyes.

In defiant answer, the male tosses Sorscha into the arms of one of his renegade disciples and draws a dagger of his own, lunging for Jace. The room erupts into chaos.

The ladies scream and squeal as Jace tackles him backward into the cards table. It collapses beneath them as Zadyn and Dover surge forward, fists flying. One of the males drags

Sorscha toward the door by her hair. I grab the nearest chair and slam it into his back with all my might. The wood shatters beneath his rock-hard form. He turns to me with unnatural slowness, but that split second allows Zadyn to land a knock-out punch to his face. I gape at him, impressed, before he pulls Sorscha and me from the room. The rest of the girls race toward us, their captors incapacitated by Jace and Dover.

"Let's go!" I shout, ushering them from the room. Dover grips Jace around the arm and hauls him off the bloodied, unconscious male beneath him. Zadyn slams the door shut and rips off the handle in the process, discarding it as he hurries us forward. Loud bangs sound from behind us as we fly down the hallway.

"Where the hell is Kai!" Dover shouts.

"One guess," Mar snorts.

As we round the corner, Kai's mess of black hair pops into view. He has the pretty barmaid from earlier pinned against the wall—her thigh hoisted on his hip, skirts splayed around her shapely legs. She writhes against him, arching off the wall as his mouth devours hers.

"Kai!" Dover grabs him, pulling him off the female. He clings to her lips as her leg slides down the length of his.

"As you can see, Dover, I am indisposed." He wrenches free of his friend's hold and dives back into the kiss. A loud explosion sounds from down the hall as the tattooed cronies spill out after us.

"We've got company," Zadyn warns.

Kai's neck cranes, and his eyes widen before he turns his attention back to the female before him.

"I'll be back for you." He nuzzles her nose before releasing his grip on her voluminous hair.

"You'd better be." She bites her lip, watching him with feline hunger. He manages to squeeze in a kiss on her hand before Dover drags him away by the collar. Kai leads us to a small door hidden beneath the stairs, and we squeeze inside the tiny supply closet, packed like sardines. The door closes, and we are bathed in darkness.

"Do you have to make enemies of every pirate you come across?" Dover huffs at Kai.

"Oh, *please*, it was one game. Besides, those pirates are richer than me, the thieves."

"Well, then, next time, you can deal with them."

"How did you know this was here?" Mar pants.

"I'm a frequent visitor of this particular closet."

"Gross," she chimes, and I can't help but laugh as the exhilaration of the chase settles in me. I'm wedged between two hard bodies. Zadyn at my chest, Jace at my back. The sound of pounding boots shakes the ceiling above us as the mob of pirates careens down the stairs.

We give it a few minutes before we crack open the door and discreetly slip out the back, giggling at our narrow escape.

When we've all snuck safely back to our rooms, Jace slips through my door. Zadyn is already there, a tense look shadowing his forehead as I give him the details of the attack.

"You didn't see who it was?" Zadyn asks. I shake my head as he pushes off my vanity and approaches Jace, his arms crossed. "You should have followed him."

Jace gives him a sardonic smile, stepping up to him.

"That would have required ditching the witch, and since she can't be left alone for two minutes and you were distracted by a certain head of blonde hair, I didn't have much of a choice. Did you even notice she was missing, or were you looking for her in Cece's eyes?"

Zadyn coughs a laugh.

"Unlike some, I can protect her without smothering her. I've been doing it a lot longer than you."

"You failed to prove that point tonight."

Zadyn snarls in his face, and I wedge myself between them.

"I can manage just fine without the two of you going all alpha male on me."

Both their eyes dart to me.

"This finger-pointing is senseless." I push them farther apart. "I'm here in one piece."

The tension seems to ease a tiny bit. Stepping back from them, I say, "I didn't see his face, but I have a sneaking suspicion that my attacker was no petty thief."

I lean against the bedpost to kick off my boots.

"Neither do I. Rumor must be spreading about you," Zadyn points out, taking up his previous spot against the vanity. "It has to be someone in your inner circle." He nods at Jace, whose face is tight.

"The only ones that know are the small council, Gnorr, Mal, Max, and Warryn. They are all sworn to secrecy. Besides, I've known them all my life. They can be trusted."

"Everyone can be trusted until they can't be. How do you know there isn't a rat amongst them?"

"My men are my family. And the same small council has ruled with Derek since his reign began. It wasn't one of them."

I sigh, moving to the vanity to lean beside Zadyn. "So we keep our eyes peeled. Next time we go out, we stick together."

"There won't be a next time. Not for a good while," Jace points out. My face falls.

"What?! That's not fair."

"It's for your own safety. The castle is safe; the city is not. You are valuable goods, and it's my head on the line if something happens to you on my watch."

"Whatever," I mutter, rolling my eyes.

Jace gives me a long look before turning on his heel and heading toward the door.

"You know," I call after him, "you should be proud of me. I think I handled myself pretty well tonight."

He pauses halfway to the door, inclining his head toward me without turning back.

"That so?"

I nod proudly. "I bit my attacker. And I broke a chair over a pirate's back."

His shoulders bounce once as he laughs.

"Get some rest, witch. It will be dawn before you know it."

I heave a groan and redirect my eyes to Zadyn.

"The chair was pretty badass." A dimpled smile slowly spreads across his face.

I answer it with a wide grin of my own. Leaning my head on his shoulder, I sigh.

"I know."

21

"One second!"

I stuff my head through the hole of a loose-fitting peasant blouse and pull my wet hair free as another round of knocks rattles my door.

"Coming!"

I crack it open and am surprised to find Sir Max standing there, his closed fist suspended mid-air as he breaks into a lopsided smile.

"Sir Max," I breathe. He steps back to bow.

"My lady." His tone is laden with sarcasm. I roll my eyes, leaning against the door jamb.

"What can I do for you?"

"King wants to see you in his study."

I straighten, my heart suddenly racing.

"Now?"

He nods.

"Did he say why?"

"Yeah, and then he tucked me in and read me a bedtime story," he says facetiously, leaning on the hilt of his sword.

"Oh, shut up."

I close the door behind me and follow him. For some reason, I feel like a kid on their way to the principal's office. Did I do something wrong? Aside from flipping Jace off behind his back a handful of times, I can't think of anything.

Max dips his head toward me.

"How's training going?" he asks in a secretive voice. I glance up at him, pursing my lips.

"It's going. Your captain is a hard ass."

"Hah! You don't have it half as bad as his men do."

"Are you kidding?" I scoff. "Since I started training with him, I've lost all feeling from the waist down." I pat my hips. My legs are still numb from this morning's session.

"He's been known to have that effect on females."

I gasp, appalled and also secretly thrilled by that implication.

What the fuck is wrong with me?

Mind out of gutter, please. I repeat—*mind out of gutter.*

Max chortles at my reaction, tossing his head back. "I'm just saying, I'm sure he's going easier on you because you're a girl."

I huff, crossing my arms. "Oh, I assure you, he is not. He is merciless."

"Maybe so," he relents, still smirking. "He's been a little on edge lately."

"Really? I thought that was just his usual winning personality."

He shakes his head, blowing out a long breath. "Match made in the heavens, the two of you."

"Excuse me?" I choke.

"I've never seen anyone get under his skin like you do. Seems like the feeling is mutual." He chuckles under his breath. "It's pretty entertaining, actually."

I narrow my eyes at him.

"Look, whatever he's got you doing in training," Max gives me a sly once-over. "Keep it up. You look good."

I roll my eyes and smack him in the arm. Angling the focus away from myself, I ask, "Hey, where's your twin? Aren't you two attached at the hip?"

"I'm assuming he's with the queen." Max shrugs his broad shoulders.

I tilt my head in silent question.

"Mal is her sworn sword."

"Ah."

We round the corner to the king's study, and Max stops me a few feet from the door when we hear arguing inside.

"The night's watch saw you sneaking back into the keep last night. Or should I say this morning?" King Derek fumes, pacing behind the cracked door. "You know better than that."

"Like you never snuck out to have a little fun at my age? We went dancing. Nothing happened," Sorscha retorts.

"Something *could* have happened. Do you not understand the danger? Whose idea was this? Was it Kai's?"

I can feel his bubbling anger all the way down the hall.

"It was all of ours," she says. "Gods, this place is like a prison."

"Yes, a prison of privilege and riches and every luxury you could dream of. You poor creature."

"I would rather be poor and happy than royal and miserable," Sorscha boasts.

"You say that never having gone without your entire life."

"When are you going to stop treating me like a child?"

"When you decide to stop *acting* like one," the king says, smacking his hand down on the desk. He looses a long breath. "I have been more than patient. It's time you stopped partying and playing dress-up and started paying attention to politics. This is your legacy. My legacy. Your mother's legacy—"

"Do *not* bring her into this," Sorscha snaps, her voice sharper than I've ever heard it.

"Whether you like it or not, you need to settle down and start making heirs. This kingdom will be yours one day."

"I don't care! None of that has ever interested me."

"Well, unfortunately, this is your lot in life. Many have it far worse."

"You mean, unfortunately, I'm your only heir." Sorscha stands. "I'm sorry I wasn't born a male."

"That is not—"

"No matter what I do, I'll never live up to your expectations!"

"You've never even tried!"

Silence ensues.

"Sorscha, I won't be here forever to protect you—to look after you," Derek says a moment later, his voice more gentle.

"I don't need looking after."

"Everyone does." He sighs, sounding exhausted. "I have another meeting."

"Your Grace," Sorscha spits a second before the door flies open and she stalks out, scarcely missing us. We stare at each other open-mouthed for a beat.

"In you go." Max nods toward the door.

I swallow hard and step forward. After one knock, the door floats open of its own accord.

"Your Grace." I curtsy to the king, sitting at his cherry wood desk.

"Serena," he regards me, rising.

"If this is a bad time, I can—"

"No, no. Please come in." King Derek gestures for me to sit in one of the high-backed leather chairs across from his desk. He walks over and perches on the corner, his posture more casual than I've ever seen. But he looks worn out. Tired.

He runs a hand over his face, drawing his beard downward.

"I never dreamt that running a kingdom would be an easier feat than parenting."

"I'll take your word for it." I settle into the comfortable leather seat.

"I'm sorry if you heard all that." He explains, "Her mother passed when she was still young. I never quite learned how to talk to her the way she was able to."

"I'm so sorry."

He tips his head in thanks. A moment of silence passes between us.

"About last night—" I start, shifting in my seat.

"I didn't call you here to discuss last night."

"Really? You're not mad?"

"Oh, I'm furious. But not with you. My daughter is...a handful." He shakes his head, making a face.

"She's been good to me. Everyone has."

"I'm glad to hear it. I just wanted to check in. See how you're adjusting."

My eyebrows lift, and I inhale slowly, considering how I feel.

"I'm...adjusting."

"That poker face needs some serious work." Derek laughs, then takes a steadying breath. "Why are you uneasy?"

"You are...slightly terrifying," I admit.

"I'm aware." He suppresses a smirk. "Is that all?"

I loose a long sigh. Then the words flood out of me like a burst dam.

"There's just a lot of pressure. We're fighting against time here, and the sooner I can free my magic and become a warrior, the better. I just want you to know I'm trying my best. I mean, I'm giving it my all. I'm taking this seriously."

I stare up at him.

"I know that. The captain says you've been making progress."

I perk up against my will. "He said that?"

"I know you and I didn't get off to the smoothest of starts. You left behind an entire life, your family, your friends—"

"Actually, I didn't," I interrupt. A look of surprise flickers over his face. "I don't have any family. Not really. My dad died, and Zadyn's really the only friend I had. My life was...pathetic."

He studies me for a long time.

"Were you and your father close?"

A sharpness tugs at my heart.

I swallow, looking over the king's face—my father's face. He waits for my answer, completely oblivious to the fact that my dad's eyes peer out from his head. Every fiber of my being wants to hold him. To inhale his scent—that fresh laundry detergent scent that always made me feel so at home. Every part of me wants to spill the truth—the entire truth. To shout that I look like him because the universe is a cruel bitch with a sadistic sense of humor.

Instead, I force a smile and say, "Very."

"I was close with my father, too." He studies his calloused hands, the masculine rings on his fingers. "It was his life's goal to find you."

"Really?" I ask, inclining my head.

"He was convinced that you would be the answer to all of Solterre's prayers." He glances at me, offering up a rare smile that softens his entire aura. "When I was a child, he would put me to sleep with stories about the ancient Blackbloods. Their heroic feats, their bloody battles. I was fascinated by the witches—their traditions and culture. I studied their ways for many years." Derek folds his hands in his lap, interlocking his fingers.

"When my father died, I made him a vow. That I would find

you. And that I would prevent your line from dying out completely." He pauses. "Your arrival here is not coincidental. I fear something is coming."

"What do you mean?" I straighten.

"Just a feeling." Leaning forward, he braces his hands behind him on the desk. "I know we don't know each other all that well, but I have this—inexplicable faith in you. Faith that you will do all my father hoped you would. Don't disappoint me." His words are without threat, making them feel confidential and hopeful.

He trusts me.

"I won't," I manage to answer. He stands.

"I do hope that in time, you can be happy here. I understand that this is not the home you knew. But I want you to know that it is your home, nonetheless, if you so choose."

I nod gratefully, warmth spreading over my chest.

22

The queen's birthday feast is even more magnificent than Kai's welcome party. The Grand Hall is bedecked in flowers and draped in gold silk panels that hang from ceiling to floor. Polished golden ornaments and fixtures hover above the sea of beautiful heads.

The ladies and I get ready together in Sorscha's chambers.* It's been ages since I've done anything like that with girlfriends. We gossip and giggle as we sift through dresses from the hefty assortment delivered to her room. I select a lacy, silver gown with a full skirt and a diamond-encrusted corset.

We dance until our feet ache. I get tipsy on Pink Poison after two sips, and the party revolves around me like a beautiful carousel. Before I know it, we're drunkenly stumbling into the hall, back to Sorscha's chambers for one of her infamous afterparties.

Surprisingly, Jace does not excuse himself this time. It's oddly refreshing to watch him interact with our friends. He still

---

* Cue: *Chaise Longue* by Wet Leg

holds himself straight and proud, every inch of him the dutiful captain, but there's a rare ease about him. Seeing him and Sorscha standing close and seeming so familiar with each other, I can't help but conjecture about the extent of their relationship. It threatens to dampen my good mood.

"Cheat!" Marideth slams her hand of cards down on the table, flinging an accusatory finger at Kai. The table shakes under her force, silver goblets of wine and ale spilling over the side. Kai holds his hands up innocently as the room erupts into chaos.

"He always does this!" Mar shouts over the noise, knocking back her seat as she shoots to her feet. "No, no, no. I am not giving you my Stygian horse! She'd throw you thirty paces if you even *attempted* to mount her!"

Kai's melodic laughter sends her over the edge. She tosses her cards in the air, and they rain down over our heads.

"I'm done with his game. If you can't play by the rules, don't play at all!"

I try to stifle my own giggles at her seething outburst. Her anger sends Dover into a laughing fit of his own and he wraps his arms around her from behind, cooing to her. She jabs her elbow into his ribs.

"Game over," the princess declares, leaning back in her chair and shaking out her lustrous curls. "What now? Shall we call for some music?"

"Do or die!" Ilsa's little voice pipes. Her white-blonde hair has already grown back to her chest in the months that have passed since she lost over a foot of it to the drunken game. Fae hair grows exceptionally fast.

Lucky bastards.

The princess claps her hands together, bouncing in her seat. Jace watches from behind her, leaning against the wall with a casual grace that threatens to break my heart. I clear my throat, redirecting my attention to the table.

"How do we play?"

"Well, first, you finish the rest of that drink"—Sorscha points at me sternly—"and then you choose 'do' or 'die.' You either do whatever we tell you to, or you have to die by telling us a truth—something wildly outrageous or embarrassing. Preferably your deepest, darkest secret." Her eyes glint.

"So, it's truth or dare," I conclude, glancing at a messy-haired Zadyn, who nods in response.

"Truth or dare?" Cece asks, looking devastating in her low-cut powder blue gown.

"Oh, that's just what we called it where I grew up," I dismiss.

"In the temple?" Kai eyes me with blatant curiosity. "Who'd you play with, the priestesses?"

"No, no," I fumble. "There were others there that were my age. A few orphans. We used to play together."

"Huh. Interesting." The slow smirk that spreads over his face is full of mischief.

"Who is first?" Sorscha bubbles, her joy barely containable.

"Me." Cece leans forward with sensual grace.

"Do or die, Ceec?" Kai twirls a lock of raven hair around his long finger.

"Do, obviously." She brings a silver goblet to her lips and takes a slow sip.

"Kiss someone in the room for ten seconds," Ilsa orders. We all look at her and burst into laughter.

Cece eases back in her chair, contemplating. Her gaze travels around the table before snagging on Zadyn, seated between us.

Her hand shoots out to grab him by the collar, hauling his lips to hers. Zadyn freezes, his eyes widening in surprise. I, however, am not the least bit surprised by her choice. When she deepens the kiss, Zadyn's eyes drift shut, one hand moving to her head, the other to her waist, drawing her closer.

I know Cece isn't doing it for show. But then again, Zadyn doesn't look like he's having the worst time, either.

The group chants as I stare at them, open-mouthed. "Five! Four! Three! Two! One!"

Cece doesn't release him there. At least two more seconds pass, and just before she pulls away, her tongue flicks out to lick his lips. She slumps back in her chair, smug and self-satisfied. Everyone around us hoots and hollers.

"Damn, Ceec." Dover laughs, tipping his glass to her.

Zadyn's face is flushed as he sits back in his chair, suppressing a bashful smile.

"I think it's Serena's turn." Cece eyes me, her honeyed voice dripping in challenge. I'm sure she's used to people shrinking beneath those cunning green eyes. But not me.

"Do." I straighten.

"Brave female," Dover commends with a silent clap.

"Serena, my love. You may wear anything in this room," Kai croons, arching a dark eyebrow. "*Except* for clothing."

I roll my eyes at him.

"Could you be more obvious, Kai?" Mar teases.

"About what? The fact that I find Lady Serena to be a truly staggering female or the fact that my greatest joy as of late is making her blush?"

Instead of a witty comeback, I stride over to the window beside Jace, grabbing hold of the rose-colored brocade curtains. With a hard tug, the heavy drape falls into my waiting arms. I turn to Kai and dump them into his seated lap.

"Hold this," I command.

Excitement dances in his ocean eyes as he rises to his feet and lifts the curtain, his arms outstretched. I tug at the laces of my dress, and it pools to the ground in a heap. Kai's eyes start to wander as I slip out of my underclothes.

"No peeking," I snap.

When I'm fully nude behind the drape, I wrap it around myself, like a towel tucked beneath my armpits. The group applauds as I do a presentational twirl.

"How chic, cousin!" Sorscha giggles as I pad over to my seat, clutching the material together at my chest. Zadyn shakes his head, laughing at me under his breath.

"Dover, you're up," I tell him.

"I've got one, I've got one." Kai twists around in his chair to peer at Dover, who's perched on the back of the couch.

"You just went, Kai!" Mar objects.

"And I didn't even choose yet!" Dover protests, holding out his hands.

"Oh, Dove, we all know you always choose do, so let's just skip it and get to the good part."

He pauses dramatically. We wait.

"A full streak, if you please. One lap around the grounds."

"Does that include the gardens as well?" Dover crosses his arms.

"Absolutely."

The ladies squeal in delight. Dover eyes Kai with a challenge in his stare as he straightens off the couch and begins to unbutton his fitted jacket. He tosses it at Mar like a Chippendales dancer before moving to the laces on his trousers, ripping each one free with emphatic showmanship.

Kai's voice halts his deft fingers. "And you can't use the main exit." He nods his head to the curtain-less window.

"You bastard." Dover shakes his head. He continues to strip, tossing pieces of clothing at the ladies, who catch them with rigorous cheers. Once he is fully naked, he struts over to the window, proud as a peacock. I do my best to keep my eyes above his waist, but even in my periphery, I can tell he's well endowed.

"Get a good look, ladies," he brags, heaving the window open and glancing downward.

"Little chill in the air, Dove?" Kai teases. Dover flips him off and climbs over the sill, his head disappearing from sight.

We all rush to the window to watch him scale the four stories down the trellis and drop onto the grass beneath. When he reaches the ground, he waves up at us.

"The party guests are probably on their way out now." Sorscha giggles, covering her mouth.

"Exactly, which is why there is no way I'm missing this." Kai hauls himself out the window and follows after him. He glances up at our heads, poked out the window, and motions for us to join. "Come on!"

"We can't climb in these dresses, Kai!" the princess yells, her liquor-laced voice echoing into the midnight expanse.

"Then take them off!"

Sorscha looks at Marideth for a moment, and then they begin to strip. Cece gives an annoyed sigh but follows suit, casting a seductive glance at Zadyn as she slides her gown over her shoulders and begins to shimmy out of it.

I refrain from rolling my eyes.

Once the ladies are down to their corsets, bloomers, and tights, they begin to file out the window.

"You're insane!" I shout at them.

"Come on, cousin!" The princess squeals as she lowers herself down.

"Please, be careful," Jace says from beside me. She waves him off with a coy little grin. I glance at Jace, who seems to have no intention of joining the escapade. Cece brushes between us, her white camisole clinging to her curves. She tosses her golden hair over her shoulder, nearly taking out my eye, and looks back at Zadyn.

"Are you coming?" Her voice is a sugar-coated dare.

He peels off his jacket and follows her wordlessly down the trellis. Their bodies grow farther away until they are ant-sized on the ground below. Dover bolts toward the gardens, covering his loins, the rest of the boisterous crew hot on his heels. An affectionate smile blooms on my face at the sound of their distant laughter.

"You don't want to join them?"

Jace breaks my reverie.

"I don't have a death wish." I nod toward the trellis. "You?"

"It wouldn't be appropriate to be seen around the castle, enabling a handful of streaking nobility."

"The breaks of being captain, I guess." I sip my wine and set it down on the ledge.

"It has its advantages," he says softly. *

Our hands rest on the window sill, side by side, our pinkies nearly touching. I'm hyper-aware of his every breath, his every move. That's when I realize I'm standing an inch from him, wrapped in nothing but a curtain. He notices the sudden tension in me as I drop my gaze.

"No need to be shy. I've seen more than a set of bare shoulders in my lifetime." He looks from me to the open window. The soft breeze bristles my hair, and I tuck a strand behind my ear.

"I'm not shy," I murmur. The sidelong glance he slides my way tells me he remains unconvinced. His gaze falls to my bare arms. He reaches out and grips one in his large hand.

"You're getting stronger."

"I know." I watch as his thumb sweeps up my arm in a way

---

* Cue: *Gasoline* by HAIM feat. Taylor Swift

that feels more than casual. I momentarily leave my body. "What are you doing?"

"I'm admiring my work."

"Your work? It's my body!" I scoff.

"That I have been training, honing, and sharpening for months."

"You are...really something." I shake my head, glancing down to where the group has disappeared into the hedge maze.

"I'm good at my job, is what I am." His answering smirk is unnerving.

"You're an ass."

He rests his elbows against the window sill and peers up at me.

"Have I or have I not made you capable of putting a fae on their back with no magic and no weapons?"

"You may have shown me the steps, but I'm the one dancing."

He scoffs. "Don't get cocky. *I* can still have you on your back in a second."

I cross my arms over my chest, leaning my hip against the window.

"The thought of that is—"

"Terrifying?" he supplies.

"Revolting, I was gonna say."

"It wasn't the night you kissed me."

I come up short.

"I thought we agreed to forget about that?" I finally say.

He's quiet for a long time, staring out the window.

"I tried." He swallows hard, then turns back to me, his gaze trailing down to my lips. "I really don't think I can."

His admission sends a flood of heat through me. I want to kiss him so badly. I almost think I'm imagining it when his hand reaches up to brush his thumb over my lower lip. He stares, transfixed, as my heart thunders behind my bones.

"I can hear your heart," he says in a bedroom-soft voice. "It's racing."

"I'm not used to you being nice to me," I lie smoothly. "I'm worried hell's about to freeze over."

"I'm never nice."

"You're nice to Sorscha." I don't mean to say it, but it slips out, breaking the moment's spell.

"Everyone is." His voice is tight as he retracts his fingers, and disappointment settles over me. "As are you. And you're an absolute menace most of the time, witch."

I don't acknowledge the mild gibe.

"I didn't know." My words are barely audible, but he directs his eyes to me, waiting for me to continue. He doesn't so much as blink as our friends' shouts drift up to us from below.

"I didn't know that you and Sorscha were...together. I wouldn't have kissed you if I had."

"We're not together. Not yet. And something tells me it wouldn't have mattered anyway. You were...unstoppable."

"I'm not like that," I say. And I mean it.

But standing here wanting what isn't mine, I feel guilty as sin.

"You seemed upset. That I went to Zadyn first."

"Not at all." He chuckles. "I felt sorry for him, actually. Poor bastard, panting after you day and night only to have you reciprocate when your judgment is impaired. It probably killed him to deny you."

"That's ridiculous. Zadyn has never *panted* after me."

Jace gives me a dubious look, angling himself to face me.

"Either you are willfully ignorant or even more unobservant than I gave you credit for."

"Neither. Maybe you're just wrong." I dare a step closer.

"Mmm, not so. Where's that famous Blackblood intuition?" Moonlight dances off the gold in his eyes.

"Buried with the rest of my magic, probably." I sigh, leaning back against the window. "I don't know what we're going to do."

"It's a problem that won't be solved by two wine-addled minds in the darkest hours of the morning."

"It's just frustrating." My eyes burn into the back of the sofa. "To have this power inside of me but not be able to understand how it works or how to free it."

"We will keep trying."

"All I have done is try." I turn to look at him. "I'm bending over backward to be what you want—what the king wants. I'm playing the part of courtier, the part of warrior, the part of witch. I feel like an imposter." He studies me as I vent. "I'm none of those things. Not really. I'm just pretending to be part of this world, and every day, it becomes clearer that I don't belong. That I'm nothing like the rest of you."

"That's because you aren't."

I look at him as he pushes off the window and comes to stand in front of me, arms crossed over his chest. His eyes burn into mine.

"You, witch, are more powerful than any of us. At least you will be when we figure out how to unleash your magic. And we will."

"How do you know that?"

"Because you're the most stubborn person I know. And you're smart. Smarter than you give yourself credit for," he adds quietly.

"Okay, now I know hell's freezing over if you're giving me a compliment."

"They're not compliments. They're facts."

"Right, because you don't do compliments."

"Oh, I do compliments. I could bullshit you with odes dedicated to your eyes. I could write songs about the color of your cheek—" He brushes a loose tendril of hair off my shoulder, leaving it naked and exposed to him. "I could tell you that the tiny freckle just beneath your bottom lip haunts my dreams."

For a moment, I think he might touch me.

Might take my face in his hands.

Might set me on fire.

"But you won't." My words are barely a whisper. There is more spoken in the look between us than either of us is able to voice.

"No. I won't."

"Because you don't actually believe any of that or because it would be inappropriate given the fact that you're courting my 'cousin?'"

He says nothing.

"Do or die," I dare.

"I'm not playing with you." His jaw is set.

"Then just answer my question!"

"Both!" He explodes. "You suffer from the impression that your willfulness is charming—endearing—when in actuality it is infuriating and obnoxious. I don't *like* you. I am not your friend. I am here to train you, not to rain praises upon you. I am meant to harden you. To make you strong. I'll leave the coddling to your familiar."

Hot tears spring to my eyes at his sudden outburst. I can think of a hundred comebacks to hurl at him, but I no longer have the energy.

"I was only teasing," I say, feeling the heat creep into my cheeks. "But it seems I've pushed you too far tonight."

Gathering up the curtain in one hand, I suddenly feel so silly and naïve. I avoid his heavy stare to hide the tears welling in my eyes.

"It's getting late. Tell the others I went to bed." I start toward the door, but he wraps his hand around my arm, pulling me to face him. Upon seeing the hurt in my eyes, a softness crosses his face, a look of regret that he quickly masters.

His voice is thick when he speaks, as if it requires some effort. "I'll escort you."

"I would truly rather you didn't." I pull my arm away and head out the door without another word.

23

The next morning, when Jace knocks on my door for training, I don't answer. I don't stir from bed to dress in fighting leathers or braid my hair back. Instead, I pull the covers tighter over my head like a defiant child.

More knocks rattle my door. Then there's a loud bang, followed by the sound of furious footsteps. Jace yanks the covers back and glowers down at me.

"Rise and shine, little witch."

"I'm not training today. Please leave."

"Are you breathing?"

"Excuse me?"

"Well, if you can talk, you can breathe, which means: training. Now."

"I'm taking a personal day." I shrug and steal the covers back from him, hauling them over my head.

"When I say you can take a personal day, you'll get a personal day."

Before I can protest, he rips the covers off, reaches down,

and tosses me over his shoulder. I shriek and pound my fists against his back.

"If you can get me to stand down, you can have your personal day."

"Put me down now!" I hiss.

"If you can't make me, then you haven't earned a day off."

Fine.*

I pull my calf back and bring it down hard between his legs. A loud groan bursts from him as he drops me, and I stumble back, colliding with the beautiful antique vanity. It knocks into the wall, shattering the mirror and sending bottles of perfumes and oils crashing to the ground. Sharp pain spikes through me as I land in a pile of tiny glass shards.

Jace stalks toward me. I grab the longest shard I can find and fling it at him the way he taught me to with a dagger. It sticks in his upper arm. He slowly lowers his gaze and pulls it out like it's no more than a splinter, discarding it on the ground.

"Your aim isn't total shit. Still missed, though."

He taps his chest and lunges forward. In a maneuver he taught me, I twist out of his grasp, reaching for the sword sheathed at his side. I whirl around and raise it above my head. For a moment, Jace seems impressed. Then he catches my wrists midair and drives his knee up into my stomach so hard that I double over, gasping. The sword clatters to the ground as my knees dig into the jagged crystals. Jace's boots crunch over the glass as he crouches before me, cold and cruel.

"Giving up so easily, witch?"

Traitorous tears blur my vision, and not just from the physical pain. Then his hand shoots out to grip me by the throat.

"You're vulnerable. Exposed," he growls, giving me a rough shake. "What are you going to do?"

---

* Cue: *Little Chaos* by Orla Gartland

I claw at his face and hands, tearing his skin with my nails. The scrapes heal as fast as they appear.

"Have I taught you nothing?" he spits.

Losing my temper, I reach out and dig my thumbs into his eyes. He staggers back, and I scramble to my feet again, lunging to gather the sword in my bloodied fists. I hold it out in front of me defensively, panting hard.

My form is total shit right now, but I can barely stand upright without swaying.

Jace approaches, eyes wild with fire. I take a swipe at him, which he casually sidesteps as he pulls a dagger from his belt.

"Better. What's your next move, witch?"

I rush toward him like a bull, but he evades me, and I go flying into Zadyn's door so hard that I fall through it, landing in a heap of splintered wood. A shrill female shriek rings out, but I don't have time to search for the source. My head swims as I slowly attempt to get to my feet.

"*What the fuck is going on?*" Zadyn shouts, rushing toward me, wearing nothing but a bedsheet.

Jace kicks in what's left of the busted door and steps through.

"Training," he says wickedly, his golden eyes red and swollen from my assault.

"This is over. Now," Zadyn snaps, gripping me by the arms to help me kneel.

"Touch her, and I will drive this clean through your chest," Jace threatens, his voice even.

"She's hurt! What the hell is wrong with you? This isn't training—this is abuse!" Zadyn growls in Jace's face, more furious than I've ever seen him. Jace bellies up to him, welcoming the challenge of male dominance.

"She's tough. She'll survive. Step back, or you'll be the one that gets hurt."

"*Don't you touch him,*" I spit from the ground, venom coating my voice.

"Are you going to stop me?" Something terrifying gleams in his eyes. A cruel challenge.

In a flash, Zadyn has him pinned against the wall. They grapple with each other before Jace lands a thick punch to his jaw. I shout and rush him, clawing at his arms, his leathers. But he's a mountain.

"Get off of him!" I pound Jace's back pathetically. He throws Zadyn to the ground and draws a second dagger.

"Pick it up," he spits, tossing the blade to the floor. Zadyn glares at him, but obeys.

"Stop it. Right now," I demand, eyeing the dagger Jace is twirling in his lethal hand.

"Make me, little witch." He rushes Zadyn, and they roll, taking out the nearby desk with a loud crash.

I frantically scan for Jace's sword, but my muscles lock when I see him lift the dagger over Zadyn's heart and bring it down.

My answering scream is earth-rending. It feels like a tether snapping inside of me. The last straw of my sanity rupturing in a flood of rage, pain, and fire. Every inch of me feels like a flame as I unleash my anguish into the world. It shoots out of me from a well so deep it actually frightens me.

Because uncapped, I don't know that I can ever rein it in again.

Everything around me fades. I see and hear nothing.

Then I am being gripped around the waist and thrown from the room.

Someone shouts my name, shaking me. But I can't open my eyes. I can't move. I am stuck in total darkness.

A splash of cold washes over my head, my face, and I suck

in a breath, trying to make sense of the whispered shouts overhead.

"Wake up," someone says, their voice edged with panic.

Slowly, my eyelids peel back. So many eyes, so many heads, peering down at me.

"Get Warryn. *Now!*" Jace's command is tight and muffled to my ringing ears. He looks down at me wide-eyed. I shift my gaze to Zadyn, whose expression is that of concern.

"She's still burning up."

"Get her in the bath," Jace says. "Ice cold."

I'm lifted into the air, then gently submerged in cool water. The icy temperature increases with every labored breath I take until the cold reaches the point of pain. I try to lift myself up. Strong hands slide beneath my arms and haul me out of the freezing bath. Someone wraps me in a towel and sets my feet on the ground. I shiver in my soaked, bloodstained night dress and open my eyes to Zadyn holding me upright on the edge of the tub.

"Are you alright? Can you speak?" he asks, smoothing the wet strands of hair back from my face. I nod in confusion, glancing between him and Jace. Their handsome faces are covered in ash. Jace's clothes are tattered and singed as he stands before me, arms crossed.

"What just happened? Did I blackout?" I croak and launch into a coughing fit. Zadyn stabilizes me, keeping me from falling back into the frigid water. Jace shakes his head in disbelief, kneeling before me on the floor. I hear loud, hurried voices outside the bathroom door.

"You set the room on fire," Jace says. "When I turned my knife on Zadyn, you erupted into flames."

"What do you mean?" I glance between them. "How—how did—"

"Your magic," Jace says, some distant cousin of pride twinkling in his golden eyes. I bolt from the room, broken glass cutting into my bare feet with every careless step until I stand before the busted door frame leading to Zadyn's room.

It is completely unrecognizable. Every surface is covered in black ash and glowing embers. Young Sir Warryn stands among the rabble, hands outstretched as a frosty chill spreads throughout the singed space, taming what's left of my destruction. The auburn-haired twins, Mal and Max, supervise from the side. Mal notices my presence and slides a curious glance my way. I can tell it's him by the cold, unflinching stare and hard-set mouth.

"Oh my god," I gasp, clutching my towel. "I—I did that?"

"Congratulations, witch," Jace says from behind me. "You earned that personal day."

I turn and fix my gaze on him, fighting the impulse to throw my arms around him. To kiss him stupid.

Instead, I walk toward him, each step determined, as I bring my fist across his face with all the strength I can manage. To my shock, it takes him to the ground.

My punch actually knocked him off his feet.

He laughs, the sound light and amused. He stares up at me, golden eyes perplexed but dancing.

"Amazing," he whispers. "Your strength."

"What the *fuck* is wrong with you?" I screech. "First you attack me, then you try to kill Zadyn?!"

"Oh, calm down. I wouldn't have actually hurt him. It was for show. I was pushing you."

"You don't use people as bait! It's barbaric," I hiss.

"It worked, didn't it?" He gets to his feet, unfazed by my assault. "You should be thanking me. You needed a shove to access your magic. And look, you burnt that room to a crisp."

"You are a manipulator," I spit. "Not to mention, your brilliant plan could have easily backfired. I had no idea what was happening to me. I was completely out of control. I could have burned you both alive."

"But you didn't," Jace amends. "And now we know your magic is triggered by strong emotion. What did you feel?"

"I wanted to kill you," I admit, recalling the overpowering emotions. "I felt rage. Pain. Fear...fear of loss." My eyes land on Zadyn's, and his answering look is filled with grim understanding.

"Now we have something to work with." Jace looks between us. He turns to a wide-eyed servant by the door. "Send for Gnorr. Tell no one what you saw." The young female nods and disappears into the hall.

"You should sit down," Zadyn says. "There's glass everywhere."

"My feet are already destroyed." The initial shock has worn off, and I wince with every step I take toward the bed. The glass shards embedded in my arms and legs are now making themselves well known.

"Is someone going to explain to me what in the seventh hell just happened?" A low-tenored female voice makes me turn my head.

Standing behind us, her beautiful face baffled, is Clemence. Wrapped in nothing but a bed sheet. Ash decorates her tangled golden hair.

I knit my eyebrows together. When did she sneak in? Oh, god. If she saw what I did, my cover is blown.

"What are you doing here?" My voice lashes out more harshly than I intend.

"We were asleep when you two burst through the door like a pair of wildcats. Seconds later, the room was on fire." Her green eyes narrow as her gaze skips between the three of us.

"Cece," Zadyn starts, "I'll explain everything, but you have to promise to keep what you saw a secret."

"Half the castle staff heard the noises and came running. The entire wing reeks of smoke." She gestures to the hall, then fixes her suspicious eyes on me.

"Please," Zadyn beseeches her. She rolls her eyes but gives a relenting nod. I glance from her to Zadyn as the realization sinks in. He stares back at me, searching for my reaction.

"Get out," I say quietly, turning my gaze away from him. "Everyone."

"Serena—" Zadyn starts. I hold up a hand, cutting him off.

"Zadyn, I don't want to hurt you. And I don't want to find out what happens if I get frustrated again. Take her and get out." My voice is cold. I don't know why I feel deceived, but the stirring of my magic is there, and I won't risk endangering him again.

"Alright." He stands. "I'll come back to check on you in a bit."

He guides Cece from the room with a hand on her lower back. I face forward, staring at the wall adjacent to my bed. The door closes, and I think I'm alone until Jace plops down beside me.

"We should move you. It's not good to breathe in all this smoke."

"I'm not moving. Please go."

"You should be thrilled right now. Instead, you're jealous that your Zadyn slept with Cece?"

"That's what you have to say to me right now?" I level a glare at him. He quirks a brow in opposition. "I'm not jealous."

"Liar. You want him to only have eyes for you." Before I can protest, he presses on. "He is even dumber than he is pretty. Bringing her to his bed, with you just on the other side of the door. That was a foolish mistake. And a dangerous one."

"I'm around her every day."

"That's completely different. This was too close to home. It leaves you exposed. It makes him vulnerable, making you vulnerable. But Cece's right. There were plenty of witnesses to what happened. We can talk to her—feed her some story—but the servants heard and saw too much. We'll need to meet with the king, gather all the witnesses, and do something about it."

"Like what? Bribe the staff to keep my little display a secret? What's the point? People are going to find out, eventually. I just want to stop pretending." I shift, putting weight on my glass-spiked palm. I wince as a wave of stinging pain splices through my hand. Jace takes it in his own and begins to tenderly pick out the shards. I watch him, feeling defeated.

"It will be the king's decision," he says. "You should be elated right now. This was a major breakthrough."

"I—"

"What."

"I don't feel anything. I feel numb. I wasn't even trying to do that."

My memory flashes back to several months ago, standing on the second floor of Tatler's books, staring at my hands after they burned holes through the table of their own accord. It was the feeling of being completely out of control.

"That was only the surface of your power," he tells me. "We're going to find out what else you can do so we understand how to control it."

My throat thickens as I glance at him. I want to lean into his shoulder. I want him to hold me and tell me I'm alright. That I'm not damaged beyond repair, and that this power is not something to fear but to master. I want someone to just tell me it will be okay.

The pain of him being so close and so far away is worse than a million glass shards embedded in my skin.

"You..."

"*What?*" he whispers, his voice fervent.

"You look so much like someone I know." Swallowing becomes difficult with his golden eyes searing into me.

"You said that to me once before. You were close?" His gaze flutters back to my bloody hand.

I nod. "It's just...hard sometimes. To look at you," I admit with a sigh. "But other than that, you're nothing alike."

He watches my face for a long time. "I would say I'm sorry about this"—he extracts another splinter—"but I'm not sorry that you finally harnessed your power. You understand why I did it, don't you?"

"Not really." I huff a laugh.

"I want you to be strong so that you can endure whatever comes your way. I want you to be steady and calm in the face of threat. It's for your own good." I stare at his fingers as they move over mine.

"Can I trust you?" The question falls out of me before I can filter it.

"Probably not."

I laugh grimly. "At least you're honest."

"I'm a realist." His golden eyes flicker up to mine. "I have no qualms about admitting that my interests lie in serving the king. I won't fail in my duty. If it's a Dragon Rider he wants, then I intend to make you a Dragon Rider. That is my sole mission right now."

And what about this? You and me? I almost ask. We had a moment last night before he went from Mr. Hyde to Dr. Jekyll and practically ripped my head off for flirting.

But to even open up that topic would be more pain than it's worth. It would require both of us forgetting about Sorscha. Me forgetting about Jack. Replacing him in my heart for a different male with the same face.

And worst of all, it would mean admitting that I have real

feelings for this person, this hard-crusted warrior, that I have been trying desperately to stomp out.

Gnorr bustles through the door, cutting my reverie short. She pushes a cart of medical supplies over to the foot of the bed.

"Heard you had quite the episode." She winks at me, her robes billowing as she stops before me. "Off you go, Captain." She tosses him a look, but he doesn't move.

"I'm staying. She is my responsibility."

Gnorr looks to me for confirmation.

"He can stay."

"Very well. At least give me some room to work, Captain."

He releases my hand to sit in the chair across from the bed, watching Gnorr go to work. She lays me back and makes fast work of healing my minor cuts, lifting up two soft, crinkled hands and floating them an inch above me. The splinters extricate themselves from my skin and hover beneath her fingertips as if her hands were magnets drawing them out. I watch in amazement as she lowers a bowl beneath them, and they gently fall into its waiting depths. She places them aside and douses a linen with a pungent clear liquid. I hiss at the sting as she dabs at my scrapes.

Gnorr asks us to give her a recap of my "episode." Jace does most of the talking because I have no freaking idea what happened when I blacked out.

"I would recommend, Captain, that you not provoke her in future. There are other ways, safer ways, to extract magic."

She finishes up with me, then insists on checking Jace for any injuries. Aside from a couple of already healing cuts, he's fine. As Gnorr is leaving, a steward passes a note to Jace. He opens it and looks at me.

"What is it?"

"The king," he says, holding up the folded paper, "heard of

your episode this morning and wants to sit in on training this week."

"You're kidding." I try to stand but get dizzy and fall back onto the bed.

"Easy, little witch. Don't go blacking out again." He helps ease me back. "This isn't a massive deal. He just wants to observe."

"And if he doesn't like what he sees?"

"Just behave and do as I tell you."

I bite my lip. I'm probably going to dream about those words coming out of his mouth tonight, only in a *very* different set of circumstances.

Speaking of which...

"I need to find Zadyn."

"He's probably—"

"Do not say he's probably with Cece."

"I was going to say he's probably settling into his new rooms since you turned his old ones into a pile of ash." Jace looks down at me.

"Well." I get to my feet. "Here goes nothing."

"This I have to see."

"Don't you have something better to do?"

"Better than watching you lay into your little guard dog? Absolutely not." He pauses. "But you should probably change out of that rag first."

I glance down at myself. The still-damp nightgown clings to me, leaving very little to the imagination. I open the armoire, throw on a pair of dark brown trousers and a thin knit sweater, and join Jace in the hall.

We track Zadyn down in his new rooms, which oddly enough happen to be closer in proximity to the princess's ladies. Wonder if that's mere coincidence.

"Knock, knock." I barge in, expecting him to have company.

Instead, we find him alone, looking distraught. He is seated at the rich wooden desk by the window, hands buried in his caramel hair.

"Hi." He stands abruptly. "Are you feeling better?"

"I'm peachy," I say with a bite. Jace enters the room behind me, and Zadyn's eyes darken as they shift over my shoulder to him.

"I was just about to check on you. There are some things I need to say." He walks around the desk, stopping before me. "In private."

"If she asks me to go, I'll go," Jace says with an edge to his voice. He stands behind me, chin lifted, chest back.

"What do you want to say, Zadyn?" I press, ignoring his request.

"Well, first of all, I'm sorry about Cece. I wasn't thinking clearly. I should have known bringing her back to my room would risk exposing you. Although I never saw *that* coming." He shoots Jace a pointed look. "I didn't mean for you to find out about her like that."

I laugh.

"So you're apologizing not because you slept with her, but because you chose to do it in the room adjacent to mine?"

"I'm apologizing because I'm *sorry*. For all of it." He lays an earnest hand on his chest.

"Why apologize to me? I'm not your mate."

My tone reeks of condescension. He looks stunned for a moment, as if I'd struck him.

"Yet you were upset when you saw her earlier."

"I wasn't upset. I had just set a room on fire by total accident. There was a lot going on." I cross my arms over my chest.

"Serena. I know you. Your face says it all. You all but threw us out of the room." He glances at Jace, watching intently by the door, before giving me a pleading look.

I know Zadyn won't say much else in front of him, and I should give him the benefit of the doubt.

I sigh and turn back. "Can you give us a minute?"

A hard expression clouds Jace's face, but he exits, leaving me to face Zadyn. The door clicks shut, and a stretch of silence ensues, where we stare at each other, unmoving. Zadyn caves first.

"You don't have to pretend it didn't bother you."

"It didn't, though. And I'm not sure why you would even think it would."

"Can you drop the act?"

"Can *you*?"

"Serena." He shakes his head. I toss my arms up, exasperated.

"You're allowed to do what you want, Zadyn. You can see who you want, fuck who you want—"

"Is there a reason I *shouldn't*?" he interrupts, taking a step closer. His chocolate eyes are wide and vulnerable in a way I've never seen. "I'm asking you now. *Tell me if there is* because I wouldn't—I won't...is there a reason?"

I've never seen him struggle for words. Usually, he is calm, cool, and collected. Smooth and polished. The perfect courtier. But for the first time, I wonder if Jace might have been right all those times he's implied that Zadyn wants me.

But that would be ridiculous. He's my familiar. He wants to protect me. He doesn't *want me*, want me. He probably sees me as a sister. A really annoying sister.

Still, I hesitate for a moment before saying, "No. You're free to do as you wish. You don't have to run it by me."

I turn away from him, studying the new room.

"If it's the fact that it was Cece that bothers you—"

It was.

"It wasn't. I told you it didn't bother me."

"I can tell you're not particularly fond of her."

"If you care so much about what I think, then why did you fuck her, of all people?" My tone is vicious.

He pinches the bridge of his nose. "It was one night. I know it's a terrible excuse, but we had been drinking for hours, and she was persistent." His cheeks flood with color. "But you have to know, I never thought that by bringing her to my room it would expose you. I had no idea Jace was going to pull a stunt like that."

"It was an unfortunate set of circumstances, but Jace meant well."

"Did he really?" Zadyn's features twist with rancor. "He threw you through a door."

"He did not. I fell."

"You always defend him. Even when he's hurting you. I'm telling you this because I care about you." Zadyn takes my hands and forces me to look at him. "Don't let your heart blind you to his faults. He's not perfect."

"I know that."

"You look at him like he's—"

"What?"

"Like he's a god."

I laugh. "No, I don't."

He sighs. "There are so many things you are running from. You need to start facing them."

His eyes are wary as they gloss over me.

"Come here."

He pulls me into his arms and I want to fight him. I want to tell him he's wrong and that he's an idiot but instead I settle into his warmth and breathe him in.

24

"The king," Jace says, selecting a heavy longsword off the weapons rack, "will be expecting you to perform like a proper Blackblood warrior. Now that your magic has manifested, the real countdown begins. He's been patient, waiting for your power to emerge, and now that it has, he will no doubt wish to speed things along." *

He presses the mother-of-pearl hilt into my palm and selects another sword for himself.

"We know you have the gift of fire," he says, turning to face me. "And I'm willing to bet that the last Blackblood has a lot more than that in her arsenal. You need to learn to call forth that power at will. To use it in tandem with your physical skills so that you are an unparalleled opponent."

Without warning, he attacks. My reflexes are fast. Not just fast from months of speed and strength drills with Jace. This is different. I'm *supernaturally* fast.

Our swords clang together as I block his swing, gritting my

---

* Cue: *The Wire* by HAIM

teeth beneath the weight of its force. Sparks fly as he runs his blade down the length of mine, then begins to circle me. I hold a defensive position, watching as he crooks his finger, urging me to attack.

I twirl the blade in my hand and thrust at his arm. He bats my sword away with barely any effort, and it clatters to the ground.

"Don't be predictable, witch," he drawls.

I bend to pick it up and cry out as his boot stomps down on my hand, the bones crunching beneath. I stumble back, gasping at my mangled hand in horror.

"You've been disarmed." His voice is filled with authority and harsh command. "What will you do? You have seconds." He circles me again like a vulture waiting to feast on my carcass. I cradle my crippled hand, feeling the pain lance through it.

"Does it hurt?" he spits, unrelenting. My answer is a glare.

"Fix it. Reach into that bag of Blackblood tricks and heal yourself."

"I don't know how to do that yet, you bastard," I hiss.

"You'd better figure it out because your enemy certainly won't wait patiently for you to get your shit together."

He advances, swinging his sword downward, and I tuck and roll to avoid being sliced straight down the middle. As soon as I'm up, I land a punch to his gut with my good hand. The force makes him bow, and I use the opportunity to drive my knee into his face. Blood stains my pant leg as he loses his balance, taking me to the ground with him. Ruined hand temporarily forgotten, we grapple on the floor, locked in a power struggle. He lands on top, his hand going for my throat.

"Pathetic! On your back in a matter of seconds. What's your next move, witch? Choke to death?" he snarls, bringing his bloody face close to mine.

He's trying to rile me. Trying to provoke me into using my magic.

Fine.

If it's magic he wants, then it's magic he'll get.

Closing my eyes, I sink into the familiar thrumming sensation beneath my skin. I reach down into myself, and when I come up, I haul whatever I can with me.

My body heats, but I don't realize how much until Jace pulls his hand back, the skin singed and angry. I throw him off and go for the sword again, stopping short when all the air rushes from my lungs.

I gasp and gasp. But no air will come.

I whirl toward him and his outstretched hand.

He's using magic. I didn't even know he had any of his own. He certainly never used it in the training ring before. My knees slam into the ground as I clutch at the phantom hands around my throat. I claw at my neck, desperate to get down a breath until I'm certain I'm turning blue.

If Jace wants to take my air, then I'll give him more than he ever bargained for.

I thrust my hands out and pray to whatever god is listening for this plan to work. A heavy gust of wind bursts from my palms and slams him back into the wall of the training ring. The chokehold releases, and I gulp down the sweet air.

"Air and fire." I tilt my head in challenge as I pant. "Wonder what else I can do."

"We're about to find out." He reaches into his belt and throws a dagger at my head.

Instead of moving, I catch it by the blade. In the hand that Jace destroyed moments ago. Only it is no longer twisted at odd angles or barking in pain. My hand is as good as new, save for the rivulets of blood streaming down my forearm from my leaking palm.

I unclench my fist, letting the dagger clatter to the ground. For a moment, I am distracted by the deep gash in my hand as it mends itself together, sealing until all that remains is a tiny pink mark. I turn it over in wonder.

That's when I see Jace's discarded sword begin to levitate.

I quickly scoop mine off the ground, gaping at the floating blade. It swipes at me as Jace leans against the training ring, looking unfazed. He's controlling the sword without even touching it. I block and parry, but the blade is relentless in its pursuit. I stumble, earning a deep gash in my forearm.

"Stop!" I shout at Jace. "I need to stop!"

Breathless, I block what would have been a fatal blow to my chest. I try mustering up some of that wind I used on him a few moments ago, but my well is dry. I can feel the magic sputter out, depleted.

Whirling toward him, I plead, "Jace! That's enough!"

That's when his sword swings around.

I see it in slow motion.

There is no time to block its trajectory, heading straight for my neck. My eyes snap shut, protecting me from the inevitable sight of my head toppling from its rightful place. I brace for the worst but feel the cool edge of the blade freeze when it meets my skin. I open my eyes to see the sword suspended in place, resting against my throat. Jace waves a hand, and it clatters to the ground.

"You're dead."

"Are you insane?!" I scream, my eyes blazing. "You could have killed me!"

"Oh, save the dramatics for the king." He brushes the dust off his shoulder.

"I will," I pant, stalking after him as he starts toward the rack. "And maybe then I'll explain to him how you nearly decapitated his only chance at championing the last potential

Dragon Rider. Or maybe I'll let you explain it to him and watch as *your* head rolls."

He snarls and advances toward me, power packed into every step.

"I would rather see you headless than on top of a dragon at this point. Just to have a moment's peace from that incessant mouth."

"I'm done training with you." I throw the sword at his feet and begin to stalk past him, wiping the sweat from my hairline. "Tell the king to find me someone else."

He catches my arm and jerks me to a stop.

"No one will prepare you better than I."

"And no one is more likely to stab me in the back while I'm not looking." I try to rip my arm away, but he tightens his grip. "For one second, *one second*, I thought you might have changed. After everything that happened yesterday, you were kind to me. I even justified your actions to Zadyn, thinking you did it for my own good. But here you are, back to your cruel, unfeeling self. You said it yourself—I can't trust you. So tell me how I can continue to train with you when I know how deeply you detest me? How you genuinely want me dead! You'd be happy if I was out of your hair and out of your life for good!"

"My life would be a lot easier without you in it, witch." His voice is quiet as his jaw twitches.

"*Why*," I demand. "*Why are you like this?*"

He tugs me forward sharply, his face an inch from mine.

"Don't you get it? You threaten to destroy every plan I've laid. I am on the brink of becoming Hand of the King. I am courting his daughter, the princess. I am expected to propose soon. Then you show up, and suddenly everything is on the verge of collapse. I can't think of anything or anyone else. I'm *obsessed* with you. Day and night, my thoughts wander beyond my control. And my head is needed elsewhere. I'm helping to inform decisions that impact an entire kingdom. And all I can think about is the moment when I can leave behind the politicking to train with you. So, yes, my life would be much simpler if you weren't here to taunt me, to tease me, to *torture* me every single day of my miserable life."

"*Jace.*" His name is barely audible on my lips.

He shakes his head in disgust and stalks away. Leaving me alone and baffled in the training ring.

~

April 2022

The apartment door slams shut like a punctuation mark at the end of a sentence. I plant my palms on the surface and force down deep breaths as I stare down at my water-logged shoes.

Three hard knocks shake my door. I squeeze my eyes closed and pray that he'll just leave.

"Serena," Jack says from the other side. I bite my lip to keep from crying out or making a sound.

"Please." The hurt in his voice is like a knife to my chest. "Baby, just let me in. I'm right here. Serena, I know you're there —I can hear you breathing. Can we just talk? Please? *Please.*"

I lean my head against the door, holding in the tears that threaten to explode from me.

"I'll stand here all night if I have to. I don't care. I'll wait."

"Jack," I croak, unable to stop myself, "just go. I can't do this anymore. I can't—" A heavy sob breaks through the surface, and I choke on my words.

"Open the door, baby. Come on," he says earnestly. Sweetly. Like he just wants to take care of me.

But I can't let him.

"I know you're scared," he says through the door, passion

saturating every word. "I'm scared too. But I want you. I want you today, I want you tomorrow, I want you on your worst day, your best day, and every fucking day in between. I don't care what happens. I just need you."

With every word, my heart thaws a bit more. But it's not enough to soften what has grown hard as stone and cold as ice in the months since my dad died.

My hand slides down the door to the lock. Jack pushes it open and stands there breathing hard, heavy raindrops dripping from his dark hair and pooling on the hardwood floor. I stand in front of him, shivering, arms folded around myself.

Jack takes one long step forward and folds me into his chest. I push my face into him, comforted by his familiar woodsy scent.

How is it possible to need someone so badly and also want to push them away at the same time?

"I love you," he whispers against the top of my head and plants a sweet, lingering kiss there. Another sob racks through me against my will.

"Talk to me," he pleads, pulling back and lowering himself to my eyeline. "Let me in." His hand strokes my face, but I can't look him in the eye, or I'll completely shatter. I keep my eyes focused on his lip ring and try to hold myself together.

"You know there is nothing I wouldn't do for you."

"You won't accept this as my decision."

"I think we need to be open to all options, don't you agree?"

"I told you I'm not getting married." I turn away from him, hardening as I strip off my drenched jacket and sink into the living room couch.

"Not now or not ever?" He follows me and kneels at my feet, his hands on my knees. "We can do this. We can have this baby."

"I don't want it," I snap. "I don't want any of it. I don't want this baby."

Lies. Such terrible lies.

He pulls back an inch.

"You don't want our baby?"

Of course I do, I want to scream. I want our baby, and I want you. Just not like this. Not when I am a shell of a person that you would tie yourself to out of obligation.

Instead, I respond with, "This is all hypothetical, anyway. I don't even know if I'm pregnant, Jack. This could all be over nothing."

"Well, you're late, and both tests came back inconclusive. But I think we're dealing with a bigger issue here, aren't we?"

"Only the doctor is going to be able to tell for sure. They have to do a blood test." I wipe away my tears with the back of my hand.

"And if it comes back that you are?" he presses. "What will you do?"

"I'll do what I have to."

"Why are you acting like you're in this alone? Like I'm some insensitive fuck who doesn't care if you keep it or not? I told you that I am in this."

"You never wanted kids, Jack."

"I do now. I want them with you." He grips my knees tightly in his tattooed hands. I stare at them while he speaks.

"I want to marry you. I told you that the night we met. Let me be here for you. Let me be in this with you."

"You proposed because you thought I might be pregnant, Jack. Don't deny it!" I say as he shouts over me, "That is not true!"

"Look at me and tell me you planned on proposing before you found out about this," I challenge. He hesitates for a fraction of a second.

"Not right away, but I knew I wanted to marry you."

I brush him off and get to my feet, running my hands down my face in frustration.

"My answer is no."

"You love me," he counters. I bite my lower lip and nod ruefully. "But you won't marry me or have this baby. You know, we're not kids anymore. This isn't some random teen pregnancy. We're adults. It's a lot harder to justify making a mistake and then just erasing the evidence."

"*There it is!*" I point at him. "Right there. This was a mistake to you. I knew it."

"That is *not* how I meant it, and you know it! We weren't careful, and now we may be facing the consequences of our actions. But we're old enough to take responsibility and deal with the circumstances."

"A mistake," I repeat, shaking my head.

"The only mistake here is sweeping it under the rug like it's nothing. Refusing to be with me because of your own pride."

"I don't want to be a circumstance you just found yourself in the middle of!" I shout.

"You're not now, and you never have been. *Goddamnit!*" he yells back, his deep voice echoing off the walls. He grips his hair at the roots and balls his fists.

"Why can't you let me love you?" *

I say nothing.

I can't.

I'm frozen in time. Speechless and numb.

"There's nothing you have to say?" His laugh is void of any humor. "*Serena.*"

My name is a plea on his lips. But his words go mute the second they leave his mouth, and I retreat further and further

---

* Cue: *The Way It Was* by The Killers

into my own fear. He continues, but I hear nothing—as if I'm submerged in water.

And I give him nothing. I stare blankly at him, not registering a word he's saying. Because I know what's about to happen.

I'm about to lose another person I love. I already feel the rift taking root. Because even if the test comes back and I'm not pregnant, we won't come back from this. He will resent me no matter what the results are, no matter what I do. And I already resent me enough for the both of us.

I am not who I was when we met. Grief has ravaged me. And the thought of loving another person so much and then watching them slip away is more than I can handle. He deserves someone whole. I am not that.

Jack is looking at me now, shaking his head, huge tears welling in his eyes. One trembling hand covers his mouth and the other grips his hip. He moves toward me and roughly grabs hold of my head. He presses his cold lips to my skin for five seconds, and I hear him say something that sounds like "goodbye."

Then he's out the door, and I'm alone.

In my head, I form a plan.

I'll have this baby. On my own. I'll try to piece myself together just enough to be a mother. I won't trap Jack into a marriage of obligation like my parents. I love him too much to watch us crumble the way they did.

But I have to leave tonight. I pack what I can fit in my car, and I start driving.

And I don't stop until I run out of road.

25

Jace's admission keeps me up all night. I am in a daze for the rest of the day, during my history lesson with Zadyn and later at dinner with the entourage. Jace doesn't show, thank god. I watch my beautiful friends exchange carefree smiles, looking light of burdens while I sit at the table, my heart heavy as stone, keeping dangerous secrets from all of them.

I toss and turn, oscillating between hot and cold, shivering beneath the silk sheets one minute and kicking them to the floor the next. Frustrated and sleep-starved, I throw a floor-length silk robe of the deepest eggplant over my bare shoulders and slip out my door as silently as I can manage.

My heart flips as I take in the tall figure outside my door. For a second, I think it's Jace, but it's just Sir Warryn.

"My lady." He bows his head. "Are you well?"

"Yes." I pull my robe tighter over my chest, feeling the chill of the hall. "I couldn't sleep. I thought I might just take a short walk to clear my mind."

"I would be happy to escort you."

"No," I decline. "Thank you, but I need to be alone."

"I was told by the captain to guard you with my life."

"And you are doing an amazing job," I compliment. "I don't see any imminent danger nearby. I'll stay close. I just need some solitude."

He looks wary but relents, nodding his head. "I understand. I will be here." I offer him as much of a smile as I can manage.

My mind drifts back to Jace. Turning his back to me in the training ring and stalking away. Just like Jack did.

I wasn't pregnant. I got my period the night after the big blowout. But by then, the damage had already been done. I knew I had pushed us past the point of no return.

After my father's death, I was so broken, so grief-ridden. I had never felt so alone. And even though I knew Jack was doing his best to ease my pain, nothing he did or said or promised would ever be enough. Nothing could fill that void except for time itself.

People say they're sorry, they send food and flowers. They ask how you're doing for the first year. But after that, they forget. The grace period is over, and you're expected to be healed, to be over it. Only those who have lived through a loss like that can truly understand. Jack tried his best, tried more than anyone else in my life to understand, but I pushed him away. I didn't want to know what it was like to love and lose ever again. After that fight, after I got in my car and drove south, he felt as far away as I did, lost at sea in a storm without a compass. So I buried my love for him where even I couldn't find it.

Until I saw Jace, and it ripped a gaping hole in an old wound. I might have thought he and Jack were one and the same when I first got here, and maybe that was what drew me to him in the first place, but I quickly learned that wasn't the case.

It's *Jace* I now care for. *Jace* I can't stop thinking about.

I can't stay away from him. And I don't want to. Pathetic as it sounds, if all he could offer me was a cold shoulder, then I would take it. No matter how degrading that is.

Maybe that's why I still need therapy.

Lost in thought, my feet lead me out onto the terrace where I first met Kai. I lean against the railing and stare out at the hedge maze beyond.*

Movement catches my eye near the entrance of the maze, and Jace emerges from the darkness, wearing a sullen expression. My stomach does a somersault. I watch as he ascends the stone steps, his posture somewhat morose from the way his shoulders curl inward. His eyes catch mine the second he reaches the top, and he slows, resting a hand on the railing. For a moment, I think he might just continue inside without a word.

But he pauses a foot away from me.

"Midnight stroll?" he asks.

I shrug. "Couldn't sleep. What's your excuse?"

He sighs and crosses the few steps to my side. Mimicking my posture, he leans his elbows on the railing.

"Guilty conscience." He looks out at the expansive grounds in their perfect condition.

"That's the worst."

A rueful smile tugs at his lips.

"It is." He studies his hands as his expression shifts.

"You have to know, I didn't mean what I said. About wishing you were dead," he admits. I give him the time he needs to continue. "It's the opposite, actually. In all my years as a warrior, as a servant to the king, I never expected that a little

---

* Cue: *Guilty As Sin* by Taylor Swift

witch would be my greatest challenge." He finally looks at me, his golden eyes electric. "But you are."

"How am I your greatest challenge? I've come a long way since the start of training. Don't say you disagree."

"That's not what I meant. And yes, you have come a long way. Your progress has been...astounding, actually. But the challenge was never in training you. The challenge has been exercising my own self-control."

I stare at him.

"Self-control, discipline, honor. Those things were never difficult for me to master. And now I fantasize about throwing all of it away in exchange for you."

My mouth falls open. He *fantasizes* about me?

Oh my god. I feel my cheeks heat.

"What's stopping you?" It's both a question and a dare.

He looks me over, his eyes undressing me.

"Look around. We live at court. We are assets to the crown. I'm to be engaged to the princess. And you're to be the heroine who will be talked about for centuries to come. I cannot escape my fate any more than you can."

"I don't believe that." I pull back from the railing. "I don't believe in fate."

"You don't think it was fate that predicted your arrival—that brought you here to this world? To this very spot at this moment in time?"

"I believe in choice. I believe we choose our paths, not fall into them."

"And what was agreeing to be the king's Dragon Rider? Was that not falling into your path?"

"I stayed to be close to him."

"To the king?" he raises his dark brows in question.

I fight the urge to smack myself in the forehead as I recall Zadyn's cautionary words when I first arrived here. He said not to mistake Jace, Sorscha, or the king for the people I knew and loved. That doing so could alter nature's course. So I hold my tongue, refraining from saying too much.

"He reminds me of my dad," I say quietly, staring out into the night. "He died almost three years ago."

Jace reaches out to brush my cheek. The surprisingly tender touch warms my skin.

"I'm sorry," he whispers. I lift my hand to rest on his wrist, leaning into his touch. He looks torn.

"I don't want to betray her," he finally says, his voice soft as night. His fingers slide to the nape of my neck, sending chills down my spine.

"I don't either," I whisper, even as our bodies draw closer like magnets. As I stare at his lips helplessly.

"We can't." He rests his head against mine, his fingers closing around my waist.

"I know." I nod. But if he doesn't stop this, then I know I won't be able to either. My stomach plummets in sweet antici-pation, and my eyes drift closed.

After another second, he pulls back, and my eyes flutter open.

"It's late. We should go inside," he breathes, smoothing my hair. I nod and follow at his side.

"Serena." He pauses before the doors. I turn to him. "If you still want to be trained by someone else, I would understand."

"Will you stop being such a dick to me at training?"

He laughs, his whole face easing of tension. It's a beautiful sight. "I'll try."

"Then no. I still want you."

He catches the meaning behind my words, his eyes soften-ing. "I'm so sorry. For how I've acted."

"Thank you." I can't stop myself from reaching out to take his hand. I give it a gentle squeeze before releasing it. We continue back to my room in comfortable silence, and I sleep soundly through the night.

~

"TA-DA."

I hold my arms up in presentation, panting as Jace and I finish sparring. Rivulets of sweat drip down my neck as I push a few slick strands of hair off my face.

The king sits on the bench lining the round space, his face a mask of indifference. He stands and slowly walks toward me. I nearly take a step back when I get a whiff of the power rolling off of him.

"Your hand-to-hand looks good," he says, measuring me up with eyes so like my own. "There is room for improvement on weaponry, but you're good with a dagger."

I make a sour face.

"Your newfound speed and strength are impressive."

I nod in thanks.

Then he turns as if to walk away. I look at Jace, perplexed, but then a spear made of pure ice is flying toward me at the speed of light. Before I have time to scream or duck, a flood of cold blasts from my outstretched hand. My intent is to block the spear from skewering me. But that isn't what happens.

The spear is met with a wall of solid ice.

Awestruck, I step forward and tap my finger against it. The wall shatters like glass, falling in a heap at my feet. I gawk at the sight.

The king smiles my father's smile, eyes crinkling. I can't help but return it.

"A deflector," he says in wonder.

"A deflector?" I ask, glancing between them.

"Deflection is the ability to wield whatever gift is thrown at you by another. Basically, you can use your opponent's own power against them," Jace explains.

"Quick reflexes for a young witch." King Derek glances at his captain.

Jace nods. "Her gifts are powerful. Raw."

"And her control?"

"Working on it," Jace answers for me.

"Keep it up, Captain. You set out for the island in two weeks' time."

"The island?"

"It's past time you met your dragon, don't you think?" Derek quirks an eyebrow at me.

I shake my head, unable to process the mixture of emotions running through me at that thought. The king starts toward the corridor.

"Oh, sir? I mean, Your Majesty?" I call after him. He waits as I approach.

"What are we going to tell the witnesses about my, uh, episode? The servants and Lady Clemence saw how I destroyed Zadyn's room. By the way, I'm really sorry about those curtains —they looked expensive."

"I've already taken care of them."

My heart sinks.

"You executed them?" I gasp.

He bursts into laughter. "No, of course not. We wiped their memories of the incident. As far as everyone is concerned, you are still Lady Serena Accostia, cousin of the king, no more than High Fae."

I clutch my chest and sigh in relief.

"Well done, Serena," the king adds before disappearing into the corridor.

I gape after him.

"The king actually paid me a compliment before you did." I turn to Jace, stunned. He looks smug.

"Admit it." I all but skip over to him. "I made you look good in front of the boss."

"You passed his test today." Jace holds up his pointer finger. "Don't get cocky."

"I think I deserve a treat for my performance today."

"What else is new," he mutters as I trail him to the weapons rack.

"Two months ago, I could barely hold a sword, and now I can take *you* on. That's something to celebrate."

"And how would you choose to celebrate?"

"A trip."

"To where?"

I hum, tapping my chin. "I'm thinking Diamond City."

"Because that worked out so well the last time."

"This time is different. I have my magic," I say, leaning against the rack. "Come on, I've never seen the city in the day."

He levels a look at me. "Ask your guard dog."

"Considering he's probably balls deep in Cece right now, I'd rather not."

Jace chokes on his own spit, clapping a fist against his chest.

"Gods, witch. Your *mouth!*" I shrug and wait for him to recover. "Still sore about that, I see?"

"No idea what you're talking about," I lie.

"Honestly, you're never satisfied."

"How so?"

Jace sighs and faces me head-on. "You don't want him, but you don't want him with anyone else."

"If I wanted him, I would take him." I take a step toward him.

"Yet you won't cut him loose." He takes a step toward me.

"He's not my dog." Another step.

"And yet you are his master."

He stops an inch away, gazing down at me. All I can think about is his mouth and how it was so close to mine last night, with no one around to see.

"You seem so preoccupied by my relationship with Zadyn." He shrugs, indifferent. "What about you and Sorscha?" I test.

"What about her?" His voice tenses, but he doesn't back down.

"Why haven't you proposed?"

An unvoiced answer passes between us, but he says, "It's not my decision. It's the king's."

He starts for the corridor, his pace quick enough that I have to jog to catch up.

"Not hers? Not yours? Neither of you have a say?"

"Not really."

"Jace. Do you *want* to marry her?" A flash of envy at the prospect rips through me. It's possible for him to have feelings for us both. He's known her longer. Not to mention, he's been courting her for months.

"I want what the king wants."

"That's a bullshit answer," I quip. He stops and turns to me. "Do you love her?" I can't stop the question from flying off my tongue. He scratches the back of his neck and looks away. Everywhere but my eyes.

"I *like* her. I was her guard for years, but I never knew her on a personal level. When the king first posed the idea, I was hesitant and honestly a little surprised that he thought me a worthy match. But I couldn't refuse him. So I had to prepare for the fact that I might marry her. I got used to the idea of us; I even began to picture a life with her."

"A life as king consort," I add.

"That has never been my goal. I'm a fighter—I like being captain," he says. "But after spending so much time with her and committing to the idea of a marriage in my head, I'd be lying if I said I didn't care for her at all."

I nod, partially relieved and partially disappointed. It would have been easier if he had said he loved her and squashed my hopes and dreams on the spot. If I thought maybe I was just an itch he wanted to scratch before getting married, I could walk away. But that tiny sliver of hope threatens to seize my body and make me do stupid, selfish things.

What is wrong with me? What is my plan here? Steal him from Sorscha? From my sister's doppelgänger? From my friend who thinks I'm her "*dear cousin*"?

I'm a fraud. And a terrible friend for even thinking these things.

It's only when Jace tilts my chin up, forcing me to look at him, that I realize my face has furrowed.

"What's happening in that head of yours, witch?"

I shake out of his grasp. "Nothing. So," I breathe, continuing on our previous path, "Iaspus?"

"Another time. I have business on the border." He smirks, shaking his head as he strides away.

26

"Two weeks?"

Zadyn leans against the railing of the spiral staircase, arms crossed over his chest, watching as I grip the polished wooden ladder and push off the ground. I fly across the expansive tile floor, seamlessly gliding past a wall of floor-to-ceiling books.

"That's what the king said."

"Then you need to stop procrastinating," he calls, eyeing me with disapproval as I zoom past.

"You're grouchy today." Sighing, I hop off the ladder and saunter over to him. "Cece not putting out?"

"Hah. You're deflecting." He runs a hand through his caramel waves, clearly vexed by my lack of seriousness.

"I just don't understand why no one will give me a break. I've got my magic, I'm kicking ass in combat—don't I deserve a little credit for all my hard work?" I slump into a chair, really milking it.

"You have been working hard, but accessing your magic and

learning to fight was only half the battle. You still can't even ride a horse. How do you expect to ride a dragon?"

"Well, then maybe we should be focusing on riding lessons rather than being cooped up in this castle day in and day out. Not that I'm complaining." I gesture to the spectacular library and let my arms flop down in front of me.

Zadyn braces his hands on the edge of the table, the veins in his arms bulging. I lose my train of thought as his chiseled bicep reaches up to push his hair back again.

When does he find the time to work out?

I can't imagine anyone being *that* naturally blessed. That would just be unfair.

His gaze narrows as a rogue lock of toffee-colored hair escapes and falls into his eyes. "You just want an excuse to go exploring."

The sound of his voice snaps me out of my gawking. I give him a noncommittal shrug, still oddly disarmed by that singular wave spilling over his forehead.

"Why not kill two birds with one stone?"

TWENTY MINUTES LATER, Zadyn leads me to a stall at the far end of the stables. Before us is one of the dark, majestic creatures I've seen Jace and the twins ride.

"This"—Zadyn grabs a saddle from the rack on the wall—"is a Stygian horse. They are the most expensive purebreds in all of Solterre."

"What makes them so special?" I ask, watching Zadyn dress the steed.

"Aside from the fact that they're larger than your average horse, they ride five times as fast. They're fierce and rare. Made for battle. Only the highest-ranking generals in the Kingsguard and the richest noblemen have acquired them."

Stepping forward, I reach a hand toward the horse. It snaps at me, bearing a full set of razor-sharp fangs as I scream in horror.

"*What the fuck?!*"

"Careful," Zadyn warns.

"What's up with their teeth?"

"Stygians have razor-sharp teeth to rip apart any threat to their rider."

"I don't think he wants me to ride him."

"It's a she. And if you think that's bad, wait until you meet Prophyria."

"Who?"

"Your dragon. Her name is Prophyria. Last of her kind."

"How do you know her name?"

"It's only been recorded in every history book for the last two thousand years."

"I'm going to ride a *dragon*," I try out the words in my mouth. They sound ridiculous. "I've never even seen one in the flesh."

"No one has in a very long time."

"Yeah, but it's like saying you're going to ride a dinosaur. It sounds so fantastical. Impossible. What if I can't do it?" I plop down on a bale of hay and glance up at Zadyn. His hands still on the horse's side as he glances at me over his shoulder.

"The Blackbloods that came before you did it. You've just begun to tap into your power, but your strength has been there all along. You won't fail."

"She will if she's unprepared."

Jace's throaty voice makes me snap my head around. Clad in all black, he leans against the stall door with sensual grace. My heart rate ticks up.

"I thought you had business at the border," I say to him.

A muscle in his jaw tightens and then relaxes. "Finished early."

"Is that what you tell your many lovers?" I ask, batting my eyelashes. He slides me a slow glare, but there is no malice in his eyes. I chuckle to myself.

"She'll be prepared. It's best she starts with something low risk," Zadyn interrupts our banter, impatience lacing his voice.

"Oh, I agree." Jace straightens off the wall and comes to stand beside me, eyes fixed on Zadyn. "Learning to ride horseback is essential. But just to state the obvious, a Stygian horse has nothing on a dragon. The only similarity is that both have backs for her to ride on."

"How else can I prepare?" I look up at him as he angles his head.

"No," Zadyn says, apparently reading his mind. He takes the horse's reins and leads it from the stall as we follow behind.

"Oh, come on," Jace drones.

"What?" I ask.

"She needs to get airborne," he insists.

"Airborne?" I all but screech.

"She hasn't even attempted to fly," Zadyn tosses over his shoulder, stepping out into the blinding sunlight.

"Fly? You want me to try to fly?"

"It's not what it sounds like," Zadyn explains through his exasperation. "It's more like hovering."

"Look, skilled witches can spell anything to fly, though I wouldn't necessarily recommend that. Nothing draws attention like a floating cow. But if you fall, hovering is your only other defense," Jace explains.

Zadyn says nothing as he motions for me to join him beside the massive horse.

"She needs to have every skill in her arsenal before

attempting to bond the dragon. Too many things can go wrong. She should be prepared for every scenario. It's her best chance at survival," Jace calls to him. Zadyn shoots him a glare.

"He's right," I say. Zadyn slides his heated brown eyes to mine. "This will be the most dangerous thing I've ever done. I have to know how to save myself."

Zadyn holds my gaze, and as he does, the ice in it thaws. Turning to Jace, he asks, "And how do you suppose you're going to teach her?"

"I have ways," he replies, smug as ever.

I toss Zadyn a pleading look.

"Alright," he says, looking past my shoulder back to Jace. "But we do it safely."

"Safe is my middle name." Jace holds up his hands, a dark smirk blooming on his full bottom lip. I fight the blush threatening to creep up my neck.

"We'll find you when we're done here," Zadyn dismisses him.

"Oh, I wouldn't miss this for the world." Jace plants his feet shoulder-width apart and crosses his arms. Zadyn and I roll our eyes and turn back to the horse.

RIDING A STYGIAN HORSE SOLO IS...TERRIFYING. It isn't helped by the fact that Hansel, the eighty-five-year-old mare, is a living terror.

From the moment I ease into the saddle, Hansel bucks and brays, seeking to flatten me on the ground beneath her massive hooves. I place a hand on her silken neck to soothe her, and the wretch actually strains her head to snap at my fingers. I pull back with a yelp.

"Steady." Zadyn stretches out his hands, attempting to

soothe her. He shifts his gaze to mine. "Tighten your grip. Lock your thighs. The more you squeeze, the more control you have. You have to show her who's leading."

I bring my thighs together as tight as I can until they strain, and Hansel simmers down a bit.

"Good. Hold that posture."

"How do I get her to go?"

"Tug the reins. Gently," he directs.

The second I do, Hansel takes off like a bat out of hell toward the thicket of oak trees beyond the stables. I squeal, tightening my grip on the reins. Wind whips through my hair as we fly through the dense forest, my hips lifting from the saddle with every punishing gallop.

"Hansel!" I shout in command, locking my thighs together like Zadyn said. That at least keeps me from flying straight off the Stygian horse as she bounds toward a sizable body of water. There's no way we'll clear it, I think to myself. But the running jump we take sails us clean across the little lake, and we land with a thud on the other side. As soon as her feet touch the ground, she's off again, faster than any racehorse alive. Thunderous gallops sound from behind, and I turn back to see Zadyn and Jace, each on their own horses, barreling toward me.

"The reins!" Jace shouts.

"What?" I yell back, seeing the panic edging their brows.

"Pull the reins! Now!" Zadyn screams at me.

Facing forward, I notice that not ten feet away, the clearing comes to a steep drop met only with mountain sky. I yank the reins back with all of my strength and pray that's enough to stop us from careening over into the valley below. My heart hammers with every long stride we take. Hansel is slowing, but she hasn't stopped.

Oh, god.

"Stop!" I shout at her. "*Hansel, stop!*"

Four more gallops, and we'll be done for.

"Serena!" someone bellows from behind.

I grit my teeth, pulling the leather so hard it skins my sweating palms. The battle cry I loose bounds off the waiting canyon below as I brace myself to go over the edge. At the last possible moment, Hansel skids to a stop mere inches before we run out of forest. Mud and debris crumble from the edge of the drop, cascading into the deep valley below.

The pounding in my ears subsides as I tug Hansel once more, and she turns toward the two males behind us.

Two sets of worry-stricken eyes stare at me as they simultaneously dismount.

Zadyn reaches me first, a horrified look on his face.

"So much for lower risk." Jace slows a few feet away from us, and I watch his gaze shift to Zadyn's hand on my leg. When his eyes find mine again, he says, "I swear, witch, you could turn a morning stroll through the gardens into a near-death experience."

I throw him a quick scowl.

"You're alright," Zadyn says, more to himself than to me. He takes the reins and leads us back the way we came.

"So clearly, the trade-off for Stygian size and speed is common sense."

The creature below me snarls as if understanding my insult. Zadyn and Jace remount, and Hansel thankfully behaves on our way back.

When we reach the serene meadow and glittering pond Hansel and I crossed during her little tantrum, Jace pulls his horse to a sudden stop and slides off.

"What are you doing?" Zadyn asks him.

Jace answers by stripping off his shirt. My jaw drops.

"We tried it your way—the *safe* way." He tosses his black

tunic on the mossy ground and slides his eyes from Zadyn to me. "Now we try it *my* way."

I don't know what the hell he means, but before I even attempt to question it, my body is dismounting and sliding to the ground. An impressed look crosses his face as he cocks his head at me.

"That actually wasn't bad."

I watch, frozen, as he tugs his boots off.

"Come on," he says. "I want to see you fly."

He dives into the sparkling stream and comes up a breath later, water cascading down his skin.

"Close your mouth," Zadyn says with quiet irritation. I shoot him a dirty look to hide my embarrassment.

I strip off my boots, pull my tunic over my head, and unlace my leather pants, pulling free the tucked-in silk undershirt that falls just past my ass. Shimmying out of the pants, I straighten to find both males staring at me.

"Have neither of you seen a female's undergarments before?" I throw my head back to Zadyn as I head for the pool of water. "Close your mouth," I taunt.

A splatter of color blossoms up his neck. I've barely dipped my toes into the inviting water when Jace holds up a hand, halting me.

"This isn't an afternoon swim. You start back there." He points to the tree a few yards behind me.

I angle my head in confusion.

"This is just here to make your fall more comfortable." His hands glide through the water's glass-like surface. "You're going to need a running start, witch."

Rolling my eyes, I trudge toward the tree. "So that's it? I just run and jump and think happy thoughts?" I flail my arms in the air.

"More or less." Jace chuckles, pushing the wet hair from his face to reveal that magnificent bone structure.

Letting my eyes close, I focus on that soft purr of magic coating my veins with anticipatory keenness. I breathe deep, inhaling the earthen scents and crisp breeze as my toes curl around the soft soil. My eyes open and I break into a run.

I take one—two more strides and leap. For a split second, I am suspended in mid-air. Then, without even time to suck in a breath, I flop face-first into the water from at least three feet above.

The surface slaps my entire front, stinging my face as a cold, dull ache blossoms deep in my gut. The air leaves me as I flap my arms and break through the surface, choking the inhaled water from my lungs.

Jace's laughter bounds off the clearing as I part my heavy mass of dark hair to glower at him.

"That fucking hurt." I splash him.

"That was magnificent," he cackles. I lunge for him, but he grips both my wrists in his hands. My belly flop is forgotten as his gaze travels down my long hair, plastered to the front of my now see-through camisole. His eyes are sober when they flicker back to mine. I wrench my wrists free.

"That was not funny." I tread away from him.

"That was only your first try." He nods toward the tree. "Off you go."

I pull myself up onto the soft grass. Goosebumps coat my bare skin as I make my way back toward the tree.

"Any other words of advice?" I call to them.

"Yeah, don't just run and then flop this time," Jace says, his words choked off by a laugh.

"Not helpful. Zadyn, you're awfully quiet over there." I look toward him, sitting on the mossy edge of the pool.

"I don't know enough about flying," he mumbles.

"Envision yourself with wings," Jace calls from the water. "See them in your mind as an extension of yourself. The goal is to stay suspended, even if only for a few seconds."

I steady myself once more, take a running start, and once again fall flat on my face.

I groan as I come up for air. Jace lounges off to the side, elbows resting on the water's edge as the sun's brilliant beams reflect off his golden eyes.

"That was worse than the first time." His voice is cocky.

I flip him off.

"This is ridiculous," I say, dragging myself from the water once more.

"Giving up so soon?" he feigns surprise, swimming toward me. I ignore him, bending for my pants.

"How about this—I'll break your fall this time."

I dare a glance back at him. "How."

"Don't you trust me?" he asks.

No, I do not trust that smirk, that face—the saintly portrait of innocence.

That elicits a scoff from Zadyn as he strips off his jacket and rolls up his cream-colored sleeves to his forearms, leaning back on the cushy blanket of grass.

I shake my head and return to home base. This time, as I sprint and leap into the air, I manage to hover there for two seconds before the wind rushes out of my lungs and I plummet. I steel myself for the cruel slap of the water, but instead, strong hands grip me by the waist and ease me down into the pool. I brace my hands on Jace's shoulders. My body slides against his, our chests pressed together, rising and falling unevenly.

The rustle of clothing pulls my attention to Zadyn, who is heading toward his horse.

"Hey, where are you going?" I call, extricating myself from Jace's intimate grip.

"I just remembered I'm having lunch with the king today. It completely slipped my mind." He doesn't meet my gaze.

Lunch with the king?

"Zadyn, are you okay?" I lean over the plush grass, searching his face.

"I'm fine." He shrugs, stepping into the stirrups and throwing a long leg over his horse.

"I'll see you later," he tosses over his shoulder and disappears through the trees.

"Did he seem—"

"Jealous?" Jace sidles up to me.

"No," I say reflexively. "Yeah."

Something tightens in me. Sadness? Guilt? Over what? Some mild flirtations with Jace? Didn't he top that tenfold when he slept with Cece with only a wall separating us?

Jace shrugs in answer, idly treading water. "He's your familiar. He's just being protective."

"Territorial, you mean."

He gives me an incredulous look. "No more territorial than you."

I open my mouth in protest. "That is not true."

"You took a hissy fit when you found him and Cece in matching bed sheets."

"Because she's not good enough for him." I pluck at the vibrant green grass lining the water.

"Will anyone ever be?" He pushes off the side and butterflies away from me, eyes linked with mine. "Other than you, of course."

"That's ridiculous." I turn to him, crossing my arms over my soaked chest.

"Is it?" Jace once again swims toward me, his lips skimming the water's surface. "Bonds like yours can be tricky. Familiars don't tend to have lasting relationships."

"Why not?"

"How can they, when their significant other will always be second to their bonded? There is a mutual sense of ownership that accompanies ties like that. It's easy to mistake those feelings for attraction." He looms closer, sharklike, as I retreat into the edge of the pool.

"Desire." Rivulets of water drip down his chin and snag on his stubble as he stands, rising to his full towering height. He braces his hands on the grass on either side of me and leans in close to my ear.

"Lust."

I shiver, and he chuckles, backing away.

"That isn't what Zadyn and I feel for each other," I say with false bravado. "He's been with me my whole life. He's more like a brother to me. A—a cousin." I shrug.

"*Distant* cousin." Jace smiles in wicked amusement, and the sight is breathtaking. I make a disgusted sound and splash at him.

"Come on. Go again." He waves his hands, shooing me away as I mutter a string of complaints. "You'll thank me one day."

I repeat the same steps as before, envisioning a pair of wings sprouting from my back, carrying me on the wind. The effort is exhausting. Jace catches me each time as I plank and fall into him. His strong arms steady me, and I marvel at how he can hold me above his shoulders without buckling or breaking a sweat. For a second, we're Johnny Castle and Baby, and I feel like I can check that fantasy off of my list.

"Tell me about your magic." I hoist myself up to sit at the edge of the pool, still submerged from the knees down. Jace swims up to me, his chiseled arms flexing as he folds them over the grass. I have to pry my eyes away.

"My affinity?" he asks, pushing his slick hair from his face. "I can manipulate air, wind."

"So you can levitate things?"

"That's part of it. A lot of fae from Aegar have mild telekinetic abilities."

"What's the other part?" I gather up my heavy hair and wring it out beside me.

"I can touch you without ever really touching you."

My hands still.

I fumble for words. "That sounds...dangerous."

He chuckles, one of his rare million-dollar smiles flashing.

"It's convenient."

His eyes close as he tips his head back to the sun. I bite my lip, engrossed by his glorious form. The water sparkles around him, its reflection brightening his tan complexion. After a moment of unrestrained admiration, I speak.

"Show me."

His eyes drift open. A beat passes before he propels himself backward, retreating from me without ever breaking eye contact. I feel a cool breeze trickle up my arm, starting at my wrist and working its way up to my neck. I would swear that phantom touch belonged to a hand, except when I gaze down, there is nothing there.

The featherlight touch dusts across my clavicle, causing my chest to pebble. My teeth clamp down on my lip to suppress the shudder threatening to rack me. Another set of hands joins in —grazing my knee, wrapping around my hips. Sliding into my hair. Teasing over my mouth. I feel everything as if it were really happening. My head falls back as the wind traces circles on my inner thighs and a tiny whimper slips out.

The touch disappears from every place it connected with my body. I instantly want it back to finish what it started. My eyes open as I lift my head.

Jace stares at me like a predator, his eyes dark and lustful, as I'm sure mine are. The silence in the air between us is palpable.

"We should head back," he finally says, his voice low and rough. I nod, unable to trust myself to open my mouth and pull my trembling legs from the water.

Jace gets out as I gather my clothes in my arms and shove my feet into my boots. Dripping wet, I don't bother to redress. I mount the horse in my underwear, ignoring Jace's eye roll.

When we reach the clearing behind the stables, we dismount and begin walking the horses back to their stalls. We both stop dead in our tracks as Sorscha emerges from the stable, holding the reins of a lithe Stygian in her gloved hands.

She starts when she sees us, a hand flying to her chest in surprise. Her eyes rake over our dripping hair, our soaked clothes, my bare legs. I can see the suspicion and confusion growing there.

"Oh, hello," she says in her silky voice.

"Princess." Jace drops into a gallant bow as I curtsy. "Going out for a ride?"

She shifts her wary gaze from me to him. "Yes, it's such a beautiful day. I thought I would take advantage. Explore the trails. It seems you two have fallen into a bit of fun yourself." She smiles, and I can see the effort behind it.

I approach her, dry clothes bundled in hand.

"I wouldn't call it fun," I say. "The captain has been training me."

Better to be honest than to have a suspicious princess on our hands.

Well, partially honest.

Jace's eyes snap to me. I avoid his gaze, concentrating only on Sorscha. Her pouty pink lips form an "o" as I rush to explain.

"My father was a fierce warrior, or so I'm told. I never knew him, but I always wanted to learn to fight, to defend myself. The captain agreed to train me. I asked him not to tell anyone. I suppose I was embarrassed." It frightens me how easily the lie slides off my tongue.

Sorscha's eyes light up, her long lashes fluttering in relief. She breaks into a beatific, genuine smile and clasps my hand.

"Cousin," she says affectionately, "why be embarrassed about such a thing? I think it's wonderful you want to honor your father that way."

"Thank you," I say. "Today's lesson ended with me falling into a stream. I'm not much of a swimmer. The captain jumped in to pull me out."

More lies. Easy, sleazy lies.

"Oh my." Sorscha's giggle is like a peal of bells. She nods to the clothes in my hands. "You should put those on before you enter the castle. Else, you'll have every servant and nobleman ogling you."

I voice a soft laugh and curtsy, pulling Hansel past Sorscha's full riding skirt. My ears pick up the conversation behind me.

"I would escort you on your ride, but I fear I've been absent most of the day. I need to check in with the king. I'll send someone to go with you. Max or Warryn," Jace says.

"It's no trouble, really. It's rare I ever get any solitude."

"I worry about you." The words tumble from his mouth, coming out ungracefully. "You're a princess. You should never go anywhere unaccompanied. Anything can happen." His concern seems to appease her.

"Very well. I will wait here. Captain," she says, tipping her head to him.

He lifts her hand to his lips. "Enjoy your ride, Princess."

He stalks forward to catch up to me, and we stay silent as we return the horses to their respective stalls. Closing the doors behind them, Jace turns to me.

"Well, that was awkward," I huff.

He shakes his head. "Why would you tell her we've been training?"

"What was I supposed to say? Do you have any idea what that must have looked like to her? Coming back dripping wet, half-dressed?" I point out.

"I know how it must have looked," he growls, and we both go silent for a moment.

"It's better than sneaking around pretending we hardly know each other when we've spent every morning together for months. It looks worse for us to lie about it and then get caught like we just did."

"You weren't exactly forthcoming in your truths just now." He leans against the stall and looks at me.

"I was thinking on my toes. You and the king want to keep this Dragon Rider thing a secret? Well, this is the trade-off. I'd rather not spark any more suspicion than necessary. Especially when it comes to the princess." I turn and head toward the door.

"What's that supposed to mean?" He catches up to me in one long stride.

"It means"—I sigh, not bothering to look at him—"I see the way she looks at you."

"And?"

"Oh, good, you're aware of it, too."

"Serena." The sound of my name on his lips stops me in my tracks. He never uses my name.

"My hands are tied here." His entire face burns with the sincerity of his words. I can see how torn he is between his loyalty, his honor, and his passion. He wants me. Just as badly as I want him. But neither of us is free to do as we like.

"If the king told you to propose tomorrow," I pose, "what would you do?"

His gaze falls to the stable floor with a sigh.

"I don't know."

"Yes, you do."

"What choice do I have? I am the king's man. I owe my life, my station, to him. He's been like a father to me. Don't you understand that?" His molten eyes fill with torment as he knots his hands in his hair.

"I do," I whisper, my voice full of regret. I swallow as I place my hand over his chest.

"I do understand. Which is why, if he asks, you have to say yes."

Jace stares at me, astonished. "You want me to propose."

"No, of course, I don't want you to propose. But I recognize your position. Just like I'm beginning to recognize my own." I offer him a sad smile and lean in to kiss him on the cheek.

"I understand," is all I say as I push through the door, leaving him alone, staring after me.

27

*Z*adyn and I eat dinner together in my room that night. He seems a little less aloof than when he stormed off this afternoon.

"How was lunch with the king?" I take a sip of wine from a crystal goblet.

He shakes his head, his brows knitting together. "Interesting."

"How so?" Setting my glass down, I lean forward.

He pauses for a moment, then says, "I think he feels... responsible for my parents' deaths."

"If anyone is responsible, it's me," I say softly.

"Please don't say that." He gives me a tender look. "Don't even think it. My parents knew what they would be sacrificing. It's no one's fault."

"What were they like?" I ask after a moment.

"I never got to meet my mother. My father," he starts, a soft smile spreading on his lips. "He was funny. Charming. Easy to talk to, easy to love."

He stares into his wine, his mind somewhere far away.

"Sounds a lot like someone I know."

Zadyn lets out a muted laugh before continuing.

"He was a shifter, too, and a fierce swordsman. He taught me everything I know. The king shared some old war stories about the two of them at lunch, some I'd never heard before. He clearly loved my parents." He sets his glass down and flattens his palms on the polished table.

"I had hoped he'd still be here when I got back," he admits quietly, studying his hands. "There's a lot I didn't get to say."

"He knew. Trust me." I reach out to take his hand.

He lifts his warm brown eyes to mine. His smile is heartbreaking. I clasp his hand tighter and peer into his eyes, his soul. We stare at each other for a long time, recognizing the loss and grief each of us knows so well. We bear twin scars.

After a moment, he clears his throat, casually slipping his hand from mine.

"The king wants me to sit on his council, to take my father's old position as his emissary."

My eyes widen.

"Zadyn, that's great. Is that...do you want that?"

"It'll give me something to do, some purpose besides babysitting your ass." He pokes me in the ribs, and I swat him away.

"Well, I think it's a great idea." I fold my napkin on the table. "You're a natural-born courtier. You're charismatic, easygoing. You make talking with people, with strangers, look like nothing."

He tips his head in thanks, reaching for his wine. "How was flying?"

"You mean falling?" I scoff, shaking my head. "It's impossible."

"You said that about freeing your magic, about learning to fight, too. And now look at you."

I sigh, tossing him a withering look. "I stayed airborne for about five seconds."

"Gotta start somewhere. If you fall off a dragon during flight, those five seconds could be a matter of life and death."

I smack my lips together. "Noted. I wish you would have stayed. You're a better teacher than Jace. A kinder one, at least."

"It seemed like you two were getting on just fine." Zadyn drums his fingers on the table, his eyes fixed on the fireplace. A tense moment passes as he holds his breath.

"Serena. I'm only going to ask you this once," he cautions. I swallow, knowing where this conversation is headed.

"It seems like something's going on between you two."

"That's not a question," I say quietly as he slides his gaze to me.

Serena, he seems to say without words.

What?

What are you doing?

I'm not doing anything. There's nothing going on between me and Jace.

Anyone with eyes can see it.

I shove to my feet, needing to put some space between us.

"It's complicated," I say aloud, stopping in front of the fireplace.

"I just think you need to be careful."

I bristle, remembering Marideth's same warning to me weeks ago.

Is it really that obvious?

"I've got it under control," I say a touch defensively, trudging over to my bed. The plushy comforter envelopes me as I flop down on my back.

"Serena." Zadyn's voice is stern as he follows me and leans against the bedpost. "He is all but engaged. To the *princess*."

"I *know* that, Zadyn. That's why I told you there is nothing.

Going. On. Okay?" I punctuate each word sharply. "We stopped it," I add, almost to myself.

"What did you stop?"

My eyes remain fixed on the canopied ceiling as I heave a sigh.

"*What did you stop*?" he presses. "Did something happen between you two?"

I snap my gaze to him.

"Nothing happened, alright? Nothing happened between us," I insist.

He huffs, pushing off the bedpost. "Oh, really? You were all but groping each other in the water today. It was sickening."

My cheeks flush with embarrassment.

"What do you want me to say, Zadyn?" I jolt upright, narrowing my eyes at him as he paces around the room. "That we're attracted to each other? We are. Sue me."

"Obviously." He whirls toward me, his face addled with disgust. "That's the problem. You're not fooling anyone. Everyone can see you *pining* for him."

"I do not *pine* for him!" I bark, planting my feet. "And this is none of your concern. Why do you even care?"

"How can you even *ask* that? You *know* why. I don't want to see you get hurt!"

"I'm not going to get hurt. I'm fine."

"You are playing a very dangerous game." He shakes his head. "With a lot of hearts."

"What is that supposed to mean?"

"Sorscha loves him. And if you don't think he's still pouring his honey in her ear to secure his spot as king consort, you are dreaming," he hisses, his caramel hair falling into his eyes. My anger flares at his accusation.

"He doesn't care about being king!"

"And you think he cares for you? He doesn't. You're just an itch he wants to scratch before settling in with a princess."

"Wow." I jerk back, stunned.

"Just tell me you're not actually naïve enough to fall for him," he fumes, his brown eyes flashing.

I already have.

"I told you. Nothing. Happened—"

"*Yet.*"

A beat passes as we stare each other down. He takes a tentative step forward and lifts his hand, but then drops it, conflicted.

His voice is pained as he shakes his head and murmurs, "You're going to break your own heart. I thought you were smarter than this."

For some reason, that last comment makes me flinch.

I slide off the bed and stand nearly chest-to-chest with him. He peers down at me.

"Let me make one thing very clear, Zadyn. I know you feel entitled to me because of this bond, but I am not yours. I don't care if you're jealous. I don't care if you think you know what's best for me. I'm not your little girlfriend who you can just boss around and control. You do not own me. You do not get to dictate who I love or how I love or anything else when it comes to my life."

The quiet words spread through the room like venom, hitting their mark. Zadyn's face drains of color.

I want to take back every word I just said, every low-blow sucker punch. I went too far.

"I'm sorry, that was cruel," I murmur.

He eyes me, his features softened by the candlelight, and leans in just above my lips.

"*You're* cruel."*

He leaves without another word.

I DOOM-SCROLL through my camera roll until the wee hours of the morning. It's become my ritual when I feel down or depressed.

Like now.

I've kept my phone tucked away in the drawer of my nightstand since I moved into this room. When I freed my magic, I figured out a way to charge it with only the zap of my fingers. This little object is all I have left to connect me to my old life. I only take it out when I need a reminder of who I am, who I was before this, and where I came from.

The screen illuminates my dark room as I mindlessly sift through photos of my old life. Pictures of me and my dad. Of our camping trips to the Adirondacks. Our old house in Beacon. The day he moved me into my New York City apartment.

A wave of nostalgia tinged with guilt hits me as I study the photos. At times it almost feels like I'm cheating on my old life with this new one.

Or maybe I'm just projecting.

I study the girl in the photos. When she's not giving the camera dirty looks, she's mostly smiling.

Was I ever as happy as I look in these pictures? Whoever that girl is, she is a stranger to me.

You're cruel.

Zadyn's words echo in my mind as the pit in my stomach returns. I groan, tossing the phone onto the bed and throwing

---

* Cue: *Bite The Hand* by boygenius

my arm over my eyes. I replay every horrible thing I said to him earlier. It was so uncalled for.

I hate myself for it.

And the worst part is that he's right. About all of it.

I'm playing with more than just my own heart. I'm screwing with Sorscha's future, her happiness, with *Jace's* future...with a kingdom that needs a strong ruler one day.

Jace would be that ruler. And he would be so good at it.

The more he and I entertain this delusion—this flirtation— the harder the fall back to reality hurts. I said we stopped it. But it isn't over.

Not in my head. Not in my heart.

I have to swear him off. I have to promise myself this will go no further than it already has—a stolen, drug-hazed kiss in the night, a handful of longing looks, and lingering touches.

It will go no further. It *can* go no further.

It ends now.

28

I knock on Zadyn's door first thing in the morning, still feeling guilty as a grade-A asshole. But he's already gone for the day. Either the king's emissary is a brutally demanding job, or he's avoiding me. Probably both.

I keep quiet during training, trying to make as little eye contact with Jace as possible and limit the banter to a bare minimum. Thankfully, he doesn't seem to be in the mood for flirtation after our conversation in the stable.

I push open the door to the towering library, expecting to find Zadyn, but instead, my eyes land on Madame Gnorr. She thumbs through a heavy tome as I slip inside.

"Serena Avery."

A sweet smile blooms on her face as she lifts her head to me.

"Madame Gnorr," I greet her. "This is a surprise."

"The king sent your young lord into the city on official business. He asked me to stand in as your tutor for the day. I thought he informed you, my dear," she says, reading my surprise.

I shake my head as she closes the dense volume. "No. He didn't. We're kind of...in a fight," I reveal, sliding into the chair. She takes a seat across from me, her gray robes billowing around her.

"That is rather common with familiars and their bonded." Gnorr chuckles.

"Why?"

"With ties so strong, it is natural for there to be a push and pull among the dynamic. Familiars are like twin spirits, an extension of oneself. A part of you lives in him, and he in you."

"I didn't realize it was so complex," I admit. "Zadyn and I fight like family. I took it too far this time." Shame washes over me once again as I remember the look on his face right before he walked away from me. It was as if I'd slapped him.

She reaches out and pats my hand. "It will pass."

"Thank you." I give her a grateful smile. "So, what are we learning today?"

"I thought we might try waking a dragon."

"You—you want me to wake the dragon? Today?" I sputter. "How?"

"We need to establish communication between the two of you. It will make bonding her easier when the time comes."

"Communication?"

"A psychic connection." She taps her temple twice before continuing on. "Prophyria has been asleep for nearly two thousand years. It would be unwise to jar her from her slumber without warning."

"Two *thousand* years." I blow out a long breath, shaking my head in disbelief.

Gnorr nods. "She has been stirring beneath that mountain,

waiting for you. Those who have tried to rouse her in the past have met untimely demises."

"If she was asleep, then how did they—"

"They say never to wake a sleepwalker." Gnorr gives me a knowing look. "It frightens them. Accidents happen. Her consciousness rests outside the bounds of time, while her physical form is in a mechanical state to protect against any potential threats."

"She's on autopilot," I mutter to myself. Gnorr tilts her head in confusion. "I think I understand. If I don't make contact with her, she might think I'm a potential threat and barbecue me."

"Essentially," Gnorr assents.

"So how do I make contact?" I ask.

She rises to her feet with all the grace of a High Fae and motions for me to follow her toward the brown leather couch in the alcove between the windows. I sit as she eases into the high-backed chair across from me and folds her hands in her lap.

"We will meditate."

I grimace. "I have to warn you, I'm not great at sitting still for extended periods of time."

"You will have no trouble." She gestures for me to lie back. With a sigh, I lift my leather-clad legs onto the long couch and rest my head back against the massive, cushioned arm.

"Close your eyes, child," she says, her voice soothing and hypnotic.

I obey, folding my hands over my stomach.

We start by counting breaths. Following them in and out. Before I know it, I'm surrounded by silence.

No thoughts. No sounds. Quiet. Peace.

I can hear Gnorr's words like background noise, but I don't comprehend them.

I wake feeling more rested than an eight-hour night of sleep.

Blinking my eyes, I glance out the window above me and bolt upright. Bright stars line the night sky, casting a soft glow on the snow-capped mountain peaks just beyond the glass.

"How long was I out?" I gasp, turning to Gnorr.

"Six hours."

I bound to my feet.

"Six hours!" I choke. "How?"

"I'm that good." She smiles, her expression self-congratulatory.

"I didn't make contact," I tell her, crestfallen. Six hours and nothing. "I didn't see the dragon."

She rises, her robes pooling around her feet, and says with a knowing smile, "You will."

∾

I DREAM THAT NIGHT. Fragmented flashes of color and movement.

Dark rock. Water dripping from a cavernous arch.

Drip. Drip. Drip.

Deep purple. Reflective scales. A serpentine movement. Something shifts, something slithers.

Rusted metal. Chains. Soft rumbles ripple through the ground—through the walls.

Heavy air.

Congested. Confined. Claustrophobic.

Something stirs. Restless. Hungry. Rubble clatters to a cave floor.

Suddenly, a fist tightens around my heart. I am unable to breathe, to move. Then in the darkness, a glowing green eye cracks open.

And looks right at me.

I sit up, gasping for air.

Someone is shaking me. Calling my name.

"Serena!" Zadyn's voice sounds far away. As if we stand on opposite ends of a tunnel. He grips my arms in his hands. I suck in a deep breath and force my eyes to open.

"She's awake," I choke up at him. "The dragon is awake. She saw me."

"I just got home, and I felt something...off. I came to check on you." Zadyn presses the cup of tea into my hands and takes a seat across from me. "You were convulsing. What happened?"

I pull the blanket tighter around my shoulders and blow on the steaming cup.

"This afternoon," I start, "Gnorr guided me into a meditation. We were trying to establish a psychic connection to the dragon. I meditated for six hours straight, but I didn't see anything."

"Six hours?" He gapes, his arms resting on his knees. I nod. "You can barely sit still for five minutes."

"I thought I was dreaming just now. But then her eyes—" I recall that piercing green, flecked with colors like I've never seen, never knew existed. "She opened her eyes, and she *looked* at me. I could feel it. I could feel the cold, the dampness of that cave. I smelled the rust on her chains. It was like we shared a mind for a moment."

"Gnorr helped open up a channel between the two of you." Zadyn sits back in his chair.[*]

I sip my tea and slowly lift my gaze to him. He stares off into

---

[*] Cue: *I love you, I'm sorry* by Gracie Abrams

the fire, one side of his handsome face shadowed and the other warmed by the flickering oranges, blues, and purples. I wonder what he searches for in those flames. His father? His mother? A better friend than me?

"I am cruel," I whisper. His warm, whiskey brown eyes slide to me.

"I never thought that about myself. I thought I was a good person. I thought I couldn't hurt anyone. I thought I *wouldn't*. But it turns out I can. I can do it with such ease, it actually terrifies me. I lie. I'm a liar now. I—" I shake my head, a sad laugh cracking my chest.

"I lie to everyone. I lie to myself, to you. And I think that if I can just work hard enough to believe my own bullshit, that will make it true. You're right about me. You see me. All of me, and it is not pretty. You deserve better. You deserve *good*. I can be nice when I want to be. But that doesn't make me good. All I am is cold."

My confession hangs in the air, settling around us like a layer of fog. Zadyn silently gets to his feet. I watch as he lowers himself to his knees before me.

"You are not cold." Taking my face in his hands, he forces me to look at him. "You're scared. There's a difference."

"Why don't you yell at me?" I shake my head, bewildered. "Why don't you tell me I'm a shit person, that I'm selfish and spoiled? Why don't you tell me that I'm a terrible friend? Why are you so understanding?"

"Because I know you don't mean it," he says, brown eyes searching mine. His thumb skims up and down my cheek in the tenderest way.

In a way I don't deserve.

"You should hate me," I whisper, tears rolling down my face and onto his fingers. "I've hurt you so many times. I've said things I should never say. I...I'm the reason your parents are dead." My voice cracks as the guilt seizes me.

"I could never hate you." He lifts off his heels, bringing his eyes level with mine. "Not even if you hurt me every day for the next thousand years. You could drive a dagger straight through my heart, and I will still be here—I will *still* love you."

The world seems to shift beneath my feet at the mention of that word. *Love.* It cracks something in my chest, thaws something hard in me.

His hands continue to sweep over my wet cheeks as my fingers glide over his wrists. I throw my arms around his neck and sob, soaking his shirt with my tears. He pulls me into his lap and gently rocks me, smoothing one hand over my back and cradling my head in the other as the tears gush from my eyes.

I eventually still against him, drained of energy and water. He gets to his feet with me still in his arms, and carries me over to the bed, laying me down and pulling the covers over me. When he starts toward the door, I catch him by the sleeve.

"Stay."

I know it's selfish of me to ask. And yet, I can't stop the word from escaping my lips. His gaze slides between me and the waiting door. Then, as if ending some unspoken debate, he runs his hand over my hair and shifts before my eyes. The small white cat standing in his place leaps onto the bed with ease. I curl up on my side with him nestled in the crook of my arm. My hand smooths down the length of his soft coat until I fall asleep.

29

Two weeks. That's all the king gave me.

They fly by in a blur as Gnorr, Zadyn, and Jace throw an overload of information my way in preparation for the big day. I pray some of it sticks.

Jace and I incorporate more flying lessons into our training, which means more close, wet encounters that threaten to break the promise I made to myself to stay uninvolved. He seems to be in agreement, his focus making him colder and more strategic in our time together.

We work on deflecting and shadow walking, which, to no surprise, proves to be an excruciating challenge. I grasp the idea behind it easily enough, summoning the shadows at will. But I'm only able to jump from one end of a large clearing to another.

"That's good," Jace calls, jogging over to me. He passes me a canteen of water and I chug it down.

"Remind me why we can't just take a boat to this island?" I glance up, sweating in the morning sun.

"The journey could take two weeks. And crossing the

Erastin Ocean comes with its own set of challenges. Shadows would be the most efficient way to get there."

"But you're coming, right?" I ask.

He nods, taking back the canteen. "Of course."

"Then I need to practice shadowing with you."

"You can barely shadow from one end of the forest to the other on your own. You'll deplete your magic if you bite off more than you can chew before you're ready," he cautions, taking a swig of water.

"I'm nowhere near depleted. I can feel my magic. I'm tired, but I'm not on the verge of collapse."

He sighs. "I'm not in the mood to argue."

Things have felt strained between us since the day Sorscha saw us heading back to the stables together. Both of us are trying so hard to behave. To keep things strictly professional.

Platonic. Student-teacher.

Because that dynamic has always worked out well, a voice inside of me quips.

I push the thought away and straighten, hands on my leather-clad hips. "Then don't. Let me have my way and we'll both be much happier for it." I give him a wide, toothy grin. He rolls his eyes and opens his arms.

"Oh," I say in surprise. "Do I just—" I awkwardly slip under his arms, trying to leave as much space between our bodies as possible.

"We have to be touching, yes," he bristles.

I heave a sigh of annoyance, gingerly stepping into him.

"For gods' sakes, witch," he hisses, grabbing me by the arms and hauling me against him. I turn my head to the side, trying not to be crushed to his chest, trying not to inhale that campfire scent that will be my undoing. He takes my arms and wraps them around his waist.

Wonderful.

"Have at it," he says above my head, clearly perturbed. I try to summon the shadows, but they move slowly, curling around our ankles and rising like smoke.

"Today, preferably," he grumbles.

"I'm trying," I snap, gritting my teeth.

In answer, the shadows spread faster, engulfing us toe to top. It takes more concentration to extend them around two people as I envision where I want to go.

Familiar darkness swallows us, a black hole with no light. Furious wind tornadoes around us as I clutch Jace's back. We cling to each other, our bodies fused together as the smoke retracts, revealing the small white stone temple at the edge of the gardens. We stand, bracing each other on the steps leading up to the towering door.

I extricate myself from Jace and laugh. "I did it!"

"Beginner's luck." The proud, crooked smile that grows on this face belies his dismissive tone.

"What are you doing?" he asks as I push open the door and step inside the stone structure.

"Taking a break." My voice echoes off the cavernous high ceilings. "I've never been in here. It's beautiful."

The floor-to-ceiling marble houses nine alcoves altogether. They line the walls, lit by floor lanterns embedded in the stone. Each alcove contains a carved marble statue amid a shrine of fresh flowers, with symbols etched into the reflective walls below. Velvet-cushioned kneelers line the walls behind double rows of candles, glowing in their glass revivers.

On the far back wall are two shrines, larger and more grandiose than the others, situated above an altar. The alcoves are encrusted in black diamond, making the alabaster statues stand out in stark contrast. Exotic flowers and gifts made of gold lay at their feet. I drift down the aisle, past the rows of pews, recognizing these two as Urhlon and Aerill in fae form.

Aerill wears nothing more than a drape around her hips, a crown of stars, and a necklace of the moon phases. Her mate is imposing and stern-faced in the alcove beside her, wearing nothing but a crown of suns.

"The gods." Jace sidles up to me.

"I gathered." I slide into the first pew, and he follows.

"That one there"—he points to the adjacent wall—"that's Silva. Mother of Witches."

I glance over at her shrine. Her alcove is painted with the five elements. Silva stands tall and proud—a crown of laurel leaves around her head. Her face is the portrait of serenity.

"I haven't prayed in a long time. I only really remember to do it when something bad is about to happen. But that's not really fair, is it?" I give him a sad smile.

"At solstice," I continue, staring at my hands, "when I denied Aerill, she told me never to call on the gods again. That they wouldn't listen. Which sucks because if there was ever a time to pray, it would be now. I don't know if I can do this. The shock of this new world, of magic, hasn't even worn off yet. I feel like I'm going in blind." I let out a long, slow sigh, like air leaving a tire.

We grow quiet, and I can feel his eyes studying me. Then he says, "You're ready."

"I'm a baby witch. I've barely even scraped the surface of my magic."

He shifts, angling himself to face me in the pew. "You'll have time to master your magic. *After* you bond Prophyria."

"And if I fail? If I die before I have the chance?"

It's the first time I've allowed myself to voice these fears out loud. I've had blinders on, refusing to admit to myself that what I'm about to do is life or death. Jace wraps his hand around mine, his eyes a searing gold.

"You are *not* going to die. Do you hear me?"

"I don't trust myself."

My words are barely a whisper. It's what I've felt every day of my life for twenty-nine years. It's my darkest secret, one I've never admitted aloud. Jace's face is stern.

"You've trained for this. *I've* trained you for this." He slides an inch closer. "If you can't trust yourself, then trust me. You can do this."

"I keep waiting for that moment." I slide my eyes toward the likeness of Silva. "When I do something truly amazing with my magic, some kind of huge feat that confirms it."

"Confirms what?" he says softly.

"Confirms that I'm really...a witch."

He curls his fingers beneath my chin and slides my face to look at his head-on.

"You're more than that. You're a Blackblood."

"I'M COMING WITH YOU." Zadyn sets his jaw, folding his arms over his chest as I shove a spare change of clothes into the thick gray sack.

"No, Zadyn, it's going to be dangerous."

"Exactly why I should be there."

"I don't need you to protect me." His eyes track me as I cross to the armoire and slip my arms through a tight-fitted leather doublet.

He scoffs, coming to lean against the wood. "That's literally the job description of a familiar."

"I can take care of myself, I promise." I fasten the closures up the center of the jacket and slide my hands into the finger-less leather gloves.

"I don't doubt that, but—"

I cut him off, holding up my hand. "Zadyn. I can't focus if I'm worried about you."

"There's no reason to worry about me. I'm a trained fighter. I fought in battles before you were even born. And having a shifter at your disposal can never hurt."

"I believe you." I place a steadying hand on his chest. "But I need to do this alone."

"Alone with Jace," he specifies. I shake my head.

"It has nothing to do with that. I promise you." I stare up into those kind, familiar eyes. "Besides, you have an order from the king as emissary, remember?"

He rolls his eyes.

"Meeting the King of Vod at the border and escorting his party to the castle doesn't even rank on my list of priorities right now. Not when you're about to risk your life." He rubs his temple with one hand, closing his eyes.

"If you truly believe I was born for this, then what's the risk?" I stare up at him, and he sighs, sliding his hand over mine, covering his heart.

"You *know* I believe in you." He shakes his head, his rich caramel hair catching on his dark lashes. I reach up and untangle them.

"I do."

A knock at my door makes me jump. Jace enters, wearing fighting leathers similar to mine and a low-slung belt of weapons. His eyes slide between us.

"It's time," he says.

Nodding, I snatch the bag off my bed. Zadyn catches my arm as I pass and hauls me to his chest. I slam into his solid form, the smell of bergamot and cedar washing over me. My arms wrap around his back and hold tight. He pulls away after a long moment and turns me toward Jace.

"Look out for her," Zadyn says, his voice rough.

Jace dips his head and holds the door open for me.

"With my life."

WE STEP out onto the lawn, the sun high in the sky. Jace turns to face me.

"Remember the plan. If you feel the shadows slipping, we go to one of the checkpoints we discussed. We don't have to make the walk in one go."

"Right." I envision the map Jace showed me yesterday with the circled pinpoints.

He slings his bag across his chest and holds out his arms for me to step into.

"You're shaking."

"I know," I say more sharply than I intend. "I'm nervous."

"You're not alone. I'll be with you every step of the way."

"Almost every step," I counter.

"Oh, shut up," he says, pulling me tighter into him. I wrap my arms around his waist and take a deep, steadying breath. Feeling the vibration of the ground beneath me, the hum of magic prickling my limbs, I summon the shadows. They snake around us until we are devoured by darkness.

We hold fast to each other as the winds toss us and tug us in every direction. I feel the sweat beading on my forehead as I strain to hold the shadows in place.

A little longer. I can hold out a few more seconds. I fight to concentrate, but my limbs start to feel heavy, lethargic.

"Serena," Jace says in the voice of the captain, "that's enough. You're fading fast."

I can't answer. I can't risk breaking my focus. My head lolls back, and Jace catches it in his gloved hands.

"Serena, checkpoint. Now!" he barks, grasping at my face.

I call to mind the checkpoint closest to the island. I can make it. I know I can. I focus on the map in my head—on the red dot.

The shadows shift as soon as my mind does. I squeeze Jace for support, and he holds me upright against him as my limbs start to fall asleep.

"Serena." He growls my name, his fingers digging into my skin. "Stay with me."

Solid ground meets my feet the second before I lose all muscle control and drop like a ragdoll. Jace is there, easing me to the ground in his arms. He kneels with my back draped across his thighs, his arms bracketing my waist.

"Hey, hey!" he shouts, panic rising in his tone. "Stay with me, little witch. Come on."

He holds my face, shaking me. It takes a moment before I can speak. My hands and arms regain feeling before anything else, and I lift my hand to Jace's wrist. He scans over me, concern marring his angelic face.

"Talk to me," he whispers, shaking his head. Dark hair spills across his forehead. "Say something."

"I could have made it," I croak. He lets out a long breath.

"Stubborn little witch," he murmurs, his thumb skimming over my cheek. I try to sit up and am hit with a wave of dizziness as I clutch my head.

"Easy." Jace's hands are at my back.

I turn from him sharply, crawling on all fours to put some distance between us. I only make it a foot away before I vomit across the rough stone beneath me. Jace scrambles toward me, pulling my low ponytail out of the way as I heave and heave until the dizziness subsides.

When I'm certain there is nothing left to throw up, I drag myself a few feet away from my mess and collapse face-first onto the cool stone. The uneven surface digs into my cheek, but I couldn't care less.

"Come on," Jace says, attempting to lift me.

"No," I croak, still breathless. "Just let me rest here for a second."

"Alright."

My eyes drift shut as Jace runs his fingers over my head, stroking down my ponytail. Calm spreads over me as I relax into his touch.

"You should have some water," he says after a while. I manage a small nod, pushing to my elbows as Jace fishes a canteen out of his pack. He lifts it to my lips, and I take in a mouthful, pushing his hand back so I can spit the foul taste from my mouth.

Much better, I sigh.

I take the canteen from his hands and sip slowly, regaining my strength.

Wiping my mouth on the back of my glove, I glance around. "Where are we?"

"The third checkpoint."

"Damnit," I swear, flopping onto my back. He leans over me, resting a hand on my waist.

"Do you know how hard it is for a novice to shadow two people? What you just did takes years to master. We're three-quarters of the way there. We can set up camp here for the afternoon while you regain your strength. See how you feel later."

I nod in agreement.

Jace pulls a large tarp from the gray sack and spreads it out as I prop myself up. He takes a few steps back and the tarp rises and expands like a balloon, forming four corners and a steep middle point. The tent stands perfectly erect as Jace turns back to me.

"Nice," I compliment. The corner of his mouth pulls up.

I glance around at the strange sand-less beach surrounding us. Crystal blue water kissed with white foam crashes against tall, jagged rocks. Behind us is nothing but flat, dark gray rock as far as the eye can see. Nothing else.

"These are the Outlands?" I ask, taking another sip of water. Above us is an expansive sky of grayish blue. Cloudless. The kind of sky that heralds a brewing storm. Jace nods in confirmation.

"We're on the Eastern border of Aeix. They call this Stone Beach."

"Fitting," I say dryly, watching Jace pull a small bedroll out of his pack and spread it on the tent floor. The gentle wind sends small ripples through the sides of the material.

"I thought it would be a safe bet for a checkpoint. The surrounding land is all but abandoned."

"Why?"

"Harsh conditions. Nothing can grow here; it's all rock. Rock and water."

I get to my feet and take a few steps toward the tide.

"Don't go any further," he cautions, holding out a hand. I glance back at him, perplexed.

"The Naiads here are vicious and starved for flesh."

"Naiads?" I ask.

"A type of water nymph," he clarifies. "Don't worry, they won't come up past the shore. They need to be touching water at all times. Just stay away from the tide, and you'll be fine."

That doesn't sound too reassuring.

"Why would the Redbloods relocate here with nothing around for miles?"

"They went further south, toward the Mydlands, where the magic is more potent. The Outlands are all brutal desert and flat rock land like this. It's not an easy or comfortable journey for travelers passing through, which is what they wanted." Jace waves a hand, and the flap of the tent pulls back.

Stepping inside, I realize it's more spacious than I thought. I sit cross-legged on the bedroll as Jace digs into his bag and extends an apple to me. I grimace, remembering how I puked my guts up a little while ago. He seems to realize it, too, as he stuffs the apple back into the bag and plops down beside me.

"The island is just over this ocean." He nods his head in the direction of the crashing waves outside the tent.

I try to stifle a yawn, but it gets the better of me.

"Sleep."

"But—" I begin to protest, but he holds up a hand, quieting me.

"We're in no hurry, little witch. Slow and steady."

I peer into his golden eyes, eyes I've known in other worlds, other lives. Heaving a sigh, I stretch out on my side and prop my head on my hand.

"Tell me a story."

He gives me a look that says, *do I look like I do stories?*

"It will help me sleep. Come on. Indulge me."

"What kind of story, little witch?"

"Yours."

He falls silent, staring into his lap as if weighing my question. I want to trace his silhouette as he hangs his head. I want to draw him, to remember this sight. The sight of a hardened warrior carrying secret scars on his heart. Heavy scars.

What weight has he carried on those shoulders over his long life?

"How do your human stories begin?" He shifts his golden eyes to mine.

"Once upon a time," I provide with a small smile, which he returns.

"Right. Once upon a time, there lived a boy in a poor village outside the city of Baegar. His mother was a weaver; his father a skilled woodworker. Every morning, he and his son loaded up a wagon of his work along with his wife's wares to take to the market. He watched his father make trades for the things his family needed. Bread, meat, game pelts for the harsh winters. Ointment for his mother's hands when they would seize from overuse. Despite how poor they were, despite the one-roomed hovel they lived in, and how little they had, the boy never felt that he went without. He loved his family. They were happy."

I study Jace as he pauses, one hand absently massaging the other. He swallows, his Adam's apple bobbing.

"One day, the boy and his father went into the village to trade at the market, only to find themselves in the middle of a raid. Soldiers from Vod had ransacked the town, busting down trade stands and gutting people in the streets. They broke into homes and looted what little valuables they could find. Took the females and set everything on fire."

Chills skitter down my arms as I listen.

"The boy and his father raced home through the streets, tripping over strewn bodies. When they arrived, the boy's mother was already dead. Her throat slit, her dress in tatters from where the soldiers... violated her. Her golden eyes, once so full of life, had gone cold and unseeing, staring up into nothing."

My hand flies to my mouth, horrified. *Oh, Jace.*

"The boy fell to his knees, clutching his mother on the slick floor. He and his father didn't hear the soldiers over their cries. Not before they shattered the window and tossed a flaming cloth dipped in alcohol inside. The curtains were the first to catch fire. Flames erupted across the liquor-soaked floor, devouring the walls. The wooden beams supporting the structure collapsed, trapping the boy between his father and his mother's blood-soaked body. He couldn't move, couldn't breathe. He struggled to push the beam as the flames grew closer, but the boy was too small. Too weak. He watched as his father turned purple beneath its weight, and his chest stilled. He would die too, the boy realized. And he would soon join his parents. The flames would hurt, but it would be over before he knew it, and then there would be no pain. Not anymore.'"

Jace's eyes grow glassy, but no tears fall as he clenches his fists around his drawn-up knees. The tendons in his arms bulge. I listen, barely breathing.

"Spots began to dance across his vision as he choked on thick smoke and swallowed ash. That's when a large male appeared in his vision, standing over him. He lifted the beam with ease and pulled the boy free before the flames swallowed him. He woke in an unfamiliar room, in a castle to the north. The Diamond Castle, his mother used to call it. The man sitting across from him, the same man that pulled him from the rubble, the man in a crown made of black diamond, leaned forward and said, 'You're safe now.'"

Jace's fists slowly release, as if reliving the relief of his salvation.

"The king raised the boy. Healed him. Gave him food, shelter, and clothes. He trained him until he could use a sword better than any of his men. Until he could ride faster. Until he was strong. Strong enough so that no one could hurt him again. So that no one could take away the things he loved ever again. In time, the boy began to show an affinity for air. He could send massive rocks flying across the training ring without ever lifting a finger. He could wield a sword without sparing a hand. And he hated it." His disgust is fervent as his eyes burn into the floor.

"He hated his gift. It was so ironic that the gods blessed him with this ability, but only after he failed to save his parents. Where was his gift when he needed it most? He was useless."

He shakes his head, a broken laugh leaving him. I bite my lip, torn between throwing my arms around him and letting him finish his tragic story.

"When he was old enough, he fought in the king's armies and worked his way up the ranks. He grew to enjoy it. The bloodshed, the torture, the killing. Each battle, he would envision those Vod soldiers sneering and laughing outside his window as his family's home was burned to the ground. He pictured their faces as he massacred and mutilated his way through the battlefields. And only when he stood surrounded by bloody remains for miles did he remember that none of them belonged to his true enemy."

Darkness twists his beautiful mouth.

His words trail off, lingering in the heavy air. The thickness makes it hard to breathe, like standing at the top of a mountain when you're not used to the altitude. I wonder if Jace realizes he's manipulating the air around us to match his mood.

"They killed your family," I say softly. He shrugs.

"The pleasantries of war. The poor villages took the brunt of it. Raids like that were common among the slums." His voice is hard. I reach for him, and his eyes snap to me as if only now remembering I'm here.

"Jace," I whisper, laying my hand on his knee. "I had no idea."

Now I see why he is loyal to the king. Not only does he owe him his life, but he loves the king like a father.

I shake my head. "I'm so sorry—"

"I didn't tell you this so you could pity me," he says without venom. I've never seen him look so open, so young.

"Pity is just about the last thing I feel right now." My eyes flicker over the strong planes of his face, the deep-set almond eyes and high cheekbones that give way to a chiseled jaw. His arms, strong and solid beneath his leathers. His broad chest.

The body of a warrior whose experience with death spans all the way back to childhood.

No wonder he is hardened. Closed-off. Who wouldn't be after such trauma?

"The story was supposed to put you to sleep." He stretches out beside me, mirroring my position, one hand propped under his head. "Now you'll probably have nightmares about the monster that I am."

He toys with a lock of my hair, twisting it around his finger.

"You are not a monster." I grip his hand tightly, eliciting a look from him. "Do you hear me? You are a warrior."

He studies me for a moment before saying, "You really should try to rest."

I scoot closer to him, draping an arm over his waist. He goes rigid and for a moment I think he's going to fling my arm from his side. But instead, he pulls me closer against his chest.

I made a promise not to go down this road, but it's just sleep. It's just a friend comforting another friend alone in the wilderness.

I close my eyes and listen to the sound of his breathing. I am asleep within minutes.

30

I wake to the sound of gently crashing tides outside the tent. Jace is sound asleep beside me—his mouth slightly parted. Wondering how late it is, I slip out of his arms and pull back the flap of the tent.

It's dark. No stars.

A small movement draws my attention. A shadowed female form rests atop a jagged boulder about ten feet from the shore. A rush of fear cinches me as my eyes adjust to the darkness, and I get a better look.

Naked from the waist up, her skin glows a pale blue in the moonlight, her lips black. Pin-straight raven hair that extends well beyond her hips blows in the breeze like a silken flag. From the hips down, her legs are fused together through the thigh and calf, webbed, like some dark, perverted variation of a mermaid. Behind her bare back, short wings that look like stretched black gossamer beat gently. The waves crash against her perch every few seconds, spraying her with ocean mist.

Her eyes, wholly black, shift to me as her full lips pull back to reveal a row of razored teeth. A soft, slow hiss makes its way up her throat. I hold my breath, afraid to move, afraid that she will climb ashore with those bony arms and drag me back into the sea with her, despite what Jace said about being safe on land.

He stirs behind me, sitting up. I beckon him, nodding toward the ocean.

"Look," I whisper as he comes to stand beside me, pulling back the flap to see.

"Naiads," he whispers back, watching as she pushes off the rock and slides into the black sea. "It's rare for them to come this close to shore," he says, his brow furrowing.

It's then that I notice the dampness coating the tent floor.

"Why is the tent wet?" I ask.

Jace follows my gaze down to the material, quickly darkening where it is touched by seawater. Before he can answer, a thin pool of water edged with sea foam rolls in, kissing our boots before retreating back toward the ocean.

Jace and I exchange a look.

We step out onto the dampened stones and stare up at the starless sky. The moon hangs large and bright, so much closer than I've ever seen on Earth, closer than I've seen in Aegar.

Large and bright and...full.

"Jace, the moon." I gape at the massive orb as another stronger pool of water laps up against our feet, forcing the tent back a few inches. I turn to him, horror frozen on my face as I breathe, "It's high tide."

"Fuck," he curses.

He ducks into the tent and emerges a second later, our two bags slung over his chest. He urges me forward, pressing his hand against the small of my back.

"We have to go. Now."

We jog up the beach as the waves roll toward us, catching up to us with unnatural speed. It's as if the nearness of the moon has accelerated the rising tide. Within moments, we are sloshing through knee-deep water, slowed despite our supernatural speed. I dare a look back. Our tent is a blip in the dark water. Distantly adrift.

That's when I see it.

The horde of Naiads streamlining toward us.

Their approach is nightmarish, cutting through the waves with alarming speed. They drift on their bellies, their dark, webbed legs zigzagging so fast the movement blurs. Long black hair jets out behind them like spilled ink. Their faces are only visible from the eyes up—those predatory, soulless eyes that send chills down my spine. Above the water, their black opalescent wings perform like sails, slicing the wind to propel them forward.

"Oh my god," I breathe, gripping Jace's arm. He turns, his eyes full of dread.

There are so many of them. We can't move fast enough.

Jace thrusts both hands out before him. A heavy gust of wind bursts from them, forcing the tide back along with most of the Naiads. But two are faster. Their dark heads disappear beneath the water. Panic rises as I frantically scan for them. The water stills around us, growing eerily silent.

I suck in a sharp breath as one of the Naiads crashes through the surface, snapping its filed teeth at me. Jace hurls himself in front of me, dagger drawn. Its teeth sink into his arm, piercing through his leathers as blood cascades into the dark water. He grunts as he drives the dagger into its rib cage. It releases him with a shrill bleat. He whirls, waving me away.

"Get back! Go!" he bellows over the crashing waves.

The Naiad violently leaps for him again, and he slits its

throat mid-air. It gives a loud gurgle before being swallowed up by the moon-kissed waves.

I tow Jace away by his good arm, my thighs aching against the thick waves as we push on. It's like moving in quicksand.

That's when the other Naiad tears through the water to wrap its spindly arms around Jace's neck. I scream as she tackles him below the surface.

"No!" I shout, my heart plummeting. Before I can think of what to do, his head explodes through the surface with a loud gasp.

"Jace!" I struggle to get to him, the water now up to my thighs. He grapples with the scrappy Naiad, her jaw fully retracted as she snaps at his neck. She's strong. His arms buckle beneath her as she strains to take a chunk out of his flesh. I reach into my belt and pull my own dagger free.

"Hey, bitch!"

I pray to God they don't shift positions in the split second it takes to hurl the knife through the air. I hold my breath as it sinks into the bony ice blue arm. Chilling black eyes slide toward me.

"Come and get me."

The Naiad tosses Jace aside and beelines for me, slithering along the tide like a serpent. I have mere seconds.

Think like a fighter.

Defense or offense. Defense or offense.

Who has the advantage here?

She does. She has the home advantage.

Defense, I decide.

I wait until she's nearly upon me before I call forth my fire. My hands heat in a split second, flames erupting from my palms. Jace fumbles toward me, bloody and horrified. I lock eyes with him and lift my flaming hands.

"Wind," I command.

As if reading my thoughts, he sends a blast of air toward me. I deflect it, aiming at the Naiad as a wall of wind pushes my fire out in a brilliant explosion of light. She screeches as her wings burst into flame. The fire devours them until all that remains is their bony frame with nothing in the space between.

The distraction allows Jace enough time to reach me. I slam into him and hold fast, summoning my shadows to hurry the fuck up and get us out of here. I feel them materialize beneath the inky water. My heart skitters as I glimpse the onslaught of serpentine bodies once again charging toward us. I squeeze my eyes shut as the shadows reach our necks. The snapping of hungry jaws looms closer and closer. Bony fingers wrap around my ankle a second before the shadows suck us up, and we evaporate into thin air.

The shadows spit us out exactly where I hoped they would. Somewhere safe, on the island. I silently thank their intuition as we fall to our knees, gasping.

"Are you alright?" Jace croaks.

"I'm fine." I crawl toward him. "Your arm."

"It's just a scratch." He winces as he lifts it.

"That is not a scratch, Jace."

He grumbles as I pull his arm toward me to inspect it. The bite is deep. "I'm going to try to heal it."

"Don't," he mutters, wrenching it back. "You'll probably fuck it up and leave a nasty scar."

"Hey!" I look up at him. "I saved your ass back there. I haven't heard a thank you yet."

"I told you to go. To run." He glares at me, suddenly furious.

"And you thought I would, what, *listen*? You think I would leave you to die?"

"It doesn't matter if I die—it's you that's indispensable!"

"*You* are indispensable, you idiot!" I shout. "I can't lose you."

"I couldn't live with myself if you died because of my stupid mistake." He claps a hand against his chest as if quelling a sudden pain there.

"It wasn't your fault. We weren't even supposed to land there, but we did. We weren't supposed to stay until night, but we fell asleep. The Naiads weren't supposed to come ashore, but it was high tide. It was a perfect storm, nobody's fault. And we're both still standing." I run my hand up and down his good arm, and he eventually softens.

Jace relents to being the guinea pig for my healing experiment. I do as he directs me, bracing my hands on his arm and calling forth light from deep within me. I visualize threads weaving together, and as I do, Jace's arm repairs itself until all that's left on his chiseled bicep is a tiny pink line.

I look around for our packs, seeking a drink of water. Then I realize they didn't make it to the island with us. They're lost at sea with a bunch of hangry flesh-eating Naiads.

"Our supplies are gone," I announce, crestfallen. "Our weapons."

"I'm the captain. Do you really think I only travel with one dagger?"

He gives me a cocky look, fishing into his boot and spilling a gold-hilted dagger onto the ground. He repeats the action with the other boot, sending another knife clattering to his feet. Then he unfastens his jacket and reaches into his breast pocket, withdrawing a miniature dagger before adding it to the pile.

"That one is my favorite. Plus, we've got one longsword." He pats his hip where his ornately etched silver and onyx blade remains sheathed.

"Just one?" I run my eyes over him, not so discreetly pausing just below his belt. "How sad for you."

I offer up a wicked grin, earning a deep, hearty laugh from him.

"You're despicable," he says, rolling his eyes. "Even with the weapons, we still shouldn't linger."

"I agree." I turn, taking in the unfamiliar land. Even in the moonlight, I can make out the red, striated rock I recognize from the renderings in the history books Zadyn showed me.

The distinct red rock of the Island of Iterre.

31

We hike through the night, weapons clutched in hand, but the journey is surprisingly peaceful. With each step we take toward the mountain, I can feel the channel between the dragon and me widening. An inexplicable magnet pulls me toward her, making it easy to ignore my burning thighs and blistering heels. We reach the base of the mountain as the sun begins to peek through the clouds, the promise of dawn.

I stare up at the Mountain of Hysphestus, marveling at its size.

"How do we get in?" I pant as we slow.

Jace points upward. "We have to go up to go down."

"You can't be serious." I throw him a look, fitting my hands to my hips. "Why can't we just shadow walk inside?"

"Because we've entered a vacuum for magic. The dragon's power, even in a resting state, absorbs all the magic within miles of the mountain. Anything we do from here on out, we'll have to rely on our physical faculties."

"Now I understand why you were such a grump about the basics," I mumble, nudging a rock with my foot.

"Come on." He motions me toward the mountain, lowering his hand for me to step into. I grapple for leverage as he props me up and I find purchase.

"So if we fall—"

"Don't." He doesn't look at me as he grabs onto the rock and hauls himself up. "If we can make it to that little ledge, there is a path that doesn't require—"

"Clinging to the side of a mountain while our impending deaths wait below?" I supply.

He snorts. We climb carefully toward the ledge some ten feet up. Jace reaches it first, pulling himself up with enviable ease. Then he reaches down and hoists me onto the sweet flatness beside him. I'm still breathing hard as he helps me to my feet.

I dust myself off and follow him up the winding path. Rock dust and pebbled ash crunch beneath our boots as we curl around the mountain for hours. The path is only about two feet wide, so we keep tight to the mountainside, wary of every sharp twist and turn.

It finally opens up to a wider ledge a third of the way up. I risk peering over the edge to assess the height at which we now stand. Jace's hand wraps around my bicep, pulling me back.

"I don't like that."

I jog to catch up to him as he turns toward the wall of rock behind us.

"Worried about little old me?" I tease.

Jace ignores me, pressing his arched ear to the red rock. I watch in awe as he pulls his palm back and thrusts it forward sharply. The rock crumbles beneath the force of his strike, leaving a hole large enough for us to fit through.

God, that's hot.

He turns back to find me gawking, open-mouthed.

"You just punched a hole through a mountain," I sputter. "I thought you said no magic here."

He shrugs, flashing me a cocky, self-satisfied smirk. "Who said that had anything to do with magic?"

Giving his arm a gentle whack, I poke my head through the dark opening.

"After you." I toss him a wary look, clearing the path for him. He steps through and holds out a hand to help me over.

We stand inside the Mountain of Hysphestus on a small ledge. A black chasm waits on the other side. As I peer down, I can feel her in a dreamless, restless sleep.

I pull back, realizing that one wrong move and I'll be dragon nip.

The ledge leads onto jagged, rock-hewn stairs that circle down to the bottom of the mountain and into the earth below. We keep quiet and close to the outer wall as we wind the descent, the only light coming from the gaping hole Jace created with the brute strength of his bare hand.

My boot catches on a loose stone and I let out a sharp gasp. Jace is fast, spinning on his heel and catching me around the waist before I tumble over the side. Our tight-pressed chests heave together in uneven synchronization.

The rock under our feet begins to rumble as something stirs below. Our gazes shoot to the ledge in time to catch the crack spidering out, disintegrating the ancient stairs. Jace throws us against the wall, but it does nothing as the entire ledge splits, and we fall.

Our shouts echo off the hollowed-out walls as we plummet with alarming speed. Somewhere during the descent, we lose contact, and the sheer terror that lances through me outweighs anything I have ever felt in my life.

I lose sight of him as we are swallowed by darkness, and the sky rains rock and debris.

My eyes close as I brace myself for the splat.

Instead, I plunge into icy water, my screams instantly silenced. Gasping, I push to the surface, my limbs threatening to seize from the cold. I flail and feel for solid ground. My hands find purchase, and I haul my heavy, sopping body onto the stone, choking up water as I go.

"Jace!" My terror bounces off the rocks, echoing in my ear over and over. I break into a heavy sob. "*Jace!*"

I wait in silence, the only sound that of water gently plunking from the walls into the waiting stream.

No response.

"*Jace!*" My wail breaks the word into three long syllables as I beat my fists against the stone.

He's gone.

"The goal is to wake the dragon, witch, not the dead."

I whirl to find him before me, water sliding down his dark hair and onto his perfect face. I scramble to my feet and throw my arms around him.

"Happy to see me?" He catches me, folding me against him.

"I thought you were dead," I mumble into his chest.

"It'll take a lot more than a fall like that to kill me," he says, smoothing my wet hair. "You okay?"

"No broken bones. I'll live." I take a step back from him, taking in our surroundings.

"Well, that was certainly one way to the bottom of the mountain," he says, glancing upwards.

"We made it to the bottom?" I ask.

"Rock bottom." He holds his arms out around him. "Literally. This way."

We drag our shivering bodies through a dark tunnel. I

clutch Jace's arm as we feel our way through the void, not even his preternatural sight offering any aid in black this thick.

I feel something. Something big, looming with every step we take.

The tunnel opens up to another massive expanse of rock. Light refracts off of a single torch, near the entrance in which we stand. In the darkness, I can vaguely distinguish the cave to be larger than a football field.

My vision is drawn to a high point above us, the only source of soft sound. Déjà vu hits me as I watch the dark water droplets pool at the tip of an overhead rock.

Drip. Drip. Drip.

They land on my forehead with a soft plink, and I blink my eyes, wiping them away with the pads of my fingers. When I bring my hand down, exposed to the dim torchlight, my fingertips are stained a deep blue.

Jace follows my gaze upward to where a female body hangs, pinned against the wall with a massive spike through the gut. Thick, sticky, blue liquid slowly, painstakingly rolls off the tips of her boots and onto our heads below.

Blue blood.

Nausea roils in my stomach as I duck out of the way.

"Oh, fuck," I spit, retreating into the black cave. I'm met with something thick and dense against my back. I turn, my fingers gliding over the slick surface. My hands collide with something hard, like bone. I feel my way up the smooth length as it tapers to a dagger-like point.

"Serena," Jace hisses.

I suck in a breath as the thing before me begins to move. It slithers along the cave floor, sweeping me off my feet. I hold on tight as it picks up speed. As I cross into view of the single torch, the moving surface below me is momentarily illuminated.

Deep purple. Reflective scales.

"Oh my god!" I gasp.

I'm being dragged along by the dragon's *tail.*

Before I can scramble off, it begins to lift off the ground. Fumbling around, my hands find one of the tall, lethal spikes. I carefully get to my feet and wrap arms around it. My stomach drops as I ascend, the way it does on roller coaster rides.

A dizzying sense of vertigo hits me as the tail curls deeper, rotating me fully upside down.

I can't stop the scream that escapes me.

The tail pauses at the sound. Blood rushes to my head as I grit my teeth, clinging to the spike with wild desperation. But my hands grow clammy and slick. Panic twists in my gut as gravity tugs at me and I begin to slide downward.

My breath whooshes out of me as I slice through the air. I land with a thud, wincing as my back connects with something flat, rising steadily up and down.

The dragon's back.

Then all hell breaks loose.

The deafening roar that follows sends the rocks above us cascading down over our heads. An explosion of blue fire shatters the darkness, kissing the rock walls and searing them white. It's hard to see anything but that blinding fire in the dark.

"Serena!" Jace's voice bounds off the cave walls.

The dragon jostles to her feet, and I slide down her back, my tailbone connecting with a solid spike. I flip over, groaning, and curl myself against it to keep from sliding off. A deep rumble comes from below me, and I know what's about to happen.

"Jace! Look out!"

Another round of dragon fire erupts.

Scorching heat that blasts through the cavern. If I wasn't so terrified, the colors of the flames would threaten to enchant me. I can't see anything but the trajectory of that fire. I can't see Jace —I can barely see my own hands in front of me as they feel around blindly.

The sound of rustling chains pulls me back to the present moment.

Think, think, think.

I push to my feet, following the sound of clanking iron as the dragon shifts, stretching her massive legs beneath me. It's like being on a moving obstacle course. I find the chain by tripping over it and land flat on her scaled neck.

Her annoyed growl echoes in my bones as I grapple for the corroded links. A heavy wind tosses my undone hair off my face, followed by a loud flapping sound. I can scarcely make out the arching, spiked wings as they stretch behind the dragon's back and begin to beat.

"Shit, shit, shit," I mutter, grabbing the chain a split second before she lifts off the ground and blasts up from the center of the earth.

My body swings through the air like a pendulum, slapping against her hard form. Ignoring my straining arms, I hold tight as she drives us higher and higher up the dark tunnel. A loud rumble rattles in her throat before blue fire bursts from her mouth and blows out the entire top of the mountain.

We break through the rock and soar into the skies.

I dare a glance down. My heart drops when I see Jace dangling from one of the tall spikes along the dragon's tail.

His grasp slips, and I wail, watching him career toward a crag of flat red rock below. He tucks into a roll as his shoulder connects with the ground, tumbling a few times before flattening onto his back. I think I see him moving as we disappear into a cloud.

The air pressure is enough to make me lose my grip, but I

am determined. I didn't come all the way here just to fall from a fire-breathing dragon.

No. Fucking. Way.

I try to dive into the channel connecting us, but am met with a wall of disorientation. Jarred from a two-thousand-year-old sleep, she's acting on instinct alone.

As I slam into her again, I plant my feet against her scales. Using the chain for leverage, I walk my way up her neck, pausing when I reach her mouth and the razor-like teeth I can only guess lie hidden inside.

I have to get higher. I have to get her to look at me. If she sees me, she'll recognize me.

When I reach the top of her head, she thrashes, her annoyance flaring. I wrap the chain around my arm for security, flattening myself against her skull. Another wild toss of her head has me coasting down the slope of her snout and flying over the edge. Her jaw stretches open. Sweat slicks my screaming fingers as the chain goes taut and I dangle inches from her forked pink tongue and the tunnel of her uvula. A loud sound rises from her throat, and time slows.

This is the moment. This is the moment where I either live or die.

In a second, blue dragon fire will spit from her mouth and torch me into dust.

Kicking my feet into her long, sharp fangs, I bound back and swing my legs upward. My fingers release the chain in time to dig my nails into her snout, arms straining to keep me in place.

I stare up into the brightest green I've ever seen.

The cat-like pupils narrow and dilate, the black engulfing the green almost entirely. Heavy, crinkled lids blink at me before reopening.

The resistance eddies from her as the channel clears, and I can hear her thoughts as if spoken out loud.

Blackblood.

Her purr is like night personified.

Dragon.

Prophyria.

Without warning, she jerks her head up, tossing me high into the air. I scream as my stomach plummets. But she dips beneath me, catching me on the massive sail of her eggplant purple wing. She descends sharply as we burst through a cloud bank, and the red rock of the mountain comes into view.

I spy Jace below—a blip on the large, flat expanse built into the mountainside. A landing strip, I realize.

He waves his arms above his head as Prophyria dips low and banks, angling her wings downward so that I slide off above Jace. I tackle him to the ground, and we roll a few times before stopping, my body pinning his, our chests rising and falling out of time.

"Hi," I breathe.

"Hi." He breaks into a gorgeous smile that crinkles his golden eyes. I ease off him, and we get to our feet.

I look to the skies. Prophyria has disappeared.

"It's not over yet," Jace says. "You have to seal the bond by successfully mounting her and taking your first ride as a bonded pair."

I walk to the cliff's edge, Jace by my side, staring down the mountain's jagged descent. Quiet settles for a brief moment. Then a brutal wind tears across the gray skies, sending the loose strands of my hair swirling around my head.

"Call her," Jace says, looking at me. A secretive smile blooms on his lips.

I close my eyes, centering myself. Deep, steady breaths.

Then I dive into my own mind—into the channel carved between us.

Prophyria, I whisper into the darkness.

A gentle nudge at the edge of my consciousness answers, like a pet brushing its nose fondly against its master. The sound of wings, beating heavy and hard, grows closer. I open my eyes to a purple-scaled shooting star as she streamlines into sight, cutting through storm clouds and diving toward us.

"Get ready," Jace cautions me.

The large gusts from her wings push back the skin of our faces, making it hard to keep our eyes open. My hair swirls around me like Medusa's snakes as I struggle to keep my feet planted on the uneven ground.

I can feel her approach through our bond like a leash pulling her nearer.

"As soon as she gets close enough, you grab the chain and swing yourself upward with all your strength. Pull hard and use her side to push off. You get on that saddle, and you're safe. And whatever you do," he shouts over the winds, bracing my arm, "don't let go." *

The earth begins to rumble. Small stones crumble from the mountain's edge, plummeting into oblivion.

Prophyria approaches at a wild speed, and I suck in a deep breath against the raging wind. Her thick, weathered wings beat fast against her sides as she lowers herself overhead. I dare one last look at Jace before I either make a successful mount or plummet to my death. He nods assuredly.

"On my mark," he shouts, barely audible above the winds.

"Three." My stomach begins to drop.

"Two." I freeze, my muscles locking.

"One."

---

* Cue: *Risk* by Gracie Abrams

I remain unmoving as I stare up at the underside of this massive creature. She casts a dark shadow above us, eclipsing what little light the sky offers. The heavy chain dangling from her worn saddle cuts through the air, threatening to take us out.

"Serena, now!" Jace's voice snaps me into action.

I launch myself forward just before the chain flies out of reach. The downbeat of her wings nearly knocks me to the ground as I dangle ten feet above the rock. But I latch onto that chain and hold on for dear life. Its aged rust cuts into my fingers as my weight takes me down a few inches.

The pressure of her upward trajectory alone is crushing. Grunting through clenched teeth, I drag myself up the iron links. Once I'm close enough, I swing my legs forward and brace my feet against her underside, using the chain's resistance to scale her body. My arms bleat, straining against the wind to maintain balance. A loud cry escapes me as I haul myself higher, until I can grab one of her spikes and climb the remaining few like a rock wall. I throw my leg over the half-disintegrated saddle and lift my head.

Then finally, *finally*, hands bloody and torn, muscles screaming in protest, I sit triumphantly on top of my dragon.

My dragon.

Our bond begins to shimmer in the darkness of my mind, like a glowing chain connecting my heart and head to hers. I grip the reins and pull, and Prophyria responds as if we share one mind. It feels as if we are one soul—she the extension of me and my will. We soar higher and higher, cutting clean through the clouds. I laugh as we break through the opaque mist, looking down at the mountain that now seems miniature from our altitude.

The moment I think about banking right, she obeys.

I let out a wild howl, and she does the same, her roar one of defiance and triumph and pure, unadulterated joy.

She is happy, I realize with a smile.

She has a rider. She has a bond again. She is awake and alive.

My power hums beneath my skin like a song to the tune of freedom and wild, wild will. I lose myself in the euphoria of the ride, the intense wind nipping at my nose and cheeks and hair. I savor the dips in my stomach as we dive and loop, decorating the bland sky with purple chemtrails.

Eventually, I steer us downward to where Jace waits, small as a speck on the cliff's edge. As we near him, I can see the elation I feel echoed on his face.

An obedient purr reverberates through my body as I call to mind a landing. The wind pushes back Jace's dark hair as we descend, casting the mountain in shadow. When we touch down, the ancient rock takes a moment to settle beneath us.

Prophyria's wings gently tuck into her sides. I grip the chain and scale down her massive side until I can make the small leap to the dusty ground. I rise from my crouch to see Jace standing ten feet away.

One look at him, and I know.

I know that everything has changed.

I know he's done fighting. Done pretending there is nothing between us.

And so am I.

His shoulders sink as he shakes his head at me. We each take three long strides forward. He reaches for me at the same time I reach for him, welcoming me home into his arms. Our lips connect at the exact moment our bodies do, his hands finding my unbound hair, mine clasping his face.

The kiss is hungry, as if we'd both been starving ourselves for months. My mind empties completely as his lips work around mine. I want to drown in his campfire scent—bottle it, and drink it. We hold each other so tight it's hard to breathe. But I won't let go. Won't allow one inch of space between us.

When he breaks the kiss and pulls back to look at me—his hair messy, lips swollen, as I know mine are—I know we have crossed a line. And there won't be any turning back.

The look we share is one of acceptance. Acceptance of the consequences. Whatever may come.

"You made it," he whispers to me, smiling.

"Did you doubt that I would?" I ask. He chuckles and leans his forehead against mine in a way that threatens to break my heart.

"You looked like a queen sitting up there on top of the most fearsome creature in all of Solterre."

"I thought I was the most fearsome creature." I smirk up at him, fingers twining behind his neck.

"You are frightening in many ways." His arms tighten around my waist. "But you don't scare me."

"Does this mean I can stop training, and you'll start being nicer to me?"

He laughs, interlacing our fingers and brushing his lips against my knuckles.

"I told you. I'm never nice," he reminds me, but a look of sadness crosses his eyes.

"What's wrong?" I ask.

"I have wanted you for so long," he admits, distracting himself with my hair, my leathers, my hands. "The only way I knew how to push you away was with cruelty. If I could make you hate me, then there would be no chance for us. I said so many things I didn't mean—did so many things I regret. I tried to hurt you purposefully. I *did* hurt you. I am more sorry than you could ever know." He is still unable to look me in the eye. I take his face in my hands and force him to look at me.

"I have wanted you since the moment I saw you. Since you

threw me in a cell and stabbed me in the leg." I laugh, shaking his arms. "And I want you now."

"Even after everything?"

"Had you done even a single thing differently, I wouldn't be standing here right now. I would not have been able to do this —" I point to where Prophyria rests. "You showed me how to be strong, even when it hurts. I needed someone to push me. I needed someone to push against." I give his chest a playful shove, earning a small tweak from his lips.

I brush my mouth against his in a gentle kiss. He stills, his eyes closing. I kiss him again, and some of that tension in his face dissolves. Another kiss and it is gone completely. He groans against my mouth, pulling me in deeper. I let him take the lead, and he devours me. My knees actually weaken as he wraps his arms around my waist and lifts me off the ground. I squeal.

Prophyria heaves an annoyed sigh at the PDA, not even bothering to be stealthy about it. Jace puts me down, and we stare at her, still holding each other.

"Now what?" I ask.

"We fly home."

❧

32

"Where is she going to stay?" I ask as we climb the large chain onto Prophyria's back.

Jace slides into the saddle behind me, wrapping his arms around my waist. My stomach does a flip. "If we leave her out in a field, word is going to travel awfully fast to the other kingdoms."

"There are lodgings suited for a dragon near the castle. They're ancient, of course, but they'll do just fine in keeping her hidden and comfortable," he says, giving my ear a playful nip.

"Unless you want us both to go plummeting to our deaths, I suggest you not distract me like that."

He lets out a dark chuckle as I take up the reins and descend into the bond.

Fly, Prophyria.

She stirs to life at the touch of my hand on her neck. Her head rears, and she opens her magnificent wings.

With a running start, we leap into the skies.

This is a feeling I will never get used to or take for granted. The feeling of gratitude that I get to ride through the skies on this beautiful, terrifying creature. That she is mine and I am hers.

Jace grips me tighter around the waist, and I ride home with my head in the clouds.

Literally.

~

ONCE WE ARE FLYING over Aegar, Jace directs me toward the mountain range north of the castle. As we make our descent toward the largest one, I spot a slight opening in the massive formation. Jace urges us onward.

"You're sure this is it?" I shout over the high winds. He nods. "That's the one."

My panic starts to rise as we near the mountain at a startling speed. I try slowing Prophyria by tugging on the chains, but she presses onward.

Down the bond, I feel a soft wave of calmness, telling me she has everything under control. That doesn't stop me from screaming my head off as we careen directly down into the mountain.

The opening is not nearly wide enough for her. We're not going to fit. We're going to collide head-on with the unforgiving mountain and end up splattered across its face.

The wind pulls at my cheeks as we plummet straight down into what will be certain death. Jace's arms brace me, his face pressed against mine. I suck in a steep breath as we shoot like a spear through the tiny opening and are instantly swallowed by darkness. My shrill screams echo off of the tunnel walls as Prophyria's spikes and talons scrape against them, giving off sparks.

Trust.

The word is spoken into my mind by a gentle voice. I count

the seconds as they pass, and while it feels like centuries, only four go by before we burst through the tunnel into an expansive diamond cave. The uncut gems refract brilliantly, creating light where there is no outside source.

With enough space to expand her wings to full length, my dragon gently parachutes us onto the ground with a soft landing.

I burst into hysterical laughter. Jace eyes me, but I can't stop. Tears stream down my face as my body is wracked by the giggling fit.

"Are you...alright?" he asks.

I nod my head, high on the adrenaline rush.

"I'm fine," I croak, hoarse from screaming. "That was beyond anything I've ever felt in my entire life."

Jace slides down the dragon's smooth side and holds his arms up for me.

"This place has been here for thousands of years. The first Blackblood High Queen, Arden, housed and bred dragons here."

"It's gargantuan," I breathe as I slide down into his waiting hands. He grips my waist and eases me onto the crystal-encrusted floor. I take in the massive size, picturing this place overrun by dragons and their young.

"The caves here are amazing." He points toward one of the dim openings. "They lead far beneath the earth. The dragons had plenty of space to play here, to fly."

Prophyria settles into a seated position, her scaled chin resting atop her front talons. It's impossible to marry the docile creature before me with the one who almost burned us alive hours ago. Placing my hand beneath her bright green eye, I gently run my fingers over her cheek. Her scales look rough to the touch but are surprisingly smooth and slick—like the skin of a seal. Beneath the uncut diamonds, she is breathtaking—

sparkling like an amethyst giant among the sea of gleaming crystals. She lets out an exhausted sigh, and I smile in response as her big cat-like eyes drift closed.

Content, she speaks into my soul.

She feels content.

"Welcome home, Furi," I whisper. "Get some rest."

Smoothing her scales one last time, I turn to Jace, who stands watching me with pride in his eyes.

"She'll be safe here?"

He nods and motions for me to follow him. "Very safe."

"I feel awful leaving her so soon."

"Dragons are very independent creatures. She hasn't flown in centuries. I'm betting she'll need a good night's rest and a big meal tomorrow."

"This might be an obvious question, but what does she eat?" I ask.

Jace looks down at me as he takes my hands and pulls me toward the entrance of a dark tunnel. He reaches up and cracks off a diamond icicle hanging above us, holding it out before him. It illuminates the space enough to see a few feet ahead.

"I'm sure she would prefer people, but a steady animal diet will keep her strong."

"Animals?"

"Deer, wolves, goats," he muses. "Good thing I taught you how to fire a bow and arrow." He winks at me.

"This is crazy." I shake my head. "I'm not even a dog person, and somehow, I end up with a dragon."

"The last of her kind." He gives my hand a gentle squeeze. "Just like you."

The dark tunnel leads us to a door at the base of the mountain, and we step out into bright starlight.

"This door is keyed to your blood," he says. I tilt my head.

"What do you mean?"

"High Queen Arden spelled it to only grant entry to Black-bloods. You're the only one who can open it," he explains, turning to me. "Do you want to do the honors?"

"I barely have enough strength to stand. My legs are shaking so badly from gripping the saddle." I wince, stretching my hips until my bones give a satisfying crack.

"If you can do it when you're on the verge of collapse, you can do it whenever. Try."

He pulls me into his arms, and I close my eyes. I lean my head against his chest, inhaling his smoky scent. As I envision our destination, the edges around us start to fray, and we are enveloped in dark smoke. It curls around our legs, gobbling them up as it spreads up and over our backs in a slow, sensual tornado. Furious winds envelop us as we are swallowed by a black hole and spit out the other side. Familiar walls materialize around us, and I open my eyes to the sanctuary of my room.

"Well done, Dragon Rider," Jace says against my hair. I lean into him, tilting my head up. Just as he lowers his face to mine and our lips begin to touch, the door flies open.

Mal and Max stand there, their twin faces wearing matching expressions of surprise. I feel the blush creep over my cheeks as I drop my hands from Jace's side. He tenses but makes no attempt to distance himself from me.

"Well, well, well," Max regales, his eyes twinkling with amusement. "She lives to tell the tale."

"Captain. My lady." Mal's cool, low voice rings out as he dips his head. It's maybe the second time I've ever heard him speak. His eyes link with mine. "The king wanted us to alert him the moment you arrived back."

"*If* you arrived back," Max mutters. Mal shoots him a scathing look. "I meant no offense! It was a dangerous mission, is all."

"Serena made it look like child's play," Jace says, glancing down at me. He doesn't bother to mask the affection brimming in his eyes. He must really trust these two.

"The king is waiting on our word. He wants a meeting in the interior throne room," Mal says, his keen eyes roaming over me.

His demeanor is drastically different from his jovial twin's. Where Max is all boisterous swagger and sloppy smiles, Mal is unnervingly quiet and abnormally still.

I nod and we follow Max to the interior throne room—a modest space in comparison to the one in the diamond cave. Our footsteps echo off the tan marble as we make our way past the alabaster pillars to stop before the dais. We wait off to the side, the entrance clear for the king.

Moments later, I feel a swell of power reverberate through the hall—a sure sign of his approach. He comes into view, looking somewhat less formal than usual—a dark, fitted jacket and black leathers tucked into knee-high boots.

To my surprise, the queen enters behind him with Mal at her side. She is cold and regal in a simple cream-colored gown and floor-length overcoat of the deepest crimson. The king starts when he sees us, sees me.

A look of disbelief crosses his features.

"I must admit, I wondered if you would make it out with your life." He stops before me. The queen stands behind him, silent and removed, hands folded elegantly in front of her. Her steely eyes are the only indication of interest as they gloss over me.

"Well?" the king asks. "Is it done?"

"I bonded the dragon, Your Grace," I say, meeting his hopeful gaze. "She is safe in Aegar."

His whole face relaxes as he blinks.

"I sorely underestimated your abilities."

I bow my head in gratitude. He shakes his head and claps

his hands together. To my utter shock, he pulls me forward and kisses me on both cheeks.

"Well done, my dear. Well done." He glances from me to Jace. "You as well, Captain. You promised a Dragon Rider. And you delivered." He claps him on the shoulder affectionately. Jace offers a small smile in return, bowing his head.

"Come," the king commands, motioning for us to follow him. "You two must be starved. I want to hear all about your adventures over supper."

The three of us dine in an intimate room with navy blue wallpaper, ornately carved cherry wood furniture, and soft candlelight. The feast before me sets my stomach rumbling as we each sink into our seats. A large roast serves as the center-piece, with cooked vegetables and hot, roasted potatoes.

We tell the king all that happened on the island, sparing no detail as per request. I realize that he isn't asking from a polit-ical standpoint. He's simply intrigued. He leans in and listens between bites as we recount our misadventures with the Naiads.

Jace recalls, more expressive than I've ever seen him, "It had me by the collar, and what did you say?" He turns to me.

"I said, 'Hey bitch, come and get me,' and I stuck a dagger in her arm." I shrug, taking a sip of my wine.

The king stares at me for a beat, then erupts into laughter, slapping his hands down on the table. I start to giggle along with Jace, and before I know it, the three of us are seized by that contagious, *can't get out a sound* kind of silent laughter that racks through your entire body.

It feels like a privilege to laugh with him. Maybe it's because being near him makes me feel close to my dad in a way that I've desperately missed. To see him smile at me—because of me—makes my heart swell.

I've never seen this side of the king. I always found him

hard to read. Benevolent but severe. Level-headed but not soft. Formidable but not cruel or self-interested.

I understand now. In public, the king portrays the cold, hard war hero; the stern authority figure to Jace's grave and obedient captain. He's tough on Jace in public. But behind closed doors, he is the loving father, and Jace, the devoted son. I can see the love between them.

We drink wine, and for a moment, all titles fall away. He is no longer king, Jace no longer captain, and I no longer Dragon Rider. For a moment, we are three friends. I feel Jace's hand discreetly reach for mine under the table, giving it a gentle squeeze.

The king shares stories about Prophyria that have been passed down through generations. It comes as no surprise that she is known for being strong-willed, brave, and, at times, reckless.

A true free spirit.

"She was bred beneath that mountain, you know," the king says. His cheeks are pink from the wine, his face is animated. "Her mother was High Queen Arden's dragon, Hyraxia. You have given her a reason to live again. In addition to bringing her home to Aegar."

He sits back in his chair, assessing both of us.

"I cannot express," he starts, "how truly proud I am of you. Both of you." His gaze shifts to me.

"I know this was not what you had planned for your young life." He lays a hand on top of mine. "Your sacrifices will not go unrecognized or be taken for granted. Not by me, and not by this kingdom. You have my sincere gratitude."

"It's been my pleasure," I answer honestly. It's been a pleasure and a gift to see my dad's face again. To hear his voice. To get to know this strange, alternate version of him. I squeeze the king's hand as tears fill my eyes. He lets go far too soon.

I blink back the tears, straightening.

"Now that we have Prophyria here, what will we do?" I ask him. He seems to ponder a moment.

"Nothing until we have to. Continue to train with the captain, hone your magic, and get comfortable with your dragon."

"We won't be doing any attacking anytime soon? No battles?" I glance between them.

"I will never throw the first stone. Lives are too precious to be lost if it can be avoided. The dragon will be a secret weapon —reserved only for when we need her most. You must learn to work with her power. You alone will serve as a conduit for her magic. You control it. Else, it will cause great destruction."

"So, I'll act as a filter for her magic."

"Essentially," Jace says in affirmation.

"Serena—" The king leans forward. "I would like for you to be a member of my small council. If you would be willing."

My mouth drops open. I glance from Jace back to the king.

"Yes," I sputter without a second thought. "Yes. I would be honored."

Derek breaks into a warm smile and claps his hands together once. He rises from his seat and the majesty of his power curls around me, like I am suddenly part of his team. Like I am protected.

"Wonderful. Rest. Both of you. You deserve it," he says and swiftly exits the room.

33

Walking back to my room with Jace, I feel that familiar thrum of nerves and excitement dancing in my stomach. I want to be alone with him. With no weapons, no interruptions, no distractions.

Just us.

When he stops at my door and leans against the wall with that casual ease, I wonder if he wants that, too.

A moment of silence passes between us.

"Do you want to come in?"

His eyes gloss over my face, drinking me in.

"You're probably exhausted right now. The events of the last two days, on top of using your magic so steadily—"

"Don't make excuses for me." I hold up a hand and twist the doorknob. "Do you want to come in or not?"

He shakes his head, growling in my ear as I push it open. "Impatient little witch."

The tickle of his breath on my neck makes my shoulders

rise. He steps inside, and I close the door behind us. It clicks shut with a sound of finality.*

We stare at each other for a moment before he rushes me, pinning me back against the door and claiming my mouth. I sigh in relief as he puts his hands on me.

Finally.

After all these months of dancing around each other, of grating sexual tension and torturous frustration, the kiss is full of heat and pent-up anger.

Longing.

His hands feel their way up my neck, fisting my hair so tightly that I arch off the door. He lowers his mouth to my throat, kissing and teasing as I undo the buttons of his leather jacket and run my hands over his smooth chest. I pull his face back up to mine, and our tongues meet, gliding over one another, stirring the dormant hunger within me.

He kisses me like I'm the air he needs to breathe. And I'm *melting.*

My tongue flicks over one of his razor-sharp canines, and a small sound escapes me. He pulls back to smile, golden eyes wicked, revealing two tiny fangs.

Calloused hands slide over my breasts before squeezing my waist, fusing my hips to his. His jacket falls to the ground, and he goes to work on mine, his lips never leaving my skin. His mouth blazes a scorching trail along my collarbone, sending a flood of warmth through me as I wrap my arms around his neck and press into him, desperate for more.

Every single touch is infused with heat, with need. And my entire body is screaming for more—for *all.*

He gives my shirt a rough tug, yanking it down over my

---

* Cue: *Ode to Conversation Stuck in Your Throat...* by Del Water Gap

shoulders. I close my eyes as he explores more of my exposed skin, aching to have less clothing between us.

I reach for the hem of my shirt, and without warning, my hands fly above my head, pinned there by invisible restraints. My eyes spring open. A cool breeze dances down my inner arms with slow, torturous agony as Jace's hands slip beneath my shirt. His fingers skim my sides as he lifts it over my head and tosses it aside. Those golden eyes turn a shade darker, devouring my body with insatiable hunger. His invisible touch drags up my legs, heading for dangerous territory, while his thumbs glide over my breasts, waking the skin beneath. I rear against him as he teases me, exploring each one with wonder until I can't take anymore. Shuddering, I dip forward to drink from his lips. He groans, releasing my wrists and crushing me to him. My fingers knot in his hair, pulling it with a sense of urgency.

He hoists me up with perfect ease, wrapping my legs around his waist and cupping my ass with his massive hands. I cry out as he spins and my back slams into the wooden bedpost. I'm pinned there, entirely at his mercy.

"I've wanted to do this for so long," he murmurs against my lips. His hips drive upward into my most private spot, and nothing has ever felt so right. "You have no idea."

His breath is hot against my pebbled skin.

"Oh, I think I do," I whisper, biting my lip to keep from crying out again.

"When you kissed me at solstice—" I strip off his shirt. "When you came to me all needy and demanding—" His mouth ghosts over mine.

"Yes?" I wriggle my hips, impatient for more.

"You were so ready for me," he grits, answering my silent demand with another thrust of his hips. I nod, unable to form words.

His hands glide over my breasts again, this time not as gently as he squeezes and pinches until I can no longer hold back the moan building inside of me.

"You have no idea the restraint it took to not give in to you. I dreamt of you that night. Dreamt of how I wanted you. Of all the things I would do to you if I ever got the chance."

He twists and throws me down on the bed. I bounce once, staring up at him in awe.

I've never been so attracted to anyone in my life.

He kneels on the floor and catches my boot in his hand, stripping it off and tossing it aside.

"I hope it's a long list." I watch him, enthralled.

"Longer than you can even imagine."

Without breaking eye contact, he yanks the other boot off, inadvertently tugging me forward. "I woke up so unsatisfied. My whole body aching for you."

Oh my god.

"Then we better get started, don't you agree?" A siren speaks in place of me, her voice husky and sensual.

The mattress dips as Jace leans over me, his kisses driving us further and further up the bed. Something small and hard digs into my back, and I break away to reach for the cell phone pinned beneath me.

"What is that?" Jace freezes, staring at the foreign object.

"It's my cell phone. I was looking at old pictures the night before we left and must have fallen asleep with it in bed."

He sits up, holding out a curious hand for it.

"What does it do?"

I scoop my shirt off the floor, draping it over my bare chest.

"We primarily use it to communicate in the human world," I explain, shifting to sit on my knees.

"You communicate through this—this little box? What kind

of magic is it?" He turns it over and upside down, studying it. I stifle a laugh at his adorable confusion.

"No magic. Just technology."

His fingers slide over the screen, nearly dropping it when it lights up. He lets out a gasp, turning the phone toward me.

"There are portraits. In your phone," he sputters, dumbfounded. I can't help laughing now as he shakes his head in disbelief.

"It's a picture. It uses this thing called a camera to freeze moments in time—like a portrait. You'd be amazed at all this thing can do. It plays music, you can play games. You can even ask it questions, and it will pretty much tell you anything you want to know."

"A magic mirror?" He glances up at me.

I gawk at him.

"What? You guys have magic mirrors here?"

He shrugs, staring at the photo, transfixed. "There were only a handful ever made, and they've been lost to time."

"Here. You do this to see the next one." I brush my finger over the touch screen, and a new photo appears. Jace mimics the motion.

"This is incredible. How do they all fit in here?" he breathes.

"It's called the cloud. It backs up photos and files and messages." Jace stares at me like I have three heads. "Never mind, it's complicated."

"This is you?" A photo of me from a year ago displays itself, and I nod. Jace glances from me to the image and back. "You're beautiful."

My skin heats at the absent-minded compliment as he gazes at the screen and swipes again. Then he freezes, and the air around us grows cold. He slowly lifts his eyes to mine.

"What is this?"

He turns the phone to me, and my mouth falls open.

It's a picture of Jack and me after a Yankees game. We got caught in a downpour on the way to the subway, and he pulled me to a stop outside the entrance. He said he just wanted to hold me in the rain. I told him he was crazy but risked the pneumonia to stand there with his arms around me. Then he reached into my back pocket, held up the phone, and snapped a photo of us—his smile wide as I stared at him adoringly.

That's the image Jace now holds up to me.

"Jace," I start as he slides off the bed.

"Who is that?" he asks, eyes flashing.

"I told you that you reminded me of someone I used to know." The words sound so feeble leaving my mouth.

"That's an understatement!" he seethes. "You told me there was a resemblance, not that we share the same face!"

"I know it's a shock, but despite the resemblance, you are not the same person. Not at all."

"Oh, I know," he growls. "Who is that? Because it sure as hell isn't me."

"His name is Jack. He was my boyfriend," I rush to explain, watching him pace. "We were pretty serious. We almost got married."

"But you didn't?" He glances at me, golden eyes incredulous.

"No, I got scared, and I left. I never saw him again."

"You loved each other," he says.

It isn't entirely a question, but I nod as he runs his hands through his hair, the movement so oddly like Jack.

"Did you think I was him? Is that why you—" He breaks off, shaking his head. "What am I to you? Am I just a stand-in for that person?"

"No, that has never been the case!" I scramble off the bed, trailing him.

"When I first saw you, I didn't know what to think. Everything was so surreal. But I fell for you in spite of myself. It didn't matter that you looked alike. I fell for the male who picked me out of the Bone Forest and threw me in a dungeon. For the male that taught me to fight and made me strong. The one who showed me it was possible to love again when I thought I never would. I fell for *you*."

I pull him to face me.

"When I first got here, and you brought me to that cell, I told you that the king was my father." I reach for the phone before he can respond, pull up a picture of my dad, and turn the image to him.

"That is my dad. I thought he and King Derek were the same person at first—I mean, look at them. He's a carbon copy of my dad before he... before he died. And this"—I pull up a picture of Sam—"is my sister."

"She looks like Sorscha." His eyebrows knit together as he takes the phone from my hands, studying it.

"Sam and I don't speak anymore. But Sorscha and Sam are nothing alike. My sister is bratty, cold, and aloof. Sorscha is... like sunshine," I admit. "I knew right away that none of you were the people I knew."

"You should have told me." His voice is less hostile than it was moments ago, and I take the opportunity to run my hands over his arms.

"Jace, I know, and I'm so sorry. When I first came here, Zadyn said that if I were to say anything, it could alter nature's course, so I kept quiet."

"And you listened to him?" he hisses, his voice rising.

"Yes, why wouldn't I?"

"Because he's in *love* with you!" He explodes, breaking out of my grasp. His shout echoes off the walls, followed by a long silence.

No, I shake my head. That's *impossible*. That's *crazy*.

"He is not in love with me—he's with Cece." My protest is weak. Unconvincing. His laugh lacks any trace of humor.

"No, he's *fucking* Cece. He's not in love with her. There's a difference."

I flinch at his harsh words.

"You should have told me," he fumes, pacing the room, hands braced on his hips.

I've never seen him so discomposed.

He turns to me. "What did you think was going to happen?"

"I don't know," I answer honestly. "Something bad. I felt like I would be messing with fate."

"I thought you didn't believe in fate," he bites, hurling his words like an accusation.

Suddenly, I feel so small.

"I—I didn't."

My answer is clearly the wrong one. Jace throws his shirt over his head and scoops up his jacket, rushing for the door.

"I need some air."

Unable to stop myself, I bound after him, still clutching my shirt against my naked chest.

"Look, I understand why you're upset, but give me a chance to explain. I will tell you everything. Jace, please."

Pathetic.

I am pathetic, tugging on his arm, begging him to stay. Maybe this is karma. He brushes me off, wrenching the door open as tears blur my vision.

I am not expecting to see a wide-eyed Marideth on the other side. Gazing between us, she says, "I wanted to speak with you. It's Dover, he's—"

She trails off, piecing together Jace's disheveled hair and my state of undress. The look of shock on her face sends a flood of shame through me. Jace stands beside me, still as a statue.

"Good gods." Marideth shakes her head, her expression falling into steep disappointment.

"Marideth," I start, not knowing what I'll even say.

"I came by to tell you that Dover's parents set a date for the wedding." Her cold voice is meant for me, but her eyes are fixed on Jace.

"I'm so sorry," I breathe, reaching for her hands. She rips them away and walks Jace back into the room, driving her finger into his chest.

"How could you," she hisses.

"Marideth." His voice is pained.

"How stupid can you be?" she snaps and glances back toward me. "Both of you. I knew, I just *knew*, from the way you two looked at each other, that something was going on. And if I noticed, then surely I'm not the only one. How long?"

She crosses her arms. The two of us, ashamed, say nothing.

"*How long?*" Her firm demand shakes free the words hanging on the tip of my tongue.

"It just happened."

"Well, it *can't* happen. If anyone else had seen this—" She slows her breath, closing her eyes and pinching the bridge of her nose. "You are courting the princess. And *you* are one of her ladies. You're her *cousin*. You're lucky she's so blindly enamored with you, or else both of your heads would be on the chopping block."

"She would never—" Jace starts.

"You don't think so? I've known her a lot longer than you have, Captain. Long enough to know that she does not respond well when you take what she is not willing to give." Her eyes slide to me. "You underestimate her. You see a bubbly little party girl who would rather sneak off to visit pleasure halls than sit in on her father's council meetings. But that female"— she prowls closer—"is capable of more than you know."

I let that sink in, wondering what she could mean.

"This was over anyway." Jace sets his jaw, refusing to look at me. "Marideth, I know I don't have the right to ask, but please. Let me be the one to tell her." He wears a tortured expression as he begs her.

"Are you mad? Don't you dare say a word to her. Just agree to end this now," she commands, eyes darting between our guilty faces.

"It's already done," Jace emphasizes as we exchange a look. His face is riddled with anger and disgust.

I've ruined everything. I want to run to him, to smooth that tension from his brow, to kiss his lips into a smile, to hold him until he breathes easy. But where we stood seconds ago, our bodies pressed together, we now stand on opposite sides of the room. It might as well be the other side of the world.

"Get out," Marideth says to Jace, her voice sounding tired.

He shoves his arms through his jacket and smooths his hair as he makes for the door, the hardened mask of the captain easing onto his face before my very eyes.

"Jace," I call.

He turns halfway back to me and shakes his head with a sigh.

Did we ever really have a chance?

The look in his eye tells me what we both already know. This was doomed from the start. Realizing there is nothing more to say, he addresses me with a cold and removed voice.

"I'll see you tomorrow."

I stare at the door as it clicks shut, his campfire scent still lingering in the air. A cruel tease indicating all that I cannot have. Marideth plops down in a chair, eyes roaming over me.

I turn to her. "Aren't you going to give me the third degree? Or lay into me about how wrong Jace and I are?"

"I've said enough tonight. And I said it because I am your friend." Her voice softens as she repeats, "I am your friend."

The words make my heart clench. Her brow knits together as she glances over me.

"And what the hell are you wearing?"

"Fighting leathers." I sigh, throwing the shirt over my head and sinking into the seat across from her.

"The truth, please." Her cunning gray eyes lay me bare as she leans forward.

Here goes nothing.

"I'm the last Blackblood witch."

"Are you fucking serious?"

I lean my head on the tip of my pointer finger. "You can't tell anyone."

"Don't worry, I'm your personal vault." She rolls her eyes.

I expect a flood of follow-up questions, but Marideth keeps me on my toes, inspecting me for a long while before opening her mouth.

"This all makes sense now. Your sudden arrival at court, that bullshit story about the temple and the priestesses, your *'courtier lessons.'*"

"I'm not a cousin of the king. I'm not from the temple, I'm just...me."

"You and Jace have spent more time together than you've been letting on."

"I've spent nearly every morning since I've been here training with him so I could bond my dragon."

"Your dragon?" she sputters.

"Prophyria," I supply, running a hand through my hair. "Jace and I just got back."

"You just got back from bonding a dragon?" Her eyebrows nearly reach her hairline.

"Mar, this information cannot leave this room."

She nods. "We all have secrets. I understand. No one will know."

We sit in silence for a long time after that.

34

Jace is quiet as we take cover beneath the brush, waiting for a deer or wolf to appear. I hold the bow and arrow, trying to still my hands. I've missed three shots so far this morning because they were shaking so badly. I didn't sleep at all last night, my heart and my conscience weighing heavy.

A twig snaps thirty yards away.

A large deer with great antlers slips around a tree, grazing in the grass. Jace nods to me. I try to steady myself as much as possible, but when I release the arrow, its trajectory is subpar. A strange wind, however, lashes out and corrects its line. It lands in the deer's heart, and he goes down without so much as a yelp.

I turn to Jace, frowning.

"Hey!"

"If I let you keep that up all day, your poor dragon will starve." He slides on a pair of leather gloves. He's barely looked at or spoken to me all morning, clearly still pissed about last night.

"Jace?" I call as he heads toward the deer. He dips down to rip the arrow free from its unmoving chest.

"Please don't be mad at me."

His eyes dart up to mine. "Why would I be mad at you? You only led me to believe you cared for me, all the while envisioning someone else."

"That could not be further from the truth!" I protest.

"Look, this conversation is pointless. It was never going to work. What we did, what we've been doing—Marideth was right. It needs to be over."

"Is that really what you want, or are you just trying to punish me?" I stalk toward him. "Look, if I had told you, would it have changed anything? I know who you are, and you know who I am."

"Who you are never fails to surprise me, little witch." He sighs, assessing me for the first time all day. "I understand why you kept it from me, although you might want to have a conversation with your guard dog about that. As for what we did...I'm the one who's practically engaged. I should have been stronger. I shouldn't have—"

"What? Kissed me?"

"Yes."

"I'm glad that you kissed me. Because even though this situation is totally fucked, I want you. I know how wrong it is, and still, I want you so badly it's driving me insane."

He stares at me unblinking as I drop to my knees, bringing us to eye level.

"We're fooling ourselves if we think Sorscha won't find out somehow and that she'll be forgiving." His fingers reach out to graze my cheek, but the touch is over far too soon. He tosses the limp deer over his shoulder, and we make our way back toward the cave where Prophyria is waking.

I feel her grow more alert as we enter the lightless tunnel. I recall how Jace took my hand as he led us through the darkness last night. My heart sinks a bit when he doesn't offer the same comfort this time around.

I feel awful. I feel lousy for what we did and what we were about to do, knowing that Sorscha is involved. I try to push the racing thoughts and warring emotions from my head. Try to focus on the reason I'm here. The reason I will be coveted among kingdoms. The reason why the king values me enough for a seat on his council.

The reason I have a purpose and a mission for the first time in my life: the majestic purple dragon before me.

She is curled up like a harmless kitten in the center of the sparkling cave. Her large tail begins to thump when she sees me, the lethal spikes kicking up loose dust and diamonds.

Blackblood.

Her voice is bright and clear in my mind. She's happy to see me.

Seeing her again makes it even more real. Last night, as I tossed and turned, I had to keep reminding myself it wasn't all a dream. That I actually did it. That I, Serena Avery, from Beacon, New York, am now a full-blown Blackblood Dragon Rider.

I'm filled with a sense of pride. I *earned* this. I worked hard. I worked through literal blood, sweat, and tears. And as my dragon scrambles to her feet and barrels toward me, bowing her head for me to stroke, I think to myself, *yes, I deserve this.*

"We brought breakfast, Furi." I present her with the deer Jace is sliding from his shoulder. The pupils of her wide green eyes become slits as she scans Jace. A hiss works its way up her throat, and I rush to throw myself in front of him.

"No, no, no—Jace is *nice*. We *like* Jace." Taking in my words, her arched back eases into a neutral position, and she sits, her flared wings settling against her. She sniffs at the dead deer.

I take a step back, pulling Jace with me as Prophyria nudges the carcass with her massive snout. In one swift movement, she opens her jaw to reveal long dagger-like fangs and chomps down hard on the deer. Blood splatters everywhere, dotting our faces and chests and turning the diamonds beneath us into rubies. She tosses the mangled body high into the air, opens her mouth, and swallows it in one gulp, her forked pink tongue poking out to lick her lips. I groan in disgust.

"Someone's a messy eater," Jace mutters.

Porphyria lowers her eyes to me.

More, she purrs.

I turn to Jace. "She's still hungry."

He rolls his eyes. "Well, she could have had three more helpings if you hadn't missed every shot you took this morning."

"I have a lot on my mind!"

"Don't we all." He sighs, hands on his hips. "Come on."

He starts toward the tunnel and waves for me to follow. I turn to my dragon, who waits patiently for another treat.

"Good girl." I reach up to pat her thick leg. "I'll be right back. Mommy's going to get you some more."

"*Mommy?*" Jace says, his voice dripping with disdain.

"Shut the fuck up," I grumble and follow him.

We hunt down two more deer and a few rabbits, tossing them into a game bag and heading back toward my hungry pet. I try not to vomit at the sight of the dead animals, never having really hunted a day in my life.

When we arrive back at the cave, Happy Meal in tow, we find it empty.

My heart plummets.

"Where is she?" I panic.

"She's probably in the lower caves, exploring."

I listen for her. Nothing.

"She's not here. I can't feel her. Jace," I breathe, horrified. He moves in front of me, grasping me by the shoulders.

"Hey, it's alright. Listen down the bond. She's a dragon, she can't have gone far."

I nod and dip into the channel, listening intently.

"She's in the forest, circling overhead."

"Let's go," he says, a sense of urgency looming in his tone. We race outside into the morning sun, and I squint up through the trees.

Nothing.

But I can feel her there on the other side of the tether.

Porphyria, I call. An ear perks up.

Come.

Her wingbeats become audible as wind rocks the forest, shaking the leaves from their branches and kicking up the ones dusting the floor. Her lean, serpentine form becomes visible as she nosedives for the forest. Her impromptu landing knocks out a handful of trees to accommodate her enormous size. Jace tackles me out of the way of a falling tree, and we hit the ground hard, breathless, and tangled around each other.

The forest begins to calm as Furi settles on the ground and takes to chomping the leaves off of a nearby fallen tree. Jace and I stare up at her, mouths hanging open.

"Furi, what the fuck!" I hiss.

Her head snaps up to me for an instant before she resumes chewing her salad. Jace helps me sit up, and I stomp toward my disinterested dragon.

"Where were you?! You had me worried sick," I demand.

Jace dusts his jacket off. "You're mommy alright."

I shoot him a glare, then redirect my attention to Furi.

"What were you doing?! Anyone could have seen you! It isn't safe yet," I press, hands on hips, fuming beside her lowered head. Her eerie green eyes blink as her reply echoes in my head.

There was danger. I went to investigate.

"What did she say?" Jace asks, coming up beside me.

"She said there was danger. In the cave?"

She shakes her head no.

Outside.

What kind of danger?

Don't know, that's why I went to investigate.

"Okay, sass."

"Did she say what kind of danger?"

"No, she just felt something off. She didn't see anything."

"Come on," he says in the captain's voice, launching forward. "I want her back in that cave, safe. And I want you back at the castle. Now."

My protest stops his determined stride. "No, we need to see what she meant! I'm not leaving her here unprotected if there's danger nearby."

Jace turns to me, a stern expression on his face. "She's a dragon, Serena. She'll torch anyone who's a threat to her. Besides, no one can get inside the cave without you."

I run my hand down her smooth, scaled side.

"Go inside, Furi. Your food is getting cold." She starts to flap her wings. "And *stay* there this time. I'll be back as soon as I can."

She gives an affectionate nudge against my mind and darts into the air, disappearing into the clouds before rocketing back down into the mountain's narrow skylight.

"Do you think anyone saw her?" I ask as we start back. Jace's face is tight—his jaw clenched and brow furrowed.

"Let's hope not. She's kind of hard to miss."

We reach the main hall and find it empty except for a few guards, none of whom seem to notice or care enough to ask about our blood-splattered leathers. I struggle to keep up with Jace's swift pace.

We round the corner to find Zadyn on the other side. He breaks into a jog, closing the short distance between us and crushing me against his chest.

"Hey," I mumble, breathing in his crisp, cool scent.

"Thank gods you're alive." His relief is palpable as pulls back to study me. "Did you actually do it?"

"I actually did it. I am *officially* a Dragon Rider." I can't help but beam up at him. His answering grin is blinding as he wraps me in a hug and spins me around. My laugh echoes down the spacious hall.

"I am so proud of you." He shakes his head in disbelief as he lowers me to the ground. "Wait, why are you bloody? What happened?" Concern mars his features as he searches for the source.

"It's not mine. We were hunting for Prophyria," I assure him, gripping his arms. "Zadyn, she's amazing. Wait until you meet her."

"She's here?" Zadyn's brown eyes widen in surprise.

"I hate to interrupt this little reunion, but we have pressing matters that require our immediate attention." Jace's comment is directed at Zadyn, and I detect a touch of bitterness in his tone. Jealousy, perhaps, seeing as he can barely keep the snarl off his face while addressing him.

"What happened?" Zadyn asks, either oblivious to Jace's hostile looks or not giving a shit.

"Furi sensed something out in the forest—some kind of danger. We need to find out what it is. She's somewhere safe, but no one can know she's here. Not yet."

"We're on our way to gather a search party," Jace says, somewhat impatiently.

Zadyn's eyes shift to him, finally sensing his indignation. He glances between us, piecing together the source of Jace's frustration. A new wave of shame washes over me. I want to crawl into a hole and die right then and there.

Without another word, Jace shoves past us, fists balled at his sides. I know he blames Zadyn for me keeping secrets, but it wasn't his fault. He was only looking out for me. I rush to catch up with him.

"I'll come with you," Zadyn says from beside me.

"No. Stay here with Serena," Jace barks, not bothering to turn. It's an order.

"I'm coming with you." Outraged at the mere thought, I wrench his arm, forcing him to face me.

"You are not," he bites, golden eyes flashing.

"Why the hell not? Haven't I proved myself? I just bonded an ancient dragon and lived to tell the tale—I think I can handle a search party."

He shakes his head, ripping his arm away.

"I don't have time to argue with you," he says, stalking off.

"You can't stop me from going, Jace. She is my dragon, and I will destroy any threat to her." The fervor in my voice slows him. My sudden rage surprises us both as my fingers begin to prickle with magic. I flex them, watching Jace's eyes fill with caution.

"Fine." He leans in close, index finger pointed in my face. "But you do as I say. When you're out there with me, you are part of my troupe. You follow orders just like the rest of my men. Both of you. Clear?" He glances between me and Zadyn.

"Crystal," I hiss, brushing past him and knocking his shoulder. Jace and Zadyn fall into step beside me, their long limbs dwarfing mine.

Jace leads us across an outdoor bridge to the other side of the castle, where the Kingsguard are lodged. The wing is more run down than the glittering quarters held by the members of court, smelling of sweat and ale. Jace stops outside a plain wooden door and pounds it with his fist.

"It's me. Open up."

"A little busy at the moment," a breathless voice calls from the other side. Jace doesn't hesitate before kicking in the door. I try not to swoon as it flies open and rebounds off the wall behind it. I peer over his shoulder at Max—his brilliant red hair flowing down his naked back as he pounds into a female whose face I can't see.

"Woah!" I quickly shield my eyes.

"Put your cock away and get dressed." Jace snatches a pair of leather pants off the ground and chucks them at Max's face. He catches them, and with a frustrated groan, disentangles himself from the female.

"Bring your brother and five more men," Jace orders. "Be ready at the stables in five minutes." He yanks the door shut behind him, his face grave as he starts down the hall again.

I turn to Zadyn.

"Did you just get back?" I ask, looking up at him. He nods. "How was the King of Vod?"

"Just as much of a dick as you'd expect." He slides his light brown eyes to me, offering a tiny smile. "Tonight's the big kick-off party."

"What do you mean?"

"In Solterre, when a king visits a foreign court, it's tradition to welcome them with five full nights of feasts and festivities. We call it King's Fair. Five nights of drinking and debauchery to rival the gatherings of Dionese himself."

"Perfect timing. I'm harboring a rebellious dragon, and this place is about to be overrun by drunken members of a foreign court for the next week." I sigh, shaking my head. "I wonder what made the king decide to come here all the way from Vod."

"He's playing the part of loyal son—guilt-stricken over

missing the queen's four hundred and fiftieth birthday. Personally, I think he's here to push Kai down Derek's throat for Sorscha."

The mention of the princess sends a new wave of remorse through me. I swallow hard. I told Zadyn I was done with Jace. That we cut our flirtation off at the knees. He has no idea that a line was crossed last night.

"It's very likely," I say, my mind far away.

We dress the horses, and Jace surprises me when he slides his arms around my waist. I blush, wondering what he's doing in front of Zadyn like this, and then I realize he's strapping a belt with a sheathed dagger around me.

Idiot, I mutter to myself.

We mount as the rest of our party joins us and ride out. Hours pass as we search for any possible threat. We find nothing.

"Either Prophyria was mistaken, or whatever was out here left before we arrived." Jace sidles up to me on his horse.

"I don't think she was wrong. Something tells me we should trust her instincts," I say, puzzled. "What do you think it could have been?"

"A mistake, I hope."

A grim silence settles.

"Your business at the border—" I slide him a curious look. "What's that about?"

He stares straight ahead and lowers his voice. "There have been a handful of disturbances, starting around the time of your arrival. A number of fae have been found dead at the border between Aegar and Hyrax. Mostly from the city and some neighboring villages."

"How many?" I ask.

"Forty so far."

"Forty?" I balk, then drop my voice. "That's kind of a lot."

"You think I don't know that? I've had my best men looking into it. There were claw marks on the bodies—as if a massive beast had struck them down. Their blood was completely drained, their eyes turned white."

I contemplate this.

"Sounds like a vampire to me."

"Vampires aren't real," he says, as if it's the most outlandish idea in the world.

"Well, what kind of animal do you know of that does *that*?" I purse my lips.

He shakes his head as if lost in a memory. "This was no animal."

"Do you think it's connected to the issue at the portal with those dead Guardians?"

"I have a sneaking suspicion it is."

Mal, Max, and Zadyn catch up to us, and my attention snags on a flash of familiar maroon.

Déjà vu creeps over me as I stare at the underside of Mal's cloak, visible beneath his arm. Gold stitching over shiny maroon silk. I wrack my brain, trying to figure out where I've seen that before. Noticing my distraction, Mal speaks, his voice dark as night and cold as ice.

"My lady, are you alright?"

I snap my eyes back up to him and force a smile. "Yes. I'm just distracted."

He gives me a tight nod and snaps his reins. His horse picks up the pace, and I stare at his back the whole way back to the castle.

35

Empty-handed, we arrive back as the sun is setting, bathing the diamond castle in a sparkling orange glow. We each break off, retiring to our chambers to dress for the first night of King's Fair.

I bring Igrid up to speed on the events of the last two days while she weaves a few thin braids throughout my unbound hair.

A soft knock sounds from the door. Marideth doesn't bother to wait for a response before trudging in, wearing a gorgeous, if not scandalous, red dress with matching shoes dangling from her hand. She scuffles directly to my bed, turns, and falls back, stiff as a board.

"Kill me," she drones, flopping her arms out beside her.

"What's wrong with you?" I ask as Igrid begins to clip tiny silver cuffs into my braids.

"The honorable *Lady Wyneth*"—her face contorts in a nasty expression—"will be in attendance at tonight's party at the behest of her and Dover's parents." She heaves a loud sigh. "If you have any trouble spotting her, she'll be the wallflower in the corner, refusing to have any fun whatsoever. *Dover* is to escort her, as the engagement will be announced tonight in front of the entire court."

"Which means you have to behave."

"I don't know what that word means," she mumbles, gazing up at the canopy. I'm quiet for a moment as I think.

"Have you talked to Sorscha about this? Maybe she could pull a few strings and have the engagement ended."

Marideth shakes her head. "Her father doesn't want to anger the nobles. Wyneth's parents are rich as hell and big in the diamond trade. The king needs their support—he signed off on the match personally. Anyway, I came for a distraction. How's your dra—"

She cuts herself off, noticing Igrid's presence. "Your puppy?"

"It's fine. Igrid knows about me."

Marideth sits up and stares at her for a moment.

"She's my friend," I tell her. Mar slides off the bed and comes to stand beside Igrid, looking at her through the mirror.

"Well, any friend of Serena's..." she mutters, toying with a strand of my hair.

"Pleased to meet you, my lady." Igrid lowers her eyes in the mirror and curtsies.

"Oh, don't do that," Mar says, pulling her upright. "You're among friends. My name is Marideth."

"Hello, Marideth." Igrid smiles and moves over to the wardrobe as Mar continues fiddling with my braids.

"Quite a dress." I nod to her.

"It's called *eat your heart out red*." Her eyes flicker up to mine in the mirror with a sardonic smile.

"Really? I thought it was called *fuck you, Wyneth red*."

She tosses her head back and howls, coming to lean against the vanity.

"Be my date tonight?" she asks, her slender shoulders sinking in.

"Obviously," I answer with a smile. In the mirror, I see Igrid laying out a garment on the bed. Pulling my robe tighter, I move closer to examine it.

"I had it made for tonight," she says, her face brimming with excitement. "Actually, I had a whole collection made for the next four nights."

I run my fingers over the silky black piece that looks more like a scrap of fabric than a dress.

"I thought it would suit you."

"Igrid." I give her hand a grateful squeeze. "Thank you."

The dress is strappy and slinky, clinging to my every curve like a second skin. A choker made of thick silver chain splits off into two panels of glossy black material that barely covers my breasts, leaving a long slit of exposed skin down the center of my chest. The breast panels form a downward "v" and knot together below my navel, where the skirt tapers out to rest on my hips. My entire back is naked down to my tailbone.

"So is the theme of the party skin?" I assess myself in the mirror. I have more flesh on display than I have covered.

"The theme is gluttony and extravagance. King's Fair makes every ball you've been to so far at the castle look like a backwater revelry," Mar says.

I sit on the bed and lace up the ties of my strappy heels, the scandalous slit parting over my thigh in the process. I smooth the dress and wiggle over to the mirror.

"Now *that*"—Marideth stands behind me, hands on my shoulders as she eyes me in the mirror—"is *eat your heart out, set it on fire, and chop it up into tiny pieces, black.*"

I break into a wide grin. I look hot.

Igrid passes me a pair of dangly earrings and slides two silver cuffs onto my wrists. The final touch is a thin metal circlet around my forehead. It makes me look exotic and sensual.

Zadyn knocks on the door, and my mouth almost drops as he appears, pushing his wet hair back off his face. I bite my lip as a single rivulet escapes down the side of his chiseled jawline. My eyes drink in his bare arms, braced on the doorframe, the low-cut leather vest that hugs his well-defined chest, and the tight black pants tucked into high boots.

Zadyn looks *sexy*.

I burst into laughter at the thought, clapping my hand over my mouth.

"Is it too much?" He raises a brow and gestures to his outfit. "Igrid picked it out—I feel a little ridiculous."

Igrid beams from behind us, lips pressed together to suppress the girlish smile Mar and I also wear.

"It's just *enough*," Marideth cracks.

Zadyn zeroes in on me in my scrap of fabric, his mouthing falling open. "Nice...dress?"

His brow ticks up. Marideth shakes my shoulders at him.

"Doesn't she look delicious?" she says wickedly.

Zadyn's eyes flicker to the ground, those long lashes casting shadows down his cheeks. When he lifts them again, they twinkle a touch brighter.

"One last thing." Igrid dips her finger into a small glass tub and dabs a pigmented liquid onto my lips. I look into the mirror at my strong, sun-kissed body—the glamoured fae ears, the daring dress, and the dramatic lip stain. I turn to Mar and link my arm through hers.

"Come on. I want to dance."

I HEAR the drums long before we reach the doors of the Grand Hall. At every other ball, the music was classical and cultured to match the composed, demure choreography. Tonight, there are no set steps. A mass of uninhibited bodies entangle on the dance floor, writhing languidly in time to the steady rhythm. The effect is hypnotic. Primal. Ancient.

The entire space is bathed in a hazy, dark red glow, creating an intimate, sensual ambiance. Fixtures of blood red rubies dangle over the crowded dance floor. A mild breeze trickles in through the open doors, setting the red gossamer curtains aflutter. Silk dancers and aerialists twist and twirl overhead, dressed in nothing but gold paint. They dangle from ivy covered hoops and glide through the air on swings.

Taking in the swarm of party guests, I realize that Igrid's wardrobe choices were more than appropriate. My outfit is modest compared to the sea of skin and lace and gold dust surrounding me.

We find most of our friends on the terrace as the sun sets over a blazing red sky. The princess is dressed as the angel to my dark, sensual devil. Her slender silhouette is on display beneath a low-cut, white gossamer shift, belted with a delicate gold chain around the waist.

Kai is absurdly handsome in nothing but a pair of loose, low slung black pants of the thinnest material and a thick chain around the nape of his neck. His black hair is gelled to look wet and black kohl lines his eyes, making their vibrant blue-green stand out even more.

We make light conversation, and I am acutely aware of how close Cece stands to Zadyn, her near-naked body angled toward him. When she leans in to whisper something in his ear, her metal bra grazes his arm. A wave of envy ripples through me as I clutch the drink in my hand, threatening to melt the goblet beneath my warming fingers.

Marideth elbows me, and I snap out of it—my limbs cooling in response.

I spot Jace making his way onto the terrace. He wears a sleeveless black mock-neck shirt and pants similar to Kai's. The onyx sword he is never without is sheathed at his hip. His intense, molten eyes lock on mine, and my heart strains toward him. Sorscha perks up as he reaches us, beaming with youth and vitality. I watch his gaze shift to the angelic fae.

He bows before her, and I try not to cringe as he presses a kiss to her delicate hand. She drifts closer, running her fingers over his chest in a way that makes my stomach churn. I force myself to look away. When Ilsa says something that snags her attention, Jace slips into the vacant space beside me.

"Really?" He gives me a sly once-over and drops his voice so that only I can hear.

"What?" I slide my eyes to him without turning.

"*That's* what you're wearing?"

"Yes, Jace. This is what I'm wearing," I say through a gritted smile. "Problem?"

He shakes his head with a soft sigh.

"I swear you were sent from hell to torture me, witch."

The words float to me on a phantom wind that kisses my ear so gently I want to melt. I can't stop myself from looking up at him. He faces away from me—jaw clenched, eyes fixed ahead. I study his profile, that of a Greek god. Classical and proud.

He turns to Sorscha, offering her his arm. As he leads her inside toward the dance floor, his fingers brush against mine so feather-light, I wonder if I imagined it. The whisper of longing.

I can feel Marideth's watchful eyes on me. I give her a sad smile, and she gives my hand a small squeeze. My friend.

Her eyes drift to the garden where Dover holds the arm of a slight, brown-haired fae. She is pretty, if not a little plain for

High Fae, dressed in a modest gray gown. Her only decoration is the diamond necklace around her delicate neck. She scans the party with wary eyes, her expression bordering on pained. Dover speaks to her every so often, clearly making an effort to put her at ease.

"I suppose I should go say hello." Mar sighs.

"Keep your fangs retracted," I warn. She nips at me with her teeth before disappearing down the steps toward her mate and his betrothed.

I find myself standing alone with Kai after Cece lures Zadyn to the dance floor with bedroom eyes, and Ilsa flits off to flirt with a half-naked nobleman.

"Excited to see your brother?" I turn to him, taking a sip of cherry wine. Kai drapes himself over the railing, making even the stone beneath him look good.

"Not particularly." He swirls his wine before bringing it to his lips and draining it. I watch him carefully, noticing the tense mood overshadowing his charm. He's not his usual quick-witted self tonight.

"What's wrong with you?" I ask. He holds up his glass in answer.

"Need a refill. Care to join?"

I nod, figuring it's better than being left alone among the rising debauchery. With every second that creeps toward dark, the party grows more and more risqué.

I take hold of Kai's arm as he leads us through the wild throng toward a table of refreshments. He hands me a short glass of clear liquid, taking what's left of my wine and draining it before reaching for another short glass of his own.

"What is this?" I give the drink a tentative sniff.

"Temporary reprieve," he mutters, clinking his glass against mine. He shoots the knuckle of liquor and wipes his mouth on the back of his hand.

"I'll drink to that." My eyes find Jace among the crowd. He and Sorscha dance, their bodies close together—her hands on his chest, his resting on her hips. I shake my head, trying to rid the image from my mind.

I know exactly how those hands feel on my hips. I still feel them, like a brand on me even now.

I redirect my attention to Kai, who's staring off, stone-faced, at the bawdy crowd. He looks so...depressed. It's almost disturbing to see someone so full of life, full of wicked fire, with an extinguished flame.

"Wanna dance?" I suggest. He gives a nearly imperceptible shake of his head. I try another approach, hoping to milk some life from him.

"Aren't you going to comment on my dress? Or lack thereof?"

He slides a lazy glance my way. "I wasn't aware you needed anyone to stroke that ego of yours."

"I don't. I just thought you might like to know what kind of undergarments one wears beneath a dress such as this." I gesture to the length of my body.

"Not tonight. Excuse me."

I follow him through the crowd, a bit concerned, as he slides into a secluded alcove with plush red velvet seats. He says nothing as I scoot in beside him.

Reaching into his pocket, he pulls out a tiny vial no larger than a knuckle. He uncorks it and sprinkles a neat line out on the table, not even bothering to check for onlookers. I glance around at the swirling crowd, but no one is even remotely phased as Kai lowers his nose to the table and snorts the line.

"Kai?" I ask as he dusts the remnants of powder from his nostrils.

"Did you want some?" he offers, casting a quick glance in my direction as he pours out another line.

"N—no," I stammer, horrified, as he repeats the action. He tips his head back and blinks his eyes a few times.

"Kai, are you alright? You don't seem like yourself." I put a hand on his shoulder, and he shrugs out of my touch, eyes fixed on a scantily clad fae female passing by our table. She stops mid-step and slowly turns to him, transfixed. Her hips swish as she draws closer, and I glance between them, noticing Kai's eyes peering out from beneath his lowered lashes. I know that look because he once tried it on me. The female leans over the table and kisses him hard.

He's using his siren tricks on her, I realize. I smack his arm, appalled.

"Ow," he blurts. Slumping back against the cushion, he waves a hand, sending the girl on her way, completely unfazed.

"What is the matter with you tonight?" I shake him. He wrenches his arm away.

"Go bother someone else with your holier-than-thou act." He sneers, two little fangs extending from his gums.

"Kai," I start, but he's already bounding out of his seat and darting away. I jump up to catch him, not bothering to watch where I step. That's when I slam into a wall of rock and rebound from the force. I am steadied by two large hands around my waist. Blinking, I stare up into familiar ocean eyes.

King Kylian is quite possibly the most beautiful creature I've ever seen. The face a more mature version of Kai's, with the same black hair and ocean eyes, he stands taller, with more muscle and an air of power that rivals King Derek's. Even in silence, there is a subtle arrogance about him. I drink in the golden crown atop his head, the light dusting of gold powder over his broad shoulders and bare chest, and the delicate body chain that skims his hard torso. His skin is luminescent, with a deep tan, as if he'd spent an ample amount of time on a beach beneath the radiant sun.

"Brother," Kylian regards Kai without so much as a glance in his direction.

If his looks weren't proof enough of his siren lineage, his voice would be. Spun straight from the darkest bedroom fantasies, the deep rumble sends a wave of chills down my bare arms. I step out of his steadying grasp to stash them behind my back. The movement earns a sharp gaze from him, his eyes threatening to swallow me whole as they scan from my head to my toes and back up again. I try not to squirm as that gaze lays me bare.

Kai's expression is unreadable when he pauses, turning back toward us.

"Oh, hello, asshole," he says, sidling up to me. Kylian huffs an unamused laugh, breaking our intense eye contact to assess his younger brother.

"Miss me?"

"Not really." Kai shrugs, his tone effusive.

"Is that any way of greeting your dear older brother? Your king?" Kylian tuts, his mesmerizing stare circling back to me. "I must apologize for my brother's rudeness. I don't think we've been properly introduced."

"Don't worry. Your reputation precedes you, *my King*," Kai pipes, brushing the underside of his nose with his fingers. Kylian takes a slow, deliberate step away from me to stand directly in front of his brother. Kai stares up at him, chin high, defiant.

Kylian's voice is a gentle caress.

"Are you high?"

His hand shoots out at a jarring speed, wrapping Kai's chain necklace around his fist and slamming him against the wall. I gasp as his head makes contact with a loud thud, causing a small crack to spider out above him.

"You're a disgrace. A worthless little waste of royal blood,"

Kylian breathes—his tone calm, cool, and collected despite the discreetly violent display. No one seems to notice. Kai's expression as he struggles against his brother's iron fist is truly heartbreaking. Shame and defeat haunt his downcast eyes. Having seen enough, I stomp forward, marching right up to Kylian.

"Hey. You." I snap my fingers in his gorgeous face. "Don't talk to him like that."

The death glare he slides my way almost sends me skittering back to hide in a corner. But I hold my ground.

"Do you know who I am?" he purrs, his voice temperate.

"I don't care if you're the Queen of fucking Sheba." I inch closer, both compelled and repulsed by him. A slow smirk spreads over his cruel mouth, but he releases Kai, allowing him to slump back against the wall. My eyes land on the mangled, dented chain around my friend's neck before he slips it off and stashes it in his pocket. Kylian assesses me, siren eyes dancing.

"Brother, if you don't marry this creature, then I will be forced to."

"Then we'll have a queen at last," Kai slurs. "Whoopee."

"My lady." Kylian reaches out to take my hand. I rip it back before his fingers even brush my skin and fix him with a tight, phony smile. His answering laugh is musical.

"Would you honor me with a dance?" he asks, suddenly the portrait of charm. This guy is a certified psychopath. Beneath that godly exterior that likely fools just about everyone, lurks a Patrick Bateman of the worst degree.

I should know. I can smell a narcissist a mile away.

Crossing my arms, I make a show of looking toward the dance floor, where the music leads the throng in primal, lusty choreography.

"I don't think so." I sigh, tossing him an uninterested glance. Kylian folds his hands behind his back as I wrap my arm around Kai's elbow. His movements are slow, heavy, and lethargic, no doubt from the drugs.

"Kai, shall we?" I elbow him in an attempt to rouse him before tugging him away from his brother.

"At least honor me with your name," Kylian says, stopping me with a possessive hand around my upper arm. I stare up at his intimidating height, the crimson shadows of the hall bathing him in a sinister red wash.

"I told your brother once, and I will tell you now. You will ask before you lay your hands on me." My voice lashes out, cold and demanding—a voice I've never been able to summon despite my best efforts. It is the voice of a queen.

I don't waste another breath on Kylian before I tow Kai through the crowd, past the patio, and down into the empty garden. We reach the fountains, and I sit him down on the stone bench beneath the alabaster likeness of Myr the Huntress. He goes limp, eyes glazing over, jaw slackening.

He's so fucked up.

"Kai." I hold his face, trying to get him to focus. I give his cheek a gentle slap, but it doesn't even begin to rouse him from his near-catatonic state.

"Kai, what the fuck did you take?"

God, I hope the fae aren't capable of overdosing.

His arms dangle lifelessly at his sides as I dip my hand in the fountain to dampen his forehead. It does nothing. With a frustrated groan, I flip him onto his belly and dunk his head beneath the cool water. He seems slightly more alert when I bring him up, blinking the water from his eyes. I dunk him again. The moment I feel his resistance, I release him, and he pushes himself upright. Turning sharply, he expels the contents of his stomach onto the cobblestone beneath us, just missing the fountain. He slides onto the ground, resting his cheek against the cool ledge. My hands are on his back, patting him as relief washes over me.

"You're okay," I breathe, my heart rate coming back to normal.

Laughter sounds from around the corner, and I glance up to see our friends step into view. They stop short when they see us, eyes going wide as they take in the scene.

"Kai!" The princess breaks away from Jace and rushes forward, dropping to her knees beside him.

"What happened?" Jace comes around Kai's other side, voice tense.

"I don't know. I think he overdosed," I explain. "He had a lot to drink, and then he snorted this pink stuff."

"Stardust," Cece supplies. Sorscha shakes her head, smoothing the dripping hair from Kai's face.

"Let's get him up," Jace says, helping to ease him into a seated position. Kai tips his head back against the fountain, still breathing hard. His sleepy eyes roll toward me as he breaks into a beatific smile.

"My hero."

I laugh in relief. "You're an idiot."

"So I've heard," he huffs, giving his eyes a rest. I get to my feet, noticing how drenched my own dress is as it clings to me. The girls huddle around Kai as Jace and Zadyn come to stand on either side of me.

"How did he get that messed up so quickly?" Jace asks for our ears only.

"He seemed off all night, and then he started pounding drinks and snorting lines. I think it had something to do with his brother."

I recall how Kai could barely look him in the eye. He didn't even try to resist as Kylian tossed him against the wall. He didn't lift a finger.

"Kylian is a sadistic bastard. It wouldn't surprise me." Jace's eyes darken.

"I had the displeasure of running into him earlier." I shake my head at the memory of his stinging cruelty. Kai is now talking more, some color returning to his pretty face. Cece and the princess help him to his feet, draping his arms over their shoulders.

Once we get Kai inside and back to his rooms, we stay long enough to order a detox brew from Gnorr and to get some food in him. When he is sound asleep, we slip out the door and disband for the evening, no longer in the mood for an afterparty.

36

The second night of King's Fair starts at sundown with a tradition called "the Hunt."

The king selects a trove of treasure to be hidden somewhere on the grounds, and it's basically a big scavenger hunt to find it. Whoever is successful in uncovering the treasure gets to keep it.

Like last night, the partygoers are dressed daringly, myself included. I wear a soft golden sarong that flashes an obscene amount of leg and a black bandeau bra knotted around a gilded brooch. Fingerless gloves cover my arms from wrist to bicep, and my hair is pulled up into a chic updo held together by two long, spiky chopsticks.

We are gathered on the sprawling lawns for the start of tonight's festivities. I stare out at the hundreds of lit torches lining the manicured expanse. Kylian sits between his mother and King Derek on a small dais that has been erected on the lawn. He leans in to say something to Derek while Ilspeth, garbed in a tight, long-sleeved red gown, oversees the crowd with her typical distaste.

The booming war drums pound three times, signaling the start of the Hunt, and the sea of fae breaks off, scattering like ants in all directions. Kai and Dover spring into action—a clear strategy already in place.

"We'll search the maze first—Sorscha knows her way around," a thankfully sober Kai says in the voice of a war general.

He and Dover lead the way, and the rest of us rush to keep up with their determined pace.

"You people take this way too seriously." Cece rolls her gold-dusted eyes beside Zadyn. She seems to be glued to his hip as of late. I haven't bothered to ask him if their dalliance has continued—mostly because I truly don't want to know the answer.

"Everyone loves a winner, Ceec," Dover calls over his shoulder. Marideth hangs back with me, noticeably more quiet than usual. She hasn't had much to do with Dover the past two nights, probably still shaken by the news of the wedding.

"The maze is massive. It could take us all night to search," Sorscha points out, gathering her skirts.

"Captain, you're awfully quiet. Isn't this sort of thing your area of expertise?" Kai drawls.

"My area of expertise involves a bit more than strategizing to find hidden treasure, Kai," Jace says mildly. "But if we split up, we can cover more ground in a shorter amount of time."

"Brilliant." Kai claps his hands together, pivoting to a stop.

Marideth slides her arm around mine. "Dibs on Serena."

"I'll go with you," Dover says to her, his tone falling short of casual and landing on hopeful. She gives a loud sigh, not bothering to look at him. "Fine."

"As will I. Captain, do you think you can handle the rest of this riff-raff?" Kai gestures to the remainder of the pack.

"I'll manage," Jace deadpans.

"Tick tock." Kai taps an imaginary watch and waves us onward. I cast a quick look back at Jace, whose attention is on Sorscha.

I roll my eyes internally, embarrassed by my own simping.

The entrance to the maze appears as stars begin to dust the sky. We split almost immediately, branching off in opposite directions. Dover falls into step with Marideth a few feet behind me and Kai. I can hear him struggling to make small talk with her. Trying not to eavesdrop out of respect, I fix my attention on the prince.

"How are you feeling tonight?" I ask, pebbles crunching beneath my heels.

"Good as new, thanks to my little savior." He flashes me an ironic smile that doesn't quite touch his eyes. "I have to say I'm flattered that you felt so inclined to help me. Shows how much you care," he teases, exaggerating a down-turned pout.

I chuckle and throw an elbow into his ribs.

"You've grown on me." I sigh. "Like a fungus."

It's his turn to laugh, throwing his dark head back to the night sky.

"Kai, about your brother," I tread. His gaze lowers to the ground as we round the corner of a perfectly groomed hedge.

"I'm sorry you had the misfortune of meeting him last night. Although, I think you left quite the impression on him." His eyes slide to me. "No one has ever dared to stand up to him, let alone speak to him the way you did."

"You didn't exactly kiss ass either," I point out.

"That doesn't count—we're family, as much as that fact shames me." He shrugs. "I learned from a very young age that word holds no real meaning to my kin beyond heirs and lines of succession."

A dark look crosses his face.

"Kylian was a ruthless child with a sadistic streak. One

394

which my father not only condoned but also rewarded. When I was thirteen and Kylian seventeen, he decided I was a threat to his imminent reign and that he needed to be rid of me. One night, he beat me senseless and tried to take off my head with a hot poker. He missed, luckily." Kai points to the slight scar beneath his left eye.

"That's horrible," I whisper. "Kai, I'm so sorry."

"I'm used to it. I've taken his abuse my entire life. Anytime things didn't go his way, I'd get a beating. If I *embarrassed* him somehow, I'd get a beating. If I took an interest in politics or even combat, I'd get a beating. Eventually, I became so used to it that I stopped feeling the pain altogether. It wasn't all for naught, though. Ladies do go wild for the scar." He waggles his brows. I don't acknowledge his attempt at diffusion.

"No one saw? No one tried to stop it?"

"My father and mother both knew. They encouraged it, actually. Said it was good practice for the future king to instill fear in his enemies and that I needed to toughen up. Kade was far enough apart from us in age that Kylian barely even noticed his existence. It spared him from being on the receiving end of Kylian's fits, which I was thankful for."

He's quiet for a moment—the only sound that of our footfalls. He stares at the ground as he continues softly, "I tried to fight back. But he was always bigger, always stronger." Kai shakes his head, sliding his hands into his pockets.

I pull him to a stop, forcing him to look at me.

"Kai. You are a thousand times better than him. Than all of them."

"Beautiful savior." He gives me a sad smirk. "Don't I know it?"

It dawns on me that there is more to Kai than I realized. I was so quick to judge him as a roguish party boy with no real cares or responsibilities other than bedding females and getting high. I wonder if he adopted that role to avoid his brother's beatings, worried that if he took an interest in ruling and court matters, his brother would see it as a threat and make another attempt on his life. But the unserious second son, the debauched frat boy with a penchant for drugs, drinks, and females, would be of no threat to his brother's crown. This act could allow him to keep his life. My heart aches for his sorrows, for his pain. For the times his parents neglected to save him. For the times he was met with a brother's fist rather than any semblance of love or affection.

I lean in and plant a light kiss on his cheek. When I pull away, his expression is perplexed. He opens his mouth to say something when a scream erupts from deep within the maze. We freeze, turning back to Mar and Dover a few feet behind. Then the four of us break into a simultaneous sprint, led by the growing cries.

Cece and Sorscha spill around the corner, clasping each other, their dresses torn and hair disheveled. They fall to the ground, panting.

"What happened?" Kai grips Sorscha by the shoulders, helping her straighten.

"Something—" She gasps for air, pointing in the direction they came. "There's something in the maze."

My stomach drops.

"They attacked us," Cece finishes for her. Jace and Zadyn's faces flash through my mind.

"What attacked you?" Kai urges, but I shout over him.

"Where are the others?"

"They told us to run, to get help." Sorscha's terror-ridden eyes snap to mine as she shakes her head and clutches Kai's arms. "They're still back there. We have to go back."

"Where is Ilsa?" Marideth steps forward. Cece and Sorscha whirl to face each other.

"She was right behind us," Cece breathes, dumbfounded.

"Dover," Kai snaps, "go with them. Get them to safety and send for help." He passes Sorscha to his friend, but she wrenches herself free.

"Sorscha," Mar starts.

"I will not leave them!" she shouts, her voice panicked. "Jace is—"

Another shrill screech interrupts her protest. I break into a run, no longer able to refrain from going after them. My heart thunders inside my chest as I will myself to go faster and faster, praying I get there in time. The others are close behind. We burst into the epicenter of the maze, a circular space with a towering fountain in the center.

We find Jace and Zadyn locked in combat with the most disturbing creatures I've ever seen.

They stand well over seven feet tall on the thick hind legs of a horse. Their heads are a perverted twist on a wolf's with an elongated snout and curling horns. Long arms extend from their humanoid torsos, ending in razor-sharp talons.

I spot Jace inside the massive fountain, sword slicing through the air as water sprays around him. I hold my breath as three creatures rush him. Jace slits their throats with a single swipe of his sword and sends them flying back on one of his winds.

"Jace!" Sorscha cries. He whirls, his eyes landing on me. My heart snags in my throat.

"Go!" he shouts before surging back into battle. A quick glance around, and I know we are severely outnumbered.

"Get the girls out of here!" Zadyn bellows at Dover before shifting into a massive *OrCat*. Cece gasps, skittering back as Zadyn tackles one of the creatures to the ground. Their jaws snap at each other as they fly through a thick hedge. I don't have time to panic, knowing that every second counts.

This is what Jace has trained me for. I am not helpless.

I am a Blackblood and a warrior.

I call forth my magic, reaching into the deepest, darkest parts of myself. When I force my eyes open, I rip open that well within me and bring forth all the raw power I can muster.

Fire bursts from my palms in a wild display. I throw my hands out, casting my magic toward the two beasts charging from either side. Their matted manes catch fire first before the flames engulf them entirely. Sorscha and Cece shriek from behind me as the smell of burning flesh cuts through the air.

A loud splash has me whirling to find Jace on his back inside the fountain. My throat locks up as one of the creatures lunges for him. The water surrounding him begins to collect like a cloud in the air above. It bursts forth in a massive tidal wave that sends the creature flying back into a nearby hedge. Water bubbles and pours from its mouth as it tries and fails to stand. My eyes snap to Kai and his outstretched hand as he drowns the creature. Clutching at its windpipe, it keels over, still vomiting water.

Kai looks at me. He doesn't pause to ask questions about my flaming fingers. Instead, he presses his back against mine, and we fight methodically, hurling our power out in tandem as our assailants attack.

When my magic begins to sputter out, I dip a hand into my skirt, ripping free the dagger sheathed at my thigh. I move through the swarm of locusts, reminding myself of all Jace taught me. I am a whirlwind of violent death as I take down one monster after another. But for the amount Kai and I alone have killed, there are still so many.

Something doesn't add up.

The problem, we realize as the first creature Kai drowned rises and charges at us, is that they aren't *staying* dead.

"Fuck," I breathe.

Kai's head snaps over his shoulder to where Dover is doing everything in his power to wrangle the females back through the maze to safety. They won't budge.

"Dover, go! Get them out!" he shouts, gathering his water affinity.

"No!" Sorscha rips her arm out of Dover's grasp. I don't wait to see what happens next.

Three creatures rush at me simultaneously. I blast them back with what's left of my fire as another materializes before me. It knocks the blade from my hand before I sweep its legs out from underneath. As the creature rises, I rip the golden chopsticks from my hair and dig them into its meaty throat. Blood spurts out, spraying across my face as I kick it back, freeing my makeshift weapons.

Jace is almost entirely surrounded now, fighting with a deep gash to his arm. Despite the injury, he is a cyclone of relentless fury. I can hear Zadyn's growls, but he is nowhere in sight. Kai is now a few feet away from me, hurling out miniature hurricanes to incapacitate the crazed, undying beasts.

But my friends and I are growing tired. I realize that without aid, we will not survive. We cannot win against creatures that won't stay dead.

Past the point of frustration, I turn and bellow at the girls, "GET HELP NOW!"

My voice is laced with pure command. Their eyes go wide as they shift to something over my shoulder.

A snarl sounds from behind me. I turn to be met with a set of knives to the face, scarcely missing my right eye. Searing pain explodes across my cheek. Blood drips from the creature's razored talons as I fall to my knees, clutching the face I'm quite certain is ruined. Tears leak from my eyes, and as they do, I feel my flesh knitting together.

I'm healing myself.

I glance up as the beady-eyed monster drives its heavy hoof into my stomach with alarming force. The air leaves me. I try to drag myself away, but the creature pins me beneath its crushing weight. Its jaws snap at my neck, coating my face with thick saliva. I grunt, holding it at bay with all my might as I call on my magic.

But nothing comes. I am tapped out.

"Serena!" Jace bellows, barreling through the fountain.

He leaps across the space in one impressive move, driving his sword through the creature's neck as he lands. The beast collapses on top of me, its blood pouring out in a hot rush of liquid. Jace looses a war cry as three more attack. He slams one of them face-first into another and skewers them both on his sword. They collapse as he wrenches his blade free and spins toward the remaining one. With a clean swipe, he takes off its head. It falls to the ground moments before its body follows.

Jace turns to me. Blood-soaked and panting.

He drops to his knees, pushing aside the monster crushing me. His hand kisses my face where I was sliced.

"Serena," he breathes.

That's when I see the beast materialize at his back.

"Jace!" I gasp. "Jace, *behind you!*"

He whirls as the creature lifts his discarded sword above its head. The trajectory threatens to slice Jace clean down the middle. There is no time for him to move.

The blade swings downward.

And the scream that erupts from me is earth-shattering.

The ground rumbles beneath my feet as a massive gust of wind bursts from a place lodged deep in my chest. It flattens the nearby hedges and blasts apart the fountain. It explodes, raining heavy chunks of marble down on us. Water sprays everywhere, coating the pebbled ground. I stand like a goddess of chaos and destruction as I unleash my anguish on the world.

Only after the calm has settled and my vocal cords have given out from roaring Jace's name, do I open my eyes.

I blink a few times, adjusting to the vibrant colors that skate across my vision. My sight is sharper, picking up on beautiful hues I didn't even know existed.

My friends are huddled together on the ground, Kai and Dover using their bodies to shield the ladies beneath them. Peaceful silence surrounds us as they slowly rise.

I can *smell* them—their scents. Each and every one distinct.

I scan for the creatures, but they have vanished without a trace. There are no bodies.

I *obliterated* them. And I don't even know how.

Jace turns to me on his knees, his eyes level with mine. I grasp his shoulders as blood trickles from my nose.

Black blood.

"She's a banshee," Cece breathes.

Kai shakes his head, his voice reverent. "She's a witch."

"The glamour," Jace whispers, clutching my arms. "You shattered the glamour."

I don't have time to worry about it before I spot Kylian standing at the opening of one of the tunnels, staring directly at me, his expression intrigued. I quickly turn my face away as King Derek's command rings out.

"Guards! This way!" His voice booms as he stalks past a wide-eyed Kylian into the dilapidated mess. He spots Sorscha trembling violently in Marideth and Cece's arms and rushes toward her, nearly crushing her in his embrace.

"Are you hurt?" he demands, looking the princess over. She shakes her head, speech evading her.

Kylian stands stone-faced, taking in the blown-out hedges and the shattered fountain. Behind him, a handful of Kings-guard rushes in. Zadyn shifts back into fae form and bounds toward us. Kylian clocks his every move.

"Take them back to the castle. Do not leave them," King Derek orders a few of the guards. "I want the watches doubled until further notice."

They hustle the princess and the rest of her ladies toward the exit. I mark their shocked faces, staring at me over their shoulders as they are escorted back toward the castle. Dover and Mar clasp each other's hands as they disappear.

Before Kai can follow, Kylian grabs him by the arm and bites out, "What happened here?"

Kai wrenches his arm away, but it's Jace who answers, breath coming hard.

"We were attacked. They came out of nowhere. It was an ambush." Jace gets to his feet and reaches down to help me up. I notice the gaping wound on his arm and brace my hands over the gash.

"You're not healing," I breathe. He nods, swallowing.

"Our bodies are depleted. I'll have Gnorr look at it later," he assures me, eyes shifting to Kylian.

"We heard the screams." King Derek walks toward us. "Are you alright?"

We nod, still numb. Derek does a double take when he looks at me, his eyes widening at my appearance. I have no idea how different I look with the shattered glamour. I detect a hint of caution in his expression as Kylian approaches. Picking up on it, Jace pulls me against him, pressing my head into his shoulder.

"Cry," he whispers into my ear as Kylian stops before us.

He's trying to hide my face, I realize.

He smooths my hair as I will my body to shake. I suck in short, uneven breaths as I clutch the material of Jace's shirt. Kylian slowly reaches into his pocket, eyes burning into the back of my head, and pulls out a white handkerchief, extending it to me.

"You're bleeding," he says, his voice twinkling with disturbing delight.

Fuck.

Jace takes the handkerchief from him and stuffs it into my hand. I remain facing away from Kylian, discreetly wiping the mess of black liquid off my lips and chin. I ball the material in my fist to conceal the thick black marring the pristine white cloth.

"She's in shock," Derek says, his voice tight. "Come."

He hurries me toward the exit, my face still buried in Jace's shoulder. Zadyn, Kai, and Kylian follow behind.

I stop short, turning back to the king.

"Ilsa. Ilsa is out here somewhere," I choke.

"My men will find her. Jace, take her back. All of you, stay together," the king says as he turns back toward the few remaining guards to search the maze. Kylian casts one last glance at the four of us, then tears his eyes away and follows Derek.

None of us says a word as we head back, battered and bloody. Jace holds me close to him, his expression tight with worry. I look up at him as he stares ahead.

"Do you think he saw?"

"I don't know," he bites.

We head straight for Sorscha's chambers, where the guards stationed outside her door are doubled. Inside, we find the three females huddled close together on the settee, Dover seated in a chair beside Mar.

They all look up expectantly as we enter. Sorscha and Cece have clearly been crying, their pretty eyes swollen and wet. Marideth does not cry; she sits holding their hands with quiet strength.

Sorscha shoots to her feet, her eyes on Jace. He moves forward to take her hands.

"Are you alright?"

She nods, her lower lip trembling. "Ilsa?"

"The king and his men are searching for her," I answer. She peers at me, her expression shifting as if remembering how my blood leaked black when I obliterated the creatures that terrorized us.

"You look different." She swallows, looking over me.

Shit. The glamour.

"You destroyed those creatures with nothing but your wails." She steps around Jace and stops before me. I hold her gaze as she wipes the tears from her face. "You bleed black."

"Sorscha, I'll explain everything. Let's sit."

As she moves back to her seat, I catch Marideth's steely eyes. She gives me an encouraging nod.

I stand before a room of skeptical, somewhat fearful faces as I take a steadying breath.

"Up until a few months ago, I thought the fae only existed in fairy tales. Then, one day, I found myself thrown from my world into yours. Jace found me in the Bone Forest and brought me to the castle. I had been glamoured since birth, living in the human world. My name isn't Serena Accostia."

I slowly glance around the room.

"It's Serena Avery. And I am the last Blackblood witch."

37

The room is silent.

"I knew you were different," Kai whispers after some time.

Sorscha shakes her head, bewildered. "The way you fought, the way you destroyed those creatures—"

"Jace has been training me since I arrived, teaching me to fight and how to unlock my magic so that I could bond Furi—Prophyria—my dragon."

I glance around the room at the group of people I have come to care for these last few months. They stare back at me, their expressions a mix of shock and confusion.

"I never meant to deceive you." I cast a sincere look at Sorscha, who sits stoic and removed across from me. "We needed to keep my identity secret, both for my safety and for all of yours. The king worried that if other kingdoms heard of my arrival, they would come for me. So he had me pose as your cousin and made me one of your ladies."

"*You're* the last Blackblood witch?" Cece says, as if she can't believe that I, of all people, would be chosen.

Bitch.

"I thought that much became clear when she exploded those hideous things into dust at the mere sound of her scream." Kai stands behind a high-backed chair, leaning on his elbows. "That would explain why my charm never worked on you."

"That has nothing to do with being a witch. I'm just idiot-proof." I smile warmly at him, and he snorts, diffusing some of the tension.

"And you—" Cece assesses Zadyn, her green eyes distrusting. "You're a shifter."

"Zadyn arrived here with me. He's my familiar," I explain.

"It all makes sense now." Sorscha's brows knit together.

"I promise I will answer any questions you have, but right now"—I glance between Jace and Zadyn—"I think we need to discuss what just happened."

Dover exhales. "What in hell were those things?"

"I've never seen anything like them," Zadyn says. "We were walking through the maze when they appeared out of thin air and attacked."

"I have no idea what they were." Kai shakes his head, dumbfounded.

"I might," Jace addresses the room. "A few months ago, there was an attack at the portal in Hyrax that ended in two Guardians killed."

Kai straightens. "Something crossed over."

Jace nods. "I've had my men scouring Hyrax, searching for whatever it was that came over to prevent it from crossing into Aegar, but we've had no luck. On top of that, there have been recent attacks on our own borders. The assaults have left a string of innocent fae dead, their bodies drained of blood. We can't confirm that the two incidents are related, but it's certainly a possibility."

"This attack had to have been planned." Zadyn leans against the settee near Cece. "Think about it. It was limited only to where we were, inside the maze. The rest of the grounds were untouched. Those creatures, whatever they were, knew where we would be. They were targeting us."

"The party, the Hunt, it was all the perfect distraction," I say.

"But to what end?" Marideth asks. "What do you think they wanted?"

"The most obvious guess is the princess, maybe even Kai," Jace says, crossing his arms over his chest.

"But they didn't seem focused on getting to me or Kai," Sorscha points out. "They were just hell-bent on killing anything in their path."

A knock at the door interrupts us. Jace opens it, taking a folded slip of paper from the steward and reading it to himself.

"The king has requested my presence. I'm sure he'll want a detailed account of tonight's events." He pauses, one hand on the doorknob, his face a mask of concern. "You should all try to get some rest. None of this will be solved tonight."

He exits without another word. My eyes catch on Zadyn as he stands.

"He's right," he says, casting a glance around the room. "It's late."

"I couldn't sleep if I tried," Sorscha murmurs, moving to the window. "Not when Ilsa is still out there."

Marideth moves to her, placing a comforting hand on her shoulder. "The king and his guards are out there now. They will find her."

Something tells me they will. But the question is: in what state?

"I WONDER how many people know about the attack last night." I slip my arm through Zadyn's as we make our way into the Grand Hall.

"Not many, it seems," he mutters.

Our eyes ghost over the blissfully unaware sea of heads gathered for the feast. Not a fae in this room seems to be on alert for any potential lurking threat.

Zadyn stayed in my bed last night, shifting back into his *OrCat* form in case of another attack. Even with the comfort of his company, I didn't sleep a wink, my mind occupied by brutal monsters and the sight of Jace on his knees, his life a moment from forfeit. I had hoped to see him this morning, but he sent word that he would be indisposed with the king for most of the day, no doubt regarding last night's ambush.

Zadyn and I snuck away from the castle this morning to hunt for Furi. I didn't dare take her out of the cave with a possible threat lurking in the woods. She took an instant liking to Zadyn, who literally had her eating out of the palm of his hand. She purred for him like a kitten, the little flirt. He was just as enchanted by my beastly pet.

"I know that whatever I did when I screamed last night blasted them apart"—I look up at Zadyn—"but I doubt we've seen the last of those creatures. My gut is telling me that this wasn't just a one-off."

"I agree. We need to be on high alert."

We descend the steps into the hall. Half the entourage is seated at one of the red velvet booths in the corner, looking worse for wear. They bear the same sullen expression, clearly having had as rough a time sleeping last night as I did. I notice that Jace, Sorscha, and, of course, Ilsa are not in attendance.

"Any word on Ilsa?" I slide in beside Marideth, who shakes her head.

"Nothing." She sighs, her chin propped on her hand. "I

don't understand. She has to be out there in that maze. She couldn't have just disappeared."

I shake my head, silently rolling through the list of things that could have happened to her. If any of those creatures got past us and took her...I don't want to consider the alternative to her being perfectly fine and in one piece.

"Where are Jace and Sorscha?"

"Who knows? I haven't seen Jace since last night, and Sorscha was called to see the king late this afternoon. She said she would meet us here." Her smart gray eyes do a quick scan of the room for the princess.

"I don't see the king, either." I note the three empty thrones behind the massive head table set up for the feast.

Kai leans across the booth. "I heard a rumor that my brother and the king were locked in a meeting last night until the earliest hours of the morning." He gives us a conspiratorial look and sips his drink. Cece turns to him.

"Where did you hear that, Kai?"

"I have spies everywhere, sweet Ceec," he says, dark charm coloring his voice. She rolls her eyes.

"A meeting without his advisors?" Zadyn asks.

"Apparently. The captain was the only one asked to sit in." Kai slumps back, one arm draped over the cushion behind Cece's abounding curls.

Something about all of this strikes me as odd. Secretive.

"You're looking particularly be*witching* this evening, Lady Accostia." Kai assesses me.

"Be more obvious, Kai," Mar mutters.

"What, like anyone's around to hear?" he says, glancing toward the massive crowd gathered for the reception. Mar and I shake our heads, not in the mood for his idea of a joke.

With all that happened last night, I nearly forgot about the shattered glamour.

As soon as Zadyn and I made it back to my room, I dashed over to the mirror, terrified I would find a stranger looking back at me.

"It's alright." He laid a gentle hand on my shoulder, seeing my horror reflected. "The difference is barely noticeable."

Maybe to him.

I turned my face from side to side, marveling at how my tan skin caught the candlelight. There was a slight sheen to it, almost as if the cells contained barely-there facets of glitter. Like the dust of a star had rained down upon my skin, kissing it with celestial brilliance. I was no Edward Cullen, but if I wasn't already sure that I was superhuman, this would be enough to convince me.

My chocolate brown hair had deepened a shade and now hung to my hips, the shine so reflective it was nearly blinding. The slight shift in color made me look dramatic, contouring the hollows of my face to look sharp and structured. I was still me, but different. Enhanced. Alluring.

I trailed my fingers along my smooth skin, over the remaining arch of my ears, over my perfectly proportioned lips. In place of canines stood two tiny, razor-sharp fangs.

"The fangs retract." I peered at Zadyn in the mirror, who, in turn, bared his teeth and offered me a demonstration. "See?"

But that wasn't the most concerning alteration.

"What's wrong with my *eyes*?"

I gasped when I took them in. Dark purple lined the outer irises, circling the deep lavender before bleeding into a hypnotic magenta around the pupils. I stared in horror as they constricted, becoming tiny black slits similar to my dragon's. I blinked, and they returned to black dots. All my life, my eyes had been plain old chocolate brown. These were the eyes of a predator. With starry flecks floating around the irises, my eyes now held an entire solar system. An entire world. Mesmerizing and mysterious and ancient.

"The slits are the sole indicator of a bonded Blackblood."

"I'm terrifying," I breathed, taking in the full picture.

"You're stunning." His eyes linked with mine in the mirror. Too concerned to offer a thank you, I turned to face him.

"If people see me like this, they'll know what I am instantly." I ran my fingers down the silken locks. I had hoped for a little more time to adjust before slapping a blaring target on my back.

"I can put a temporary glamour on you, more of a damper, really. It should cover up the eyes and the skin," he said, tilting my chin up to examine my face. "But it will fade, so we'll have to keep redoing it until we find a more permanent solution."

When Zadyn was through with me, I looked a little more normal.

"Something different with your hair?" Kai pokes, snapping me back to the present moment. I glare at him.

Zadyn had done a well enough job at glamouring my eyes and lessening the iridescent skin. My irises were brown again, although there was a hint of something deeper beneath, giving them a warmer tone than usual. I prayed the glamour would hold until we were alone again, and he could give it a refresh.

I ignore Kai, glancing around at the endless rows of red-clothed tables situated throughout the room.

"I need a drink," Mar grouses beside me.

"Same."

The two of us extricate ourselves from the pack and head toward the refreshments.

"My lady."

I turn to find Kylian behind me, his towering figure once again naked from the waist up. Tonight, he wears a necklace of brilliant golden suns stretched across his broad chest, from shoulder to shoulder. At the center of each one is a large crimson ruby. His gilded crown is of the same make, situated perfectly on his mess of dark hair.

The sight is breathtaking.

"King Kylian." I give a small curtsy, never taking my eyes off him. Mar pauses a few feet ahead of me, looking back at us.

Kylian reaches for my hand, drowning it in his own and bringing it to his lips. I fight the flood of heat that kisses up my skin from where his mouth touches, knowing he's throwing his siren power at me full force. I hate to admit the effort it takes on my part to resist.

"You look well despite the events of last night," he murmurs, his voice dangerously sensual. His eyes roam over my scantily clad body.

"How kind," I deadpan. He lowers my hand but does not release it.

"The feast is about to begin. I would be honored if you would sit by me. There is much I wish to learn about you."

"Going to pester me for my name again?" I peel my hand from his, quirking my brow.

He gives a soft, lovely laugh and leans in to whisper in my ear, "Oh, I already know exactly who you are."

My stomach clenches.

I don't know how much he saw in the maze last night, but he certainly caught the tail end of my display. Definitely heard the banshee shriek. Heard me wailing Jace's name over and over as I racked the earth with my agony and blew those creatures apart. He saw the black blood leaking from my nose despite Jace's effort to shield me from his view. I don't know if he got close enough to see the purple-slitted eyes, the dead giveaway of a bonded rider, but he knows a lot. And he's not about to show his hand. He wants to play a little while longer.

"Lady Serena Accostia, cousin of the king," he says in earnest, ocean eyes wide with false naiveté.

Oh, he's good. Which means I have to be better.

While everything in me wants to claw at him, to kill him for hurting Kai, hurting my friend, it dawns on me that this might be an opportunity to spy. He's endeared to me—that much is clear. And I don't trust him as far as I can throw him. But I do want to know what his overnight meeting with the king entailed. And why Jace was involved.

The moment I think his name, he materializes on the other side of the hall. Those trademark golden eyes connect with mine. His face is a mask of quiet fury, glancing between me and the King of Vod.

Envy, I realize.

I force myself to turn back to the dark king.

"It would be my pleasure."

He holds out a rippling bare arm, and I slide mine through it, my nails lightly grazing his skin. He mistakes it for an accident, but that doesn't quell the chill I catch racing up his bicep. I nod to Mar that all is well. She seems to read my mind, covertly nodding and heading back to our booth. Kylian leads me to the three gilded thrones at the center of the head table. He pulls out an empty chair for me, and I slide in as he takes his place on the throne beside me.

"I must admit, it's not often I come across a female so spirited." The backhanded compliment lands softly, and I return it with a sweet smile. "Color me intrigued."

"Me, spirited? I have no idea what you're referring to, my King."

He chuckles.

"I witnessed your bravery last night in the maze. Such heroics in the face of death."

How long had he been standing there? How much did he see?

"Most females would see a threat and run, but instead, you ran toward it. Even lesser males would have cowered. But not you."

I want to slap him just for the little *females* comment, though I truly believe he thinks he's paying me a compliment, the ignorant bastard.

"I'm not most females." I shrug.

"That much is clear."

"Anyone would have done the same to help their friends." I flash him a demure smile, lowering my eyes and bringing them up again to peek through my thick lashes.

"I don't think they would." He angles his upper body toward me and leans in, half-caging me in with his impressive arms.

"I can't help but feel responsible." He sighs. I fix my eyes on him. "The attack happened at an event meant to celebrate my arrival. You were only in that maze because of the Hunt. The moment we realized something was wrong, King Derek and I rushed to get there. I only wish we could have made it sooner. Though by the time we arrived, it appeared you had the situation quite in hand."

His eyes roam over my chest and legs, not bothering to be subtle. "Beautiful and lethal."

He tips his head back, taking a slow sip of wine.

A trumpet sounds, and the guests begin filling in the empty spaces at the endless sea of tables.

"I have many talents," I say. "Did you uncover anything more about the attack in your search?"

"Unfortunately, not. But thankfully, it was contained to the maze. Where those creatures came from and what they wanted remains a mystery."

I figured as much.

"Don't be worried." He reaches out, concern coating his features as his finger grazes my chin. "King Derek has doubled security around the castle and adjusted the wards. There will be no repeat of last night."

If I wasn't already convinced of what a bastard he was, I would read his words as caring—empathetic. But I don't think there's a heart in there capable of any such emotion. So I lean into his touch ever so slightly, giving his ego the desired stroke and painting me as the damsel rather than the powerful Blackblood capable of inflicting dragon fire on his sorry ass.

"Tell me, my King—" I offer up a coy smirk, treading carefully. "What brings you all the way to Aegar?"

His poker face remains perfectly intact. If he's surprised by my sudden interest in him, he doesn't show it.

"It has been many years since I've seen my mother. I was due for a visit. I must admit, however, that I do have ulterior motives." He lowers his stunning eyes before flashing them back up to mine.

"Such as?" I say, hoping he drops a major bomb at the mere sight of my batting lashes.

"Such as finding a wife."

"Is that so?" I can't help the way my eyebrows shoot up in response, remembering how the nobles told Zadyn that Kylian had refused to take a wife and queen consort. So what changed his mind?

"Aegean court is full of lovely, eligible bachelorettes. I'm sure you'll have no trouble finding a worthy wife here."

"Lovely as they may be, I'm looking for something...special. Suffice it to say my tastes are more"—his hand glides over my bare knee, and I fight the urge to take the fork on the table and jab it clean through his hand—"refined."

"Something special?" I challenge. "Is the King a secret romantic, or are you referring to an advantageous alliance?"

"Perhaps a little of both." He hits me with a wicked smile.

"I don't believe that for a minute." I sigh, facing forward again. "You desire a love match?"

"That's certainly part of it. I have refused many marriage offers over the years from princesses and highborn females—the most desirable matches in all of Solterre. But none of them were my equal and, therefore, would not be fit to rule beside me."

The fanfare of trumpets announcing the arrival of the king and queen sounds from atop the massive staircase, pausing our conversation. They descend the steps side by side, Sorscha trailing behind them in a cropped fitted golden breastplate, a cream-colored skirt with a long train, and a sparkling tiara in her done-up hair.

She and the queen settle into their thrones, and the king remains standing. He lifts a golden goblet, addressing his court.

"Friends, courtiers, and honored guests," he booms. "I welcome you to the third night of King's Fair. Tonight, we honor and embrace the valiant King Kylian of Vod by feasting on the finest meat and mead Aegar has to offer. We are forever grateful for the tranquility between our two great nations. Let us toast to many more years of peace and prosperity!"

The crowd roars and applauds, lifting their glasses. Kylian smiles and nods to the masses like a goddamn Kennedy. King Derek holds up a hand to hush the room once more.

"Tonight is a momentous occasion indeed. Not only do we celebrate King Kylian's stay at court, but we have happy news to share. Raise your cups to toast the recent engagement of my heir, the Crown Princess Sorscha Accostia, to my newly appointed Hand of the King, Jace Fallyn."

38

My heart stops.

It stops dead in my chest as tunnel vision threatens to knock me from my seat.

No, no, no.

My eyes shift to Sorscha and Jace as they get to their feet beside the king. Jace interlocks their fingers and lifts their joined hands in the air triumphantly. The crowd erupts into wild cheers as I fight to get down a breath. It would take a trained eye to notice that their twin smiles don't quite reach their eyes.

"Wish them everlasting fortune and happiness!" The king toasts and sips from his goblet. The crowd again threatens to deafen me with their taunting cheers. When Jace looks at me, his mask momentarily slips, revealing the regret behind those golden eyes. It's gone before I can blink.

"You and the captain seemed quite close yesterday. Or should I say, the Hand? I was surprised to hear of his involvement with the princess." Kylian tuts, interrupting my racing thoughts. I school my face into a mask of indifference.

"He and the princess have been good friends to me since my arrival at court. We have all grown close in recent months."

"Yes, I had heard of your humble upbringing in the north. How tragic for a beauty as rare as yours to be cloistered behind temple walls all your life."

He really did his homework, didn't he?

"I'm here now, aren't I?" I paste a smile on my face, shifting to face forward again. "And I plan to take full advantage of my freedom."

"That shouldn't be difficult to do with a dragon on your side."

My blood goes cold as I slowly turn to him.

"Oh, did you think I didn't notice your little nosebleed? Those unmistakable eyes? That glamour won't last another hour." He leans back in his velvet-lined throne, his sparkling eyes roaming over me. "You are even more of a surprise than I originally thought."

"I have no idea what you're talking about," I bluff.

He chuckles. "You remind me so much of myself."

What an insult, I refrain from saying aloud.

"How so?"

"Stubborn, willful, with great power at your disposal. Determined to get what you want." His voice dips low as he slyly glances toward Jace. I follow his eyeline for a moment before snapping my gaze back to him. "Don't worry, your secret is safe with me. Both your secrets, I should say." He places a hand over where his heart should be.

"I think you're mistaken." I force an amused smile onto my face as I sip my wine.

"That would be a first." He smirks, crossing one long leg over the other.

"You have no idea what I want."

"You wear your heart on your sleeve, Dragon Rider. It's a

shame that he's unavailable. But you know, you can do so much better than a low-born fae rat masquerading as Hand of the King."

I want to rip out his throat for talking about Jace like that. The pinpricks of my magic begin to gather at my fingertips. I will it to remain subdued.

"You are a queen. And you are fit for a king as powerful as you," Kylian whispers in my ear, his body suddenly very close.

I beam at him, my voice full of ire when I say, "Let me know if you find one anywhere."

He stares as I rise from my seat, wine in hand, and tip my head to him.

"Please excuse me."*

Without waiting for a response, I file through the tables toward the door. Alone in the abandoned hallway, I drain the rest of my wine and toss the goblet into a nearby potted plant.

Deep breaths, I remind myself. Hold it together until you're alone in your room.

"Serena," Jace calls from behind me.

My heart sinks, but I don't turn or slow my pace. He catches up to me with those damned long legs and pulls my face into his hands, forcing me to look at him.

"Hey, hey, hey. Stop," he whispers.

"A promotion and an engagement. Congratulations."

"I'm sorry. I'm so sorry—there wasn't enough time to tell you." His eyes search my face.

"It's fine, Jace, you don't owe me an explanation." I peel his hands from my cheeks and push past him.

"Yes, I do. Serena, please. Just give me a chance to explain."

"There's nothing to explain. This is over. It was over before it even began. So I'm not sure why you're standing here."

---

* *Cue: Moon Song* by Phoebe Bridgers

He gives me an obvious look. "You know it isn't over. Last night, you almost died—"

"We both almost died," I interrupt. "And because of that, I broke the glamour and gave myself away. Because of what we mean to each other. We knew this was coming."

I shove past him again, my stride steady and my focus ahead.

"And yet you're still surprised." He blocks my path, forcing me to skid to a halt.

"I'm not, Jace." I sigh, closing my eyes. "I'm tired. I'm tired of fighting my feelings for you, knowing I can't have you. I'm tired of hoping for a miracle that ends with us together. And I'm tired of seeing you dangled in front of me on Sorscha's arm." I shake my head. "You know, you said you weren't in love with her and that your feelings for me were real, but you sure put on a convincing show whenever she's around."

"And how am I supposed to act?!" he exclaims. "Appalled? Disgusted by the fact that the king has given me his only daughter and his crown one day? Any feelings toward Sorscha aside, I am grateful to him. For giving me a life I could only dream about."

"So, I guess a beautiful princess is just a sweet little bonus," I bite.

"That's not fair, and you know it." He seethes as I stalk away.

"Life's not fair. Get used to it. I wish you all the happiness in the world."

I wait for his stinging comeback, but instead, he pivots topics.

"What were you doing with Kylian?"

"He asked me to sit by him. Said he wanted to get to know me."

"Tell me you didn't fall for that line of bullshit," he growls. I toss him a pointed look.

"I'm not an idiot. I just wanted to find out how much he saw last night."

"And did you?"

"Yes. I did. He saw everything. He knows."

Jace scowls, his jaw tightening. "He can't be trusted."

"You don't think I know that?" I toss my hair over my shoulder. "The timing of his arrival here is suspicious. I intend to find out why."

"By seducing him?"

"By any means necessary."

"You're playing with fire. *Serena*." He tugs on my arm, pulling me to face him. "He knows you're the last Blackblood. This is exactly what we wanted to prevent from happening."

"This was always going to happen." I jerk my arm away. "Other kingdoms were bound to find out, eventually. And I don't think he would be stupid enough to *steal me away* in the night. The king would be on his ass in a second."

He sighs, shaking his head. "I hope you know what you're doing."

"You know what, Jace?" I take a step closer, angling my face up to his. "Who I spend my time with and what I do is none of your concern. I have to go."

∼

I TAKE a big swig from the bottle of liquor I found in Zadyn's room.

The glass presses against my lips, stifling my sobs. I swallow down the wrong pipe and go into a coughing fit, choking on my own spit. I force out slow, deep breaths until my chest eventually softens and my throat unlocks.

"You look terrible."

Mar slips through my door quietly. I toss her a desolate look and hold out the bottle. She takes it and sips, easing into the seat beside me.

"To loving men who are engaged." I reach for the bottle and give a half-assed toast to no one.

"I'm not sure how much longer I can do this," I admit after a long silence.

"Do what?"

"Survive Jace," I say. "I can bond a dragon, I can take out a bunch of raging beasts with one scream, but this I'm not sure I can do."

"You love him," Mar states.

I nod sadly. "And so does Sorscha. It's so obvious. She looks at him like he walks on water. And it is killing me. I know it's wrong, I know how selfish I sound, but I can't stay away. I can't turn off my feelings."

"Then you need to prepare yourself for what is about to happen." She eyes me evenly, her gray stare cutting through me.

"Jace and Sorscha are engaged. They will rule together as king and queen when Derek steps down. You have to let him go, or you will be the one left hurt and alone in the end."

"I can't stay away from him. I've tried, Mar."

"You're going to have to."

"Why? Did an engagement ever stop you from being with Dover? You just steamrolled right over the whole idea, right over Wyneth."

A flash of hurt flickers in her expression, and I slightly regret bringing that up.

"That's different, and you know it," she says. "Dover is my mate. That trumps any marriage of convenience orchestrated by his parents. Not to mention, in your case, it would be treason. Sorscha is a princess, the heir to the throne."

"I understand that, but you yourself said that there was no life for you without Dover. That's how I feel about Jace."

"Sometimes it does feel like that," she admits. "But I know who I am without him. Would it break me if I lost him? Yes. But would it kill me? No. No matter what, mate or not, he's just a male. I won't let loss define my life. Define me." Her fervor simmers into something softer as she lays a hand on my shoulder.

"Sorscha is my princess and my friend, but so are you. She may be willfully ignorant at times, but she has eyes, and after last night—the way you reacted when Jace was attacked, how he fought, how he killed to protect you..."

I think of the moment he saw me fall to that horrible creature. The way he screamed my name, the way he cut down those creatures like he would tear the entire world apart to get to me. That's when I realized I would do no less.

"Do you think she knows?" I ask, sobering.

"I think anyone that gets within thirty paces of you two knows. But I think she's been willfully blind up to this point. I don't know how much longer you can count on that."

And here I thought we were being discreet.

Zadyn surprises me by bursting through the door, eyes wide and face flushed. We leap to our feet, startled.

"Ilsa's dead."

"Oh my gods," Marideth breathes, clasping her hand to her mouth. "No."

"What happened?" I ask, boy drama forgotten.

Zadyn steps into the room and closes the door behind him. He hesitates, looking at Mar. "I'm sorry, Mar, you may not want to hear this."

"I do." She steels herself, taking my hand and squeezing hard. "I need to."

Zadyn sighs and continues. "Her body was strung up from

the ceiling in the Grand Hall and dropped in the middle of the dance floor. She'd been dead for a day already. Her body had been drained of blood, just like the victims of the border attacks."

"The creatures from the maze did this," I say. "And if her blood was drained, too—then they must be the ones behind the border attacks. But why kill her and then make a public show of it?"

"To send a message. A warning that the castle isn't safe." Zadyn glances between us. "We're on lockdown until the guards finish searching the grounds."

Jace.

My heart sinks.

He's undoubtedly out there searching for the danger. If he gets hurt, and the last time we spoke, we were fighting, and I was giving him hell...

"I'm going out there." The alcohol hits me the second I step toward the door. I wobble on my feet before Zadyn reaches out to steady me.

"You're not going anywhere like this. You're drunk."

"I am not!" I protest, my tongue feeling thick.

"Would you just listen to me for once?" He rolls his eyes, taking the nearly empty bottle from me and shaking it to prove his point.

"Oh, fine. We can just sit here like helpless idiots while others do all the work," I grumble, tossing my arms up in the air.

"I need to find Dover," Mar says, bracing my shoulders.

"But we're on lockdown." I make a taunting face at Zadyn, who ignores it.

"I dare the guards to try and stop me. Besides, no one takes lockdown seriously around here." She shrugs.

"They should when there's an actual threat," I point out, but she waves a hand.

"There are guards everywhere right now—lockdown is probably the safest time to be roaming the halls. But you. Are you going to be alright?"

"Yes," I assure her. "Are you? You and Ilsa were close."

She swallows, eyes momentarily glossing before blinking back to normal. Marideth isn't one to show emotion. I know she will cry, but she will do it in private or with Dover. She has a kind of quiet strength that can only come from surviving true hardship.

"I'm alright. I need to check on the others. Don't do anything stupid." She shakes me once before slipping into the hall, leaving Zadyn and me alone. He gives me a concerned look.

"I don't want to talk about it. Not tonight," I murmur, trudging toward the bed.

We sit in anxious silence for hours until a guard knocks on the door to let us know the castle is clear. It must be near midnight when a softer knock sounds. Zadyn answers it to a trembling Cece, her golden hair undone and a knit shawl wrapped over her nightgown.

"Cece," Zadyn breathes. Her beautiful face contorts in sadness as tears spring from her eyes. He pulls her into his chest.

"Ilsa," she sobs, her body shaking. My heart aches for the female I've never liked. Her best friend was mutilated and hung up for the entire court to see. I wouldn't wish that on my worst enemy.

"I don't want to be alone right now." She peers up at him, her green eyes sad and hopeful as Zadyn smooths her face.

"I'll stay with you, of course." Wrapping her in another tight hug, he strokes her hair and glances at me over her shoulder, silently asking for permission. I don't understand why he needs it from me, but I give him a nod.

Of course. Go be with her. She needs you.

And you?

I'll be fine.

He imparts me with one final look before taking the trembling beauty by the hand and leading her back toward her room.

39

I lay in bed far longer than I should, my hangover riding me viciously after guzzling that bottle of liquor. I know I should get up. Go feed my dragon. Hit the training ring. Check on my mourning friends.

Be anything but a hungover slug.

My door clicks open, and Jace slips through, not even bothering to knock.

"Sure, come on in." I prop myself up on my elbows.

"Ilsa's dead." He slides onto the bed.

"I know." I sigh. "Zadyn told me last night. It's terrible."

I still haven't had time to really process it. I've just been trying to unravel this knot and figure out how to prevent it from happening again. "Did you find anything?"

"No."

"How did they even get in here to...to plant her body?"

He shakes his head, rising to his feet. "I don't know. I don't know how they were able to breach the wards again."

"Zadyn said Ilsa's blood was drained like the others."

"It was. They hung her up like swine to send a message. It

was a threat, and now everyone knows the wards have been compromised. It makes our security look unstable. Weak." He paces, hands on his hips.

"But now we know those creatures are behind the border attacks. And since they started after the portal was breached, they could be responsible for that, too."

He nods in agreement.

"You said that they just *appeared* in the maze?" I ask.

"Yes, but the question is how? The wards around the castle should have kept them out." He runs a hand through his dark hair, clearly perturbed.

I knit my brows together as I think.

"Who's to say they aren't an exception to the wards? If those are the same creatures that came through the portal, then maybe the wards can't recognize them. Maybe it's a different kind of magic—magic not of this world."

Jace glances at me.

"It would make sense. If they aren't from Solterre, then our magic wouldn't protect against them. It wouldn't know how. Which doesn't bode well for us," he adds.

"That and the fact that they don't stay dead," I mutter, staring out the window at the gloomy day. Jace pauses his anxious pacing.

"Your scream worked on them. *You* worked."

"You were about to die," I whisper, holding his gaze. "I just snapped."

He inches closer to the bed.

"If you hadn't screamed, then I wouldn't be standing here right now. You saved my life. All of our lives."

A long silence falls.

"You shouldn't be here," I say quietly, dropping my eyes to the comforter.

"You're the Dragon Rider—you're high priority. And aside from that, as my trainee, you are my responsibility."

"That's such bullshit." I toss the covers back and plant my feet on the ground. "The princess is the *highest* priority, not to mention your fiancé, and yet here you are. Bothering me."

"Would you rather I go to her then?" he challenges.

"Don't do that." I point at him. "Don't ask questions you already know the answers to."

He leans against the bedpost and says, "I wanted to finish our conversation from last night."

I pinch the bridge of my nose and close my eyes. "What more is there to say?"

"Plenty, little witch." A sigh empties from his chest. "I wasn't expecting things to happen like this, but the attack in the maze scared the king. If Sorscha had been hurt or killed, his line would have died with her. He said he couldn't allow that to happen—that she needed to marry immediately to come into her power and start producing heirs. That was what we discussed in our meeting. He moved me up to Hand so that I would be of a worthy enough station to marry her. We worked out the details, drew up the contract, and it was settled."

"You drew up the contract, and it was settled." I laugh. "How romantic."

He drops his eyes to the ground. I know it's no one's fault and that my anger is misplaced on him. These are just our circumstances. Still, I can't help the acid that leaks into my voice.

"What was Kylian doing there?" I try for a more agreeable tone.

"Discussing Sorscha's betrothal with Derek. Kylian and his mother had initially vetted Kai as a match, but something changed his mind, and he went to the king to withdraw him as an option. Then he put his support behind me."

"That's suspicious. Why wouldn't he want Kai on the throne after the attack?"

"I don't know," he admits.

I hop off the bed. "I'll find out."

"What does that mean?"

"It means that I am going to charm him and get to the bottom of it. Something is not right here, and my gut is telling me he has something to do with it." I head toward the wardrobe, but he blocks me with his rock-hard body.

"What are you doing?" he demands.

"Getting dressed, obviously. The service for Ilsa is starting soon."

"I mean, what are you *going* to do?"

"I'm *going* to start stripping in five seconds, so unless you want an eyeful, then please leave."

I step around him, continuing to the wardrobe.

"I was referring to Kylian." Frustration seeps into his words as he comes up behind me. His breath tickles my neck, sending a shiver down my spine. I turn to face him. An electric charge passes between us as we stare each other down. He walks forward, forcing me back until I hit the wardrobe.

"Jace," I warn. He leans in, pressing his lips against my ear. My eyes fall shut.

"I didn't like you talking to him," he growls.

I feel it in my knees.

"What a coincidence. That makes two of us."

"And I really don't like how he looks at you." He palms the wood, caging me between his arms.

"That shouldn't matter to you."

"And yet it does, little witch," he whispers, pulling back so that his golden eyes burn into mine.

I scoff.

"You don't get to be possessive. You are *engaged*, Jace. It's official. I am trying my best to let you go, to put my feelings aside, and here you are—doing whatever it is you're doing. I won't share you with someone else." I close my eyes and swallow the glass shards in my throat. "You coming here, doing this—it's cruel. It's cruel to try to make me forget that you aren't mine, only for reality to come crashing back in the moment we're not alone. Do you know how cheap this makes me feel? When I know you have feelings for both of us?"

"My feelings for her are nothing like what I feel for you. I care about her, but not like that. I don't love her, I love—" I press my fingers against his lips, silencing him.

"Do not finish that sentence. Please. I know you care about her. And it may not be love now, but that will easily change because you're you, and she's Sorscha. So, I can't do this. I won't."

I find the will to push him back and turn away, pressing my head against the wardrobe.

He waits a long moment before striding to the door and leaving me alone.

I KNOCK LIGHTLY on Sorscha's door before the service.

"Yes?" her soft voice calls.

I crack it open to find a slightly dimmed version of the dazzling princess seated at her vanity, head resting in her hands. She wears no makeup. Her eyes are swollen and red, her lips less rosy than usual. It's not exactly the state I would expect to find a recently engaged princess in, but then again, her best friend was just killed.

"Oh, cousin," she breathes, turning in her seat. "Come in."

She tightens the tie of her silk robe as I take a seat across from her. Her disorientation is evident. Vacant amber eyes peer out from her heavy lashes, looking through me instead of at me. She must be in shock.

"I guess we aren't really cousins after all," she muses. "It's too bad. I so enjoyed having a cousin. I never had a sister..." She trails off, her voice light and airy.

Remorse tightens my throat as I swallow. She's been more of a sister to me in the past few months than my actual sister ever was.

I repaid her with deceit.

"I'm sorry I had to keep it from you," I say with sincerity. "It was for everyone's protection. But you have to know that I care for you. For all of you."

She nods, barely managing a slight smile.

"How are you holding up?" I ask. She shakes her head.

"I don't quite believe it, even though I saw her with my own eyes," she recalls, her voice devoid of emotion.

Definite shock.

"Jace and I had just gotten to the dance floor when it happened. She just fell from the ceiling. Dropped like a little ragdoll. At first, I thought it was one of the silk dancers—just an acrobatic trick. Then I saw her. It was so loud. For someone so slight, when she fell, it was so loud."

Oh, god.

I scoot my seat closer.

"We are going to find whatever did this to her, and we are going to put an end to it so it can never hurt anyone again," I vow.

"I don't understand how it happened. Any of it. One minute, she was right behind us, and the next... If Cece and I had noticed sooner—"

"You can't blame yourself, Sorscha." I take her hands. "It's no one's fault."

That's when I notice the massive rock on her finger. I can't

432

tear my eyes away. She notices my distraction and retracts her hands, twisting the ring around her finger.

"It's a bit tacky for my taste, but I'm told it belonged to my mother." She glances down at it.

"No, no, it's beautiful. It suits you." I sit back. "I never got a chance to congratulate you."

The words taste like ash in my mouth.

I feel like a deceitful, lying piece of trash.

"It's not exactly how I pictured getting engaged. It was horribly unromantic. Father called me into his chambers, I signed a few papers, and it was done. I thought maybe Jace would take me somewhere private after—somewhere lovely— and get down on one knee. Propose. But I realize now that's a little girl's dream." She fiddles with the ring around her manicured finger.

"There's nothing childish about wanting a romantic proposal."

"There was no proposal of any kind," she clarifies. "It was all just agreed upon, like a business contract. The attack pushed Father to speed things along. He wants me to make heirs as soon as possible."

"Is that—is that what you want?"

"I love being a princess—" She turns to face the mirror and begins to untangle the plaits of her loose braid. "But I've never wanted to be queen. I love my freedom. I love throwing parties and kicking up trouble. I love to have fun. I fear that will all come to an end when I am married with children. That kind of behavior isn't fit for a wife and mother, let alone a queen."

"Oh, Sorscha. I'm so sorry this wasn't what you hoped for."

She shrugs. "I always knew this was what I was meant for. My worth lies in my ability to create heirs, to continue my line."

Shaking my head, I say, "You are worth so much more than that. You are not just some machine meant to reproduce."

433

I watch as she begins applying cream to her smooth arms.

"I know I'm a disappointment to him," she says with a heartbreaking smile. "He wished for a son. Or a daughter like you. Someone strong, smart, capable. The way you destroyed those creatures in the maze, the way you swing a sword—I'll never be able to do that. I'll never be able to run a kingdom, and everyone knows it. That's why he wanted me married off to Jace or Kai—although Kai's really no better than I am. The only difference is he's a male. I suppose that's why he decided on Jace in the end."

"Don't say that, Sorscha," I whisper. "Never discount yourself like that. You are just as good as any male. And I know that the king loves you."

She is quiet for a moment, contemplating something.

"It could be a lot worse. Jace is everything I could have hoped for in a match. He was my guard for so long. We never even noticed each other, not like that, until my father posed the idea to us. He's not my typical type, but maybe that's why I like him. He's not a spoiled, privileged prince. He's not—"

"Kai?" I supply with a knowing smile. She shakes her head, giving a small laugh in return.

"No, Jace is nothing like Kai. He's a challenge to me. He's brooding and serious. He doesn't show affection—he doesn't show *any* strong emotion one way or another."

She lifts her eyes to mine in the mirror.

"Except when you're around."

My chest locks as I struggle to hold her gaze.

"Sorscha—"

"It's obvious he cares for you, cousin." She resumes applying her cream, working her way up her slender neck and onto her face in small circles. "You anger him. You push him. And the fact that he lets you, that you elicit such strong reactions from him, well, it says quite a lot." She pauses, her eyes flickering up to mine with an intensity I've never seen before. "I don't want to know what's happened between you up to now. I just want to make one thing clear. I'm going to marry him. Because if this is all I can do right in my father's eyes, then I will not fail. So whatever is going on, it needs to stop."

She redirects her gaze to her reflection and begins to apply foundation to her face.

"I understand." I won't insult her by denying it.

I move toward the door and pause, turning back to her. "We never meant to hurt you."

"You didn't. Nothing can hurt me now." Her grave words hang in the air as she continues with her face, and I quietly exit the room.

40

Hell in a handbasket.

That's where this is going.

I finally have everything I wanted—friends and a purpose. Fuck, I even have a *dragon*. And I'm screwing it all up for a guy.

I cannot believe myself.

No more, I promise myself. And this time, I mean it.

Night four of King's Fair is canceled out of respect for Sorscha and Ilsa's family. I stand at river's edge, between Zadyn and Marideth, our friends gathered close by.

The turnout for Ilsa's sendoff is overwhelming. Hordes of High Fae nobles and courtiers gather behind us for the service.

My eyes snag on the princess down the line. Her face is removed and stoic beneath a sheer black veil. Jace stands at her side, dressed impeccably for his new role as Hand of the King. His posture is not so easily shed—hands folded behind his back—still the captain at heart. They stare forward, and I wonder if Sorscha had a similar talk with him about the nature of our relationship.

I pry my eyes away and glance down at the floating plat-form staked to the water's edge. It is fashioned entirely from gathered sticks and flowers. Beneath its ethereal archway rests a white bed where Ilsa lies, small and still. She is dressed in a simple white gown with long sleeves, her silken platinum hair arranged around her like an angelic halo. Her skin is dusted with color to hide the blueish decay already setting in. She looks peaceful as sleep itself atop the float, surrounded by mementos and the most beautiful floral arrangements I've ever seen.

The High Priest leads the congregation in a prayer in ancient fae. Then a female in robes similar to his steps forward and begins to sing, her voice pure and angelic. The crowd joins in the sad and ancient song, cracking something in my soul.

When it concludes, and the echo of their joined voices has faded from the air, a fae couple who I assume to be Ilsa's parents, carry a burning torch over to the float. They bend to light it together. The rope is loosed from the stake, and it begins to drift away. Flames slowly engulf the altar as her parents hold each other, heavy sobs wracking their bodies.

Then it begins to rain.

The droplets fall onto my cheeks, mingling with the onslaught of quiet tears. A wave of anger washes over me for the innocent life taken.

So wasteful, so unnecessary.

Jace once said that one day, when the time came, I would be able to kill. I didn't believe him until I was dagger-deep in those creatures. And now I can safely say that to protect my friends, to protect my loved ones, I would kill and kill and do it gladly.

If it means preventing innocent lives like Ilsa's lost.

DRAINED AND DEPRESSED, I sneak away after the service, needing distance from everything and everyone.

I sit on the cool cave floor, back propped up against a massive crystal stalagmite, watching Furi munch on the squirrels I caught for her. I stare at the grotesque sight, feeling nothing but numb. She swallows and lets out a loud burp, and I gasp.

"Furi! Where are your manners?"

Excuse me.

It's okay, girl.

She eyes me keenly.

The Blackblood is sad.

My friend is dead.

There is more you mourn. The captain.

What are you talking about?

I can smell him on you.

So what? I was with him this morning. That doesn't mean anything.

He is not for you, Blackblood.

Great, not you, too. I know this. He's engaged. It's over.

That is not why he is not for you.

What are you talking about, Furi?

You belong to another.

What? No, there is no one else.

Isn't there?

Okay, I'm not about to discuss my love life with my dragon.

When do we ride?

I sigh, running my hand over her slick scales.

Soon, I promise. When it is safe. You were right about the danger. We were attacked a few nights ago by these...creatures.

What creatures? Why did you not call for me, Blackblood?

Because Furi, I had it under control. I took care of them.

Next time you are in danger, you call. I will come. I will fight. I will protect.

You're loyal, Furi. But I wasn't about to endanger you. If anyone had seen you, it would have put a target on both our backs.

Let me see the creatures.

How?

Open your memories to me.

I close my eyes, stilling my hand on her face, and think back to the night of the attack. The swarm of beasts coming at us one after another. Their undying rage, their brute strength.

Stryga.

What?

The Stryga is what they were called in the world of my mothers.

You know them?

They are the spirits of those who died before their time—cursed with an endless cycle of death and rebirth.

What do you mean?

Rather than create a new world for the souls of the dead to inhabit, our gods created a form capable of reanimation. The Stryga do not die, for they are already dead. With each cycle, the soul grows blacker until all that remains is an incurable thirst.

Thirst for what? I ask, already knowing the answer.

The eternal vessels survive on the blood of the dead.

"Oh my god." I leap to my feet. "The creatures from the portal came from your home world. This confirms everything. I have to get back—I have to tell the others. Thank you, Furi." I peck her on the cheek.

"I'll be back soon."

I BARREL THROUGH THE DOOR, breathless after racing back with my discovery, to find Zadyn already waiting in my room.

439

"Where have you been?" He gets to his feet, his voice tense.

"Oh, hey, mom," I tease, closing the door behind me. I shrug out of my jacket and toss it on the chair. "I have big news. Bad news, but big news. I went to see Furi."

"And?"

"And she knows what those creatures were. I showed her my memories, and she recognized them from her home world. They're called Stryga." I sink into a chair, gazing up at him. "They're beings who met early deaths, and their gods were too lazy to create an afterlife for them. So, instead, they created these immortal vessels to house the souls so that they would just die and be reborn in a never-ending cycle. And guess what keeps them running?"

"What?"

"The blood of the dead," I answer, leaning my elbows on my knees. "It's them. The Stryga are the ones who tore through the portal and killed those Guardians. They killed all those fae at the borders and attacked us in the maze."

"There were dozens of them." Zadyn's brow furrows. "And these Stryga—they're strong enough to kill a Guardian?"

"They must be." I shrug. "But if Furi is right about them, then our wards will do nothing to keep them out. We have to tell the others. Come on." I rise, making for the door, but Zadyn stops me.

"Hey, slow down," he says, taking my hand. "Everyone is... mourning right now. Give them tonight to grieve. We can share what you learned tomorrow."

I sigh, frustrated with myself. "You're right. I hadn't even considered that. I'm just in another world right now."

Where is my empathy? My compassion? I'm so morally gray right now, I barely even recognize myself.

"What's going on with you?" Zadyn asks softly, his warm brown eyes concerned.

"Nothing. What do you mean?" I sit back down, crossing one ankle over my knee, and start ripping the laces of my boots free.

"You're distant."

I say nothing.

"Is it Ilsa?"

"No." I chuck off my boots and pour myself a glass of water. After a long sip, I swallow and clarify, "I mean, of course, I'm upset about her, and I'm angry that she died, but...I don't want to talk about it."

"This wouldn't have anything to do with Jace and Sorscha's engagement, would it?"

I sigh. I knew there would be no avoiding this conversation with Zadyn, but I'd hoped he'd give me a little more time to let the dust settle before launching right into it.

"Look, if we're going to talk about this, you need to promise not to judge me. I just need someone to listen."

His kind eyes soften. "I would never judge you, Serena. What happened?" He takes a seat across from me and waits.

So, I tell him.

I confess to what Jace and I did after I told Zadyn it was over. I tell him what we did after I bonded Furi. I tell him what a terribly selfish person I am. And then we're quiet for a long time.

I sigh, leaning over the table, and bury my face in my arms. "Well? Am I the worst person ever?" My voice is muffled as I peek up at him.

"Not even a little. You fell in love with someone you can't have. It will pass, and you will heal. I'm not minimizing your feelings, but Serena—" I prop my chin up, and Zadyn reaches out to brush a strand of hair out of my eyes. He tucks it behind my ear and lowers his hand.

"Blackbloods live a long time. You will probably fall in love a thousand times before you find the one you want to spend forever with."

"Don't tell me you believe in *the one*, Zadyn. When the fae live for thousands of years?"

He nods, his brown eyes searching mine. "What is a mate, if not *the one*?"

"And witches mate?" I ask doubtfully.

"Of course. And believe me, when you find that person, when you find your soul's match, it will make every love that came before seem inconsequential."

"How do you know that?"

"I just do." He shrugs with a sad smile. I stare at him for a long time.

"Have you had that? The kind of great love you're talking about?"

He sits back in his seat, saying nothing.

"Well, have you?" I nudge his foot with mine.

"I've loved many females."

For some reason, that makes my cheeks flush with envy. I force myself to press on.

"That isn't what I asked."

"I did find my great love." He smooths his hand over the table, his eyes tracing the motion.

"What happened?"

"I wasn't hers," he says, lifting his gaze to mine.

Who wouldn't want Zadyn?

"Wow." I blink. "What a fucking idiot."

He bursts into contagious laughter, and I allow myself to join.

"Just tell me your great love isn't Cece," I amend through the fit of giggles.

He nearly chokes. "Cece and I—we just enjoy each other's company. We all need our distractions."

"Yeah, I'm sure the conversation is absolutely thrilling."

"You're an ass," he says, tipping my chair back with his foot.

"And that's why you love me."

I stand, planting a kiss on his cheek before heading to the bathroom to get ready for bed.

41

On the fifth and final night of King's Fair, I am dressed to kill.

To destroy.

To demolish.

Tonight is a masked ball, and as the penultimate conclusion of the festival, it promises to be the most extravagant.

Igrid has outdone herself with the final look of her collection.

It consists of a cropped, onyx metal breastplate that fits me like a second skin, contouring my body into this hard, shiny thing. It gleams like molten obsidian under the light, coating my curves in cured lava. The black skirt is paneled—a strip in front and a strip in back—held together by black chains around my hips. Igrid styles my hair poker straight, reaching like a seamless sheet of silk to my hips. The black metal mask fits over the bridge of my nose and the contours of my cheeks tightly, held in place by silver chains.

"Look at you," Igrid breathes, grasping my shoulders and

spinning me toward the mirror. "Now you look like a Dragon Rider."

I look fierce. Tough. Sexy.

I turn and wrap her in a tight embrace.

"What's that for, missy?" She pulls back, blue eyes wide.

"For being my first friend here. I'll never forget it. You were kind to me when I needed it most."

"It was easy to be kind to you." She squeezes my arm before retreating from the room.

Voices sound in the hall, drawing my attention. I gather the panels of my skirt in my hands and make my way to the door, reminding myself not to trip in my four-inch heels as I swing it open.

Jace and Zadyn stand outside my room, locked in some heated debate.

"—talk some sense into her for once. She won't listen to me," Jace says.

"I wonder why." Zadyn's tone is flat.

"I'm sorry, do you have something to say to me?" Jace takes an intimidating step toward him. "Because I think there's a lot to be had out between you and me."

"Oh, I could say plenty, but I won't do that because she—" Zadyn notices me shift inside the doorway and does a double take when he sees my getup. Jace follows his distracted gaze. I feel both sets of eyes travel up and down my body as they fall silent, argument temporarily paused.

"What are you two looking at?" I stand with my hands on my hips, waiting for an answer.

"You're going to let her do this looking like *that*?" Jace gestures to my body.

"First off, she's free to do whatever she wants. And second, I don't see how what she looks like is any of your concern," Zadyn says, breezing past me into the room to pour himself a drink from the diamond decanter. He leans against the table as he takes a sip, his black sleeveless shirt clinging to his muscled torso.

"What are you two going on about?" I cross over to Zadyn, holding out my hand for a sip.

"We're talking about you quite literally flirting with the enemy," Jace says, clutching his mask in his hand.

"It's not real. It's acting." I wave a dismissive hand. "Playing a part to find answers that might be useful to us."

I take a swig of the liquor and hand it back to Zadyn. The two of them track me as I move to the mirror and slip on a pair of dangling diamond earrings.

"While I can agree that Kylian is dangerous, Serena knows what she's doing," Zadyn says. Jace scoffs at him.

"Of course, you agree with her. Why did I expect you to do anything but pacify her?"

"You know what? I really am not a fan of this overprotective bullshit. I appreciate your concern, but I can take care of myself." I shoot Jace a dark look in the mirror.

"You're so damn stubborn." He runs his hand through his hair in frustration.

Good.

I hope I get under his skin half as deep as he gets under mine.

"Look, I'm not stupid enough to go anywhere alone with him. It's just a little harmless flirting to get him to open up, to trust me."

"He won't stop at flirting," Jace bites, his eyes bugging. "You give him a few coy smiles, some innocent touches, and he will take whatever he wants. Do not encourage him."

I turn and stalk up to him, stopping an inch away.

"Is this because you're actually worried for my safety or because you don't want me within ten feet of any other male?"

Jace growls in my face, his upper lip curling back. But Zadyn is there, a buffer between us, preventing him from getting any closer.

I knew that would rile him. And that's exactly the reaction I had hoped for.

"We'll be close by. If he tries anything or so much as touches her without permission, he loses a hand," Zadyn says, his voice a calm threat.

I turn from both of them.

"Don't you two have girlfriends to worry about?" I lean a hip against the vanity, crossing my ankles, then toss a glance at Jace. "A fiancé in your case?"

"Cece is hardly my girlfriend," Zadyn huffs, turning red. But Jace goes still as death.

"It's beside the point," I say with finality. "I'm doing it. Now, can we go so I can make my grand entrance in this masterpiece and watch his jaw crack hitting the floor?"

I straighten, smoothing my skirt. When none of them answers, I glide forward, linking my arms through theirs, and tow them into the hall beside me.

"Would it be terribly cliché to tell you how devastating you look?"[*]

Draped across the red velvet alcove with a considerable amount of leg on display, I glance up to see Kylian standing over me, bare-chested save the epaulet of raven feathers covering his broad shoulders. His thick-lashed siren eyes peer at me from behind a simple black mask.

I told the guys to make themselves scarce to give Kylian an

---

[*] Cue: *Devil Like Me* by Rainbow Kitten Surprise

opening. They're undoubtedly close by—hovering—even though I can't see them from my vantage point.

"Never cliché if it's true." I flash him a killer smile.

"Well, in that case, you're stunning. You're just missing one small thing."

I sit up as Kylian slides into the booth beside me and opens his fist. In his hand appears a velvet rectangular box, which he extends to me.

"Open it," he urges, his naked chest grazing my elbow. I give him a beguiling smile as I pry open the box. I can't help the gasp that escapes me.

Rubies.

A three-inch wide choker of dazzling rubies.

My fingers ghost over the glittering scarlet gems as I clutch my chest in false sentiment.

"I can't accept this," I breathe.

"Yes, you can. I had it made specifically for you." He pushes the necklace toward me and I give him a look. He had it made after knowing me for less than five days?

"Put it on me?" I will my voice to sound girlish and hopeful. His stunning eyes flash before he eases the choker around my neck and takes his time clasping it. His hands slide over my shoulders with the proprietary touch of a male who thinks he owns someone, body and soul.

Kylian leads me to the dance floor. With the eyes of a thousand on us, I play the part of enamored prospect. Standing in his arms, I realize he's one of those men who takes up all the space in the room. He sucks up the air, leaving none for the rest of us.

Everything about him is inviting. Alluring. Attractive.

I know it runs in his bloodline, this compelling siren magic. I can't trust anything I feel around him. I can't trust how my body reacts to his touch, how he draws me close and looks down at me with searing intensity.

I wonder what it would be like to be loved by him. To have him lay me down on a soft bed and ravish me. He would tear the clothes from my body using only his teeth. He would kiss every square inch—

I cut the thoughts off abruptly, my eyes snapping up to his as the spell shatters.

Was he just in my head?

Those were not my own thoughts. Which is slightly terrifying. A slow, sensual smile spreads on his lips. A smile that tells me I'm right.

He pulls me into a dance before I can think of what to say.

"I'm sorry about your friend," he says, his voice lullaby soft.

Are you now.

"Thank you," I force out.

"Were you close?"

"I didn't know her for long, but I liked her a lot."

"It's tragic, really, the loss of a life so young. The responsible party will be found and dealt with. I give you my word." His voice reeks of false promise. "I hope tonight can offer you a small diversion, if only temporary."

"It's off to a promising start." I flash him a million-dollar smile as Jace whirs past with Sorscha, neither of them looking too thrilled behind their masks. I can sense his watchful eyes on me.

"I was wondering if I may call on you tomorrow. Take you into the city for a bit of fun."

"Tomorrow? I'm booked." I heave a dramatic sigh.

"Is that right?" He pulls me tighter to him, a hound on the scent of challenge.

"It is."

"The day after then."

"I'll check my schedule."

He chuckles as the dance comes to an end and tips my chin up—something urgent bubbling beneath the soft touch.

"Busy female." He shakes his head, his eyes roaming over my face. "Let me spoil you."

"Sounds tempting."

"Oftentimes, just on the other side of temptation is pleasure. A painful sort of pleasure, but pleasure nonetheless."

"The King is a hedonist. How shocking."

"We all have vices." His cruel mouth twists into a devastating smile, and I have to struggle to keep my mind closed to him, to keep him from invading my thoughts and planting his own there.

He leans down, his voice caressing my cheek. "I'm afraid I'm about to add you to the list of mine."

Jace, Zadyn, and Kai stand together, off to the side, their faces tight and stances tense. Kai's expression is a mixture of disgust and horror. Zadyn's fists are balled at his sides, and Jace's hand slides not so subtly to the hilt of his sword.

But I can't bring myself to care.

Not with Kylian standing so close and smelling so good. I inhale his intoxicating scent and force myself to hold his gaze without blinking.

Those sea-blue eyes drift to my mouth, and a wild thrill shoots through me. A sense of power at the thought of him wanting me. He draws closer, slowly lowering his lips to mine as my eyes flutter shut.

I'm no longer playing a game.

I've become the game, and Kylian is winning—conquering —just a hair's breadth away from claiming his prize.

My fingers curl into the feathers of his shoulder piece, and I find my lips parting for him.

The moment they touch, the screams erupt.

I jump, putting some distance between Kylian and me. My hand flies to my mouth as if it could erase the almost kiss.

But that's not the biggest problem.

Because the shouts surrounding us are growing louder and more urgent. I reel toward Jace and Zadyn, who are already cutting through the masked crowd to get to me.

That's when I see them. The beastly creatures from the maze are everywhere, clawing people down and feasting on their blood in horrifyingly gruesome displays. Their massive black forms transform the room into an instant nightmare.

Kylian draws his sword and dives into action, cutting down any creature that gets within a foot of me. I snap myself out of my frozen horror, dashing for Jace and Zadyn, but I lose them in the frantic mob. My voice is swallowed by the surrounding chaos as I scream their names. I trip over dead bodies and bloody limbs, trying not to gag and praying that no one I know or love is amongst the fallen.

People push and pull in every direction as the Stryga continue to attack. With the crowd this thick, using magic would do more harm than good. I won't get a clear shot at the beasts without someone else getting hurt or worse—killed.

If I can reach my friends, I can shadow us away.

But I can't find them. I can barely see over the swarm of frightened fae. I need to get to the dais—to a higher vantage point.

Suddenly, the ground begins to shake.

And the chandeliers begin to fall.

One after another, the ruby fixtures clatter to the floor, their magic tethers snapped. A new wave of screams breaks out as the massive chandeliers crush the beautiful fae beneath their weight.

I can't watch. I have to do something.

I reach for my dagger while summoning my magic, but something hard clamps down around my wrists, and I feel my magic sputter out and die. My knees buckle, but before I collapse onto the floor and am trampled, a set of arms breaks my fall.

I don't see who they belong to before I fade into darkness.

ertigo.

My dad told me that when my mom was pregnant with Sam, she was laid up for months in bed with vertigo. Everything bothered her. Lights, sounds, even strong smells. For the entire third trimester, she sat in a dark bedroom with no light, no TV—nothing. I wasn't allowed in her room for weeks on end, and as a little girl, I didn't understand why she wouldn't see me.

I wake in blackness with an intense headache, dizzy to the point of nausea.

Vertigo.

I blink into a dark, drafty space, seeing nothing. My hands are met with the resistance of a cold metal chain as I try to lift them. A knot forms in my stomach when I yank again and realize I'm chained to the floor.

My entire body feels heavy and lethargic, like I've been drugged. I feel around in the black, over the coarse, cold ground beneath me.

What happened?

The last thing I remember was dancing with Kylian, and then the hall erupted into screams and chaos and...

Those beasts—*the Stryga*—were there.

Oh my god.

Jace and Zadyn. Kai and Mar. Dover, Sorscha, Cece, the king, Igrid...My head spins. All of my friends. They could be dead.

And I'm...I have no idea where I am.

"Serena?" a voice whispers in the darkness.

"Who's there?" I croak. My throat is raw, as if I'd swallowed sandpaper.

A tiny flickering candle appears before me, illuminating half a face. I blink.

"Kai?" My voice cracks as I choke out his name.

"Thank gods. Hang on. I'm getting you out of here," he says over the jangle of metal.

"Where—" My bound hands reach out, brushing against a row of metal bars.

Am I in a cell? A dungeon?

"Where are we? What happened?"

"I'll explain everything, but we need to stay quiet if this is going to work," he warns. "Can you use your magic at all?"

I try. I try to call it forth, but nothing comes. That's when I remember.

"Blood ore. I'm wearing blood ore chains."

"That's what I figured," he mutters. My eyes adjust to the darkness as Kai holds the candle to the lock and, with one hand, slips a key inside. It doesn't fit. He goes through each of the keys on the rusted ring, and on the seventh try, the lock clicks open.

Relief floods through me as he eases the barred door open and scrambles toward me, dropping to his knees. He throws his arms around me tightly, and I lean my head against him, unable to hug him back with my restraints.

"Thank gods, you're alright," he whispers against my hair.

"I've never been happier to see you," I murmur. "The others?"

He pulls back and shakes his head. "I don't know. I was knocked out during the chaos. I didn't see. Come on, we can't linger," he urges, making to lift me. The chains yank me downward.

"I'm chained to the ground."

"Fuck," he hisses. "It's too dark in here. I can't see enough to swing a sword, and even if I could, I might take off one of your hands."

"There has to be a key somewhere." I eye the iron ring in his hand.

"Blood ore is spelled—there is no key."

"Where there's a will, there's a way. Isn't that what they say?"

Kai and I go utterly still.

"My little brother, the traitor."

Ice creeps up the back of my neck at the sound of Kylian's voice.

Gone are the honey-dipped tones and seductive purrs, replaced by the cold, calculated voice of a cruel king. He takes a slow step through the open cell, towering over us.

"I always knew you were a detestable little earthworm, but have you no loyalty to your blood? To your dear, dear older brother? To the crown?"

An iron fist shoots out and grips Kai by the neck, slamming him against the stone wall so hard that dust and debris crumble around his head. I let out a choked cry as he dangles Kai off the ground, his feet kicking for purchase.

"Have you no respect for your *king*?" His manic voice rises.

"Leave him alone!" I roar, rearing against my chains to reach him. Kylian slowly, like a possessed doll, turns his head toward me. A brilliant and horrifying smile spreads across his proud face.

"My love," he breathes, dropping Kai so fast he crumples to the ground, gasping for air. "How I hate to see you bound and chained like this."

"You did this to me, you asshole."

"And I regret it wholeheartedly. Do you think it brings me pleasure to see my future queen rotting away in filth and decay?"

"Future queen?" I hiss.

"That is why I've brought you here. You have done what no one in hundreds of years has managed to do." He pauses for dramatic effect, splaying a hand over his chest. "You have stolen my heart. You are my equal. The last Blackblood Dragon Rider. You will make a worthy queen, and we—" He closes the gap between us and slides his hands into my hair. His grasp borders on rough—like when you find a puppy so cute, you just want to squish it in your hands.

"We will rule *everything*," he concludes.

I spit in his face.

"Such venom." He chuckles, wiping the spit from his cheek with one long finger and licking it up. "And yet it tastes so sweet."

"You sick son of a bitch."

"You know, this mouth—this *filthy* mouth—is my favorite part about you."

"I will destroy you," I promise.

"My love, you are powerless. That's what the blood ore is for," he muses, releasing my hair with a toss. "But like any mare, you'll need to be broken. Trained into submission."

"I will never submit to you, you fucking psycho," I hiss.

"Perhaps you just need the right motivation."

Kylian whirls and roundhouses Kai in the face. I cry out, rushing toward him, only to be jerked back by my restraints.

"Don't fucking touch him!"

"Don't stress yourself, love. My mealy-mouthed little brother can take it. He would be honored to serve his future queen and sister this way."

"I will never be your queen! I will never be yours!"

"You say that now, but you lie. You lie to yourself about the way you want me. The way you desire me. I expected you to be grateful after the lengths I went to in order to get you here. I played the long game for months. I put on the performance of the century. I ripped this world *open* for you. For us."

"What do you mean, you ripped this world open?" I demand as the pieces of the puzzle all come together. "The attacks at the castle, the portal in Hyrax..."

"I destroyed those Guardians. Quite easily, actually. Shredded their minds like tissue. And then I negotiated like any good diplomat and king. Safe passage for my foreign friends into these lands in exchange for their undying allegiance—and I do mean *undying*. Any creature that crosses through that portal has sworn fealty to me and my crown."

"Oh my god," I whisper.

"What have you done!" Kai bellows, charging him. He doesn't even get close before a phantom wind slams him backward.

"Stop! *Stop it*, Kylian!" I cry.

"Alright, alright." He sighs, his power releasing Kai. "I can see you're still agitated from your long journey. I'll leave you to contemplate my offer. Kai and I are due for one of our talks. Isn't that right, brother?"

"Go to hell." Kai grits his teeth, struggling to sit up.

Kylian chuckles and starts down the dark corridor. "Bring him," he says to an armored guard outside the cell.

My jaw drops when Mal steps out of the shadows, his flaming auburn hair momentarily illuminated. I gasp, astounded, as he grabs Kai and tows him from the cell. I scream my friend's name as he is torn away from me, only guessing at the horrors that await him for trying to free me.

"It will be alright, Serena," Kai says as they disappear into the dark. "We'll find a way."

I slam my fists into the ground as I'm left alone again. The chains dig into my skin, drawing blood as I fight against them.

Worry overtakes me.

The names and faces of my friends flash through my mind in a torturous loop. I don't know if they're dead or alive. I don't know what torture Kylian is inflicting on Kai right now while I sit here powerless in a cell.

I don't even know where I'm being kept.

Prophyria suddenly pops into my mind. She said to call her if I was in danger.

I close my eyes and quiet my anxiety to dip into the channel between us. But I'm met with a sealed-off wall, thick as brick. I pound against it with my mind. And it doesn't budge.

The channel is sealed. Which means either the blood ore has affected my ability to communicate with her or she's...

No, I will not go there. I would know if my dragon was dead. I would feel it in my soul.

I have to get out of these chains. But how? Without the spell and without a key, I'm useless. I'm entirely at the mercy of a psychotic king hell-bent on marrying me for world domination. As if my experience with men couldn't get any worse. This one takes the whole damn cake.

Something scratches against my neck. I reach up and feel over the cool gemstones. Kylian's ruby choker remains around my throat, thick and heavy. Only now it feels more like a collar.

A collar built specifically for a leash.

⌒

I DON'T KNOW how much time goes by as I am starved and dehydrated to the point of immobility. Moving takes too much effort, so I lie frozen on the floor, every breath labored.

I will die soon if someone doesn't come to my aid.

But Kylian needs me too much. Wants me too much. Which restores some hope in me that I will not be left down here and forgotten.

A few minutes or hours later, an armored guard slides open my cell and unlatches the floor chains. The second he pulls me up, I collapse from weakness. My head lolls against cool metal as he carries me from the darkness. I have to shield my eyes against the harsh light after days of being entrenched in pitch black.

I'm laid down on a soft chaise lounge in a dim damask room. Someone lifts a cup to my lips. I take a tentative sip, worried it might be drugged, but as soon as I get one gulp down, I take the cup in my own hands and chug the water greedily. Gasping, I hold my hand out for more. I am obliged, feeling some life flood back into me.

"Good girl."

I lift my eyes to Kylian.

He takes the cup from me when I'm finished and sits down on the cushion beside my limp form.

"Eat." He holds out a piece of bread, and I rip it from his hands, stuffing it into my mouth as he watches.

"Where is Kai?" I manage to croak between bites.

"In his room, of course." Kylian gives me an innocent look.

"Don't bullshit me."

"I'm not. Your little friend took quite a tumble down the steps yesterday. He's getting some much-needed rest."

I stare at him for a moment.

"How can you be so cruel? He is your brother!"

"That means nothing to me. He is a liability," he says, his face expressionless.

I shake my head in utter disbelief. "You really are a sociopath."

"Are you feeling better? There are some matters we need to discuss." He moves toward a large desk situated in front of a wall painted with a giant map of Solterre.

"Where are we?" I demand.

"Home, my love."

"Home...we're in Vod?"

He nods, sitting down at the desk to sift through some papers. His attention remains fixed on the documents while I grill him.

"Where are my friends? What did you do to them?"

"Oh, I lost track of them amid the chaos." He waves a dismissive hand.

"You orchestrated those attacks. All of them." I plant my feet on the floor, testing my strength. I won't be able to stand, not yet. "You are the reason all those fae are dead. The reason Ilsa is dead. You brought those creatures into Solterre—into Aegar and the castle!"

"I did it for the greater good. King Derek is a weak ruler. He always has been. I've been preparing your place here long before you even arrived in this world." He looks up at me. I wait for an explanation, my nails digging into the cushion.

"When my mother wrote to me of your sudden appearance in Aegar, I initially thought to wed you to my brother. If you survived bonding the dragon, of course. You would have been no use to me dead."

Ilspeth, that bitch.

I knew she couldn't be trusted. How many times had I caught her sizing me up? Quietly observing from the sidelines.

She had been plotting and scheming this entire time—conspiring with her son to get me here.

"But I grew impatient," Kylian continues. "Desperate to lay eyes on the infamous Blackblood Dragon Rider. So, I journeyed to Aegar. The moment I saw you, I knew you were my future wife—my queen. My brother wouldn't have the faintest idea what to do with a female like you. I just needed to put your dalliance with that captain to an end. Convincing Derek to promise him to that disgrace of a princess was so easy. That little attack in the maze was all it took. It was the perfect solution. And the civil unrest it will spark in Aegar will be the cherry on top of a successful execution."

"What are you talking about?" I shake my head, not understanding. He chuckles, redirecting his attention to his desk.

"Derek naming his nit-wit daughter and a low-born bastard as his successors is enough to start a civil war. People will never accept him as their king. And everyone knows all that little brat is capable of is looking pretty. And now they've lost the only thing they had going for them—their Dragon Rider. By the way, I've been meaning to ask you—" He finally looks up, a mad twinkle in his eye. "Where is she? The dragon."

"I will die before I tell you a thing," I spit.

"Ah, well, we shall see. Now, onto more pressing matters. What kind of flowers would you like for the ceremony? Gardenias are in season, but I find the smell quite irritating—"

"I'm not fucking marrying you!"

"Oh, come now. Don't deny what you know is between us. We had a moment when we danced, didn't we?"

"You were using your siren magic on me! None of that was real. And I was putting on a show to get close to you because I knew—I *knew* in my gut that you were behind all this. I hate you. I hate you, and I will *never* be your wife."

"But don't you see how alike that makes us?" he asks.

"You're a cunning little liar. We are masters of deception, you and I. We, Serena, are cut from the same cloth."

"I am nothing like you, and I will never marry you," I say through clenched teeth.

"I could always force you," he muses. "But then, what kind of male would I be? I have a reputation of benevolence to uphold."

"Hah!" I bark. "Benevolence? Are you actually that narcissistic? If you had any decency at all, you'd take these chains off and let me go home. But you're a coward. You're afraid of me. You're not *half* the male Kai is. You're *pathetic*."

The pen in his hand snaps in half.

"You *are* home. And I don't want to hear my brother's name on your lips again, wife." He shoves out of his seat and walks around his desk to me.

"You might want to watch the way you speak to me, my love. My patience only extends so far." Kylian kneels at my feet, his hands smoothing over the rough blood ore chains on my wrists.

"You are powerless. Entirely at my mercy," he whispers, his lips close to mine. "I can make you do things. Anything I want. And you would have no choice but to obey me. Is that what you want? Do you want me to make you do things? Would that excite you?"

I snarl at him, baring my tiny fangs as he squeezes my face in one hand.

"It can be enjoyable, surrender. Submission. It can be freeing. I can show you if you'd like."

"No," I grind out.

"Then at least be agreeable." He releases me with a shove. A gesture of degradation. "If you give me what I ask for, I won't have to take it."

He stands, not bothering to veil his threat.

"My dragon will come for me. My friends will come for me."
I glare up at him as he motions a guard forward to drag me
from the room.*

He smiles dazzlingly as I'm towed away.

"Oh, I'm counting on it."

---

* Cue: *Nothing's Gonna Hurt You Baby* by Cigarettes After Sex

43

JACE

My hands glide over skin smoother than the finest silk.

She writhes like a serpent in my arms, her limbs wrapping around me tightly. Legs over legs, arms around my neck. She could crush my bones, and I wouldn't care. I would beg on my knees for her to do it again.

The taste of vanilla and cinnamon coats my tongue with every sweep of her lips as she grinds into me. My fingers thread through dark, heavy hair as she purrs beneath my touch. I slide the thin straps of her slip down her shoulders and angle my lips to the crook of her neck, planting soft kisses all the way down the perfect slope of her chest. She pins me on my back, and I marvel up at her.

My strong, beautiful warrior. My little witch.

Her slip slinks lower, pooling around her waist, leaving her perfection exposed, and I heave a groan of frustration, unable to stop myself from bucking against her weight on my lap. Her violet eyes flash, the pupils narrowing to slits before they drift shut, and her head tilts back in pleasure. My hands run down the length of her body as she leans down to offer her lips to me. Fusing her face to my own, I open my mouth, desperate to devour her, only to be met with thin air.

My eyes fly open.

I'm alone, twisted in bed sheets, rock hard, hips grinding against nothing.

She isn't here.

She never was.

I sit up, running my hands over my face, shaking the torturous mirage from my head. These dreams have haunted me ever since she was taken.

I spotted her wide eyes through the frantic crowd just long enough to see a name form on her lips.

My name.

I tried to fight my way through the thicket of bodies. I shoved and pressed and did all I could short of cutting down innocents to get to her. I raged against the sea of fae and monsters, but it was futile.

Blinding horror washed over me as blood ore chains were clamped around her wrists, and she dropped like a ragdoll into the waiting arms of one of those vile creatures. Then they vanished into thin air.

I wasn't fast enough.

I failed her.

Kylian, the queen, and Mal disappeared along with Serena and Kai. I know that was no mere coincidence.

Kylian's arrival at court was timed too perfectly to be happenstance. The attacks on the castle started the day after he stepped foot on the grounds. He knew of Serena's identity. And I suspect he knew of it before he even touched down on Aegean soil.

Kylian had an informant—someone privy to the truth about Serena's identity. I'm willing to bet my life that person was Ilspeth or Mal. Or both.

This entire thing was an elaborate ruse. A plan to take Serena. What better way to throw us off Vod's scent than by pinning the attacks on a rogue pack of foreign monsters? By turning Kylian and his mother into innocent victims?

Those creatures are just puppets. And Kylian and Ilspeth are holding the strings.

I've spent every waking moment going over and over it in my head. Drilling it with the king and coming up with a suitable course of action.

I haven't eaten and I've barely slept. Each time I do, she haunts my dreams. A cruel taunt to trick me into believing she's safe in my arms, only to wake to an empty bed and remember she's out of reach, hurt or dead, being tortured or gods only know what else.

I bound out of bed, shameful dreams forgotten, as I quickly dress and arm myself to the teeth with weapons. Minutes later, I'm knocking on the door to the king's council room.

"Come," he commands.

I storm in to find him alone, bent over a map, his face a mask of tense concern.

"I'm going to Vod. Today. I can't wait another minute."

"Jace." Derek comes around the table to take my shoulders.

"Zadyn is already on his way there. Following her scent like a crazed hound." I heave a deep sigh, shaking my head.

"He'll be there any day and will report what he finds." His tone is soothing. I envy his level-headed nature. "In the meantime, I have men searching for leads all over Aegar, to be certain."

I insisted on going with Zadyn, but Derek was adamant about me staying behind in case of another attack. I don't foresee that happening now that they've got what they want. Serena.

"Is this what being Hand means? Sitting on the sidelines like a coward while others fight the battle? I'm being wasted here." I toss a hand in the air.

"Your presence here is necessary. Not every battle is yours to fight." His kind brown eyes hold mine.

"How can you be so calm?" I shake off his touch and pace around the room, hands on my hips. "This is the very thing we feared happening from the start."

He turns to me. "We're doing all that we can short of starting a war."

"You don't think she's worth a war?" I snarl. He sets his jaw.

"Hasty decisions lead to sloppy execution. There is no room for error. You'd do well to remember that." His voice is laced with royal authority.

"We've wasted too much time already," I argue, staring out the stained-glass window.

"I won't send you to Vod unless we know for certain that's where they are. We need to consider the alternatives," the king points out.

"There are no alternatives. They're in Vod. They have to be. I should have seen it sooner, should have connected the dots," I mutter, disgusted with myself.

"No, it's I who should have been more cautious about welcoming Kylian into our home. My court has become overrun with traitors. Ilspeth, Mal, and Kai have committed treason."

"Not Kai. I know him. He hates his brother and mother—he didn't know about this." I shake my head.

It's Mal's betrayal that stings the most. I trusted him. Fought beside him. Even considered him a friend. I always attributed his fierce loyalty to Ilspeth to being her sworn protector—

simply doing his duty. I thought nothing of his little crush, but now I think there was more to their relationship than any of us knew.

Why else would he betray his kingdom? His brother?

I try to slow my breath to quell the rising panic. "The fact that Prophyria can't even locate her means they've bound her magic. She's alone, helpless, and at their mercy. They don't need her whole; they just need her alive. Let me go," I beg, wearing him down.

He studies me for a moment before turning back to his map. "I will ready a fleet to sail for Vod."

"She doesn't have that kind of time! It's been too long already!" I shout, slamming my hand down on the table. "*Let me go*. Now. I can make it there faster without a troupe."

"You need backup, Jace."

"I need to get to her. Every minute she's in their clutches..." I trail off, chest heaving in anger, fists aching to punch a hole through the wall. Vod has taken enough from me.

They cannot have her, too.

Derek puzzles over my state of rage, his brows knitting together. Then his expression shifts into realization.

"Jace." He comes to stand at my shoulder, turning me to face him. "You love her."

I set my jaw, saying nothing.

I don't care that he sees, I don't care that he knows, or that I'm engaged to his daughter. The only thing I can think about is Serena and her safety.

It's all-consuming.

"If you care about me at all, you will let me go," I grit.

Shock flashes in his eyes as he removes his hand and nods.

"Find her. Your men will be right behind you. Get her back, and then we will figure out what comes after."

I throw my arms around him, and he claps me on the back.

"Thank you," I say against his shoulder before tearing from the room to find the female I once detested.

To find the little witch I fell in love with against all logic.

To search for the source of my assured ruination.

TO BE CONTINUED....

ACKNOWLEDGMENTS

First and foremost, I need to thank you, my dear reader. This book was born out of my lifelong love of fiction and fantasy. I hope it makes you laugh, makes you cry, lifts your spirits, and challenges you. This is a story about healing, self-discovery, and finding the magic within you when you feel like all is lost.

May you always find your way to the self you are meant to be.

I would be nowhere without the support of my family. Mom —you have always encouraged me to follow my dreams, no matter how big. Thank you for your endless support and patience, and for letting me annoy the crap out of you with my ever-changing mind. I love you more than words.

To my amazing ARC team, beta readers, and friends that helped me fine tune and proof—I would not have had the confidence to release this without you. Thank you to Yoanna for helping me shape this story and to Alex for letting me talk your ear off about my ideas. To my new friend and editor, Kara —I'm so thankful that book club brought you into my life!

Gotta give thanks to God. Your blessings are endless, and I am eternally grateful.

To my dad—I know you are always watching over me and guiding my spirit. I know this would make you so proud. Thank you for passing your love of books on to me.

And thank you for the parts of me that I love most.

ABOUT THE AUTHOR

Marina Laurendi is an American writer, singer, songwriter, creative, and book lover. This is her debut novel. She intends to write more unless people throw tomatoes and beg her to stop.

Visit www.marinalaurendi.com/books to learn more.

facebook.com/theworldofmarinalaurendi

x.com/marinalaurendi

instagram.com/marinalaurendibooks

tiktok.com/@marinalaurendi

pinterest.com/marinalaurendi

goodreads.com/marinalaurendi

youtube.com/@marinalaurendi

threads.net/@marinalaurendi

amazon.com/author/marinalaurendi

Made in the USA
Middletown, DE
04 April 2025

73636229R00284